THE FUN FACTORY

THE FUN FACTORY

The memoirs of Arthur Dandoe, 1907–1910

Edited & Arranged by Chris England

For Susan.

First published in Great Britain in 2014 by Old Street Publishing Ltd

This paperback edition published 2016

www.oldstreetpublishing.co.uk

ISBN 978-1-910400-23-4

Copyright © Chris England, 2014

10 9 8 7 6 5 4 3 2 1

A CIP catalogue record for this title is available from the British Library.

Typeset by JaM

Printed and bound in Great Britain.

EXPLANATORY NOTE

THE memoirs that make up this volume came into my hands quite unexpectedly one day. When my wife and I moved into the house in Streatham where we have now lived for nearly fifteen years we became friendly with the elderly lady who lived in the ground-floor flat of the large house next door, a Mrs Lander. One day we happened to be talking about my interest in comedy and comedians, and she said: "Of course, my grandfather knew Charlie Chaplin."

"Really?" I said, thinking to myself: yes, and Lloyd George too, no doubt.

"Oh yes," Mrs Lander said. "They were really quite thick, apparently."

It seems incredible to me now, looking back, but I didn't really pursue the subject. Eventually Mrs Lander moved to a residential care home, and then a few months later her daughter dropped round to tell us that sadly she had passed away.

"She wanted me to thank you for your kindness," the daughter said, "and asked me to make sure you had this."

The battered old trunk she left me - which was brown,

reinforced by wooden ribs, and secured by what looked like an army belt – had been used as a repository for the memorabilia of a career treading the boards. There were wooden swords and shields, in the Roman style, and a lion skin (somewhat past its best). There was some old-fashioned football kit, a red shirt with a lace-up collar, long white pantaloons, and big boots that laced above the ankle. There was also a big black cape, of the sort you might see a magician wearing, and a top hat.

Underneath all this, lying flat at the bottom of the trunk, were papers, including posters from old music hall and vaudeville bills, mostly featuring the sketches of the great Fred Karno. Tucked in amongst these charming relics were old black-and-white photographs of groups of young men and women posing together, sometimes in theatrical costume and make-up, sometimes formally dressed, often in front of steam locomotives.

Who were they, I wondered, and what had they been doing?

I inspected the old photographs more closely. Surely that dapper young fellow with the toothy smile was Charlie Chaplin? And who was *that* one, standing over to one side, captured in an instant glowering at young Chaplin as though he would cheerfully throttle him till his eyes popped out?

Well, the answers were to be found in a brown leather satchel right at the bottom of the trunk, in the memoirs of the owner, one Arthur Dandoe, comedian.

I have no reason to doubt that they represent a truthful account, and where Dandoe touches upon verifiable historical fact he is invariably accurate – considerably more so than his contemporary managed in his 1964 autobiography, at any rate. Indeed, this memoir covers a period very swiftly – one might almost say, dismissively – dealt with in that other volume, and seems to have been written in response to it, in the spirit of setting the record straight.

Readers can judge whether or not Dandoe is to be believed regarding more personal matters. In editing the papers, I have confined myself, more or less, to the addition of a few historical notes.

C.W. England
Streatham, May 2014

PART 1

1
COLLEGE LIFE

"SO tell me – how did you get started?"

That's what people always seem to want to know, as though finding out how mundane, how matter-of-fact, how accidental everything was at the kick-off will reassure them that it could all have happened to them, if only...

In point of fact the vast majority of theatrical performers I have met in my long and interesting life had the great advantage of being born into the game, never knowing anything else. Look no further than Chaplin's autobiography. He paints a vivid, one might almost say *melodramatic*, picture of a childhood as the offspring of two music hall personalities. His father was a bona fide headliner, a baritone purveyor of faintly ribald singalong items who drank himself to death at the age of thirty-seven, and his mother was also a singer, who went by the name of Lily Harley. She lost her voice, and subsequently her marbles, and Charlie's first exposure to the joys of being on stage came (he says) at five years of age. He had to stand in for her one night at the Canteen in Aldershot when she couldn't face it, sang a song – "Jack Jones", it was – scored a notable hit (of course, or it wouldn't be in the book), and he was on his way.

I, on the other hand, unlike Charlie – and unlike Stan, whose father was a notable theatre impresario, and unlike Groucho and the boys, who were child performers with uncles and aunts in the vaudeville business – wasn't born into it.

So how did *I* get started?

I take you back to Cambridge in the time of the old king, Edward VII, when the years, oddly (and evenly), began with "ought". He was an enthusiastic visitor to the halls, by the way, old Bertie, used to come in disguise, but everyone recognised him, of course. His face was on the coins, after all.

So back in ought seven, it must have been, a glittering generation of carefree young things disported themselves about the old university town, sipping champagne in the sunshine on the banks of the Cam, flirting, carousing, occasionally dipping into a book or two, little dreaming that they were enjoying the last golden decade of the British Empire, and that the whole world order was just a few short years from changing for ever.

I was there too. Well, someone had to clean up after them, pick up their empties, make their beds, collect up their soiled laundry. And that someone was me. Arthur Dandoe, aged seventeen.

Not born into the theatre, you see. Born into servitude.

I'd lived in and around the college all my life. The school I went to until I was fourteen was just up the road. The little terraced house vouchsafed to the Dandoes by the college in its beneficence was about a hundred yards outside the main gate, up Trumpington Street.

All of my family belonged to the college, and had done going back into the mists of time. My mother, bless her, worked morning, noon and night in the kitchens, turning out exemplary breakfasts, luncheons and five-course suppers day after day. I wish I could say now that I miss my mother's cooking, but the plain fact is I hardly ever got to taste any of it, certainly not during term time. Her best work was destined for a higher class of palate than mine.

Lance, my brother, six years older than me, had returned to college dogsbody status after a stint in the army. He had served in Southern Africa during the conflict there, and despite many attempts by me and the other lads to get him to tell us tales of derring-do and glamorous hand-to-hand fighting with the filthy pig-faced Boer, I only ever heard him use three words to describe his active service. These three words were: "I shit meself."

And there was my father. He was the head porter, which gave him a certain amount of status about the place. No one, whether he was a plummy-voiced undergraduate, a crusty old brainbox, a college servant or – it has to be said – a family member, ever addressed him as anything other than "Mr Dandoe". Woe betide the unthinking fool who popped his head into the porter's lodge and said something like, "I say, porter chappy...?" or, worse, "I say, Dandoe, be a good chap and hail me a cab, there's a good fellow..."

The back would straighten, the nose would crinkle, the thumbs would work their way into the waistcoat pockets, and my father would say: "I've lived and worked in this college for nigh on thirty year, man and boy. I've risen, in that time, to the position of head porter, like my father before me, and as such I believe I have earned the right to be addressed as '*Mister* Dandoe'."

He would lurk in his little room in the porter's lodge, which was built into the side of the original fourteenth-century archway at the main gate, like some gigantic spider. The invisible strands of

3

his web stretched out to the furthest extremes of the college, and he was sensitive to its minutest vibrations. Nothing got past him.

All his hopes of the Dandoe line continuing its tenure of the porter's lodge were vested in me, and I was a sad disappointment to him on this score. He seemed to have more or less given up on Lance, partly I think because when his eldest left to join the army all those years ago he put his king and country before the college, and to my father's way of thinking that was simply the wrong way round.

"One day, lad," he was fond of saying to me, if possible within earshot of Lance, "all this will be yours. You'll be master of all you survey."

Every time he'd say this I would grind my teeth a little bit more.

My father got it into his head, as part of his grand plan for me, that I should familiarise myself with all aspects of college servitude, and in this spirit he allocated me a staircase, O staircase, to be precise, and I began a period as a probationary bedder. Now, college bedders – or *bedmakers* to give them their full title – were invariably women, usually matronly figures chosen precisely because of the sheer unlikeliness that they would inflame the passions of the young gentlemen of the college. As you can imagine, I was not overly thrilled to count myself amongst their number.

I got my own back by perfecting a wicked impersonation of my father with which I'd entertain the other college servants behind his back. I got his voice off so pat that I could actually put the wind up folk if I spotted them slacking. On one occasion I came across two of the bedders sitting on the stairs having a good old chinwag when they should have been working. I tiptoed up to a spot one flight below them and just out of sight, and realised,

4

gloriously, that they were having a right old go at my father and his ways. Picking my moment – just when one of them had ill-advisedly described the old man as "a tartar of the first order" – I bellowed at the top of my (or rather, his) voice: "So! *That's* what you think of me, Clarice Thompson!"

I then climbed the stairs and peeked round the corner to find that Clarice was in gibbering hysterics and her companion, most gratifyingly, had fainted clean away.

Lance claimed outright that I could never fool him, though, so imagine my joy when our father caught him one Sunday having a sly smoke in the Wren chapel.

"Lancelot Dandoe! What in the name of all that's holy do you think you are playing at?" he cried, outraged, to which Lance, without turning round to look, retorted: "Fuck off, Arthur, you little bastard. I know it's you."

"Oh! I...! Oh!" my father spluttered, incoherent with anger.

"Fuck off, I said, or I'll kick your bony arse for you, you scrawny little shite..."

Lance was twenty-three, and had been in the army, remember, but he was still carted unceremoniously out of the chapel by the lughole, looking like nothing so much as my father's pet orang-utang.

On this one particular morning, the morning of the day when it all started, I'd helped out with breakfast, I had whizzed around the rooms on O staircase with the duster, and I'd popped back to the kitchens, where Mum was able to slip me a piece of cold bacon and a couple of slices of bread. I had a bolthole near the library, behind a big ugly black-green statue of William Pitt the Younger, a celebrated college old boy, and I tucked myself away there to get outside my bacon sandwich and read a 'penny blood'.

You'll remember these, I'm sure – little flimsy storybooks packed with lurid adventures of pirates and cowboys, kidnapping and murder. (I forget how much they used to cost, now...)

My favourite tales were the ones set in America. Partly it was the grandeur of the place, the huge snow-capped mountain ranges, the mighty plunging canyons, the vast, sweeping desert plains. If you'd been born and brought up in Cambridge then you could get a kick out of almost any geographical feature grander than a slight incline. Mostly, though, it was the freedom it seemed to represent, the freedom to go where you wanted, be what you wanted, to rustle cattle or prospect for gold, to stake your claim for a piece of the New World.

So there I was, hidden behind a likeness of one of our great Prime Ministers, when suddenly a horny hand grabbed my collar and yanked me out. I spluttered, showering crumbs and half-chewed bacon over my father's coat.

"There you are!" he cried. "I might have known you'd be skiving off somewhere. What about your staircase? What about your beds?"

"Fimmished..." I coughed. How did the old spider know I was there?

"Well, then why aren't you laying out the luncheon in the Great Hall?"

"I was juft..."

"How on *earth* do you expect to ever get the lodge with this sort of attitude? Do you think your grandfather rose to become head porter of the college by lazing about the place? Do you think I gained that position in my turn by slacking off and back-sliding?"

"Don' wamp it..." I mumbled, still struggling with a mouthful of crusty bread. I don't know where the nerve came from to answer back on this particular day. Ordinarily I'd have let the storm blow itself out.

"I beg your pardon!"

"Don' wamp lodge. Don' wamp be head porper...!"

My father had hold of the lapels of my jacket, and in his frustration he began to shake me, which didn't help me to get rid of the mouthful of sandwich.

"Well ... what *do* you want, then, tell me that? Tell me what glorious plan you have devised for yourself?"

I took a breath, a couple of furious chews, and swallowed. Then I looked up at my father, his exasperated face shining red.

"I ... want to go to ... America," I said.

"America!" he scoffed, investing that one single word with every morsel of scorn he could muster. "I suppose we've got this trash to thank for that bright idea, have we?" He snatched the story from my hand and flicked through it contemptuously. "Well, young man, you can do the late rounds for me all this week. That'll give you some time to think about the error of your ways."

There was a curfew in operation at all the colleges and any student spotted on the streets after eleven at night by the 'bulldogs',[1] could be fined the finicky but traditional sum of six shillings and eightpence – a third of a pound – and repeated infractions could result in a student being sent down, which meant sent home. Cambridge, you see, thought so much of itself that the only way was down once you left the place, even though geographically speaking it was so near to sea level that almost everywhere else was up.

The college, too, could levy a fine, called 'gate pence', to be paid to the porter, whose job it was to apprehend any bright spark trying to avoid stumping up this pittance by clambering in the back way. The well-oiled undergraduate would regard this as a kind of local sport and would think nothing of dumping you on your backside in an ornamental lily pond before shouting "Hullooo!!" and disappearing over the horizon. My father, understandably, had tired of this treatment over the years, and, as soon as I was big enough to take care of myself, doing the late rounds became his preferred punishment for me. Actually, I didn't mind too much, as I soon realised that if I managed to catch anyone and get gate pence off them I could trouser it myself.

Later that evening, then, after the nobs had had their five-course dinners and their brandies and their ports, and everyone else had toddled off to bed, I was dawdling behind some bushes in New Court with a clear view of the single-storey bath house. I'd heard some rustling in the street outside as I passed the back gates, you see, and I suspected that someone was about to make an attempt.

Sure enough, after a moment or two I heard the telltale straining of some hero launching an assault on the north face of a lamp post, and then a leg was slung over the wall, followed by a backside, and finally a complete human form lay silhouetted against the lamplight playing on the building opposite.

To my astonishment, it was a woman. She was wearing a green frock, padded out by a number of petticoats, by the look of things, and she paused for a moment, panting in a most unladylike fashion from the exertion of the climb, before beginning to slide a shapely leg gingerly down the roof towards me.

I was delighted, because if some young rogue was trying to sneak a lady into his rooms then he was committing a serious sending-down offence and I should be able to extract a little more than just gate pence from him to keep his secret.

I watched for Romeo to make his appearance, but strangely there was no sign of him. Juliet, meanwhile, was leaning rather precariously over the guttering, and suddenly lost her grip, toppling headfirst into one of the large bins full of kitchen refuse. Well, I'm not sure what was in there that particular night, but nothing you'd want to be upside down in, that's for sure. I broke cover and went to lend a hand. The lady had toppled the big bin over on its side by the time I reached her, and was truffling around in there looking for something. With an "Aha!" of triumph, she emerged, clutching her prize – covered in bits of potato peel and suchlike but still recognisably a rather fancy wig with lots of ringlets.

It was then that the penny dropped.

"Good evening, Mr Luscombe," I said. Mr Luscombe was a first-year student, a friendly, cheerful chap whom I rather liked. (When I said earlier that his leg was shapely, you have to remember that it was quite dark, and the mind sees what it hopes to see, often, doesn't it...?)

"Oh dash it all!" he moaned. "I hoped I was going to get away with this. Damnation!"

I assured him that his secret was safe with me, and he clutched my arm.

"I say, do you mean it? Stout fellow, stout fellow indeed..." He clambered to his feet and brushed kitchen rubbish from his frock, then looked around furtively.

"I'm afraid I'm going to have to trouble you for the late charge, though, Mr Luscombe, if you would be so kind."

Luscombe's hand went for his trouser pocket and then remembered that neither trouser nor pocket was there.

"Oh, hang it all! I say, listen, Dandoe, you're a decent fellow, I know, and this must look dashed odd to you. How about you pop up to my rooms in a few minutes and I'll see you right. And perhaps, what, a little bit extra, eh? What do you say?"

Well, Luscombe was all right in my book. Some of the other gentlemen of my acquaintance – including, I may say, Mr Luscombe's humourless older brother, who had left the college to join the family business the previous summer – would lounge around pulling a face as though something had died on their top lips while I made their beds for them in the mornings. This Mr Luscombe, though, always had a smile and a cheery word or two, and so I nodded, and he darted off into the darkness like a startled rabbit.

I, meanwhile, carried on with the late rounds, ambling around the old courtyard and up to the Wren chapel, little realising that the course of my entire life had just been dramatically diverted.

2
THE SMOKING CONCERT

BY the time I got round to O staircase and tapped on his door, Luscombe had transformed himself back into the pink-faced young fellow that I knew, now wearing a mauve smoking jacket and dark trousers. A cigarette and a fire were on the go, and there was a small kettle dangling in his fireplace steaming away.

"Hallo, Dandoe, old chap," he cried. "Come in, come in, let's have a cup of tea, eh?"

I thought about offering to serve the tea up, but then thought, what the hell. If he wanted to play at being friends, then why not?

"You must be wondering what on earth I've been doing this evening?" he asked with a nervy laugh. I merely shrugged, as though I apprehended young gentlemen scrambling over the walls dressed as women every night of the week.

"Well, you'll have heard of the Footlights Club?"

I hadn't.

"Oh surely? The Footlights Club, no? *The Honorary Degree?* It was an absolute smash last summer, everyone was talking about it? Rottenburg wrote it. You must have heard of Rottenburg? Harry Rottenburg? The Rotter?"

I assured him that I knew of no Rottenburg. His face fell.

"Oh. Well, look here then. The Footlights Club is absolutely the premier dramatic society in Cambridge. Their shows are all comedy and music, none of this dreary highbrow stuff, *The Taming of the Thing* or *The Merry Wives of Wherever*, no, no, just the most tremendous fun. I've been simply desperate to join, and tonight after supper they were having auditions in a room in Magdalene. The Rotter's speciality, as it happens, is female impersonation, and I've been getting together a little item for a smoker in college next week..."

I must have been looking blank, for he paused to fill me in.

"A smoker? A smoking concert. We have one every term in the Old Reader. Very informal, really. Chaps do a turn, or a song they've written, or a poem, or a dance. There's a fellow called Hulbert[2] in the first year at Caius, apparently he's the most terrific clog dancer."

Luscombe handed me a cup of tea.

"My turn, do you see, is going to be an address in the character of the Master's Wife, Lady Marjorie. So I took the old costume along with me to the audition this evening, and do you know what those rotters at the Footlights did? They kept me waiting until the very last, and then finally while I was onstage, in character, doing the little monologue that I've worked out, they pinched all my own clothes and disappeared into the night."

He wore such an expression of pop-eyed outrage that I had to laugh, and after a moment he began to giggle as well.

"I didn't even notice they'd all gone right away. I thought I wasn't getting many laughs. Really, those rotters! They've got my wallet and everything..."

Mention of his lost wallet reminded me that I was there to collect gate pence from him, and also the "little bit extra" that he had mentioned.

"It's past midnight, Mr Luscombe," I began. "I should be on my way, really..."

"Oh yes, yes, my dear fellow, I'll see you right, of course..."

He pottered about looking for coppers on the dresser, but I could see that his mind was on something else, and suddenly he turned to me with a thoughtful expression on his face.

"I say, listen here, Dandoe. I wonder if you would like to help me out."

"If I can, sir, of course," I said, a little wary.

"Well, look, it's about my turn, my monologue. You see, I want it to be a big surprise at the smoker when I come on as Lady Marjorie, and if word gets out it'll ruin the moment. You see that?"

I supposed that made sense.

"So I was thinking, since you've already seen, I mean, the cat's out of your particular bag, as it were, perhaps you wouldn't mind having a quick look and letting me know what you think...?"

"I ... er..."

"Stout fellow! It'll only take a moment to pop the kit back on and I'll be right with you!"

I tried to say there was no need to make this a dress rehearsal, but he'd already shot into his bedroom like a rabbit down a hole, and I could hear petticoats a-rustling. After a minute or two the bedroom door opened a few inches and Luscombe's voice declaimed from within: "Gentlemen, would you give your best attention please to the Master's wife, Lady Marjorie."

Then the door was flung open and in he strode in the green dress and the wig once again.

13

"Good evening, my boys, and *my* what big boys you all are...!"

I knew pretty well what Lady Marjorie herself was like in real life, having served afternoon tea at the Master's lodge. Mr Luscombe had the lady's querulous tone off pretty well, and he certainly looked the part, and as I watched him recite his monologue a curious thing began to happen.

It was the first time I'd ever seen anyone trying to perform comedy. I'd never been to a pantomime or a circus, never even set foot inside a theatre, and yet as I was sitting there I felt my mind begin to whirr and click, little hammers hammered and tiny cogs ground their teeth together. It was an extraordinary sensation. I found myself assessing each line, each movement, each little aspect of the impersonation as it went by, mentally ticking off the bits that I thought would work and crossing out the bits that wouldn't. Yes, that's not bad, I was saying to myself, exaggerate that a little more, repeat that, lose that. I was really starting to enjoy myself, actually, and before I knew it he'd finished and was looking at me.

"You didn't laugh," he said, crestfallen.

"I'm sorry, sir," I said.

"I thought 'good for your blood' would get you going, I really did." He slumped forlornly into the easy chair opposite.

"Yes, now that's a good line, but you should bring it in a lot more often."

"More often, you say?" he frowned.

"I think so, yes." I could see, suddenly, that he was feeling a little bit sensitive, and so I hesitated to say anything further, but he pressed me.

"And have you any *more* bright ideas, Mr Dandoe?"

I took a deep breath to get my thoughts in order. "Well, I think you would find it much easier if you were to sit down rather than standing. Most of your audience will know Lady Marjorie from having tea at the lodge – in fact why don't we pretend that the whole performance is an afternoon tea at the lodge…"

A spark of interest ignited in my companion, and he leaned forward in his chair.

"Now you're sitting like a man in a dress," I said, emboldened. "Knees together, and perhaps to one side. Yes, that's better, and back absolutely straight. That's good. Now suppose we put a little table here with a cup and saucer on it, then … then, you can use Lady Marjorie's little trick."

"Whatever do you mean?"

I couldn't believe I was the only one who'd noticed this. Lady Marjorie was a fearsome woman with a voice like a foghorn and a physique that made you believe she could knock down a horse with a single punch, but she liked to affect a feminine weakness, making out that lifting a cup and saucer full of tea was the most tremendous burden.

"Would you be so *very* kind?" she would simper, obliging some young chap to leap to his feet and hand her a cup which she could very easily have reached herself from a table only a couple of feet away. I was always sure that she did this with the sole intention of having young male consorts bending in front of her so that she could ogle their firm athletic backsides.

"Yes! Yes!" Luscombe shrieked, delighted. "The very thing! I've seen her do it a dozen times! Let me try…"

We quickly devised a little bit of business whereby his Lady Marjorie would require someone from the audience to lift the heavy cup and saucer for her, and then leer lewdly at his rear end for a moment, seen by the audience but not the unwitting stooge.

Lady Marjorie was utterly fanatical about rowing. "A boy

15

should row," she'd pontificate at the drop of a hat. "It's good for the blood!" Luscombe had already used this line once in his routine, but I reckoned – I don't know how, it was instinctive – that he needed to repeat it over and over again and its impact would build. Before long the script had developed to a point where tea was good for the blood, walking was good for the blood, parsnips were good for the blood, and looking at saucy French lithographs in the privacy of your own home was good for the blood.

Hours slipped by unmarked, consumed in gleeful invention, and as the dawn began to light the chimneys on the far side of the New Building our conversation had turned to other amusing college characters. I found myself demonstrating my own party piece: my impersonation of my father.

"That's priceless, you know?" Luscombe gurgled between laughs. Both of us had become pretty hysterical by this time, and were laughing at almost anything.

"I'm serious," he insisted. "You could do that at the smoker. You *should* do that at the smoker. It would be an absolute smash hit. I'll speak to Browes, he's organising the whole thing. Do it, say you'll do it. It will be a *sensation!*"

Which is how I found myself a week later, still not quite believing it, in the Old Reader, about to make my theatrical debut. There was a little raised stage, with a pianist improvising some agreeable plinky-plonk while a noisy audience of a hundred and twenty souls paid no attention to him whatsoever.

I peered out through a gap in the hastily strung black curtain that formed the impromptu wing. The room was packed. A fug of smog hung down from the low ceiling, being fuelled by dozens of cigars like the chimneys of some great industrial metropolis. Champagne corks popped and young male voices brayed and hee-hawed boozily.

Standing there out of sight in my father's clothes, a cushion padding out my tummy, my left leg trembling apprehensively of its own accord, the week just past seemed like a bizarre dream.

I remembered Mr Luscombe's excitement as he told me that he had fixed it with Mr Browes, who was organising the smoker, for me to perform, and the churning of my guts as I realised there was no way to back out of it.

I remembered lying awake at night in the tiny room I shared with Lance, gripped with terror, and nudging my brother into the land of the living.

"Lance? You awake? I want to ask you something."

He sighed, rolling over to face me, one eye open. "What?"

"When you were in Africa...?"

He groaned. "When I was in *Africa*? Lea' me 'lone..."

"You were scared, weren't you?"

"I told you, didn't I?"

"Yes, but how did you ...? How did you ... manage, when you were really scared? How did you manage to carry on?"

"I tried to stay downwind of as many people as I could so that they didn't know how scared I was."

"Seriously, Lance."

"Well, I'll tell you this. It was always worse before than it was during."

"Really?"

"Unless you were one of the blokes who got shot in the head or had an arm blown off. Then it was worse during. Now go sleep..."

"Lance, listen..."

I told him about the smoker, about what I'd somehow agreed to do, and he rolled over and looked at me, before saying: "There's nothing to be scared of. How many of 'em are going to have repeating rifles? How many of 'em are going to try and chop you to bits with machetes?"

"Not too many, probably..."

"Exactly. Now go to sleep..."

There was a rustling, as of a big and complicated frock, and Mr Luscombe was beside me, also peering out.

"Decent crowd!" he hissed. On the other side of the curtain another cork popped, and half a dozen boisterous voices wha-heyed as their owners thrust their glasses forward for a refill. Luscombe suddenly hiked up his skirt and retrieved a hip flask from his trouser pocket. "Here," he winked, "bit of Dutch courage. Why not?"

I took a sip and felt the spirit trace the shape of my insides in fire.

"Why Dutch courage, I wonder, when it's *Scotch* whisky?" Luscombe was musing to himself. "Do the Dutch even make whisky? And what do they have to be so damn timid about? Living next door to all those Germans, I suppose. Ha!"

Mr Browes, the tall, athletic young fellow who was in charge of the evening's proceedings, pushed past us and pinned a sheet of paper to the wooden panelling, out of sight of the audience. Luscombe nudged me in the ribs.

"Running order," he whispered, shouldering his way forward to get a view of it past about eight chaps in boaters and stripy blazers. "These fellows are first," he said, "then me. Crikey, I was hoping not to be so early. You're midway through, after the clog dancing."

The fear gripped me once again. The fear of failure, of making a fool of myself, and in front of these people, who already held me in such low regard (if indeed they gave me a second thought).

Mr Browes completed a hurried headcount of the boaters-and-blazers, and then, satisfied, bounded past us and up onto the stage. The piano player tinkled to a little flourish of an ending and shut up, which is more than you could say for the packed and sozzled crowd.

"Gentlemen! Gentlemen, if you please!" Browes bellowed, and gradually heads began to turn in the direction of the little dais and the hubbub slowly subsided.

"Gentlemen," Browes began, in a more conversational tone now he had their attention. "Thank you for patronising our little entertainment this evening. It is still not too late to participate if you feel so inclined. See me during the interval and if you have your sheet music, or if Edward knows the ditty you have in mind, then I'll happily squeeze you into the second half." There were one or two lewd haw-haws at this, though quite where the double-entendre they thought they had spotted was lurking was beyond me. "And now," Browes went on, "let the revels commence!"

The first part of the evening went past in a blur. I think the opening item was a song by the chaps in boaters, accompanied by the pianist, a jolly little ditty about why you should always have champers in your hampers. There was a verse in it about all the different ways of popping your cork which they were inordinately proud of.

Then it was Mr Luscombe's turn.

"Wish me luck!" he grinned, and then stepped out into the light. His Lady Marjorie started a touch uncertainly, it seemed to me, but once he got his first big laugh under his belt – actually, for the bit of business that we'd devised together in his rooms – his confidence grew. By the end he was getting uproarious laughter every time Lady Marjorie opined that something was "Good for the blood!", and he left the stage to a thunder of applause.

Flushed and triumphant, he bustled into the wings and grasped me by the hand.

"My dear chap!" he whispered, "what tremendous fun! And I have you to thank, you know! Yes indeed!"

I was happy for him, and naturally pleased that my contribution had made a difference. Mostly, though, I was envious. He had finished.

The jovial mood that Luscombe's performance had generated in the room gradually dissipated during the next few acts, which were not, it has to be said, the absolute apex. One, I remember, was a rather mournful poet delivering sorry odes on the theme of lost love. Fellows were not just yawning as he droned on, they were actually shouting the word "Yawn!", but the drip didn't take the hint.

Then there was the clog dancer. Everywhere you looked people were holding their ears and uttering oaths with absolute impunity. One or two were caught out by the suddenness of the cloggist's finale and so he was greeted with a bellow of: "...ost confounded bloody racket I ever ... oh, he's stopped."

Beside me in the wings Browes was frowning at his running order. The evening was spiralling helplessly down the drain, and we both knew it.

"Right-o," he hissed as clog boy traipsed off with derision ringing in his ears (ours were just ringing). "You're next..."

Browes hopped up onto the stage and held his hands up for quiet (ever the optimist).

"I am sorry to have to tell you, gentlemen, that the college authorities have informed me that your behaviour so far this evening has left something to be desired..."

A choral "Oooooh!" rose from the audience, half-pleased with themselves for the raucous good time they were having, half-outraged that anyone might dare to criticise them for having it.

"And ... *and* ... they have instructed me to make way for our esteemed head porter, Dandoe here, to speak to you for a few moments. Gentlemen, please...!"

There was a murmur, now, of sullen displeasure. I began to doubt the wisdom of the conceit I had devised, but it was too late now. Concentrating hard on holding back the trembling in my limbs, I walked out to the middle of the stage in a fair imitation of my father's arthritically shuffling gait. The combined effect of that, the padding round my waist, the borrowed bowler hat and striped (second-best) waistcoat, and the cigar smoke blurring people's vision meant, I'm sure, that most, if not all, of the assembled company, took me for the genuine article.

There was silence. Utter, horrible, silence. A second, two, three...

My brain suddenly emptied of all thought.

"Well, come on then!" came a voice from the back, cutting through the silence. "Get on with it, for goodness' sake!"

The casual rudeness of it, the lack of respect that they felt towards me, or rather towards my father, snapped me back to myself. I wasn't going to fail, not in front of these people.

"First of all," I barked, "I've lived and worked in this college for nigh on thirty year, man and boy. I've risen, in that time, to the position of head porter, like my father before me, and as such I believe I have earned the right to be addressed as '*Mister* Dandoe'."

Emboldened by anonymity, several of the audience ventured another "Woooh!" at this, which they'd never have done to the old man's face, I'll tell you that. I fixed them with a stern eye.

"Second, gentlemen. I have been sitting over in the porter's lodge this past ... half hour..." (taking out much-prized pocket watch and checking) "...and I'm exceeding sorry to have to report that the racket you are making in here this evening ... well, I can hardly hear it. I'm very *disappointed* in you all."

Bemusement mostly, as I looked around, but one or two titters beginning to ripple across the room.

"Ordinarily I look forward to your college smoking concerts, because the amount of disturbance you cause will usually bring the head porters of other colleges round to my lodge to complain, and otherwise I don't get to see them much socially..."

By now they were starting to get it, and were beginning to laugh.

"Poor Dr Leather has a very important lecture to deliver tomorrow morning at the history faculty, and he was relying on you to keep him awake this evening long enough to finish copying what he was going to say out of Dr Simpson's latest book. Well, I'm sorry to have to report that because of your half-heartedness a very distinguished academic career lies in ruins."

Confidence building, I stuck my thumbs into my waistcoat pockets and strummed a little tum-tum-tiddle on my padded belly, as was my father's wont when about to reminisce about previous generations.

"The smoker of Michaelmas term 1782, which I remember well, because it featured a young Arthur Wellesley doing the Wellington boot dance with which he later made his name, got such applause that plaster fell willy-nilly from ceilings as far away as Trumpington."

Huge belly laughs, now, from everyone in the place. I could see gents turning to one another, asking who the devil I was, and some shrugs in response.

"If you gentlemen are unable to organise a smoking concert that draws complaints from at least as far away as St Catherine's, I'm afraid we are going to have to forbid the use of the Old Reader until such time as you learn how to do one properly."

The gauntlet thrown down, the ancient room reverberated to cheering, whistling, stamping, howling, a row like you've never heard before. I stood up there in front of the bedlam and had the curious sensation all of a sudden that something was missing. You know what it was? It was the fear.

In its place was something I have always since thought of as the power. Or rather: The Power.

Time seemed to slow down for me. I knew, I was absolutely certain, that everyone in the Old Reader at that moment was in my thrall. I held them in my hand. I didn't know what I was going to say or do when they stopped cheering, but I did know that I would know, exactly. It was the finest feeling I'd ever had in my entire life.

As the laughter rolled around the room, I watched it, detached, serene, like a scientist watching an experiment going exactly according to plan. Through the haze of smoke I could make out individual faces, eyes fastened on me, mouths open in laughter or anticipation of laughter. And there, amongst the blazer-clad goons who had drifted round there after finishing their drippy song, I caught sight of a familiar face. Watching. Not laughing. Just watching.

My father.

3
OH! MR PORTER!

HE was looking directly at me. I was wearing his clothes, and his hat, and a parody of his paunch, and the better part of the population of the college, which was his whole world, was laughing at me. At *him*.

All this I spotted in the blink of an eye. I was able to register the sudden sight of him, digest it, consider its implications, set it aside for later, even as the laughter rolled on. The Power did this for me. I seemed to be operating at a different speed to the rest of the world, like the man in the H.G. Wells story whose trousers catch fire.[3]

And then it was over.

Browes was bounding out onto the stage again, leading applause for me, and I walked off slowly, carefully remaining in character, already wanting to do it again, and wondering how I was going to explain myself.

"Well done!" Mr Luscombe was saying. "Didn't I tell you? You were a sensation...!"

Others clapped me on the back, wanting to share in my

triumph. That clog-dancing fellow trod on my foot with his big wooden boot, but I hardly noticed. What was I going to say to my father? I should have known – nothing got past the old spider.

I slipped out through the library and out of the side door into the cool night air, leaving another group of bright young things to warble on about punting to Grantchester, or some such, and I stood with my back against the ancient stonework for a moment to gather my thoughts. Lance lurched around the corner and immediately spotted me.

"Now then, Arthur, before you say anything. I never let on," he said, as he trotted over, his hands raised defensively in front of himself.

"Of course not," I sighed.

"I never, I swear!" he protested, detecting the sarcasm in my voice. "He heard the rumpus and came over to see for himself what was going on!"

It had the ghastly ring of truth about it, I had to admit. That I should be onstage pretending to be my father berating the audience for not making enough noise, thus inspiring them to make more noise, and that that noise should then have been what brought him over to see what was happening, well, it was one of those naturally occurring moments of perfect comic irony that you can't make up. I grunted, letting the lump off the hook.

"He wants to see you," Lance said, grimacing in an unusual moment of fraternal sympathy. I shrugged and set off over to the lodge, the condemned man, to take my punishment (without hearty breakfast).

I shoved open the heavy old door slowly, setting the ancient hinges squealing. For once, though, my father wasn't standing at the ready behind the counter, alerted by his early warning system.

"Hello...?"

His voice came from the back. "Come through."

I nipped behind the counter and into his little back room, which was as snug and warm as a toasted muffin. There was a fire going in the grate and my father was sitting in his old comfy chair (his father's before him). He waved me over to a stool opposite and I sat there with my hands on my knees for long agonising moments, waiting for the thunderstorm to strike.

"I was wondering where my second-best waistcoat had got to."

"Sorry," I said.

He looked me up and down as though seeing me for the first time. I didn't know what to do to break the tension, so I took his bowler hat from my head and handed it over to him. He nodded, took it from me and set it on the small table at his side.

"Would you like me to do the late rounds tonight?" I said finally, unable to stand it any longer.

"I would appreciate that, Arthur, thank you."

More oddly appraising silence followed, and then I ventured: "I'm sorry, if seeing what I did this evening was ... embarrassing for you. I didn't mean..." My sentence tailed off and he completed it for me: "...for me to see you at it, I know, I know. Well, I've got two things to say to you, Arthur Dandoe, and I sincerely hope you'll pay attention to them."

Here it comes, I thought, bracing myself.

"When I saw you up on the stage there tonight, well, I don't mind telling you I got the shock of my life, I did. I saw you up there, dressed like me, speaking my words in my voice and heard all the gentlemen in there laughing and cheering, and do you know what I thought to myself? Do you?"

He wasn't raising his voice. In fact he was frighteningly calm, and I'll tell you what I was thinking to myself. I was thinking, this is the angriest I've ever, ever seen him. Even more angry than when Lance left and joined the army without telling anyone.

"Um ... no...?"

"I thought to myself, well, Dandoe. Here's a nice thing. Look at them all, laughing at you, laughing at your funny little ways. What does this all mean, I wonder...?"

He looked me right in the eye.

"I'll tell you what it means, my lad. It means they like me. They really like me."

Eh?

"Oh yes. It means I, George Dandoe, am more than just a college employee, the senior college employee. I'm beyond that now, oh yes, way beyond. I'm a college *institution*."

He beamed.

"And do you know what else I thought?" he went on. "I thought to myself: look there, Dandoe, there's your son. He's had none of what all these other men have had, none of the privileges, none of the advantages, and look at him. He's as good as every last one of them. Better even. They're hanging on every word he says."

I was stunned. Staggered.

"Good luck to you, son. You showed 'em, eh? Oh yes! You showed 'em all! Well done! I'm proud of you. I mean it."

He leaned over, took my hand and pumped it enthusiastically, a warm smile spreading across his face.

"Now come on, look lively. Off with that waistcoat, and whatever else you've stuffed under there, you cheeky beggar..." – here he patted his tummy, more jovial than I'd ever seen him – "and then round to the Old Reader. Some of those gentlemen will need sending on their way if they're not to be locked out of their own colleges..."

A couple of minutes later I was outside in the night air once again, shaking my head at my father's reaction. I'd lampooned him in front of everyone, and he'd loved it! Well, you could have taken the proverbial feather and rendered me more or less horizontal with it.

The smoking concert was over by the time I reached the Old Reader, and it had dissolved into a loud and raucous drinking party. If anything, there was even more smoke than before, and you could see it swirling and drifting by the gas jets on the wall.

"Excuse me? Gentlemen? Could I have your attention?" I bellowed at the top of my voice. "The front gate will be closing in ten minutes. Those of you from other colleges should be on your way now."

It was as if I was invisible. The Power clearly did not extend to the delivery of mere factual information. I gave up on them – after all, if they wanted to risk the wrath of the proctors' bulldogs it was no business of mine. I stepped off the chair and took down one of the long poles to open the top windows, thinking to let out some of the smoke. I was reaching up to the first window, when Mr Luscombe rushed over and grabbed my arm.

"For goodness' sake, put that down!" he hissed.

"I was just letting in some air," I protested, but he was already hustling me briskly through the crowd.

"I know, I know, but there's someone I want you to meet, and it would be better if he didn't know you really were a porter. You see the fellow in the striped blazer?"

I did.

"Well, that's the Rotter!"

28

"The rotter?"

"From the Footlights Club."

"You mean the one who stole your trousers?"

"Exactly so."

I drew myself up to my full height. "I see, sir. What do you want me to do? Do you want me to sling him out of the gates on his backside...?"

"No, no, no, no, *no-o-o-o!*" Luscombe urgently grabbed my arm again to hold me back. "He was in tonight, he saw the smoker and wants to talk to you, to me, to *us*! Come on!"

Harry Rottenburg – 'The Rotter' – was the president of the Footlights Club and – although I didn't know it at that moment – he was the university's leading theatrical celebrity. He was holding court at the far side of the room, surrounded by a dozen or more acolytes gazing at him worshipfully over the rims of their champagne glasses. The Rotter was somewhat older than his courtiers, having been a student himself some ten years earlier, and he now was a senior member of the university's engineering department. His nickname was rather misleading, as "rotting", or being a "rotter", was undergraduate slang at that time for joking or sending someone up. Luscombe dragged me over and we hovered at his elbow, waiting for him to draw breath, which he did presently.

"Mr Luscombe, there you are. I congratulate you, sir. An excellent turn."

Luscombe beamed. Praise from the Rotter was praise indeed. The Rotter was a burly figure, with broad shoulders and a square face that looked like it had been knocked about a bit. If his speciality, onstage that is, was playing female roles, then they must have been exclusively female characters who had played rugby union for Scotland (as he himself had).

"And I apologise for the high jinks with your clothing last time we met. I sent a man round to your rooms with the items. I trust they arrived safely?"

"Oh yes, thank you," gushed Luscombe. "And there's no need for apologies, really. Excellent rotting!"

"Well, there we are. And this is your man, is it?"

"Dandoe," Luscombe put in, before I could speak for myself. "This is Dandoe, yes. Excellent chap."

"I congratulate you too, Mr Dandoe, most entertaining." The Rotter offered his hand and I took it. A huge, meaty fist it was too. "Here's the gist," he went on. "I'm putting together a show at the New Theatre. It's practically written, and I dare say we'll be able to find something for the two of you. What do you say?"

I was dumbstruck. Luscombe looked as though he had died and gone to heaven.

"I'd be deligh ... that is to say, *we'd* be delighted, wouldn't we, Dandoe? Yes indeed we would," Luscombe jabbered, and before I could say a word on my own account it was all arranged, and the Rotter swept grandly out of the Old Reader with his retinue in his wake. Luscombe was quite beside himself with glee.

"Did you hear? We are to be in a Footlights show! How absolutely bally splendid!"

I was sorry to bring him down to earth, because surely it was impossible for me, a mere college servant, to take part.

"Ah, no, because I told Browes to tell the Rotter you were my manservant, my gentleman's gentleman, do you see, and they would have no problem with that, it would be perfectly fine. It was all I could think of at the time, it was all rather sprung on me, and I wasn't sure whether he liked you or me. But if you're my man, do you see, he can't have one of us without the other, so it fits the bill rather splendidly, doesn't it?"

Well, whether it did or it didn't, I'd felt the intoxicating thrill of the Power. I wanted more, and whatever it took I was going to make it happen.

4
THE VARSITY B.C.

In the event, rather than try to pull the wool over my father's eyes, I decided to come clean right away – well, the next day – and tell him about the conversation with the Rotter. Remarkably, it turned out that he was quite happy to accommodate my absence in the evenings, as long as I was prepared to make up the hours late at night – more late rounds – and early in the mornings. The crucial factor, I think, was that Mr Luscombe had decided to describe me as his gentleman's gentleman. There were few ways in which a college servant could hope to improve himself, other than graduating to head porter, but being taken into private service by a wealthy gentleman when he left the college was certainly one of them.

And so, shortly thereafter, Mr Luscombe and I found ourselves taking part in Mister Harry Rottenburg's newest venture, a production called *The Varsity B.C.*

There was a busy hum about the university at that time. You couldn't miss it, even if you were only serving the port at High Table. The chatter was all about dinosaurs, and fossil bones which somehow proved that giant lizards had once ruled the earth. Back then, in ought seven, these bones were being discovered all the time.

Some of the finest minds in Cambridge were absorbed in the business of connecting these prehistoric monsters with animals that still lived on the planet, hoping to shed light on some of the murkier corners of the theory of evolution. Others, like the Rotter, were thinking along different lines, such as: "I say, wouldn't it be an absolutely spiffing lark to make a model of a brontosaurus and have it eat a chap?"

So while on one side of town the archaeologists and anthropologists pored over ancient ribs and bits of spine, on the other the engineering department were devising a complicated system of wires and pulleys, weights and counterweights that would allow the Rotter to climax his new show with a full-size moving brontosaurus – its head and neck, at any rate – with room in its mouth for a human snack.

And who do you think was in line to be lizard lunch? That's right, yours truly.

The conceit of the show, as you can probably guess from the title, was to depict Cambridge in prehistoric times. Rival groups of cavemen from rival caves would compete in a variety of activities which aped – *rotted*, I should say – college life, with the whole scheme enlivened by the appearance of the mechanical dinosaur.

Mr Luscombe and I had relatively small parts to play, as cavemen from 'St Botolph's cave'. I was Caveman 4, and I'm pretty sure that Luscombe was Caveman 3. There was a deal of standing around in animal skins, and numerous scenes in which twenty or more of us were running around trying to bop one another on the head with papier-mâché clubs. Caveman 4's moment in the sun came near the end. It turned out, wouldn't you know it, that I had been secretly working to further the interests of the Trinity cave, and I got my comeuppance when I was devoured by the brontosaurus.

One evening the company were just finishing a run-through in the club's private rooms, which were above Catling's sale rooms near the Corn Exchange, and I was busy dispensing whiskies-and-waters when Browes burst in, mopping his face.

"I say, you chaps, I've some frightful news!" he cried.

"Whatever is it?" the Rotter said, steering him to a chair, while I ghosted alongside, manservant-like, stiff drink at hand.

"A fellow on my staircase is writing a thesis..." – a collective shudder went through the company at the very thought of this – "about ... well, about good old Brontie, actually!"

"No!" someone gasped.

"Yes, I assure you, so I told him – in strictest confidence, of course – about the climax to our show. I thought he, of all people, might be amused, but do you know what he said?"

"Go on," the Rotter said, upper lip stiff as an ironing board.

"He said to me, he said: 'Browes, you priceless ass! Don't you know that the brontosaur was *herbivorous*?'"

After a moment Rottenburg smiled, and snorted, relieved: "My dear chap, so we got the name wrong. We'll just call her 'Herbie' instead. Problem solved..."

"No, no, no! *Herbivorous*! It only ate plants! It couldn't possibly eat a chap! The whole ending's ruined!"

There was a grim silence. The Rotter shook his head slowly from side to side, much like Brontie herself. Did I mention, by the way, that Brontie was female? She had to be, do you see, because of a truly awful line in the closing number about her being one of the Brontie sisters.

"I'll have to give this some thought," The Rotter declared suddenly, then strode urgently out of the theatre. "Some serious thought!"

———

Next evening we all gathered again, desperately worried that the whole show had been fatally undermined. Cigarettes were smoked, carpets were paced. Everyone was convinced that the show was done for, but we reckoned without the never-say-die spirit of our president. He burst in with a big grin on his face, flourishing a drawing he himself had done.

"I've added a small scene, solves the whole thing. The chap, do you see, Dandoe here, has to spy on the other cavemen to find out what they are up to. Do you follow me? So he dresses himself up as a tree, ergo, dear Brontie can chomp him up with a clear conscience. *Voilà!*"

A resounding cheer went up at this elegant solution, and I doubt whether the man who discovered the actual brontosaurus ever had acclaim to match it.

And as fellows like the Rotter and Browes and Lord Peter Bradshaw thumped me genially on the back it really felt like we were all in this great enterprise together, as equals.

As the opening night approached, however, I began to wonder just how equal we all were. Because when the two technicians from the engineering department, Rottenburg's assistants, Mr Ernest and Mr Kenyon, began supervising the installation of the monster, it became dazzlingly clear to me that the reason why I, of all people, had been selected to be Caveman 4 was that being eaten by the mechanical dinosaur was actually going to be pretty bloody dangerous.

The beast weighed a ton for a start. It consisted of a solid wooden framework, strong enough to hold three men inside, covered with canvas which was painted to look like the giant reptile's skin. Then there were – I don't know how many. Seven? Eight? – huge blocks with pulleys on, any one of which could have killed a man on its own if it came loose and fell on him, not to mention the further tons of scaffolding which Mr Ernest was reckoning on using to attach the whole contraption to the ceiling. As the man who'd be standing on the spot marked with an X, I quickly saw that if the slightest thing went wrong I was the one for the chop.

The only way they could make a victim – me – disappear whole into Brontie's mouth was by positioning Mr Ernest inside the neck to haul me in bodily, with Mr Kenyon further up holding onto Ernest's ankles. No fewer than eight others were concealed in the wings, yanking on ropes, pulling levers, throwing sandbags on and off, and they just couldn't seem to get it right.

I was watching from the wings with my heart in my mouth the first time they tried to lower the head to the stage and smashed the chair they were using for target practice into matchwood.

On another occasion the neck started careering up and down uncontrollably. The stagehands were trying to grab hold of a counterweight which would have brought Brontie under control, but it kept bobbing out of their reach. Finally three of them caught the creature's head as it smashed heavily into the stage for the umpteenth time, and Mr Ernest and Mr Kenyon slithered shakily out onto the floor.

"Most invigorating," Mr Ernest said, an idiotic grin on his face.

Finally, well after midnight on the day before the opening performance, Brontie was deemed safe enough to attempt to eat me. I said my line (and a silent prayer), the monster's head came down, my leaf-covered torso disappeared into its jaws, Mr Ernest grasped my arms, and we all swung up into the flies.

Despite the triumphant cheers and whistles from the rest of the company, I had a strong suspicion that my first appearance on the stage could easily turn out to be my last.

———

Come the opening night the New Theatre was packed to the rafters with students and local townsfolk, all drawn by the Rotter's proclamation that this was to be the first time a great dinosaur had been portrayed on the live stage anywhere in the world.

Mr Luscombe and I peeked out through a small gap in the curtain at the crowd milling about, finding their seats.

"I say," Luscombe hissed. "Did you hear?"

"Hear what, sir?" I whispered.

"Word is that some big noise from London has come up on the train specially to see Brontie in action."

"What sort of big noise?"

"Oh, our director has contacts, you know, in the London theatre. Sssh! Here he comes...!"

The Rotter shoved his big, square rugger-pug face in between ours and surveyed the scene.

"Full house! Good luck, gentlemen, which is to say, confound it, *bad* luck. Break a leg, I mean. Break all your legs!"

He shovelled us ahead of him into the wings and gave Mr Ernest the signal to begin. The curtain rose, and we were off.

The show itself trundled along agreeably enough to begin with. The Rotter stomped around backstage as his small army of cavemen galloped on and off for the various scenes and musical numbers. Every now and then there would be an unexpectedly big laugh, and he would note down what had provoked it on his script with a scrawled tick. Then he would resume his nervous pacing, occasionally pausing to give a silent pat of encouragement to someone with a huge paw.

Although the audience were enjoying themselves, there was a palpable air of anticipation about the place. Everyone was waiting to see this much-vaunted brontosaurus. The Rotter himself was pacing nervously, sometimes reaching up to twang one of the control ropes above our heads.

Finally, towards the end of the evening, it was the moment. A flurry of hushed activity suddenly bustled around the contraption, and Mr Ernest and Mr Kenyon wriggled into its neck. The ropes were pulled taut, and the eight stagehands took the strain. I hadn't time to watch any more, because I had to be onstage.

Trinity cave were having a secret pow-wow, discussing their plans for the big contest on the morrow. Suddenly they noticed that a small shrub was inching towards them, as if to hear better. In a trice I was exposed, I stood up, and I delivered my line, my only line of the show: "I did what I did for the sake of the cave! The dear old cave!"

Brontie let out a terrifying roar (which is to say, a stagehand called Nicholas bellowed into a barrel). This was the cue for everyone else in the scene to scarper, except me. One or two ladies in the audience let out an excited shriek of anticipation.

And nothing happened.

I glanced over, and saw the Rotter frantically lashing one of the ropes backwards and forwards. It seemed to have snagged in its pulley high up in the ceiling. The Rotter waved desperately at me to fill, and booted young Nicholas up the backside. Brontie promptly let out another, slightly aggrieved, dinosaurific roar.

I remembered something I'd heard, and for want of anything better to say decided to impart it to the audience.

"Uh-oh! That sounds like it might be a brontosaurus, you know," I said, putting on my best scared face. "Those of you who have been keeping up with your studies will know that the name brontosaurus means 'Thunder lizard'. So named, I'm told, for its terrifying roar..."

Nick, obligingly, let loose with another blood-curdling bass bellow, and the audience looked expectantly over to the side of the stage. I could see what they couldn't, though, that the Rotter was still trying to free the snagged rope.

"Although..." I said, and watched the eyes snap back to me. "Since its diet was in fact exclusively vegetarian, some of our finest scientists now believe the thunder may have emanated from the other end entirely."

The laugh I provoked with this line washed over me like a breaker and I felt the tingle of the Power once again. I could see the white dress shirts and black dinner jackets stretching to the back of the stalls, and the browns and greys and blues of the folk in the upper circle.

I heard the Rotter give a stifled cry of triumph and realised that the rope must be free, but I wasn't ready to be eaten just yet.

I stepped forwards off my mark and down towards the footlights.

"I spent the morning hunting, don't you know?" I found myself saying. "Not terribly successful, I'm afraid. I was trying to bag a very tricky kind of dinosaur. The Ran-off-as-soon-as-he-saurus...!"

Huge laugh. I watched it, waited for it, bathed in it.

"What you don't want, though," I went on, when the moment was just right, "is to come across one of those fearsome predatory dinosaurs. Something like the He's-got-it-in-for-us..."

Another good laugh. Suddenly Brontie uttered the most bone-chilling roar. I glanced to my left and saw that the Rotter, his face purple with rage, had grabbed Nicholas's barrel and was howling all his frustration into it. I quickly reckoned maybe I had pushed my luck far enough, and skipped back to my spot, quaking with pretend terror.

"Ooooh!" went the audience now as Brontie's massive head lowered itself slowly from the flies, and one or two clip-claps of applause broke out.

"Raaaargh!" went the Rotter.

The jaws slid neatly over my head and shoulders and I reached up to grab Mr Ernest's clammy hands.

"Ran-off-as-soon-as-he-saurus, that's a good one..." he was chuckling to himself. The great contraption swung into the air. I could hear the muffled sound of the audience's applause, suitably impressed. Then suddenly...

Twang!

Something snapped, something gave, and the head, having moments before disappeared triumphantly into the sky, now hurtled down and smashed into the floor. The audience, startled and unsure as to whether this latest development was intentional, half-laughed, half-screamed. I was thrown out – regurgitated, as it were – and rolled halfway across the stage. Without my weight in it, the dinosaur's head lurched up again and banged into the metal walkway, which was masked from the audience's view by the tab. In the wings the Rotter was furiously waving me to my feet, clearly intent that Brontie should eat me once again.

I turned to the audience.

"I told you she was a vegetarian," I said.

Down came the head once more. Again I grasped Ernest's hands – he not so cheery, now, in fact rather pale – and we bounced upwards. We made it four or five feet off the floor before slamming violently down again. After a moment we could feel the whole frame shuddering as though someone were jumping up and down on top of us, and then all at once a great rattling, rustling, bumpi-ty-bumping on the canvas right above our heads, and it all stopped.

The audience were laughing hysterically, now, at something. I peered down at the small portion of the brightly lit stage that I could see at my feet and was astonished to see the Rotter sitting there, in decidedly unprehistorical costume, holding his head and moaning. Evidently he'd been bouncing onto the top end of the creature, trying to provide enough counterweight to lift us clear, and had slip-slided all the way down the neck, ending up in a heap in full view of everyone.

Suddenly there was an ominous creaking from above, followed by a snapping, and then the whole mass of wood, and painted canvas, and rope, and pulleys crashed to the ground and splin-tered around us. The audience hooted with glee. Mr Kenyon crawled out of the wreckage over towards the orchestra pit and then vomited copiously over the kettle drums.

"Curtain," the Rotter moaned in a tiny voice, clutching the area of his kidneys. "Curtain, damn it all!"

———

The audience leaving the New Theatre that night were thoroughly satisfied. The script had been funny, the songs agreeable, and then everything had fallen spectacularly to pieces at the death. What could be better? The next best thing, always, to an absolute smash hit is a notable catastrophe.

The Rotter and his engineering cohorts set about rebuilding and repairing their pride and joy almost at once, and I was dispatched up to the theatre bar to fetch drinks for everyone.

I had just finished loading a dozen Scotch-and-waters onto a tray when I heard a sarcastic little cough from behind me.

"That's a powerful thirst thee've got there, young feller," said a voice with a thick sort of accent I couldn't quite place. I turned to grin at the speaker, who was a dapper little chap in a sharp suit and very shiny shoes.

"Yes, sir, and I'll be back for another dozen in a minute. Excuse me..."

When I returned a few minutes later the bar was empty except for this gentleman, who was perched on a stool and, it seemed, was waiting for me. I slipped behind the bar and began pouring out more drinks.

"You were in t' show just, weren't you?" the man said, narrowing his eyes at me appraisingly.

"Yes, sir, I was."

"You were t' lad in yon creature's mouth, were you not?"

"Yes, sir, that's right."

"Now then, that big red-faced feller tumbling down the neck and ending up scratching his head in the middle of the stage. I'm right, aren't I? That weren't meant to'appen?"

"Er, no."

"Pity. That were t' best bit."

I'd filled my tray again by this time, so I smiled an end to the conversation and excused myself, but my companion hadn't finished.

"You know, I came all the way up from London to see that beast. Thought it might be something I could use."

I realised then that this chap must be one of the Rotter's theatre contacts, one of the men he was hoping to impress.

"It's very clever, really, how it works, and it was fine in rehearsals. I'm sure Mr Rottenburg could explain better than I what happened. I'll run down and fetch him..."

The man held up his hand and said firmly: "No. Don't fuss yourself. It's not for me. No, laddo, it's you I wanted to speak to. Now I'm watching you running up and down stairs carting drinks and I'm thinking you're not one of these gentleman student types. I'm right again, aren't I?"

"You are, sir," I said sheepishly.

"So what are you? Servant of some sort?"

"I work for one of the colleges, yes, sir, general dogsbody work, portering and so on."

"I see. Well, now listen to me. I saw how you handled yourself on the stage tonight when that whatsit fouled up, and I'm telling you straight that I liked what I saw. Now I'm not saying I'm never wrong, but I will say it hasn't happened above once or twice since I've been in this business."

I started to grin at this, but he didn't, so I quickly reined my grin in.

"If you ever decide that you want more than general dogsbody work, portering and so on, you come and see me. You got me?"

He handed me his card, and shook me by the hand. I didn't know what to say, quite, so I said: "Thank you, Mister...?"

"Westcott. Frederick Westcott."

Then he popped his hat on his head and looked me up and down in a solemn fashion.

"When you know me better you'll know I don't say this lightly," he said. "But you've got it, young feller me lad."

"What?" I said.

"It."

And he turned on his heel and left. I looked at the card he had given me and the name Westcott wasn't anywhere to be seen. The inscription read:

"FRED KARNO

MASTER OF MIRTH AND MAYHEM

The Fun Factory, 26–28 Vaughan Road, Camberwell, London SE5"

I didn't know it then, but my life had just changed for ever.

5
THE HOUSE THAT
FRED BUILT

 it was that I found myself, a blur of a fortnight later, on a train to London, going to seek my fortune.

My father's solemn goodbye and firm handshake were accompanied by a rather smug and knowing smirk, as though he had no doubt at all that I would shortly be scuttling back to Cambridge with my tail between my legs begging to be allowed to make beds again.

My mother and brother were utterly unperturbed by my departure. When I told my mother I was going to London to make a name for myself she greeted the announcement with a casual "Bye bye, then, dear!", as if I had just said I was going to the market to buy eggs, and then turned straight back to the four square feet of pastry she was just then engaged in rolling flat. Lance barely looked up from polishing the Master's shoes to grunt the following resonant and emotional valediction, which has remained imprinted upon my memory ever since.

"Off to be a clown, then, eh? See you when you grow up."

To begin with, I hadn't given much thought to my conversation on the first night with the dapper gentleman in the theatre bar.

On the last night, though – at a sumptuous drinks party for the cast, hosted by The Rotter himself, to which I was graciously invited ... to add myself to the serving staff – I fished the mystery gent's card out of my back pocket and showed it to Mr Luscombe, whose eyes popped out on stalks. Metaphorically, of course. If he'd been able to do it for real he'd have been sure of a living on the halls for the rest of his days.

"Good Lord!" he exclaimed. "You know who this is, don't you?"

I shrugged.

"It's Karno! Fred Karno, of Karno's Speechless Comedians. Well, that's what they used to call them, back when they weren't allowed to speak. He's one of the biggest – no, what am I saying, he's *the* biggest name in the music hall!"

Once he'd recovered himself – a couple of brandies and a breath of fresh air later – Mr Luscombe explained his pop-eyed excitement. He was a great enthusiast of the music hall, if a secret one, as his parents and his po-faced brother would never have approved of his wallowing amongst the lowlife of London, as they called it. He reckoned he'd seen all the great names, just names to me then, as he ticked them off for me on his fingers.

"George Robey – the Prime Minister of Mirth – Little Tich, Gus Elen, Wilkie Bard, Vesta Tilley. And Marie Lloyd I saw once, marvellous fun! Karno, though," and Luscombe prodded me in the chest to emphasise the point, "Karno is the nonpareil."

"Why, what does he do?" I asked, not knowing what a nonpareil was but imagining some kind of novelty act, possibly involving animals.

"Not he himself, though he is the mastermind. His company performs his pieces, little plays that will make you laugh and will make you cry. The last Karno turn I saw was called *The Bailiff*, with Fred Kitchen. When he offers his arm to the poor woman who has lost everything there's not a dry eye in the house, I assure you. And yet when he and his assistant, Meredith, are trying to gain entry to a house, all his little schemes and plots had the place in tucks. Kitchen, do you see, would say, 'You do such and such, and then I do so and so, and then ... Meredith, we're in!'"

He seemed surprised that I did not immediately fall about laughing at this.

"Meredith, we're in!" he cried again. "That's the recurring phrase, do you see? And now you tell me that Karno has offered you a start? Why, man, what are you waiting for?"

Mr Luscombe dictated a letter for me to send to the great Fred Karno, and he was even more wretchedly nervous than I was as we watched the college's daily postal arrivals for a reply. When it came, a few days later, the envelope contained only another business card, exactly like the one I had been given in the theatre bar except that on the reverse side, in a firm and confident hand, a single word was inscribed in capital letters: "COME."

Luscombe was thrilled and heartily pooh-poohed my misgivings. Was not the address right there on the card? "Just take a cab from the station to Coldharbour Lane, and ... Meredith – you're in!"

The run down to London was but a short hop by train, but I felt like I'd landed on another planet as I stepped onto the platform and looked around at the terminus. Huge black iron arches vaulted way overhead, like a monstrous satanic parody of the college chapel's ceiling. Everywhere folk rushed, trotted, skittered and ambled about their various business, gentlemen

47

peering urgently at their pocket watches, small gaggles of children tugging their nannies towards an excursion train, and here and there new arrivals with little piles of luggage looking as lost and intimidated as I felt.

I wandered out into the street, where huge brick buildings thrust up four, five, six storeys high in all directions, and suddenly good old Cambridge, which had always felt so stately and grand to me, seemed like a cramped and claustrophobic warren.

Traffic of all kinds clattered, clopped, parped, crapped and wheezed this way and that. It was dizzying, bewildering, too much to take in. I felt a bit of Dutch courage was called for, and I was a grown-up making his way in the world, after all, so I nudged my way through the door of a public house called the Railwaymen, which was full, pretty much as advertised, with railwaymen.

By mid-afternoon, with a couple of pints (and then a couple more) on board, I was sufficiently confident to ask for directions to Camberwell, and eventually I found my way to the street specified on Mr Karno's card.

When I finally turned the corner I had to stop for a moment to take it in. I can't be certain, but I think I may have pushed my hat back in order to scratch my head in amazement.

A row of houses up a short side street seemed to have been knocked together, or combined into one enormous premises with huge double doors at the front. These were flung open wide, presumably to let the summer air circulate, so passers-by could see that inside it was an absolute hive of activity. Outside, no fewer than four double-decked motor omnibuses were parked in a row along the kerb, big painted signs on the sides bearing the legend "Fred Karno's Comics", where you might ordinarily expect to see "Bovril" or "Pears Soap".

I had reached the Fun Factory.

And just at that moment dozens of people of all shapes and sizes began to issue forth. Dapper young gentlemen, elegant young ladies, all dressed to kill, some of the ladies flourishing brightly coloured parasols, they spilled down the short slope and out onto the road, laughing, chattering, greeting one another with exaggerated good humour, and began to pack themselves into the omnibuses until the vehicles' aching suspensions creaked. On and on they came, a hundred, two hundred of them.

Then some even more affluent-looking middle-aged chaps strode confidently towards waiting broughams, a handful of fabulously dressed women glided miraculously after them, then a couple of stragglers ahoy-hoyed and skipped up onto the buses' backboards, until the short street was empty of pedestrians, save for a few slack-jawed gawkers like myself.

Suddenly, all at once, the heaving convoy puffed and chuffed and parped and clopped and wobbled into motion, dividing at the end of the street as half went left and half right, with a few local children who had come to wave these fantastical creatures off trotting along in their wake, bowling their hoops along the pavement.

And then there was silence. I took a deep breath, tiptoed tentatively up to the big double doors and peered inside ... where I saw the damn'dest thing. You'll hardly believe me when I tell you, but there was an ocean liner in there, just sort of looming up, large as life. The sort of thing that made me wish I had a half bottle of some sort of cheap booze in my hand, so I could look down at it accusingly before forswearing the demon drink for ever.

In the gloom at the back of the building I saw a light, and there was a little office with windows in its rather wobbly-looking walls.

The door was ajar, and a man in shirt sleeves was hunched over a desk inside. I went over and tapped lightly on the glass window in the door.

"Excuse me, sir...?"

The man looked up at me, a harassed expression on his face. He was around forty, I supposed, losing his hair and his temper.

"Finally! Here take these..." he said, striding over and thrusting a fistful of papers into my hands.

"What ... what are they?"

"Well, it's the bills, the bill matter, of course. What are you waiting for? Off you go, chop chop!"

I had no idea where to go to, of course, so I just stood there like a goof, and the man seemed to gather that he had made a mistake. He looked at me quizzically. "Are you not the printer's boy?"

"No, I beg your pardon, sir. I'm Arthur Dandoe."

The man sighed heavily, then grabbed his papers back from me.

"Arthur Dandoe, eh? Is that name supposed to mean something to me? Come on, lad, I'm a busy man. Tell me your business and let me get on."

I ventured into his office, where a fresh-faced youth I hadn't noticed before was standing in the corner smoking a cigarette. This one watched me coolly as I fumbled in my pockets for Karno's card, which had temporarily gone astray.

"Well, come on, spit it out," the harassed older chap said.

"Um, right, yes," I stuttered. "The thing is, I'm looking for Mr Fred Karno."

"Are you now?"

"Um. Yes, I am."

"Well, good news," the fellow said, burrowing in another pile of papers, looking for something. "You've found him."

My beer-fuddled brain frankly struggled with this. This was clearly not the same man that I had met in Cambridge.

"You mean, *you're*...?" I said.

"No, no, no, no, not me," the man said. "I'm Alf Reeves, if it's any of your business. That's Mr Karno over there."

Reeves pointed at the smoking youth, who gazed at me enquiringly down his nose. He was quite short and had to lean back quite a way to achieve this. Now I was even more baffled. I think I may have felt something go pop in my cranium.

"You're...?" I managed.

"Yes, that's right, I'm Fred Karno. What do you want?" the youth sneered.

I found my tongue, and explained, haltingly, about the conversation I'd had with the shinily shod man in the theatre bar, and how I had come to London from Cambridge to take him up on his offer.

"Oh, well, that's just marvellous, that is. That's just dandy!" he said, in a manner which quite definitely suggested that it was neither marvellous nor dandy. Then he aimed a vicious kick at a waste-paper bin, sending it skidding across the room. Alf Reeves sighed, ran his fingers through what hair he had left and narrowed his eyes at me.

"If I had sixpence for every time some youth strolled in here and claimed that Mr Karno himself had told them to come and present themselves to me for a career in the musical theatre, do you know how rich I'd be? Eh? Do you have any idea?"

I felt so deflated suddenly that I could only shrug.

"Well, not that rich, actually. I'd have about four bob. It doesn't happen all that often. So you met The Guv'nor, then, did you? Well, well. And what did he have to say to you when you met him?"

"Actually he said I had 'it'," I ventured.

"And what, might I ask, do you intend to do with 'it'?" Reeves enquired. "Are you going to eat 'it', wear 'it', sleep in 'it', do a little dance with 'it'? It smells like you might already have drunk most of it."

I just smiled at him, a thin, watery smile, like an idiot. Reeves sat back slowly and sighed, the weary sigh of a man who has been left in charge while whoever is supposed to be making the decisions is off having fun somewhere else.

"All right, all right," he said, suddenly bursting to life again and starting to scribble a note to himself on a scrap of paper. "I'll set you on as a super, no harm in that."

At this Reeves glanced up at the youth as if for his approval, and got a surly shrug in response.

"The pay's five bob a week," Reeves went on. "I'll have you back here tomorrow first thing to make a start. Now, then. Where do you live?"

"Um ... Cambridge," I said.

"But you're not planning to go back and forth to Cambridge every day, are you? In town, I mean, where are you living in town, in London?"

"Actually I haven't anywhere to go," I admitted.

Reeves turned to the smoking youth, who was still inexplicably seething at me as though I'd pinched his lunch or something. "Freddie? You're heading down to Streatham, aren't you? Take Arthur here to Clara Bell's. Tell her he'll be paid at the end of the week. Now run along, there's good lads. I've a thousand other things to be doing."

The youth Freddie closed his eyes and sighed, as though he'd rather tackle anything else but the onerous chore of taking care of me, then he grabbed a jacket and hat and stalked out.

I caught up with him out on the street. He was striding along unnecessarily quickly, I thought. I really couldn't imagine what I had done to offend him, and fell anxiously into step alongside him.

"So," I ventured after a minute or two of sulky perambulation. "I really did meet Fred Karno in Cambridge, then?"

"Sounds like it, doesn't it?" this Freddie said, a grim set to his jaw.

"Well, why did you say you were Fred Karno, then?"

"I'm Fred Karno junior, that's it, see?" he suddenly burst out. "You met The Guv'nor, my father, the *famous* Fred Karno. You follow?"

I nodded. I followed. We strode on towards Brixton Hill.

"I work with Mr Reeves on the *administration* side," Freddie junior eventually offered, managing to make administration sound like cleaning out sewers. With a toothbrush. "So usually when a stranger walks in off the street and asks to see Fred Karno, it's me he's looking for, do you see? Muggins. The dogsbody."

Suddenly Freddie spotted the tram for Streatham going past us and darted after it at a gallop. I followed suit, and managed to leap on board just as it was setting off again. I found Freddie inside and collapsed into the seat opposite him, and couldn't help noticing that he looked somewhat disappointed that I'd made it.

Clara Bell's house was actually very conveniently situated for someone working in the theatrical business, particularly for Mr Fred Karno senior's company. The late-night trams ran down from the West End through Brixton onto Streatham High Road until all hours, so that performers could be sure of making it home whenever their various engagements finished. This meant that this whole part of the world – Brixton, Streatham, Balham – had a significant thespian population.

Freddie didn't say a word more to me, but I had plenty to look at as we went along. The outskirts of London seemed to sprawl for ever, an endless repeating sequence of shop fronts, gardens, churches and green open spaces.

The tram stopped alongside a wide green common, and I was watching some carriage drivers leading their horses to a row of stone troughs to drink when I suddenly spotted Freddie striding away over the grass. He'd slipped off, the swine, without saying anything. Well, I grabbed my bag and scurried after him.

I could have done without having to rush, as it seemed to stir up the beer I'd had with the railwaymen, which was sloshing around inside me. Halfway across the common, with Freddie hightailing it into the distant yonder, the whole place began to spin like a crazy whirligig, buildings and trees flying past my ale-addled eyes, and I had to sit in a heap on the grass until it all calmed down.

By the time I was able to stand again Freddie had made it over to a three-storey town house and was ringing the bell. I caught up with him before the door was opened, and I leaned heavily against the porch for a moment. As I did so I glanced over at the house next door. Like the Bells', it was three storeys high, with steps leading down to a basement entrance as well as up to the front door, and suddenly I was half sure I saw a pale face, a woman's face, watching me from the window on the first floor. Then the door opened and there stood Clara Bell, a cheerful little woman with her sleeves rolled up, wiping her hands on her apron.

"Hallo, Freddie!" she cried, inexplicably pleased to see the lad. "What's this? Surprise visit?"

"Delivery," Freddie muttered, wafting his hand at me.

"Are you not coming in for a cup of tea?"

Freddie just shook his head, turned on his heel and left, the charmer. Clara Bell seemed remarkably forgiving of this behaviour.

"Well," she said, clapping her hands together. "Alf sent you, I suppose, did he? You'd better come in. I'm Clara. You've just missed Charley, I'm afraid, he's doing three a day. I suppose you can have Ronny's room, he won't be needing it any more. You can give me a hand putting his stuff into his trunk."

As she chattered away Clara led me in, along the hallway and downstairs into the scullery, where she bustled around getting out cups and saucers and a teapot.

"We'll have some tea first, shall we...?"

"Arthur. Arthur Dandoe."

"Pleased to meet you, Arthur. And this..." she exclaimed, as a tiny whirlwind sped in from the garden and thumped into her midriff, "...is Edie. Say good afternoon to Arthur, Edie."

The little dynamo turned out to be a four-year-old girl, clutching a doll in her little arms. She turned shy at the sight of me and wouldn't show her face, nor would she let her mother go about her business either, so we all stood together there as I told Clara how I came to be there.

"Aha," she said. "I expect young Freddie was thrilled to bits to see you, wasn't he?"

"He hid it quite well if he was," I said.

"Well," she said cheerfully. "You've landed on your feet, I'm sure. There's hundreds of young lads up the Corner[4] who'd give their right arm to join Karno's. Not that he's much on the lookout for boys with one arm, as far as I know. Well, now since you've come from Alf, I'll trust you for your rent until you get paid on Saturday night," she went on. "But just bear in mind that Charley, my husband, works for Karno's and is one of Alf Reeves's oldest friends, so if you come up short we'll just get our money directly from your wages the next week, before you even see them. Understood?"

After a cup of tea and a slice of rather heavy fruit cake I was shown up to a room on the top floor. There was a single bed, bowed in the middle, together with a wardrobe and a chest of drawers which were stuffed – sort of half full, actually, as though he'd gone away on a trip – with some fellow's belongings.

"This was poor Ronny's room," Clara said rather wistfully. "Such a shame..."

She tugged a trunk out from under the bed and began to fold poor Ronny's shirts, trousers and socks and pile them inside. I was wondering what poor Ronny might say if he were to come back and find me in his bed, with all his belongings packed away.

"So he's definitely not coming back, then?" I said, passing her a pair of rather battered slippers.

Clara shook her head sadly. "Oh no, I should say not."

Which was all I was going to get on that subject. "I thought I caught a glimpse of your neighbour when I arrived earlier," I said. "A pale lady, watching me from the first-floor window..."

Clara sucked a loud breath between her teeth and began shaking her head again.

"Poor woman," she said. "Poor, poor woman."

And with that she left me alone in the room, to the rather gothic accompaniment of a loud thunderclap from outside that shook the glass in the window frames.

I looked at my new home, which then began to spin slowly. That slice of cake wasn't sitting very well on all the beer, or else the nervous tension of my unpromising welcome at the Fun Factory was making itself felt. I sat heavily on the bed, and noticed for the first time a brand spanking new gas fire in the fireplace, which was nice. Sitting on the floor in front of it was a bowl of water, as was the custom, to keep the room from getting too dry.

I threw up in it.

6
A NIGHT IN AN
ENGLISH MUSIC HALL

I woke with a pounding head and the dim recollection that I was to start work that day and that I was to be a "super", whatever that was. A *super*, eh? Not too shabby!

Clara furnished me with some breakfast, not that I could manage much, and I was formally introduced to young Edie's dolly, whose name, rather splendidly, was Miss Churchhouse. Then the three of them, Clara, Edie and Miss Churchhouse, kindly walked me to the tram stop.

When the tramcar arrived Clara called to the driver to be sure and set me off at Coldharbour Lane, which he duly did, and I found my way back to the Fun Factory easily enough. It seemed deserted, especially in comparison to the hubbub of the day before.

Alf Reeves blinked at me for a moment when I presented myself again at his office, but then he recalled our meeting the previous day and snapped his fingers.

"Dandoe, Arthur Dandoe, of course. Come with me. I want to show you something."

He led me out into the cavernous workshop and over to the enormous construction taking on the shape of an ocean liner that I'd seen the day before. One or two lads were rolling their sleeves up and just getting to work on it, and a considerable amount of banging was coming from somewhere behind it.

"You see this, lad?" Reeves said, waving a proprietorial arm to take in the whole gigantic contraption. "What does it look like to you?"

"Well, like a part of a great ship, Mr Reeves," I replied.

"Precisely so. You have heard, perhaps, of the *Lusitania*? Of the *Mauretania*?"

I had, naturally. They were the two enormous and luxurious ocean liners of the Cunard line that had been launched with a great fanfare not long before.

"Well, this," Reeves announced grandly, "is the *Wontdetainia*, ha ha, and God bless all who sail in her." He banged it with his fist and this made a clanging sound. "It is the set for our newest production, which begins next week, and it's not a wood and canvas and plasterboard fake. It's sheet metal, see, just like the real thing, and real rivets, put together special by some laddies from the docks. The end panels are hinged – here..." – he strode along to a point towards the front of the ship, pointing – "...and as the whole thing moves slowly across the stage the bow will fold into the wings out of sight, while the stern unfolds correspondingly on the other side, to give the illusion that we have fitted something even larger than the theatre itself onto the stage."

I nodded, impressed, and Reeves led me round the back to see the platforms where the actors portraying the passengers would stand, and some fearsome-looking mechanisms concealed there.

"And then behind, look, we have these three hydraulic rams, which will simulate the rocking motion of the sea, backwards and forwards and side to side – port to starboard, I must remember to say, apparently – to make the effect completely convincing. It is all mightily exciting, you agree? It is also the most expensive stage machine that we, or anyone else, have ever constructed, costing upwards of two *thousand* pounds..."

I whistled, staggered by the sum. Reeves grimaced.

"So it had better damn well work, or we shall be ruined. Well, not ruined, exactly, but belts will be tightened, let's just say that."

We walked back round to the front and he put his arm around my shoulders.

"When this show opens next week, my boy, you will be a super."

"I'll try my best, Mr Reeves," I said in what I hoped was a businesslike fashion, and waited for him to tell me what a super actually did.

"In the meantime we have only a week before we shift this lot up to the Paragon and it all needs to be painted. So hang your jacket up, there's a good lad, grab a brush and a ladder and off ye go!"

And with that he strode off to take care of a million other things, all of them more important than me, it seemed.

Great gallon buckets of whitewash waited over by the wall of the scene dock, and there was nothing for it but to pitch in, so I put a ladder up against the flank of the mighty *Wontdetainia*, clambered up and began to slap the paint onto the metal.

To either side of me were young men engaged in the same work, holding their paintbrushes at arm's length, both of them, as if to keep themselves as far as possible from the point at which actual manual labour was occurring. Neither deigned to speak to me for a good while, but eventually their curiosity got the better of them.

"What are you, then?" asked the one to my right. "Are you a super?"

"I think so," I said, but to be honest I still wasn't sure what a super was.

"What show are you in?"

"Show? I'm not in a show."

"Well, you're not a super, then, are you?"

"He's an ordinary," the chap on the other side cracked, and they both sniggered.

"You two are supers, then, I take it?" I asked.

"We are," they replied simultaneously, then waggled their little fingers at one another to avert bad luck.

"Well, what is a super?"

"What *is* a super?" the one on my left repeated, incredulously.

"Yes, if you don't mind my asking. It's my first day."

"A super," the other answered with a patronising simper. "A super is an *artiste*, my dear. The principals perform their routines. We provide the spectacle."

"Who is going to want to come and see *this*?" his friend asked, a little indignantly, banging the *Wontdetainia* with a camp little clang. "A great hulk of metal, that's all it is, but imagine when a hundred people are hanging off it, waving their kerchiefs and throwing down streamers, shouting farewell to their loved ones. We will make it ... *magnificent!*"

It dawned on me then that 'supers' was a fancy way of saying that they were not especially important. Supernumerary, in fact. Human scenery. Inhabitants of the very bottom rung of the show-business ladder (not counting the outright unemployed, of course, who don't have a rung and have to sit on the floor). And I, poor insignificant Arthur Dandoe, wasn't even important enough to be able to call myself one of them.

Well, that's just ... super, I thought to myself.

Towards the end of the afternoon, as I broke off from painting to flex my aching fingers a moment, I became aware of a growing hubbub behind me. I looked over my shoulder and saw that the scene dock, which had been echoing and empty all day, was filling up once again with exuberant characters, gentlemen and ladies, all chattering away, greeting one another loudly, exactly as they had the day before. One or two looked up approvingly at the progress of the *Wontdetainia*, and hullooed a greeting at a friend they had spotted on the ladders above.

Then I saw that all the men who had been working the whole day on the ship were sliding urgently down and grabbing their overcoats, before joining the swelling throng below to spill out onto the street and head for the buses and broughams.

Silence followed, an eerie, echoing silence, and I was alone.

This turned out to be the routine. The Fun Factory would be a hive of activity all day and then, come teatime, the place would fill up with assorted performers and supers who would bustle around, chattering and gossiping, until the time came to be carried off to theatreland, leaving me on my own without so much as a "Cheer-o!" or a "See you tomorrow!" I would then make my solitary way back to the Bells' house in Streatham, where Clara and Edie would share their supper with me, and then I would either end up playing with Edie and Miss Churchhouse, or, if I was quick enough (please, God), escaping upstairs to read one of my penny bloods in peace.

By the end of the week I was heartily fed up with this show business, to be honest, and ready to slink back to Cambridge. My hands were cramped into claws from painting, and the white-wash was so dazzling in the summer sunshine that even after I'd left the cursed *Wontdetainia* behind for the day I could still see it as an after-image burned into my retinas, little dark portholes floating about in my eye water.

It wasn't just the tedious work, though. After all, if I'd remained at the college for the summer I'd have been whitewash-ing the walls of staircases O to T. It was that the fun folk at the so-called Fun Factory had made me feel about as welcome as Jack the Ripper. Even Lance was better company, and he could go days without speaking to me at all.

In due course I met my landlord, Clara's husband, Charley Bell, and you couldn't exactly call him a cheerful advocate for a life on the boards either. He was working three shows a night, playing in a Karno sketch called *London Suburbia*, in Balham, then Chiswick and then Highgate, and so was usually still in bed when I left in the mornings, and gone out by the time I got back to the house.

One morning, though, he appeared, bleary-eyed, in the door-way of the scullery as Clara, Edie and I were having breakfast, and we were introduced. Perhaps it wasn't the best time to catch him, but he seemed a man of few words. When asked about the previous evening's performances he ventured that Balham was "thin", Chiswick "as good as could be expected" and Highgate "rowdy".

Charley had been with Karno for years, and had played the original "Naughty Boy" in the sketch *Mumming Birds* – about which much *much* more later – so I was eager to ask him about the company. Most of all, though, I wanted to hear something, anything, that would make me feel it was worth hanging around for. He shrugged and poured himself a cup of tea.

"It's a job, I suppose," he said. "No better nor no worse than plenty of others."

I sipped at my own tea, contemplating the miserable prospect of painting another half acre of metal panelwork, and decided that this particular job was not all it was cracked up to be.

By the end of that gruelling afternoon, muscles aching, pores clogged and ears untroubled by even a half-friendly conversation, I'd pretty much made my mind up to pack it all in. I'd stay long enough to get paid for what I'd done, but that was that. To Hell with the blasted Fun Factory! It was all Factory and no Fun, it seemed to me. Mr Luscombe would be disappointed, but, well, he'd just have to learn to live with it.

Once the mob had left and the hubbub had subsided, I was clambering down from the side of the accursed *Wontdetainia*, ready to wend my weary way back to Streatham, when Alf Reeves came bustling out of his office, wrestling his arms into his jacket as he hurried along. For a moment he looked surprised to see me, but then seemed to place me in his mental scheme of things.

"What are you...?" he began, and then: "Oh yes, I recall. You have no show to do yet, do you?"

"No, Mr Reeves," I said. I suppose I must have looked pretty fed up. He cocked his head to one side, thinking.

"Tell you what. Would you like to see some turns this evening?"

I reviewed my plans for the evening, which revolved mostly around trying to escape from playing with a small child and her dolly, and said that I wouldn't mind.

"Wash up, then, quick as you can. I've to go up the Mile End Road. Bit of business to take care of. Come and see what we're up against, eh?"

Outside Alf was waiting for me by his motor car. I'd seen motor cars close up before, of course, even though they were still something of a rarity on the streets. Several of the more affluent and fashionable young gentlemen at college had purchased them, and very proud they were of them too.

It was a gleaming new Ford, which, as the saying went at the time, came in any colour "so long as it's black". (This one was blue.)

Reeves fiddled about with some switches or knobs inside the machine and then emerged with a starting handle, which he handed to me.

"You do know how to use this, don't you?"

"I'm afraid I don't," I replied. His face fell.

"Curse it all!" Reeves took the handle back from me and shoved it into a socket low down at the front of the vehicle. "I was hoping I wouldn't have to do this. I really dislike it – it has a kick like a mule if you don't get it just right. All right, now watch me, and then next time you'll know what to do, won't you?"

Reeves cranked the starter handle round a couple of times, and then leapt out of its way as it sprang back, narrowly missing his shins. He glanced up at me, licked his lips, then approached it warily to give it another go. This time he managed to get the engine turning over, and he yanked the handle free and scuttled round to the driver's seat.

"In! In! In!" he cried, and I hurried round to the passenger side and climbed aboard.

Reeves let off the handbrake, a gout of smoke guffed out of the machine's rear end, and we rolled away from the little gaggle of gawking street children that had formed.

It was, as I say, my first ride in a motor car, and I remember feeling quite vulnerable. Everything on the road seemed to be larger and more robust than our flimsy carriage, which felt like it was going to tip over at every turn, and Alf's style of driving involved rather more near misses than seemed strictly necessary.

"Freddie got you settled at Clara's, then, did he?" he shouted, veering round a grocer's cart.

"Yes, Mr Reeves."

"Oh, I'm Alf, you can call me Alf. You mustn't mind Freddie, you know. He's a nice boy deep down."

"I'm sure he is," I said, although it has to be said I wasn't, not at all.

"His father won't let him on the stage, at any price, and so naturally that's all he's ever wanted, you see?"

Before long, mercifully, we were barrelling down the Mile End Road, which was nice and wide and straight and with fewer things we could possibly smash into.

"This is the Jewish part of town," Alf explained, and I suppose the character of the streets did seem subtly different to those of Camberwell and Streatham. A lot more beards about the place, I think that had something to do with it.

"You get some very good crowds round here," Alf went on. "Do some really good business. Good sense of humour, your Jewish audience, and Jewish comedians are all the rage at the moment, you know."

He turned down a side road and pulled up with a jolt opposite a brightly lit building, the front of which was plastered with music hall bills. A queue of people snaked down the steps and along the street, chattering, in boisterous mood, waiting to be admitted to the evening's performance.

"This place is called Forester's," Alf said, pulling up on the handbrake. "One of the smaller houses, but there's a good bill on tonight. Come on..."

I stepped out of the motor car and headed for the end of the queue, but Alf took my arm and led me down a passage along the side of the building to the performers' entrance. We went up some stairs and into the backstage area, where Alf guided me through the throngs of folk making themselves ready, looking for someone in particular. Everyone we passed had a greeting for him, ranging from a deferential "Evening, Mister Reeves!" to a cheery "Alf!", until we reached the object of our quest, who hailed him with a booming "Alfred! Hail fellow well met! Well met indeed!"

"Ah, George, there you are," Alf grinned, shaking the hand of a formidably confident chap of around forty. The man had luxuriant eyebrows and was rather affluently turned out in a well-cut suit with a gold watch chain draped across the front of his checked waistcoat. "Can I ask a favour of you, do you think?"

"My dear chap! Anything, anything at all!" George beamed.

"This..." Alf pulled me closer by my sleeve, "...is Arthur Dandoe, he's new with us. Just stick him somewhere where he can watch, and keep him safe until I get back, could you? I need to go to the Paragon, couple of hours probably."

"Eh? I haven't heard it called that before," said George. "But if you've got to go, you've got to go. Arthur, my boy – shall we?" He shook my hand briskly and led me to the prompt corner, where he explained to the stage manager that I was his personal friend, and that I was to be given the best possible view of the show.

I hadn't the first idea who he was at that point, but from the way the stage manager jumped to attention and offered to go and fetch me a beer and a beef sandwich, I gathered that George was a figure of some importance. For the first time since I'd come to London, I was actually beginning to enjoy myself.

The show began. From my vantage point in the wings I could see a swath of audience down below, family groups, gangs of office boys, clerks, a few rougher-looking sorts, ruddy-faced, getting a little the worse for wear, and a healthy sprinkling of the dark-clad and swarthily bearded gentlemen I had seen in the street earlier.

What I noticed at once was a much more ribald interaction between stage and crowd than I had seen before. The audiences back in Cambridge were genteel and restrained by comparison, and the acts onstage were having their work cut out just gaining the attention of the room. Some of them were just not up to it, and their voices strained reedily upwards like a teacher trying to bring a classroom of rowdy boys to order.

A little spectacle held the crowd better. Two chaps dressed like circus gymnasts rode bicycles around the stage in crazy circles, interweaving at breakneck pace. It seemed that they must collide at any moment, cracking their limbs or spilling their brains onto the apron, but they were masters of their routine and exited to the first decent round of applause of the night.

Later a gentleman in evening dress addressed the audience on the subject of a large glass tank full of water, in which a lithe young girl swam like a mermaid, not coming up for air nearly often enough. The man would describe various feats, which the mermaid would then perform.

"And now," the gentleman cried, "Marina will eat a pie!"

And she did, rising to the surface to collect her treat, then sinking down to her knees on the floor of the tank and munching away until the whole thing was gone before allowing herself another breath. The audience were fairly captivated, principally I suspect by the fact that she was a lithe young lass not wearing very much and that sooner or later she'd climb out of the tank absolutely soaking wet to take her bow.

A curtain came down so that the tank could be carted away by stagehands, and a cockney coster singer of supreme cheeriness cavorted about on the forestage, tweaking his braces with his thumbs and singing about eels. In the meanwhile I became aware of a slight figure pacing nervously in the wings beside me. His beard and get-up mimicked those of the Jewish contingent in the audience, and I could hear the fellow muttering as he ran through his jokes.

I suppose I was peering at him rather, principally because I had the suspicion that he was much younger than he was trying to appear, when he suddenly turned and glared at me, as much as to say: "What the devil are you looking at?"

I stared back at him, and after a moment of two of frosty hostility he stomped off muttering to himself. I frowned quizzically at the stage manager, who shook his head in a long-suffering manner.

"This is his first time as a solo turn," he whispered. "He was here with Casey's Circus a while back and sweet-talked the boss into giving him a go. He's been giving us hell with his music cues and such. Nothing's good enough for him, and he's not happy with the running order, like we'd change it just for *His Majesty*..."

The band struck up with a tune I didn't recognise, but it seemed to strike a chord with the Jewish contingent, and I could see them nudging one another, as if expecting now to see one of their own.

What they saw, though, was a slight figure stepping onto the forestage, clearly a slip of a lad pretending to be older than he was, with a mountain of black crêpe piled on his head and a further waterfall of the stuff cascading from his chin in a parody of the style favoured by most of their number.

"Cohen's the name," the youth began. "Sam Cohen. I was talking the other day to my friend Levy, I was, and do you know what he said to me...?"

He then proceeded to relate, line by line, a conversation between himself and his absent friend – who didn't seem, from what I could make out, to be the brightest spark. And thus his whole act seemed to be made up of "then I said such and such..." and "to which Levy said so and so..." so that you had the substance of a slick two-handed patter act, except with just the one hand, if you follow me.

His first jokes, such as I could make them out as he was affecting a very nearly incomprehensible Jewish accent and his voice lacked power, seemed to have originated in America, concerning as they did "a debt of some seventeen dollars and fifty cents".

None of this went down at all well, and it was downhill from there. After a couple of minutes or so, I heard the first loud clang of a penny landing on the stage, followed by another, then another. Sometimes money arriving onstage during your act is a good sign, but on this occasion you could tell that the coins were being thrown really quite hard. Could have been worse, though. I once saw a singer hit full in the face by a dead cat hurled from the stalls.

The lad froze as the full horror of the growing hostility towards

70

him sank in. An orange cannoned off his head, knocking his home-made wig askew, and then more loose change arrived. He peered out over the footlights, as if puzzled that these people were unable to perceive the genius in what he was doing.

A rain of pennies and halfpennies settled the matter finally, and as he withdrew I even saw a shilling or two bounce off his back, so desperate were the audience to see it.

He rushed into the wings and past us, his cheeks fairly ablaze with humiliation, ripping his wig and beard off as he fled and leaving them where they fell.

Onstage the master of ceremonies was trying to get the audience to calm down for the headline act of the evening. I was suddenly aware of George alongside me, shaking his head philosophically.

"I think they preferred that act when it had two people in it," he murmured. "And two different people at that."

I nodded, but I was distracted. I was sure I'd seen, again, that when the youth flung his props down and stormed through the pool of light thrown by the lantern on the prompt desk, the eyes that flashed defiantly at me were purple.

7
THE MAYOR OF MUDCUMDYKE

"...OWn, your very owwwwn!" bellowed the master of proceedings above the hubbub. "Mistah ... George ... Robey! Ey thank yew!"

Hang on a mo', I thought. I'd heard that name. George Robey, the Prime Minister of Mirth, was one of Mr Luscombe's favourites.

Robey had transformed himself. His already luxuriant eyebrows were heavily accentuated with make-up and were now two huge black half moons covering most of his forehead. A little round derby perched up top, with two small tufts of dark, curly hair sprouting above his ears. His jacket was a couple of sizes too small and his trousers and shoes a couple of sizes too large, and he supported his weight on an achingly slender ribbed cane which looked like it might snap at any moment.

The crowd were still rowdy from their success in banishing the upstart beginner, but Robey stood before them with a look of benign puzzlement on his face. He began telling tales of an everyday life not so very different to their own, except that everything about him said "fallen on hard times" as clearly as if he had it written on a sign hanging round his neck. All his stories were designed, I could see, to make the audience feel smarter than Robey himself, and he was the unwitting butt of every one of them. He even became indignant that he was not getting the sympathy he felt he deserved.

"I am not heah," he protested, "to become a laughing stock!"

As I watched the audience, not a couple of minutes earlier a rabble throwing missiles and shouting abuse, calm down, relax and begin to laugh as one, I realised that I was seeing The Power in action. Robey was a master of it, in complete control.

"Desist!" he cried haplessly, meaning them to continue, and they did.

I found that I was not laughing myself. It was funny, I could see it was funny, and I wanted to laugh, I really did, but I didn't want to miss even a moment of the experience. It was as if I was thrilled beyond laughter by Robey's display, and was already processing it, dissecting it, taking it apart in my mind to see how it worked. And in my youthful arrogance I felt that I had been shown a vision of my own future, that I too was capable of this mastery.

Too soon Robey was done, and exited the stage to rapturous acclaim. I gave the next acts a few minutes, but they were pale shadows in comparison. I was on pins, anxious to commune with the master, and hurried round to his dressing room as soon as I thought decent.

"Come!" he boomed in response to my knock, and there he sat at a large mirror with a pot of cold cream, wiping away at his huge eyebrows.

"Come in! Sit!" he cried, wafting his arm at a battered but comfortable armchair. "How d'ye like it? Eh?"

"Um ... marvellous. You were marvellous!"

"You're very polite," Robey smiled. "Bit of work to do after that walking calamity just before me, but *in extremis* we find ourselves, don't you think?"

"I'm sure you are right," I said.

"So, you are under Alf's wing, are you? I often think of Alf as a mother hen, clucking around his chicks, making sure they all get their peck of corn, don't you know?"

I smiled, nodded.

"Good fellow, Alf. Salt of the earth. And if you can make your way with Karno you'll not go far wrong. Some very fine comedians he has brought on in his time, and no mistake. Fred Kitchen, now, he's as good as anyone, and Harry Weldon, too. Karno won't pay them a quarter of what they're worth, but they won't leave him, because they're safe, they feel comfortable. It's guaranteed work, fifty-two weeks a year, and they never have to go out and sell themselves. It's never their name on the bill, it's always Karno's, and Karno's name will always bring a crowd. Now maybe a crowd would come to see good old Fred Kitchen, or Harry Weldon, but they'll never find out, will they, because they haven't got the nerve.

"Now, say what you like about that sorry youth tonight. He may have stunk worse than a week-old halibut, but it took courage to go out there like that. Especially with that material, by the way, which was somewhat second-hand, and second-hand old hat at that. Some of Karno's lads could do with striking out on their own and testing themselves. They won't, though, because they don't see the bigger picture. Not like me. But then I have the benefit, you see, of a Cambridge heducation," he announced grandly.

"Really?"

"Oh yes, I am the finished article, you might say, both comedically and intellectually."

"Which college did you go to, if you don't mind my asking?"

"Of course I don't mind, young man, of course not. Cambridge, of course, as I said..."

"No, I meant which Cambridge college? I am from Cambridge, you see, and I know them all."

"Oh?" His eyes narrowed.

"Oh yes, I used to play cricket with porters from all the colleges. Jesus, Emmanuel, Clare, Trinity Hall, Peterhouse..."

Robey looked a bit shifty now. "Ahem, indeed, indeed. What was the second one?"

"Emmanuel? You were at Emmanuel, sir?"

"Now, you see, you are running ahead of yourself. What I said was I had the *benefit* of a Cambridge heducation, which is to say, my tutor was a Cambridge man, yes, my tutor was heducated at ... um..."

"Emmanuel College?"

"Just so, my tutor, the man who gave me the benefit of *his* Cambridge heducation..."

"I see..."

"...when I was at *Oxford*." Robey allowed himself a little beam of self-satisfaction at having turned this round. I judged it was time to shut up. In any case just then there was a knock on the door, and Alf Reeves's head poked into the room. The rest of him seemed reluctant to follow.

"Alfred, there you are. Time for a snifter, what do you say?"

"No thanks, George. I find it hard enough to control that blasted jalopy when I'm sober, and I should get this lad back to his bed."

"Suit yourself. Goodnight, young man. A pleasure to make your acquaintance." George reached over to shake my hand, and as Alf retreated into the corridor I felt myself pulled in close for a last private word.

"I trust we can keep our earlier conversation, ahem, about my heducation, between the two of us? One doesn't like to brag, you know?"

━━━━━

That night at Forester's was my first experience of music hall, and I fell in love with it. I saw success and I saw failure, and the heady balancing act between the two. I had a glimpse of what it was like to be a member of that secret brotherhood behind the scenes, how special that felt. Best of all, in Robey's performance, I saw the Power in action, and I knew that was what I wanted to do and where I wanted to be. How to get there, of course, that was the tricky part, but all thoughts of slinking back to the college were put to one side.

I was sure that I had, that very evening, met a man who would have a profound influence on the course of my career, and my life.

What I didn't realise was that I'd actually met two.

8
FRED KARNO'S ARMY

THE next day, the Saturday, I was painting again, but now I was painting with a purpose. With every brushstroke I was calculating where the painting might ultimately lead me. Onwards and upwards.

Saturday night was pay night, my first. Clara told me that the tradition was that all the performers from all the various Karno shows currently playing in the halls of London would head back to the Fun Factory at the end of the evening for their packet, and after dinner she dispatched me back up to Camberwell to join them.

When I arrived the double doors were thrown open to the summer evening, and at least a couple of hundred people clustered around the gas lamps to gossip and swap stories while they waited to collect their wages.

As I stood by myself I found my eye taken by a group of girls from who-knows-what show. They were all dazzlingly attractive, with their hair piled up on top of their heads, and dressed to be looked at, I reckoned, with their tight, brightly coloured bodices and long, flowing skirts. So that's what I did.

One in particular held my attention, and she did seem to be the ringleader, holding court almost, making all the others laugh with comments she passed about the men within their orbit. She was quite short, buried almost under a pile of blonde ringlets, which I thought most becoming, and I liked the way she seemed to fizzle with pleasure as she amused her friends, keeping them in a constant giggle.

As I watched her, trying not to make my interest too obvious, I realised to my horror that she had turned her sardonic spotlight onto me. All the girls in her group were looking straight at me, and burst into a gale of tittering as the blonde girl whispered a crack at my expense. I felt myself colouring up, and then she set her head back confidently and walked straight over to me.

"Hallo, Lonesome," she began. "We were just saying, my friends and I, that we hadn't seen you around here before. Are you fresh meat?"

"I suppose I am," I replied, more than a little flustered, not only to be talking to this creature, who, close to, was quite dazzling, with bright green eyes, perfect teeth and a face that looked like it only knew how to smile, but also to be doing so under the scrutiny of everyone she knew.

"I'm pleased to make your acquaintance," she said, holding out a small gloved hand. "I'm Matilda Beckett, but everyone calls me Tilly, Tilly Beckett. How d'ye do."

"Arthur Dandoe," I said, taking her hand with a small formal nod.

"Ooh, that's not bad. Did you think of that yourself?"

"Think of what?"

"That name. Dandoe. It says you're a dandy, man-about-town

kind of style, but the 'oe' brings just a hint of the clown. I like it."

I shrugged. "I didn't think of it, it's just my name."

"No! Your real name, and here am I thinking it's a bit of bill matter!"

I smiled, trying desperately to come up with something, some gambit to make an impression, as she chattered on.

"I was thinking I might get myself a new name when I – fingers crossed – move up from chorus to artiste. A *nom de plume*, sort of thing. Tilly de Plume, that's not bad."

I must have looked baffled, because she felt the need to explain.

"I'm chorus, you see. Most of these people here are supers, which is to say, walking scenery, but me and the girls are chorus, because we actually have something to do in our show. Chorus is above super..." – here she began illustrating this little hierarchy with her hands – "...then next above chorus there's artiste, when you have something to do all by yourself or you actually have lines to speak, then there's featured, then there's principal, and then the number one."

"And then?" I said.

"Well, and then it's the Guv'nor, I suppose."

"And then?"

She laughed and slapped my arm. "I don't know, silly! And then ... *God*, I suppose!" She glanced back towards her group, and, to keep her talking to me, I ventured: "And what do *you* do, the chorus in your show?"

"Ah, well," she said. "The show is *The Yap-Yaps*. Do you know it?" I shook my head. "It's set on the seafront at Brighton, very nicely painted, and the young gentlemen and ladies – that's us – promenade along the ... erm..."

"Promenade?"

"Just so, we promenade along the promenade, and by and by a breeze gets up and blows our dresses up around our ankles, you see, cheeky, which gets the groundlings going a bit. Not this dress, in fact, but one specially made to catch the draught from these great fans which are down in the pit pointing upwards as we pass. You with me?"

I was.

"Then a second time the breeze is stronger, and maybe there's a hint of a nicely turned calf, a knee even. And then finally, once every red-blooded male in the place has a crick in his neck trying to sneak a peek, there comes the most tremendous gust, which blows our skirts right up over our heads and we all run from the stage in our frilly drawers screaming our heads off."

My expression as the mental picture this conjured was playing in my mind's eye must have made her think I disapproved, as she went on: "Not high art, exactly, I know, and I dare say we've set the cause of female emancipation back by a decade or two, but there it is. You do what you have to do, don't you, to get on?"

"Don't the men in the show find it ... distracting?" I asked. I was sure I would have.

"Oh no, no, we never have any trouble in that regard. All the chorus men are specially selected, you see, from those of – how shall I put this? – a more ... *artistic* disposition."

"They're interested in higher things?"

"No, no, roughly the same height. Just different. They're interested in different things. And so what about you, Arthur? What do you do?"

"Oh, I've been busy painting this monstrosity," I said, indicating the hulking form of the *Wontdetainia* louring in the darkness above us.

"Oh, I see," she said, looking up politely, taking in the scale of the project. "But I meant onstage. What show are you in?"

"I'm not," I said. "I haven't done one yet."

"What, none at all? Not one?"

I shrugged. I shook my head. Tilly took a step back.

"Why, Arthur Dandoe!" she cried. "You mean to tell me you're not even a *super*? You're the lowest fellow here, you mean to say? Why, you're *nothing*, nothing at all!" She pretended to come over all flustered – at least I hoped she was pretending. "This won't do! I can't be seen talking to you. I've my career to think of!"

And with that she flashed me a dazzling smile and skipped back to her friends, who had a good old cackle at my expense.

Suddenly a frisson of excitement flashed around the dock like ball lightning. The supers murmured giddily to one another: "Fred's coming! It's Fred Karno! He's crossing the road now!"

Ties were straightened, lips were pursed attractively, busts prodded and realigned, and all eyes turned towards the double doors. I confess I too was staring at the entrance, eager for another glimpse of the dapper little fellow whose single scribbled word – "COME!" – had dragged me here from my cosy perch up in Cambridge, if only to demonstrate that he did actually exist.

Just as it seemed the assembled company might spontaneously burst from sucking its guts in and sticking its chests out, a young man, shortish, baby-faced, with slicked-back hair and an apologetic look slipped in through the huge scene dock doors, to be almost blown back out into the street by a couple of hundred people exhaling in disappointment. It was Freddie, of course, not enjoying himself one bit.

Karno junior blushed and then began setting up a trestle table and a couple of chairs for himself and his assistants. While his back was turned the whole great barnful of people rearranged itself, as if playing a huge and brilliantly co-ordinated practical joke on him, so that when he plonked a couple of great ledgers and cashboxes down on the table and looked up the entire assembly was waiting in orderly queues in front of him. Everyone seemed acutely aware of both their own status and that of everyone else in the place, and so this process had occurred with the absolute minimum of fuss.

I was staring open-mouthed at this spectacle, when suddenly Tilly grabbed my arm urgently.

"Do you want to wait all night? Come on!" she hissed, pulling me into the line alongside hers.

Freddie blinked and coughed and smiled a watery smile, then sat down to begin paying the mob. Maybe twenty minutes of shuffling later the fellow in front was telling Freddie his name and the show he had been doing that week, adding ingratiatingly as he collected his earnings: "So nice to see you again, Mr Karno. Remember me to your father, won't you?"

Freddie grunted, as every single one of the supers he had so far dealt with had had something similar to say, and the fellow departed. I stepped up.

"Arthur Dandoe, remember me? I've been working on the *Wontdetainia.*"

"Dandoe ... Dandoe ... Dandoe..." Freddie mumbled, running his finger down page after page of names until finally he came across mine. "Ah, here you are. Right at the very *bottom of the heap.*"

This resonated deep in my subconscious, along with Tilly giggling "Why, you're *nothing*, nothing at all...!"

He counted out my money and tipped the coins into my palm, expecting me to leave directly, but I stood my ground.

"It'll be more next week, you know, once the show goes up," he said, frowning.

"Yes," I said, resolved not to remain at the bottom of the heap a moment longer than necessary. "I was wondering whether I might speak to your father, please, on a matter of some importance."

Freddie snorted. "I'm sure you were. Well, he's over the road, paying the featured artistes, and all supers are strictly forbidden from forcing themselves upon him on a Saturday night, and that goes double for painters and decorators. Understood?"

Crushed, I nodded, and stepped out through the double doors and into the darkness. I looked around for Matilda Beckett, but her queue had been paid more briskly than mine and she'd disappeared into the night. Over on the far side of Coldharbour Lane a public house called the Enterprise was lit up, the windows and doors thrown open to catch the summer breeze, and the sound of loud, mostly male, mirth and merriment carried across the deserted street. I couldn't make out what was being said, but from the rhythms of the laughter I gathered that someone was holding court and his adoring courtiers were lapping up his every word.

That's where I should be, I thought to myself, over there. Surely Fred Karno didn't spot me on the stage in Cambridge and think, there's a likely lad who'd make a perfectly adequate job of painting my scenery. He'd want me to walk over there and make myself known to him.

The Enterprise was fifty yards away, but it might as well have been a hundred miles. I took a step out into the road to cross over towards the lights, but another loud gale of laughter blew away my nerve, and I stopped again. Just then a small figure emerged and trotted over to me. It was Charley Bell, my landlord.

"By God," he said, "I've had a bellyful of that. Come on, let's go home. Good of you to wait for me ... Arthur, isn't it...?"

"That's right," I said, and, after one last long, wistful glance over the road, I hurried after him towards the late-tram stop.

9
WONTDETAINIA

FINALLY the *Wontdetainia* was pronounced finished, and rehearsals could begin. A great crowd of supers gathered in the Fun Factory's scene dock and all eyes were on the mammoth construction, all trying to work out whereabouts one would be seen to the best advantage. Everyone was absolutely determined to be on the ship itself.

"After all, who looks at the quayside when there's a ship leaving?" one super near me said, chewing his lip nervously.

By the time the stage manager, Mr Bryant, emerged from the office and came to address the crowd, it was like a coiled spring. Greyhounds waiting in the slips, as the saying goes.

"Morning everyone," Bryant said, waving a sheaf of papers above his head, and the hubbub quietened at once. (On your marks...) "Now, I'm going to want some of you on board the ship ... (Get set...) ... and some of you down below, so if you'd all..."

All at once there was a thunder of feet, a clack of heels, and a massive mob-handed game of musical chairs was under way.

Spotlight-crazed supers scrambled up the ladders like a marauding army assaulting a fortified town. Ladies elbowed gents aside in most unladylike fashion, the elderly were crushed underfoot, the infirm left to go hang.

I was able to stake my claim to a goodish spot at a railing, and looked down to where the tidal wave of supers was now falling back and resolving into small pools of the thwarted, remaindered and disappointed. Bryant stood peering up at us, a long-suffering expression on his face, then nodded briskly to the technicians in charge of the huge hydraulic rams.

At first the rocking was slow and gentle and really rather enjoyable. The supers near me grinned as though they were on a ride at a funfair.

Then the rams were cranked up a notch, to show the *Wontdetainia* crossing the Bay of Biscay. A chorus girl clutched a hand to her mouth, while others gripped the railings in front of them, their knuckles showing white. Finally Bryant announced that for the climax of the piece the *Wontdetainia* would find herself thrashing through a great storm.

"Oh my good Lord above!" murmured the gentleman alongside me, gritting his teeth.

The technicians paused a moment, malevolently, then cranked the rams up to full power. The ship bucked and dipped, and there was screaming, retching, crying and pleading yells of: "Stop! For pity's sake, stop!" The sickly-looking chorus girl could stand it no more and threw up in a gentleman's top hat. Admirably discreet, you might think, except that she was atop the ship and the gentleman holding the hat was way down below at ground level.

"All right, stop!" Bryant bellowed. "Stop!"

Down we came, a far more subdued bunch than had swarmed aboard the *Wontdetainia* like a pirate crew just a short time before. There was a pitiable moaning from all parts, with many clutching their stomachs or being helped into chairs by friends.

We gave way to the principals – Shaun Glenville, a small, wiry, athletic young man playing a tipsy purser, and Charles East, a twenty-stone human leviathan, who was the ship's captain. A few of us winced as East clambered aboard the *Wontdetainia* for the first time, fearing that it might not be able to cope with his bulk. He was a massive fellow, who used to dine nightly on a whole leg of ham – which was a show in itself, by the way.

The whole flimsy contrivance, involving card sharps, a rich heiress and a detective in disguise, was funny enough, but it was clearly going to take second place to the spectacle of the storm-tossed liner itself, especially the carefully choreographed chase-in-the-storm sequence, involving passengers (us) and furniture flying through the air from side to side.

As I watched I began to understand why Mr Karno had been so unimpressed by poor Brontie. It must have seemed a puny effect indeed in comparison to this.

―――――

At the weekend we somehow got the great liner broken up and loaded onto carts. There were dozens of us, all the occupants of Karno's lowest rungs, and it took several trips, but eventually we managed to get the whole contraption all the way from the Fun Factory up to the Paragon in Mile End, where we bolted it all back together again. It must have been a strange sight for anyone up at the crack of dawn that Sunday morning, seeing parts of an ocean liner drifting majestically over Southwark Bridge, while the barges slunk down the river below.

When the time came for the dress rehearsal I found my mark, and as I looked around I noticed that a number of gaps had appeared here and there. The sickly chorus girl was no longer with us, and neither was the man who had been next to me, murmuring entreaties to his maker.

"Hullo there, Arthur Dandoe," said a soft voice behind me. I turned and discovered that my new neighbour was to be little green-eyed Tilly Beckett. Things are looking up, I thought to myself. Tilly was every bit as attractive as I remembered, but maybe not quite so full of beans – indeed she looked positively apprehensive.

"This old thing is a real monster, isn't it?" she said, stamping her heel onto the deck. "You know Angeline has been fired, just like that?"

"Really?" I said, not knowing who Angeline was.

"On the spot. I mean, I know she threw up into that man's hat..." Ah, so *that* was Angeline. "...but dear me, they're brutal. Brutal! They know, you see, that they can get a hundred new chorus girls just by going up the Corner and giving a whistle, so they might as well have ones that won't puke up all over the shop. Margaret's fired, as well, and Nell, and Winnie. A few of the men too, I heard. Anyone who looked a bit green about the gills..."

She shivered and drew her shawl tighter about her shoulders. "I tell you, I nearly lost it myself that last time, when it was the storm, and Lord knows I can't afford to miss this go." She looked up at me, and sidled a little closer along the railing. "Let's you and me be a couple, like, then you can hold onto me, and maybe it won't be so bad. What d'you say? Are you game?"

Well, I was game, right enough, and as she slipped her arm under mine I found I was actually looking forward to it quite a lot.

"Here we go everyone!" cried Mr Bryant, and we all braced ourselves. There was a muted sort of a chugger-chugger-chug from behind, but nothing much else happened.

"Cue!" Bryant shouted, and again there were faint stirrings down at the back of the stage. The *Wontdetainia* did not budge. We were in dry dock.

Bryant skipped up onto the apron and stagehands appeared from all corners to confer. They peered at the machines, gave them the occasional desultory tap with a mallet, scratched their chins, shook their heads. Tilly's arm clasped mine and she rested her head on my shoulder while we waited.

"Don't worry," she said. "Something like this always happens. They'll sort it out, they always do."

The longer it went on, though, the less it looked like anything was being sorted out. We began to hear snatches of the discussions below, and the words "...no good ... water pressure too low..." and "...may have to cancel..." sent shivers of apprehension through the assembled company.

Eventually Bryant came to the front of the stage and sent us all away. There was no point in everyone hanging round all day, he said, and we should all be back at six o'clock. It didn't sound promising.

I turned to ask Tilly if she would like a walk, or a cup of tea somewhere, but she was already skipping off with some friends, so I just found myself shuffling out with the rather despondent crowd.

The supers milled about on the street outside the theatre, and I could hear them all muttering darkly about the jobs they could have been doing instead of this one (a likely story). If the turn was cancelled, of course, it would be a week without pay for everybody.

Before long I was the only one left on the pavement there, fed up, wondering what to do with myself until six. I decided to go for a walk – that was cheap. As I strolled up the Mile End Road, Miss Tilly Beckett was on my mind. It's difficult to feel you've impressed a girl when you have a vivid memory of her saying: "Why, you're nothing, nothing at all!"

Still, though, there was the memory too of her arm through mine and her head on my shoulder and the smell of her hair, but then the thought that the sketch which had brought that delicious proximity about was probably done for turned my mood dark again. I suddenly realised that I'd been walking out in the sun for some considerable while and had worked up a powerful thirst.

On my way to a pub I happened to glance in at the window of a tea shop, and who should I see but Tilly Beckett sitting there all by herself. I carried on past, being a silly, self-conscious youth with no real idea of how to talk to a girl, but after a couple of strides I took a deep breath and summoned up the nerve to go back and step inside with a determinedly casual air about me. Tilly looked up when the little bell on the door tinkled, and her face positively lit up when she recognised me.

"Oh good! Good! Come and sit with me!" she said, beckoning me urgently to her table. "Sit! Sit!" I did so, and she leaned over conspiratorially to put her hand on mine, at which my heart actually did what hearts are said to do at moments such as this: it skipped a beat.

"I'm *so-o-o* glad to see you, I can't tell you," she gushed. "I've been nursing this pot for an hour and a half now. That woman's started giving me filthy looks so I had to tell her I was waiting to meet someone, and now here you are! She can't ask me to leave now, can she? Ha!"

Tilly shot a look of purest triumph towards the counter, behind which there sat a beetroot-faced old troll who clearly felt it was high time more money was spent in her establishment, so I ordered another pot of tea for two and some teacakes.

By the time these dubious treats arrived Tilly had explained that she had thought to visit a friend who lived nearby, but that friend had been out, and we'd moved onto fevered speculation as to whether the show would actually go ahead that evening.

"I heard a rumour that the water pressure in this part of the world is simply too feeble to operate all those hydraulic whatnots, and that there might be nothing for it but to abandon the whole week's booking. Maybe more."

"So maybe the wretched *Wontdetainia* is sunk with all hands before it even embarks on its maiden voyage," I said gloomily, and she grimaced.

"Well, I dare say we'll find out soon enough," she said. "Now, shall I be mother?"

I helped myself to a teacake as she did the honours teapot-wise.

"Now then," she said. "I was thinking it might be fun if we were married. What do you think?"

A sizeable chunk of teacake suddenly headed down the wrong pipe. I began to splutter, and Tilly had to come round behind me to thump me on the back, whereupon the offending morsel shot out of my mouth and cannoned wetly into the little vase in the centre of our table.

"Have a sip of tea now, there we go. That better?"

"Mmm..." I said, then: "*Married*, did you say?"

"Yes. I was thinking it might be a lark. What do you reckon?"

It's a measure of how far gone I was, I suppose, that I actually started thinking about it.

"Well ... I... er ... um... Are you sure? I mean, we hardly ... know each other..."

I ventured this gingerly, feeling the point ought really to be raised but not altogether wanting to put her off.

"What's that got to do with anything?" Tilly demanded.

"Well..." I stammered. "Perhaps we could walk out together a few times ... see if we hit it off...?"

"We get along all right, don't we?"

"Yes, yes, we do, I suppose, but..."

"There we are, then, what more do we need? Now, I'm thinking we'd be travelling to America to start a new life together, leaving behind everything and everyone we know ... whatever's up?"

I must have looked shocked, I suppose. "Oh? It's just ... America?"

"Yes?"

"Just like that?"

"Yes?"

"Well, I was just thinking, what about the show? I mean, maybe it will be all right after all, and will go for a few weeks, and then we can get a bit of money together and we'll be able to afford..."

"I'm *talking* about the show, you chump! You know, we should pretend to be married, for our story, in the show. You surely didn't think I was really proposing to marry you in real life, did you? What sort of a girl do you take me for, Arthur Dandoe?"

"Ha ha! Of course not! I was being a character," I blurted out. I felt my face flush hot, and my collar suddenly felt about three sizes too small. "I was thinking I'd be a theatre entrepreneur, worrying about his latest show, and whether he'll be able to afford to ... to ... you know, marry his lovely leading lady and whisk her off to America, the land of opportunity, for the fresh start they both ... um ... long for. Something like that, you see?"

Tilly frowned, chewing this over. "Yes, that's not bad. I like that. Not bad at all. You have to have a story, I reckon. Don't you? Or else it's just the deadliest thing imaginable, standing around, being human scenery. And, you know, the audience don't need to know it, as long as *we* do, do they?"

I nodded and let out a long, slow sigh of relief that we were at last both on the same page of the script, so to speak. She carried on.

"So we're leaving on the *Wontdetainia*, heading to America to make our fortunes. And hey, perhaps someone is trying to stop us. How about that? So we're happy, but we're also just that little bit anxious."

"We're eloping, then, are we?"

"Yes, yes. My father hates you, thinks you'll never amount to anything, and he wants me to marry a vicar, with a big hook of a nose, like a beak..."

On and on we went, embellishing this little tale, until you'd have thought the whole *Wontdetainia* sketch was going to be about the two of us. Our pan-faced hostess eventually made her displeasure at our dragging out a single pot of tea for the whole afternoon too plain to be ignored, and I paid and we made our exit. Tilly popped off to visit the friend who had been out earlier, so I nipped into a hostelry called the Saracen's Head for a swift couple of jars and then made my way to the theatre, feeling much better about life.

Yes, things were definitely looking up. I turned into the alley which led to the stage door ... and saw a fire engine standing there.

The theatre was on fire!

I started to run up the alley. The firemen, three of them, were leaning on the back of their wagon, smoking cigarettes, which they'd hardly do in an emergency. I nodded to them as I squeezed past, and saw that a broad hosepipe was leading from the engine into the theatre, holding the door open.

Intrigued, I followed the pipe, which led up to the back of the stage, all the while becoming aware of a pumping noise getting louder and louder. I stepped out from the wings onto the apron and there, in all its glory, was the *Wontdetainia*, rocking back and forth as though cresting a mighty Atlantic swell. The hydraulic rams were operating at full capacity, thanks – it turned out – to the extra water pressure supplied by the fire brigade.

"Not bad, eh?" said a voice behind me. I walked to the front of the stage, shielding my hands against the lights, and peered down into the darkened stalls. A figure was standing there, a stocky, dapper little fellow, hands on hips, surveying his handiwork.

"Mister Karno," I said. He raised a quizzical eyebrow. "I'm Arthur Dandoe," I said.

"And what are you doing here, Arthur Dandoe?" Karno said, his tone ever so slightly mocking.

"Well, um, I'm to be on the ship," I burbled. "I'm a super."

"I'm sure you are," the boss replied, turning on his immaculately shod heel. "I'm sure you are just as a-super as can a-be. Well, things to do, people to sack, on we go!" he cried, giving me a little wave as he went on his way.

"Mister Karno," I heard myself shouting after him. He turned at the rear of the stalls and looked back at me. "I'm Arthur Dandoe. We met in Cambridge. I wrote. You said to come. I came."

I stopped. The world stopped. Karno began to walk slowly back to me.

"Well, well, well!" he said. "Well, well, well, well, well. It's the young man who was etten by the giant dinosaur, is it not?"

"That's right, sir," I said, my heart hammering.

"I said to come and you came," he said. "And now you're one of my supers, is that it? And what have you done for me so far, Arthur Dandoe?"

"Well, I ... um, nothing, onstage, yet," I twittered. "I've been here two w-weeks and the whole time I've been painting that." I pointed at the good old *Wontdetainia*, lurching away on the stage.

"So tell me this, Arthur Dandoe," Karno said, fixing me with a gimlet gaze. "Why did you come? Hmm? To be a painter?"

Only one thought came to me and I blurted out: "You said I had 'it'!"

Karno grinned. "I did, didn't I? I said you had 'it'. I recall t' conversation now. I don't say that often, you know, and I'll tell you another thing, when I do say it, I'm hardly ever wrong."

He paused for a moment, turning something over in his head, it seemed to me.

"Well, now, if you've got 'it' we can't waste you as a super, can we, or painting scenery? That'd be nothing short of criminal – or do you like it on t' very bottom rung?"

"No, sir," I said, hoping that was the right answer.

"Remember this, Arthur Dandoe. It's up to you, it's always up to you. No one else. It's your responsibility. You must push yourself forward. Make yourself heard. Stick your head up above the crowd. You need to get to the next rung, then climb over whoever's in front of you to get there. Push yourself forward."

I put on a determined expression, which seemed appropriate, and nodded enthusiastically.

"Come and see me in t' morning, ten sharp. We'll see what we can do with you."

"Thank you, Mister Karno."

"Call me 'Guv'nor'. Everyone does." He gave a little wink, smiled and was about to head off again, but I must have been emboldened by his words, because I said: "Er, Guv'nor?"

"What now?"

"It's just that ... you have the fire engine's pump connected up to your hydraulic rams there..."

"I have, and I've brought those lads all the way from Merry-weathers of Long Acre to do it. What of it?"

"Well, last summer the fire brigade came to the college where I worked," I said. "And connected up their pump to the college plumbing by mistake, and it was very powerful. Burst some of the pipes, blew one old don clean off the water closet."

Karno smirked.

Old Mr Kirkham, it was, who'd ended up in First Court, soaked through, with his trousers round his ankles, looking for his spectacles.

"If that pipe doesn't hold you'll have an absolute tidal wave of water heading straight for the front rows."

Karno scratched his chin. "Really?"

"I'm afraid so."

For a moment I was afraid my warning had taken the wind out of his sails, but then the Guv'nor turned and winked at me.

"Well. That would be a shame, wouldn't it?"

10
HIS BIG BREAK

I will never forget the gasps of astonishment as the audience at the Paragon caught their first glimpse of the mighty *Wontdetainia* sailing serenely across the stage. Tilly and I looked down from on high at the upturned faces and eyes wide with amazement as the brass band played and the streamers spun down out of the sky.

The ingenuity of the folding panels was impressive enough, but once the ship reached the open sea and began its realistic rocking motion, the crowd burst into spontaneous applause. They nudged one another with glee and pointed, then, at the green faces of we supers hanging grimly to the rails in the throes of our all-too-realistic seasickness. They gasped and squealed at the ominous creaking and thumping from the hydraulics, and then all at once the over-worked pipes succumbed to the extra pressure and burst at the seams, gushing hundreds of gallons of icy cold water across the stage and into their laps.

People ran for their lives to the exits, and stood, dripping, out on the Mile End Road to the amazement of passers-by, cursing the name of Fred Karno and shaking their fists up at the theatre building as though it was somehow to blame.

Despite this utter debacle, though, the Guv'nor strode in through the double doors of the Fun Factory the next morning just before ten, beaming all over his face, clutching the morning's newspaper in his fist.

"See this, Alf?" he shouted up to Reeves, who was supervising some fresh scene building up in the roof space above our heads. "Front page!" He slapped the paper with the back of his hand and bustled towards his office, pleased as Punch, nodding greetings as he went. He saw me waiting for him outside the door and tossed the paper to me without breaking his busy little stride.

"See? You were right about that water pressure, then, lad. Be with you directly..."

He went in and I glanced over the report of the previous night's mayhem. The writer made it sound like an unmitigated disaster, but the item covered very nearly a quarter of the front page and gave prominent and numerous mentions of the name of the show, and the ambitious and spectacular set, and the outrageous cost, and the name of the theatre, and the name of Mr Fred Karno.

While I'd been reading the paper a couple of other fellows had come over to Karno's door. The older of the two – a tall, rangy chap, smartly turned out, with slickeddown hair – paused before knocking to indicate that the younger – a short, slightly built youth, also in his Sunday best – should wait outside to be called, then he marched straight in.

So much for me, I thought to myself.

The younger youth sat down opposite me and looked at me with a steady gaze, which I found unsettling, though I couldn't quite have said why at first. I returned his look, as if to say: "What are you looking at?" and before I could stop it and without either of us saying a word I found myself in a full-blown staring contest. I knew it, and he knew it, and I knew he knew it, and he knew I knew it.

So I stared and he stared, and he stared and I stared, and as I did I suddenly put my finger on what it was that was so unsettling about this youth's level gaze. It was this. His eyes, the irises, that is, were a startling deep purple. This couldn't be, could it, the same youth, that Sam Cohen, who had suffered that calamitous humiliation...? The thought was enough to make me break off looking at him, and his lip curled in a slight sneer of self-satisfaction, this boy, which made me colour in embarrassment and defeat.

I looked at my feet, so as not to have to look at him, this purple-eyed freak boy, and so found myself tuning into the conversation in Karno's office.

"So how was America?" Karno was saying.

"It went very well, Guv'nor, they sure seemed to like us," the tall slicker replied.

"No thought of staying out there, then?"

"Guv'nor!" came the reply, affecting to sound indignant, hurt at the very suggestion. "I'm your man, through and through."

"Is that so, is that so indeed?" The Guv'nor sounding thoughtful.

"I'm not saying there weren't offers, mind."

"Oh-ho!"

"And good money too."

"Oh-ho again! Better money than I'm paying you, is that what you're saying?"

"The money's not the important thing," the slick dude claimed, unconvincingly to my eavesdropping ears, and to Karno's too, it seemed.

"Don't give me that bunk! The money's always the important thing, Sydney. You know it, and I know it. So is that what this little social call is about, then? You after a little pay rise...?"

"No, Guv'nor..."

"Because, you know, I might have something in here for you, now I come to think of it..."

There was the sound of a cupboard door being opened, and Sydney the slicker protested at once.

"Guv'nor please! Put the big hat away! I've come to ask you about another matter entirely..."

I learned later that the Guv'nor had a novel way of dealing with requests for more money from his players. He'd bring out an oversized hat – there were two in his cupboard, an enormous bowler, I think, in the winter, and a vast straw boater for the summer months – to demonstrate what he thought of the claimant and his swollen head. Prop sarcasm, it was, and it usually had the desired effect, I'm told.

"Well then?" A low thump, which may have been the Guv'nor putting his feet up on his desk.

"It's ... it's about poor Ronny Marston..."

My ears pricked up at mention of that name, my predecessor at the Bells' house.

"I... Well, I blame myself, Guv'nor," Sydney said, a little catch in his voice.

"Interesting," Karno replied, with a little cough. "I blame you too."

"Oh? Really? I see. Right-o..."

"You are the number one of a Fred Karno company, and everything that happens to that company is your responsibility. You got that?"

A reverent pause followed. Whatever had happened to this Ronny Marston, whose name only ever seemed to be mentioned with the word 'poor' preceding it?

"Fortunately the perfect remedy is at hand," Sydney started off again, perking up.

"Oh?"

"Yes, my brother, Charlie. He's waiting outside. He's been with Wal Pink, and Casey's, and he got good notices in *Sherlock Holmes* with Mr Saintsbury. He's a quick study and he'd be a perfect fit, and I was thinking...?"

"That I might set him on?"

"Exactly..."

I glanced up at the purple-eyed boy opposite. He was holding his breath, hanging on every word, every nuance of the conversation inside.

"And if I do, you'll pay no more mind to these other 'offers' you've had, is that it?" Karno's voice was taking on a sarcastic and rather calculating tone.

"Guv'nor! I never said..."

"I heard what you never said. Heard it very well. Anyway, I've seen your boy, and he's clever enough, but he's too young..."

"He only looks young close to. With make-up and a wig he can play anything you like."

I snorted derisively at this. The boy opposite stiffened and glared at me, a frown darkening his features, and I could sense him wondering, as plain as anything, whether I knew of his crushing night at Forester's. I met his strange purple gaze and nodded, ever so slightly, and this time he was the one who coloured and looked at his feet.

"That's as may be," Karno was saying. "The plain fact is there's no vacancy just now."

"What about Ronny Marston's place?"

"Filled!"

"Already?"

Footsteps approached the door, and I gathered that Karno's visitor was being shown out. The brother and I both stared at the floor, as though we hadn't heard anything of any interest whatsoever. The door opened.

"Yes, filled!" said Karno, gesturing flamboyantly in my direction, "by young Mr Dandoe here. Stand up, lad. Sydney, Arthur. Arthur, Sydney."

The tall chap, Sydney and I shook hands. He glowered at me in a cool and unfriendly manner, and glanced over at his brother with a slight shake of the head and a tiny shrug.

"Pleased to meet you, Sydney," I said.

"Syd," he said, summoning up some politeness out of his disappointment. "Syd Chaplin. Come on, Charlie, let's go."

———

Now, it's probably useless for me to pretend that you won't have spotted the arrival just now of a key character into the story. I've kept him in the background as long as I can – after all, this is *my* story, not his, and his highly *selective* autobiography is available (one mention, that's all I get, one measly, solitary little mention!) should you wish to plough through the thing. In case you have more sense, however, let me now take a moment to bring you up to date with the careers of the two Chaplin brothers, Sydney and Charlie.

They were half brothers, actually, with the same mother but different fathers. Charlie's dad married their mother a few months after Syd was born and gave the baby lad his surname, and Charlie himself came along four years later.

Charles Chaplin senior was a singer on the halls, of middle-ranking fame on either side of the Atlantic, who drank himself to death at thirty-seven. The boys' mother, Hannah, was a singer too, but her career petered out and she scratched a living as a seamstress in between periods in the Lambeth workhouse, and, not to put too fine a point upon it, the Cane Hill Asylum.

Throughout their childhood, then, Syd, as the elder, was obliged to look out for young Charlie as they were bundled from one Poor Law school to another, and for their mother too. At sixteen he went to sea, taking a post on a mail boat to the Cape, first getting an advance on his wages which enabled Charlie and Hannah to take new lodgings in Kennington.

By the time Syd had completed a handful of voyages, young Charlie had begun a career on the stage, first as one of the clog-dancing act Eight Lancashire Lads (even though he was a proper Cockney sparrer), and then as a boy actor in straight plays. Syd decided that he too wanted to tread the boards, like his brother, and his father and mother.

Funnily enough, it was Charlie who gave Syd his first break. Charlie was appearing as a pageboy in a touring Sherlock Holmes play and talked the management into taking Syd on in the role of a foreign aristocrat called Count von Stahlberg.

When a second tour of the same show was mounted Charlie retained his role, but Syd's went to someone else – most likely the manager wanted to hire a nephew or something – so he took another posting as an assistant steward on a Cape mail boat. On this trip he was persuaded to take part in a scratch entertainment, at which he did some comedy songs and a few impersonations, and became the talk of the ship. I imagine that, much like I did at the college smoker, he felt the Power for the first time, and became intoxicated by it. After that he was determined to make a career in comedy, and nothing else would do.

Back in London once again, Syd abandoned his maritime career and managed to talk his way into the Wal Pink company, appearing in their briefly notorious romp *Repairs*. He was quite a hit in this messy house-fixing-up sketch, and was able to return the favour he owed Charlie, landing his younger brother the role of an incompetent plumber's mate.

Wal Pink himself was a self-regarding braggart of an author and producer who confidently expected that *Repairs* was going to catapult him into the top rank alongside even the great Fred Karno, but the reviews were discouraging, the bookings dwindled, and the rats began to abandon the sinking ship. Charlie quickly left to join another outfit, called Casey's Circus, and then it just so happened that the Guv'nor turned up to run his eye over the ailing Wal Pink routine. He liked the look of the heavily moustachioed lead actor and offered Syd a job.

Syd Chaplin's rise within the Fun Factory organisation since had been little short of meteoric, as they say – except meteors, by their nature, are hurtling downwards, aren't they? I've never quite understood that one – and within three months of joining Karno as a pantomimist, Syd was deemed ready to lead his own company, heading off to America as the drunk in *Mumming Birds*. Now he was back, and making a play to get the Guv'nor to take his kid brother on. Which was spoiled – inadvertently, as we have just seen – by me, your 'umble narrator. Oh well. How sad. Never mind.

"Now then, young feller," Karno said when we were alone. "I'll put you into *Jail Birds* – on trial, kind of style, understand? – an' we'll see whether you've got 'it' after all, shan't we?"

For the rest of that week my feet barely touched the ground. The *Jail Birds* company I was to be joining was on tour in the North, but as it happened there was another company rehearsing *Jail Birds* down in London, so I was dispatched to learn the ropes with them first. I didn't yet know all the ins and outs of Karno's organisation, but I quickly gathered that a supporting player in a Karno sketch was like a cog in a machine. A beautifully tuned machine, with immaculate timing, but a machine nonetheless. You couldn't get out of step with the other cogs, or the whole thing would grind to a halt. Also, the Guv'nor might need to remove a cog from one machine and transfer it to another at any moment, so there was no point in trying to build up, cut down or otherwise alter your part.

So it was up to Walworth Road to the Miracle first thing every morning to do a full day's rehearsal, and then over to the Fun Factory to catch one of the Karno motor buses up to the Paragon to be a super in *Wontdetainia*.

I quickly got the hang of *Jail Birds*, which was a mostly phys-ical routine without too much in the way of dialogue, set in a quarry where prisoners were breaking rocks and moving them about. There was an escape plan, which the guards thwart with a deal of tightly choreographed chasing around and bumping into things, and a bit of a free-for-all at the end, which was one of the Guv'nor's principal trademarks.

It was hard work, though, and didn't leave me any free time at all that week, which was to be my first and last as a passenger aboard the *Wontdetainia*. Although I was excited about the chance I had been given, I wouldn't have minded asking Tilly if she would like to repeat our afternoon tea together. As it was, though, the only real chance we had to speak at all the whole week was as we clung to one another on board the heaving mechanical ship.

Playing, you will recall, at being a married couple. Tilly was enjoying the game of playing her character to the full, and would whisper: "What do you think America will be like?" and "Will we still be able to get a nice cup of English tea?"

On one occasion she breathed: "How many children shall we have, do you think, darling?" into my ear, which affected my composure more than somewhat.

On the last night I couldn't hold out any longer, and whispered the news in her ear, my dramatic step up from lowly super to probationary number five in a Karno touring company. It went down big, as they say in the States.

"No!" she suddenly cried out loud, grabbing my arm and gaping at me in disbelief. This would have been a very gratifying reaction, except that we were in the middle of the sketch at the time so it rather punctuated the action onstage, causing everyone – principals, supers and audience – to stare up at us. Tilly flushed and buried her face in my chest until the sketch picked up where it had left off. After a moment or two I could feel her shaking with mirth.

"How awful! I'll be for it now!" she whispered. "How about *you*, though? You're the next big thing!"

"I'll only be on trial, you know."

"Oh, pooh" she breathed. "Karno's got his eye on you, that's plain enough!"

Back at the Fun Factory, where all the various companies gathered at the end of the evening to collect their pay, Tilly abandoned her giggling chums and stood with me. She slipped her arm under mine, pulled me to her in a rather proprietorial fashion and beamed. I felt like the king of the world.

Then I noticed all the other supers looking squintways at me. They all seemed to be pretty much seething. Chaps who'd been warming up to me and generally giving me the time of day were now scowling in a surly fashion. A suspicion began to dawn.

"Tilly," I whispered. "You didn't tell anyone that I'm leaving, did you?"

"Oh, I may have mentioned it here and there," she twinkled.

The rumour had spread like wildfire, leaping from dry stick to dry stick and consuming them all in the red heat of its jealous flames. I didn't realise then, of course, that no super had ever been given a featured part in a Karno sketch. Ever. It had never happened before. Tilly stayed close by my side, basking in the glow she herself had created around me, smiling and waving at all the lesser mortals.

One of the fellows who'd been painting the ship alongside me, who'd been rather snooty that whole time, sidled over to offer his heartfelt congratulations.

"You will mention my name to Mr Karno, won't you, if you get the chance?" he said, and I'm sure I would have done, as well, if he'd ever deigned to tell me what it was.

Freddie Karno junior arrived, as before, to set up his counting tables, and such was my new-found status that the mob parted deferentially to allow me and Tilly to go first. We strolled slowly forward, rather like royalty, and the riff-raff bowed their heads and fell in line behind us.

Junior had his ledger open ready, and looked up to see me standing before him.

"Arthur Dandoe," I said.

"I know," Freddie said curtly, and I could tell right away he wasn't all that pleased to see me. "I know who you are. Everybody knows who you are. You're the super the Guv'nor's sending up to take Ronny Marston's place."

I grinned modestly (I hoped) but said nothing, and we eyed one another.

"Do you know how long I've been on at my father to give me a go?" Freddie demanded. "Do you?"

I didn't. And he didn't tell me, but I imagined it was quite a while or he'd hardly be banging on about it.

"I thought when that whole Ronny Marston business happened, that was it, it was obvious. That would just be the perfect start for me. I as good as begged him, my own father, and he said he'd think about it, oh, he was still thinking about it, well maybe, or you never know, and then boom! Out of the blue, here's *you*! I'll tell you. I'm just about ready to pack this lot in! I am, straight!"

"I'll mention your name if you like," I offered, then bit my tongue.

His face hardened. "You do that," he said, and slapped my money for the week into my hand, scratching my name out of his ledger with what I thought was unnecessary violence.

Alf Reeves was hovering nearby, having bustled over from the Enterprise. It turned out he was waiting for me, and he took my arm and led me outside for a private word.

"You mustn't mind Freddie, you know, Arthur," he said. "He's not a bad fellow, when you get to know him. He's as sorry as anyone about poor Ronny, even though it sounds like he's only thinking of himself."

There it was again – "*poor* Ronny".

"Whatever was it that happened to...?" I began, but Reeves thumped me cheerily in the chest.

"So! It seems like the Guv'nor had plans for you after all, eh? Capital! Delighted!" He pumped my hand enthusiastically. "Now, it's Bolton, isn't it, yes, and it's a half week, so most of them'll be down tomorrow for a couple of days, loved ones and so on, so you can go back up with them on Tuesday. They've been using a sub since, well, you know, but he's needed elsewhere, so you'll be stepping straight in. Euston station, ten o'clock train. Look out for Frank O'Neill, he's company managing. Good luck!"

With that he was off, with a hundred other things to take care of, no doubt, and while I was processing that information Tilly came out, skipped over to me and stood very close. I could smell her perfume, feel the weight of her as she leaned on my arm and pressed herself against me.

"Now then, Arthur Dandoe," she said softly. "When you're a big success, and can have any girl you want..." (now there was a distracting idea) "...you won't forget me, will you?"

"Um ... forget you? Forget *you*? I should say not."

She smiled, a dazzling smile, and then suddenly pulled herself up on her tiptoes and kissed me quickly on the lips. Then off she went, skipping back inside to join her pals.

I should have gone back in, but I was embarrassed. I should have found her and asked if she would like to spend the following afternoon together, but I was afraid that if I went back in all conversation would cease instantly and two hundred pairs of eyes and ears would track my every move. And nobody does their best courting under those conditions, do they?

So I made my way home, and lay awake all night thinking about that kiss.

11
JAIL BIRDS

THE day before I headed off to start in *Jail Birds* I packed my carpet bag, then unpacked it and packed it again a couple of times. I was as nervous as a kitten in Battersea Dogs Home, and couldn't settle. The part I had learned to do was straight-forward enough, and I had it down pat, but I couldn't stop thinking that I was only on trial, and wondering who was to be judge and jury.

A cup of tea, that's what I needed, so I stuck my head through the scullery doorway, but there was no sign of Clara. I popped into the parlour, as she called the best front room, and there she was, her nose pressed up against the window, half hiding herself behind the curtain, fascinated by something happening in the street outside.

"C'm'ere, c'm'ere!" she hissed when she noticed I was there, and beckoned me to her side. "D'you see? There look!"

I peered out, immediately steaming up a patch of window pane, which I set about wiping with my sleeve. To my astonish-ment Clara slapped my arm down.

"Don't do that. They'll see you!"

Finding a clear bit of glass to spy through, I saw the woman from next door standing by her front gate. It seemed that she had had a visitor, who was just now making her farewells, a small but forceful lady, who had an expensive-looking brougham waiting at the roadside. The two of them embraced, the visitor raising a gloved hand to wipe away a tear from her friend's cheek.

"D'you see who it is? Do you?" Clara whispered. "'Tis only Marie herself!"

"Who?"

"Marie Lloyd! You great ... tuppenny bit!"

"Is it?" I gasped, and leaned forward to gawp pretty shamelessly at the legendary queen of the music hall. Clara, mortified with embarrassment now, tried to pull me back out of sight, but she was too late, and Marie Lloyd gave our house a cheery wave and a salute before stepping aboard her transport. Our neighbour watched her go, then turned and walked slowly back up her path, flashing a wan smile at our window. Clara turned away, shaking her head sadly.

"Poor woman," she said. "Poor, poor thing."

"But who is she?" I wanted to know. "And why is Marie Lloyd, of all people, coming to call on her?"

But Clara would only shake her head, before disappearing into the scullery, where after a moment I heard the sound of the kettle being filled, and her voice singing: "*Oh, Mr Porter, what shall I do...?*"

———

Funnily enough, the train to Birmingham that went on to Crewe – although Marie Lloyd wasn't really singing about *trains*, was she? – was the very one I was catching the next morning.

I made my way up to Euston station and into the Great Hall, a mighty echoing chamber that dwarfed anything the good old college had to offer, with its sweeping, curving staircases and its ornate panelled ceiling. Like a cathedral, it was, I thought, dedicated to the worship of the steam engine.

A statue of George Stephenson stood on a plinth at the far end, and this was where I had arranged to meet my new colleagues as none of us would recognise one another on sight. It seemed that this landmark was a popular meeting place, and a short, fat fellow with a red nose was already leaning with his back to the monument, puffing away on a cigarette. He had a rather garish checked suit on and a bow tie, like a newspaper cartoon of a comedian.

"Excuse me, sir. Are you with Karno's?"

A look of pop-eyed indignation appeared on the man's face, and he flushed bright red.

"Am I with *Karno's*?" he cried, taking a theatrical step back in amazement. "Do I *look* like I am with Karno's, sir?"

"Yes," I said. "Yes, you do."

"Well, I am not, sir. As a matter of fact, I sell brushes" – and he tapped his suitcase with his toe end – "and I might add that I am very well respected in that trade, sir, *very* well respected. Now buzz orf! *Karno's* indeed...!"

I buzzed a little way orf to one side as he chuntered away to himself and surveyed the throng of busy people passing through the station, or sitting on the bench seats lined up on either side of the concourse. Where did it come from, I wondered, that brush salesman's disdain for the very idea that he might have been a comic? Did he not realise that being a comic was a far superior way to spend one's life?

"No, I am *not* this Arthur Whoosis!" the cartoon comedian was loudly insisting. "I sell brushes. Now buzz orf!"

Another hapless fellow was backing away apologetically, and I tapped him on the shoulder.

"Excuse me," I said. "Are you looking for Arthur Dandoe?"

"Ah! That's you, is it? Excellent. Right, follow me…" I followed him as he hustled through a ticket barrier, waving a pair of tickets high above his head, then along a platform and up onto a train, where he ushered me into a compartment. Three others were already waiting inside: two young chaps who looked more than a little cowed, and a tall fellow with slicked-down hair sitting with his arms and legs crossed, an air of barely suppressed fury about him.

"Here he is, Syd, I found him," my companion said breathlessly.

"Finally!"

"Yes. Well…" The fellow who'd fetched me smiled at each of us in turn, as if trying to inject a bit of sunshine into the compartment. "Now, let me see. I didn't even introduce myself, did I? I'm Frank O'Neill, company manager. This is Mr Sydney Chaplin, our principal comic…"

The principal comic's eyes narrowed.

"… And these bright sparks are Mike Asher and Albert Austin," O'Neill continued. "Gentlemen, this is Arthur Dandoe."

"We've met," Syd Chaplin muttered, and then began grinding his teeth, so no one was in any doubt that he was displeased to see me.

"I'm sorry we weren't all waiting for you as arranged," Frank continued, with the kind of forced breeziness a manager will sometimes employ to try and mitigate a star performer's sullenness. "Only Syd doesn't like to hang about in public places. He gets recognised, you see, and people start making a fuss."

Syd Chaplin grunted scornfully. There was a sharp whistle from outside and the train began to ease its way out of the station.

As we glided out through the suburbs, no one speaking, I realised that our leader had been regarding me appraisingly for an uncomfortably long while.

"So you're the Guv'nor's new blue-eyed boy, then, are you?" he said, once he was sure he had unsettled me completely.

"Oh, I don't know so much about that," I said, trying to sound cheery.

"Oh yes, everyone's talking about *you*, aren't they?" He looked to Mike and Albert for confirmation, and they nodded dutifully. "Look at these two," he laughed. "They're just eaten up with curiosity about you!"

Mike and Albert both flushed and stared at the floor.

"Now then," Syd continued. "It's my understanding that you're with us on trial. Well, you're not the first, not by a long chalk, and I dare say you won't be the last neither. Lot of 'em don't last too long, do they, Frank, the Guv'nor's little fancies? They can't stand the spotlight, the expectation, they drop by the wayside, and he moves on to someone else as if they'd never existed."

Frank O'Neill gave me a wan little smile, and Syd sat back, folding his arms smugly.

"So the Guv'nor saw you in a show, I suppose, did he?" Syd mused. "What company would that have been for, if you don't mind me asking?"

"Um, the Footlights Club in Cambridge."

"Oh-ho, college boy, is it?"

"No, no, well, that's to say, I used to work in a..."

"Don't worry, we've got nothing against college boys as long as

115

they pull their weight. Davy Burnaby, he was in that Footlights Club, wasn't he, Frank?"

"Mr Concert Party," agreed Frank, enigmatically.

"And he does all right for himself on the halls. He'll never be exactly in the top rank, you know, but he'll not starve neither."

Frank nodded, and with that, our leader began to gaze out of the window and the conversation dried up completely.

I felt about as welcome as a turd in a tin bath.

———

Over lunch in the restaurant car – the first time I'd ever had a meal on a train, I had beef, I remember – Syd held court again.

"So you weren't a student, you say? What were you then?"

"I was a college servant," I said.

"Good, solid, reliable position. You've got something to go back to, then, when – I mean, *if* – you decide to pack all this in. Isn't that right, lads?"

Mike and Albert nodded eagerly.

"Is that what happened to Ronny Marston?" I said.

There was a loud clang as Mike dropped his fork onto his bone china plate.

"I mean to say, did *he* just decide to pack it all in?" I asked. "Ronny Marston?"

Under the table, somebody kicked me sharply on the shin. I looked to Syd for an answer to my question, but the safety curtain had come down once again and the meal concluded in puzzling silence. Was the guilty flush on his cheek merely because he felt the responsibility of his position as company leader, I wondered, or was there something more?

When Syd got to his feet and led the way back to our compartment, Mike Asher surreptitiously grabbed my arm and held me back. He watched until the other three were well out of earshot, then he hissed: "Don't you know better than to talk about Ronny bloody Marston?"

"*Poor* Ronny Marston, you mean. Why?"

"Why, he says! After what happened to him!"

"I don't know what happened to him. Nobody seems to want to tell me anything about it."

Mike gaped at me. "You really don't know?"

"For God's sake, man, *tell* me!"

After a moment he leaned forward over the table, confidentially. "Well, you know the expression 'breakneck speed'? That's what the reviews say about us, usually. 'The action takes place at breakneck speed – *Brighton Argus*.' So forth. Well, one night Ronny ran on at breakneck speed, slipped, fell off the stage, landed on his stupid head, broke his stupid neck."

"No! Did he...? I mean, *is* he...?"

"No, no, he's alive, but they don't know if he'll walk again, the poor chump."

"How did he come to slip, for Heaven's sake?"

"Ah, well, for that we must look to the Rufford Bioscope."

Most music hall bills in those days would have something like the Rufford Bioscope. Down would go the lights, down would come a big white sheet, and a projector would show jerky, oddly speedy moving pictures of this and that, slice of local life stuff, like workers spilling out of a factory, or a horse and cart going by.

Real-life flesh and blood acts would hate to find themselves following the Bioscope in the running order, for two reasons.

Firstly, the mood of the audience would be calmed to the point of torpor. Secondly, the calico sheet that was used for the projection was prone to waft around in draughts, so the projectionist would spray it generously with a gelatinous mixture which weighed it down and kept it flat. It also, inevitably, oozed all over the stage, making the place extremely slippery.

Usually the curtain would come down and a front of tabs act would go on – a banjo singer or something – so that the stage could be mopped. But on the night of poor Ronny's mishap this individual had been pronounced too drunk to appear, and so there had been no gap between the Bioscope and *Jail Birds*. Hence Ronny's entrance, at, as Mike had pointed out, breakneck speed, was followed immediately by his exit, ditto, poor fellow. Still, he may have been the first to have a music hall career cut short by the moving pictures, but he sure as hell wasn't the last.

"The reason we are not talking about it," Mike whispered, "is that the stage manager swore blind afterwards that he'd told Syd we'd be straight after the bloody Bioscope, and to be sure to tell us all to be extra careful, but I'm telling you Syd never said a word about it."

"Careless," I said.

"Careless my backside! What happened to Ronny could have happened to any one of us," Mike said indignantly, "and Syd wouldn't have minded. Just so there was a vacancy for his precious brother to fill."

"No," I said. "You don't really think...?"

Mike put a finger to his lips, then wriggled out into the aisle.

"Just watch yourself, that's all I'm saying. Come on, we'd best get back..."

As I followed him through to the next carriage, I wondered just what I had got myself into.

Back in our compartment, Syd Chaplin had stuck his feet up on the banquette opposite and lit up a cigar. We continued North in frosty silence, until suddenly our leader clapped his hands and stood up.

"How long till Bolton, Frank?"

The company manager checked his pocket watch. "We're due in around twenty minutes," he said.

"Right, let's get on with it then."

All of a sudden there was a flurry of activity. Everyone but me seemed to know what to do. Mike and Albert reached up to the luggage rack and pulled down a medium-sized trunk, while O'Neill pulled down the blinds so that no one could see in from the corridor, and Syd began unbuttoning his jacket. I just blinked, puzzled.

"Here." Syd took a costume from the trunk and chucked it to me. "Get this on."

He'd given me a comical sort of convict suit, arrows on it, like a loose-fitting pair of pyjamas. Syd himself was now struggling into something similar, while Mike and Albert were dressing up as prison guards.

"You see, college boy, this is how we drum up a crowd for *Jail Birds*. It's one of the Guv'nor's oldest and best schemes, tried and tested."

Syd seemed to share a look with O'Neill -- or did I imagine it? - and then he went on.: "There'll be a Black Maria waiting for us at the station. Mike and Albert manhandle us along the platform while we complain at the top of our voices about the horrible injustice of it all, making as much of a racket as possible.

You with me? What we want, you see, is as big a crowd as possible following along, watching us all the way to the Black Maria, because then, just as the desperate criminals are being shoved inside... Ho! We make a break for it, off we go, hell for leather, into the town, and the mob pursues us, d'you see? You and me."

"Thinking we're desperate criminals," I said. Syd gave me an encouraging punch on the bicep.

"That's it, you've got it. We lead them a little bit of a merry chase around the town centre, and end up, da-daaah! Bang outside the theatre! Meantime Mike and Albert have brought the Black Maria round, they arrest us, and we all turn round and say 'Karno's Matchless Comedians in *Jail Birds*, all this week, at this theatre!' See? Nothing to it."

"And you've done this before, have you?"

"Yeah, yeah, many times. Never fails. It's an absolute copper-bottomed cert, this one, isn't it, lads?"

Mike and Albert nodded their agreement. It was all right for them, I thought. Their part of it sounded a good sight easier than mine.

———

Shortly afterwards the train pulled into Bolton. O'Neill kept us waiting until the platform was crammed with passengers, then out we came pushing and shoving and making the maximum kerfuffle.

"Make way! Make way there!" Mike bellowed. "Officers of the law transporting dangerous murderers! Stand aside!"

Folk gasped, and a busy murmuring began. Mike and Albert wrestled us over to the back of the waiting Black Maria, trailed by a growing curious mob, and bundled Syd inside, while he declaimed hammily: "Will no one give me justice, sweet justice!"

"You'll get your justice on the gallows, mate!" one bloke shouted. It occurred to me suddenly that some of the locals were getting a little wound up and wouldn't mind dishing out a bit of justice of their own.

At that moment Syd booted the doors open wide. One hit Mike in the face – I saw him take the blow with the palm of his hand – and the other smacked into Albert – who may actually have been taken unawares – and down they both went like a pair of felled oaks.

"Run for it!" Syd yelled. "Run for your life!"

I pelted off up the cobbled street, gaining a good head start on the mob. I heard Mike shouting "Stop! Help!", and somewhere a police whistle sounded. Now footsteps, running footsteps, dozens of them, could be heardat my back.

The street led up a slight incline to a main road at the top. Realising I didn't know which way to go, I turned to Syd.

"Which way's the theatre?!" I shouted.

He wasn't there.

I skidded to a halt and looked back. Hurtling up the cobbles towards me came a tidal wave of local citizens. Behind them I could see the Black Maria. Mr Sydney Chaplin, lead comic, was climbing out in leisurely fashion, dusting himself off. He was smirking his fat head off.

There wasn't time then to try and work out what was going on: a particularly mean-spirited practical joke, or something more sinister. I had two choices. Give myself up or run like hell. Some extremely hefty-looking chaps with teeth missing were managing to run after me and roll up their sleeves at the same time.

I decided to run like hell. Up to the junction, no time to toss a coin, I went right. The theatre was my only possible hope now, so I had to find it. On I galloped, knees pumping, past shops, past terraces of houses whose doors opened right onto the pavement. Fresh pursuers were maybe only a foot or two away, and the hot breath of the mob was on my collar, which they were longing to feel.

"Stop! Thief!" came the cry from behind. Clearly somebody hadn't been paying attention – I was supposed to be a murderer.

I was tiring as I hurtled up what seemed to be a main sort of street now, but I was young and in reasonable shape, and no one was gaining on me. If anything, the crowd from the station were falling back. I began to think I was going to make it, if I could only find this damned theatre. I ran past a group loafing outside a bakery – oh, that's rather good, must remember that one – and one of them made a grab at me, which I easily batted aside, and then ... yes! Up at the far end of this thoroughfare was a large building with a telltale magnificence about it. A tram went *Ting!* and eased slowly aside to reveal the glorious legend: Hippodrome! Sanctuary!

Almost there! I looked for the rescuing Black Maria. No sign of it. More shouts from behind. "Grab him! Stop him!" Another whistle. Well, nothing for it but to make a dash for the theatre itself and take refuge inside. I gathered myself for the final sprint ... and out went the lights.

I came to a second later, sprawling on the road outside a butcher's shop. The meat monger himself was standing over me, holding a great leg of pork in triumph above his head. I still had a moment. I scrambled to my feet to complete my mad dash for safety, only to find myself grasped firmly from behind by an unseen hand. No! I wasn't going to let myself be taken. I swung round and let fly at my captor, connecting cleanly with his jaw. There was a wet and bony sort of splat, then the sound of teeth rattling, and down he went like a sack of spuds. Off came his helmet, and his whistle bounced into the gutter.

I'd punched a policeman.

In all honesty, I can't recommend spending a night in jail. Especially not – and I say this from bitter first-hand experience – after receiving a right royal kicking from the larger part of the population of a northern industrial town.

Early the following morning I gasped myself up into a sitting position on my plank – it really didn't deserve the name of bed – and gingerly tried to enumerate my injuries. One eye was pretty much closed, but I was able to prise the swollen lids apart and satisfy myself that it was still in working order. I seemed to have escaped with all my teeth loosened but intact, although I could only just open my mouth wide enough to count them. Breathing was painful – maybe a cracked rib or two. And the fingers on one hand were like a little collection of black puddings. I tried to stand, but the cell immediately began to swim around alarmingly, so I sat back down again quickly.

I had a little time then, wincing whenever another unsuspected bruise made itself known, to think about Sydney Chaplin's hilarious prank.

Clearly it was one part putting the new boy in his place, mixed with three or four parts of payback for spoiling his plan to get his younger brother a job with Karno. I wasn't thrilled about it, but I realised that Syd was the number one, the top dog, and if I was going to get the favourable notice I needed from him I'd be well advised not to let my temper get the better of me.

Which is why, when the bolt eventually shot back and the door swung open to reveal a police constable and then Syd Chaplin himself, I didn't immediately leap to my feet and grab the bastard by the throat. Also, as it happened, neither leaping nor grabbing was on the list of activities I felt capable of just then.

"Ha! Well, good morning! Look at you!" Syd exclaimed, nudging a surly-looking constable to welcome him into Chaplin's World of Mirth.

"Hnnnf...!" I croaked.

"Well, you almost made it, they tell me."

"Mmmmgrmmf...!" I said, spitting blood into the piss bucket.

"By the time we got the Black Maria round to the theatre you were already in custody, you see, and if only you hadn't thumped one of His Majesty's finest we might have been able to get you out, but they insisted that you needed to learn your lesson."

The constable whacked the palm of his hand with his truncheon, seemingly keen to enrol me on a refresher course.

"So what do you say, sir?" Syd declaimed dramatically. "Is he free to go?"

After a long moment the constable grudgingly stepped aside, and Syd helped me out of the cell.

As he helped me out of the police station, into a cab, and then eventually into a comfortable armchair at the digs where I should have stayed the night before, Syd was solicitousness itself, quite unrecognisable as the superior character from the previous day.

"Now then," he said finally, as he brought a cup of tea and a biscuit through for me from the landlady's little kitchen. "You do look in quite a bad way, you know, old chap. Quite a bad way."

I felt in quite a bad way too, and was thinking that a drop of Scotch might suit my situation rather better than a cup of tea. The effort of asking, though, kept me quiet. Syd perched on the adjacent settee and patted my knee, which made me hiss sharply through my wobbly teeth.

"Sorry!" he said, withdrawing his hand quickly. "So-o-o-o... I was thinking, if you wanted to drop out, then everyone will understand. No shame in it, or anything, and don't feel you're letting anybody down. I'm sure the Guv'nor will give you another go when you're mended, of course he will, and I'll just wire down to London now for a replacement, so don't you worry about a thing."

In a flash I saw what he was up to. The replacement would be his brother, of course, who would be installed in a Karno company before the Guv'nor knew anything about it, while I joined poor Ronny Marston in the ranks of the forgotten. Poor Arthur Dandoe, they'd call me!

"It's for the best," he said, laying his hand on my shoulder with extravagant care and then heading for the door.

"Mo!" I grunted. Syd turned.

"What's that, old chap?"

"Mo!" I insisted. "I'n no' dro'ing ou'! I be fine, rea'y! Just nee' couple hour' res'."

Syd looked doubtful. "Really?"

"Rea'y!"

"You're absolutely sure?"

"Yeshhh!"

"You want to do the show tonight, you mean? In your present condition?"

"Yeshhh! Yeshhh! I do!"

Syd's face hardened.

"Well. On your own head be it," he said. Then he gave a single nod, and left without another word.

I sat there in that strange Bolton parlour all by myself, feeling pleased with myself at first for not giving him the satisfaction of my stepping aside. Gradually, though, it became clearer and clearer to me that I was going to find it very difficult to get through a performance of the energetic, harum-scarum mayhem of *Jail Birds* that evening. Particularly considering that when I tried to take a fortifying sip of tea I couldn't get any of my swollen fingers through the handle of the teacup.

Still, somehow I had to drag my aching carcass through that evening's performance without bringing the whole thing down, or else my career as a Karno comedian was over before it had begun.

That evening I sat in the dressing room at the Hippodrome and caught sight of myself in a mirror for the first time. My face looked like I'd been hit by a prize fighter, who'd been driving a locomotive engine at the time. On the top of my head there was one of those goose-egg-style bumps with a little tuft of hair on it that you might see in the funny pages, maybe after Mutt has hit Jeff with a pan.

Mike Asher, stout fellow, trotted off to the stalls bar to fetch me a whisky. While he was gone, Frank and Syd came in. The company manager peered at me, whistling through his teeth.

"There's no way this chap should be going onstage tonight," he pronounced.

"I agree with you, Frank," Syd said. "But he insists."

"Is that right, Arthur?" Frank asked. I nodded vigorously. It hurt like hell and the room began to drift out of focus.

"See?" Syd said. "Now all I'm saying is that it would be as well to have a replacement ready, in case he sees sense and decides to step down from tomorrow's performance, or in case he really fouls things up tonight and we decide we absolutely have to make a change."

"A replacement?"

"Now, as it happens, my brother is coming up tomorrow morning to visit me for a couple of days. He's more than capable, and he'll be Johnny-on-the-spot, won't he?"

Frank looked dubious. "I'm not sure the Guv'nor would be too happy about that," he said.

"I'm the number one," Syd said. "And, as the Guv'nor said to me the very last time we spoke, the number one takes responsibility."

Frank turned back to me. "You're sure you can manage?" he said.

"Yesh," I croaked, sitting down in my chair heavily, and just about managing to make it look deliberate rather than the semi-faint that it was. Frank shot Syd a searching look, and our number one raised his eyebrows.

"Well," Frank said. "You know my view." And with that he and Syd left, and Mike returned with a large tumbler full of fiery Scottish anaesthetic. I told him that Charlie Chaplin was on his way to Bolton, and he tutted softly to himself.

"Oh well, one good thing," Mike said then, cheerfully. "At least we don't have all the bother of getting you changed, do we?"

I looked down, and realised that he was right. Under my coat, I was still wearing my bloodstained jail bird costume from the afternoon before.

A short while later I stood in the wings waiting for *Jail Birds* to begin. The whisky had done the trick of perking me up, but the pains in my jaw, my ribs and my head were still humming away.

Then the front man of the chain gang was shuffling out into the spotlights, and we were under way. The chain tugged at my leg as Mike stepped onto the stage, and then I followed as best I could, lurching along like Quasimodo.

It was fortunate, I suppose, that the sketch was set in a prison yard, because my bruises and cuts, coupled with my painful doubled-over gait, looked deliberate, part of the scenario. And after a moment or two I realised that I was the one the audience was watching, and I was the one they were giggling at, as little suffering noises escaped inadvertently from my battered lips every time I was obliged to change direction. At last I was permitted to stand still, to be addressed by the prison governor, and a deep sigh of relief brought me another laugh.

Through my one good eye I caught sight of Syd, at the other end of the line, frowning, puzzled at the audience's sympathy for me.

After that I managed to limp through a sequence where we were supposedly breaking rocks, even though I could barely lift the sledgehammer, and just leaned on it. This seemed to strike a chord with the audience, too.

So far so good, but I knew the difficult bit was coming up. The jail birds hatch an escape plan. Syd is the ringleader, and I had a number of lines to speak during the discussion, making suggestions and so forth, without which, well, there was no scene, no story, no comedy.

"All right, gather round lads," says Syd, once the prison guards have gone off, reaching round and clapping me heartily on the back.

"Aaaargh!" I went, and the audience laughed again. Clearly they enjoyed their torture up there in the hard north. I could taste blood in my mouth.

"We need to make a break for it, boys. Any ideas?"

My cue. Here we go, I thought. All or nothing. Death or glory. I gathered myself, took a deep and agonising breath, and came out with: "Awrawr wre reten dobe rarsons!"

It was loud enough, at least, but nonsense, and lights danced crazily before my eyes. Syd looked at me, and I could see him thinking. He could help me out, or he could simply let the sketch fall flat.

With a huge effort I gathered myself for another go.

"Awrawr wre reten dobe rarsons!"

Even to me it sounded like a dog trying to talk. I felt, rather than saw or heard, the audience begin to shift from one buttock to the other. Syd smirked.

Suddenly Mike Asher piped up. "What's that you say, Lumpy?" he asked, cupping his hand to his ear.

My heart jumped with a sudden burst of hope, like a drowning man being thrown a lifebelt. I grabbed Mike's sleeve and mumbled my line again, and Mike – bless him – forwarded it on to the world at large. "Lumpy says why don't we pretend to be *parsons?*"

The other jail birds laughed, and the audience joined them. Syd's eyes narrowed, but he was enough of a pro to see that the sketch could now continue, and what's more, he could hardly miss the fact that the audience seemed to like the idea of 'Lumpy', a prisoner that only his best pal could understand.

Miraculously, Mike and I managed to get through all of my dialogue, with me groaning along like a sub-human creature, and he translating Lumpy's noises into intelligible language. We established ourselves as an impromptu little comic double act as we did so. Even Syd seemed to be seeing the funny side by the end of the bit.

The finale, though, was a different matter. It was a finely choreographed piece of chaos, with prisoners and guards galloping around in all directions at (as you will no doubt recall) breakneck speed.

There was no hiding place. I simply couldn't manage a run, and even the effort of remaining standing was taking its toll.

We reached a point where I was supposed to be the centre of a piece of frenetic action, and I found myself stuck, as if rooted to the ground, right in the middle of the stage. I was supposed to bolt once around the yard and then off into the wings, pursued by silent Albert Austin, my other travelling companion of the day before, playing a prison guard. I was *supposed* to do this ... but my legs simply would not answer.

I could see the audience clearly. The butcher who had laid me out with his leg of pork was in the middle of the front row, with a gleaming white shirt front dazzling me beneath his shiny chin. It crossed my mind to see if I could spit blood all over it, salvage some small satisfaction from the evening, but then the room started spinning.

Albert started running towards me, expecting me to flee, but I just stood stock still and watched him. He slowed, he skidded to a halt, he reached out uncertainly to apprehend me, not knowing what else he was supposed to do, or what on earth we would do *then*, when suddenly I shot up into the air!

I was as surprised as he was, and he was standing there clutching at his heart! Neither of us had seen Mike coming, and he had just scooped me up in his arms and raced off, once around the yard and then into the wings. My hero! Until he dropped me in a heap by the prompt desk, that is, where I lay, moaning in agony while he clutched at his back, gasping. We caught each other's eye, then, and burst out laughing.

"Oh! 'on't memme raugh...!" I cried, grabbing at my poor ribs, which only made Mike laugh even more.

"What's that, Lumpy?" he chortled, slumping down to join me in sprawling on the floor.

Onstage, *Jail Birds* reached its raucous conclusion to rousing acclaim. The next thing I knew was that Frank and Syd were standing over us.

"Well, I don't know about you," Frank said. "But I think that will do very well, don't you?"

He looked pointedly at Syd, who looked down at the pair of us, gave a little snort.

"I suppose so," he said.

Mike helped me to the bar, where I bought him the pint he so richly deserved. Every bone in my body was sore. I hadn't felt the Power, I had only felt a monstrous swirling kaleidoscope of aches, pains and panic. And there was plenty more of the same to come tomorrow.

But I was a Karno comedian.

PART II

12
IT'S A MARVEL 'OW 'E DOOS IT BUT 'E DO

WHO knows? Maybe if Charlie Chaplin had taken my place in his brother's *Jail Birds* company, maybe he'd have had my life and I'd have had his. *There's* something to think about.

Maybe *I* would have become the most successful and popular comedian the world has ever seen, with my mansion in the Hollywood hills and a full-sized Wurlitzer organ in the hallway, while *he* would be living in his granddaughter's box room in Streatham.

Maybe Ronny Marston could have been the pre-eminent comic actor of his generation, if only... Poor Ronny Marston.

When the two-month *Jail Birds* tour finished, I was on tenterhooks to know what Mr Karno's plans for me were. I had hopes that Syd Chaplin and Frank O'Neill would have had good things to say about my contribution. Those bits of business involving the prisoner Lumpy, which Mike Asher had brilliantly improvised, had proved so popular that I'd had to continue to make myself up to look beaten to a pulp even once my various injuries had healed completely. And although tinkering with the script (such as it was) was generally frowned upon, *surely* I'd been given some credit for that.

Anyway, whatever Syd and Frank had to say, it must have done the trick, because over the next few months Karno began to groom me for bigger things. He began to team me up with his oldest and most trusted hands, so I could learn the tricks of the trade. To begin with, he put me with Fred Kitchen in a well-tried sketch called G.P.O. Kitchen had a distinctive lisping delivery that seemed to make everything sound funnier. He had a curious shambling walk, too, onstage and off, a sort of shuffle, with the occasional little skip-step in there. The Guv'nor, you can be sure, had worked out how to make the most of this, by ensuring that Kitchen always wore shoes that were a couple of sizes too large.

G.P.O. featured Fred as Perkins, which was pretty much a catch-all name for the many lead characters created for and by Karno's leading man. He'd also played a Perkins in *The Bailiff*, the sketch that Mr Luscombe had so enthused about, and so I wrote to my erstwhile mentor that I was appearing opposite the great man at the Met on Edgware Road. The very next day he appeared at the stage door, bubbling with excitement.

"I say, Arthur," Luscombe jabbered, as I took him (or, more accurately, let him take me) for a quick drink before the show to calm him down. "Appearing with Fred Kitchen! You know what...?" He dealt me a healthy slap on the back. "Meredith – you're in!"

And I was. I did another stint then with Billie Ritchie as the principal comic. Ritchie was a wiry little chap, with a mop of black, curly hair and a little toothbrush moustache bristling away on his top lip. Onstage he was wont to wear trousers that were a couple of sizes too large and a jacket that was a couple of sizes too small, and he walked – well, waddled, more like – with his flat feet at ten to two and his knees spread bandily apart. He always carried a cane, a springy one, which he liked to twirl, and often used to prod an antagonist in the chest or behind, and the whole effect was generally topped off with a battered derby hat. His stock in trade was the downtrodden underdog everyman, battling the injustices of the world with his unquenchable spirit.

Sound familiar? I should think it does.5

I learned plenty from those shows and those old hands, and Karno also made sure that I saw other acts that could teach me a thing or two. Little Tich, T.E. Dunville, Mark Sheridan, George Robey of course, Vesta Tilley and Marie Lloyd – all were weighed and measured.

But the man I learned the most from was the Guv'nor himself. I picked up all sorts of pantomime techniques, a whole dictionary of mime gestures, from Karno. When a man is amazed, for example, he tips his hat back and scratches his head. When he is thinking, he frowns and scratches his chin. I used to wonder how such exaggerated moves came to mean the thing that they meant, but obviously, originally, they must have come from life, mustn't they? I always used to get a kick out of seeing someone, in real life, scratching his head in amazement, or wringing her hands in dismay, not because they wanted to convey these things to an audience, but because that's how their very bodies reacted in these situations, because that was the truth.

One key element to Karno's comedy was a quality he called "wistfulness". Time and again in rehearsals at the Miracle I remember him slowing down a scene, and murmuring: "Wistful, keep it wistful..." – reminding the actors to tug at the heartstrings as well as going for the funnybone.

He himself had been a performing gymnast as a young man, so when he made the transition to pantomime he brought a whole range of specialist skills with him. One time, I remember, tired of trying to explain, he demonstrated a flawless rolling fall for us, right there in his smart suit and shiny shoes, bobbing up to his feet again with the spring of a sixteen-year-old.

"There," he said, brushing the dust from his sleeves. "That's how we used to do it."

I was fascinated by this glimpse of the Guv'nor's former career as a performer, and after the rehearsal I plucked up the courage to ask him about it. He cocked his head on one side and regarded me with half a smile for a moment.

"Come over to t' house," he said then, to a background of astonished gasps from those close enough to overhear, and I followed him as he trotted over the road from the Fun Factory to his home at number 28 opposite.

Inside he led me into the kitchen, and I sat there at the table while he trotted upstairs to look something out. I didn't want to do anything to tarnish the moment, so I sat very still with my hands on my knees, like a schoolboy waiting for the headmaster.

As I listened to the Guv'nor's footsteps clicking to and fro across the wooden floor upstairs, I suddenly became aware that I was not alone. I risked a glance over my shoulder, and there, almost on top of me, as if he had just materialised out of thin air, was a wild-looking elderly man. His hair was white and wild, sprouting in all directions at once, with odd-coloured bits in it, and he was wearing only a dark tartan dressing gown, beneath which his bony shins and bare feet were visible.

"Aaaagh!" I gasped, as this apparition smiled, revealing at most three teeth, and reached out to me with one skeletal hand balled into a fist. Slowly the fingers unclenched to reveal a small mass of dirty-yellowish putty.

"Cheese?" the vision offered.

"N-no, thank you very much."

"Go on, it's Wensleydale," the old geezer wheezed.

"Really, I'm fine, thank you."

"I think I've got some Red Leicester if you'd rather..."

All of a sudden he clambered up onto my lap, shoving one bony kneecap into my groin, and began rubbing some cheese against my face, trying to force it between my lips.

"Cheee-eee-eeese!" my assailant keened happily.

"Ahem!"

A little cough from the doorway. Abruptly the assault was over, and the ancient figure scampered off up the passage and away up the stairs. I wiped my face quickly with both hands and looked up.

There was the Guv'nor, slightly flushed, clutching a leather-bound album in one hand, while with the other he guided a buxom and cheerful-looking woman towards me.

"Arthur, may I present Mrs Karno?"

"Arthur Dandoe," I spluttered, scrambling to my feet and offering my hand. "Charmed, I'm sure, Mrs Karno."

"Please, call me Maria," Mrs Karno smiled. "So, Fred, this is the lad you've been telling me about, the one you've such high hopes for?"

"One of 'em," Karno grumbled, and it was clear that he was irked to have this opinion aired in front of me. I, of course, was thrilled to know I had been the subject of discussion between them, and Mrs K banged on regardless.

"Yes, the lad who's been doing so *well*," she said, still smiling, and I preened a little at this, I'm afraid. "I remember you saying. Syd's brother."

Thump. Down to earth I fell.

"No, no, dear, this is t'other one," the Guv'nor mumbled, waving a hand dismissively in my general direction, and I shrank another couple of inches.

"Well," Mrs Karno clapped her hands together. "I'm sure you two boys have things to discuss. Why don't I...?" She and the Guv'nor shared a glance, and she nodded and set off upstairs after the cheesy old codger. Probably to tie him down to something.

Karno sat down at the table and began flicking through the album, looking for whatever it was he had meant to show me. Neither of us said anything at first, until he noticed a stray lump of grubby-looking Gloucestershire on the table between us, and noticed me noticing him noticing it. He picked it up daintily, between forefinger and thumb, and walked it over to a waste scuttle, then washed his hands at the sink. Back at the table, he sniffed, embarrassment in the air, and said: "You met my father, then, I see?"

"I did...?"

Karno nodded slowly.

"You won't mention to anyone ... the...?"

"The cheese?"

I promised him faithfully that I wouldn't ever tell anyone anything about it. "You mustn't mind what Maria said, you know. She's only taking an interest in young Chaplin because I told her t' story of how I came to take him on."

I waited expectantly, hoping he would enlighten me.

"Syd, you see, has been on and on at me to bring Charlie on board ever since I first got him off Wal Pink. He's always playing t' big brother, see, has always looked after the boy because their father died years ago and their mother, poor soul, is not all there. But Karno's is not a charity, and I didn't think the lad was ready. After that *Jail Birds* tour of yourn I called Syd in, as I'd a mind to send him back to America, and he tells me straight he won't go.

"'What's this, Syd?' I says. 'A mutiny?'

"'If you like,' says he.

"Well, I told him there's no more money for him, and he says it's nowt to do wi' money, he must put his family first, and if I won't take Charlie on then he'll be off, and the two on 'em'll work up an act together, or maybe run back to Pink's. I could see he'd got himself proper worked up, and so I reckoned it like this: either Charlie will be up to it, in which case everyone wins, or he won't, in which case Syd will see it as well as anyone else, and I'll be able to say I gave him a fair go and get rid. And as it 'appens he's doing fine, so far."

Karno began to leaf through his clippings.

"Some of you young lads don't know you're born," he said. "I hear you complaining about doing three a night and it makes me laugh. I was in a travelling circus when I was your age, and on Sheffield Fair Ground one New Year's Day, how many shows do you think we did?

Naturally I had no idea.

"Twenty-two!" Karno cried. "Twenty-two shows in a day! Not just a ten-minute turn, either, a full on affair. I did the double trapeze, the horizontal bars, I was ringmaster for the Fortune-Telling Pony, I had to introduce the so-called clown *and* pick the audience back up afterwards, I was in a sketch called *Dead and Alive*, and played three parts in *The Drama of Dick Turpin*."

"Twenty-two times?" I said, astonished.

"Twenty-two times, and was paid one and ninepence for my trouble."

I listened to him telling me stories of his youth, and knew this was an indication of a growing bond between us, knew that all this was a good sign, good for me, good for my future career. All the while, though, somewhere in my central nervous system, I had registered the knowledge that I was the "other one".

13
THE NEW WOMAN'S CLUB

WHENEVER we were playing in London, the routine was that we would gather on a Saturday night at the Enterprise to collect our pay from the hand of the great man himself.

It was my habit, on those Saturday nights, to position myself by the window so that I could see across the road to the Fun Factory, where Freddie junior was even then dishing out the dosh to the supers and chorus girls. My fervent hope was that I would catch a glimpse of lovely Tilly Beckett, whom I hadn't seen since we last set sail on the *Wontdetainia* together. She would pause at the end of Vaughan Road. I would then stroll over from the Enterprise, looking prosperous and successful – to which end I always wore my best suit and hat to be paid in – and would offer to escort her home. That was how it always played out in my head, anyway.

As I kept my vigil on this particular night, a pint of ale for company, I looked around at the gathering of Karno principals. I felt that what I had joined was far more than just a bunch of new workmates. It was like a secret society, in a way, a fraternity that extended well beyond the limits of the Karno organisation to include every comic and comedical actor who worked or who had ever walked upon a stage.

The Power was part of the secret, for we had all felt it at some time or another. It set us apart from the herd, and once you had looked down from the apron of a stage and seen the faces turned up towards you, hanging on your every gesture, your every word, how could you ever again be content to be the man on the Streatham omnibus?

And in this secret society, we all somehow instinctively knew our place. We knew that the top echelon was occupied by the great solo artistes, Little Tich, George Robey, Marie Lloyd, those that followed in the footsteps of poor mad Dan Leno, who was then four years dead but still remembered with love and reverence. Clara Bell used to say, whenever it started to rain, that it was "the angels crying with laughter at Dan".

Karno's principals held a high rank, but they were denied the very top rung by the knowledge that it was Karno's name that put the bums on the seats. Some were content with this, but others, like Harry Weldon, burned with the desire to prove themselves worthy of top billing in their own right. They were always held back, though, by the knowledge that the Guv'nor offered them security and a guaranteed weekly wage.

And so on down the bill, past the trick cyclists and the mermaids, the coster singers and the nigger minstrels, until you came to those "billed amongst the wine and spirits", as we used to say, a reference to the very bottom line of a music hall poster, or worse still, "sharing a line with the Biograph". We were all "in", because at some time or another someone somewhere had decided that we had "it", but we all knew our place as surely as we knew our own names.

144

That place could change in the blink of an eye, mind you. Take Fred Kitchen, for example. He was working as an understudy when one fine day the principal comic decided to throw his weight around a bit. Dickery, his name was, and he thought he'd play sick, show Fred Karno how valuable he was by going missing for a couple of nights. Well, the Guv'nor didn't blink, and shoved young Kitchen centre stage, where he blossomed, and overnight he was an understudy no more, while his erstwhile superior was sliding backwards down the greasy pole.

Karno himself – sitting over there at his rickety fold-up table, scratching figures into his ledger – was an interesting case study for this imaginary hierarchy. As the master employer he held dozens of artistes' lives and their very standing in the world in the palm of his hand. Yet he had been a performer in his day, and a good one, who had given it up, and do you know what? All those who actually practised their art nightly on the stage, who felt the Power coursing through their veins, secretly felt themselves placed higher on the ladder than the good old Guv'nor. You'd never say it out loud, least of all to the man himself, but it was true.

Charley Bell, never one to hang around of a Saturday, strolled over to me and said: "I'm off home – you coming, Arthur?", and I was just about to give up my window seat for yet another week when I caught sight of a little blonde bob in the big double doorway, lit up brightly by the lights from inside the Fun Factory. I pressed my nose against the glass, trying to make sure it was really her. It was – surely it was…

"Arthur…?" said Charley, on pins to go.

"No, you're all right," I said, as casually as I could manage. "I'm good for one more, I reckon."

Charley followed my eyeline across the street. "Aye aye, it's like that, is it? Well, happy hunting, my lad, happy hunting..."

Tilly was strolling slowly towards the corner of Vaughan Road and Coldharbour Lane, quite alone. I watched her as she paused beneath a street light – instinctively knowing, like a good super, where she would be seen to the best advantage – and looked both ways down the street, a move which enabled her to toss her lovely hair in the light, and crane her perfect neck.

Well, this was as propitious an opportunity as my many fevered imaginings had devised, so I determined to grasp it. I took a deep breath, jammed on my hat, shoved my way out of the pub and set off across the road.

When I was halfway there, a casual and worldly smile (that I had been practising) fastened to my features, I saw that she had suddenly been joined by someone – Freddie junior, damn his eyes! – who was striking up a conversation with her. I tried to veer away, but just then saw that she had spotted me, so I had to press on. The confused messages my brain was sending to my legs at this point meant that I ended up doing a few paces of a strange, uncertain bandy little skip not unlike a two day-old foal finding its feet for the first time.

Freddie guffawed. "That's very good! What sketch is that from?" he said. I ignored him, my face burning, and turned to Tilly.

"A very good evening..." I began, touching the brim of my hat.

"My, my, aren't we formal?" Tilly smiled. "Is that any way to address your wife?"

"Eh? What?" said Freddie junior.

"Um...?" said Muggins, your narrator.

"That's right. Oh, we had such plans once upon a time, didn't we? To go to America and seek our fortune?"

146

"Indeed we did," I said. Tilly gave me another radiant smile, raising an eyebrow as if she wanted to signal something to me, but I was too overwhelmed – or just too plain dim – to pick up what it was.

"Now, Freddie, what was it you wanted to ask me?" she said, turning her full attention back to the baffled junior Karno.

"Well, um..." he said, "to be honest, you've rather taken the wind out of my sails. I was going to ask if you had plans for tomorrow afternoon...?"

"Oh, Freddie, I'm sorry, I do, I do have plans. I'm going to be taking a stroll in Hyde Park with Arthur here, aren't I, Arthur?"

"Oh, yes, that's right," I said.

"And then maybe some afternoon tea somewhere. We have been parted for such a long while, you see, and have such a lot to discuss, don't we, my dear?"

"We do," I said. I was conscious of not really contributing to this fiction, so I added an apologetic little shrug.

"I see," Freddie said. "Well, I hope the weather keeps fine for you. Goodnight to you both." He traipsed forlornly back into the Fun Factory, where, it has to be said, there were plenty more fish in the sea. Tilly gave him a winning smile and a little wave as he went.

"Thank goodness you appeared, Arthur!" she said, once he was out of earshot. "I was afraid he was going to proposition me again."

"Again?"

"Oh yes, he's a persistent little chap. I'm afraid he'll never amount to very much, though, poor Freddie. So, shall we say Speakers' Corner, at half past two?"

She stood up onto her tiptoes and kissed me quickly on the cheek, then she skipped off into the night, leaving me standing there, my head spinning.

147

I had the opportunity to put poor Freddie straight the very next morning. I was pacing up and down Charley and Clara's garden, thinking. Suddenly I heard a voice hailing me. I looked around and saw our neighbour, the mysterious friend of Marie Lloyd, looking over the garden wall. She was wearing gardening gloves and a headscarf (as well as a full range of other clothes, naturally) and seemed to be engaged in a little light pruning.

"Hallo-o!" she called, beckoning to me. I walked over to introduce myself. "You must be Clara's lodger. I'm Edith. I'm very pleased to make your acquaintance at last."

She peeled off a glove and we shook hands. Her hand was cold, though it was a warm spring day, and she had little colour in her cheeks for all the work she had been doing. A small, half-moon-shaped scar showed clearly on her cheek, and I tried not to stare at it.

"And you work for the celebrated Fred Karno, I suppose, do you? Like Charles?"

She seemed surprisingly thrilled to have this confirmed.

"Tell me all about it!" she said. "How do you find Mr Karno? And how do you come to be working for him?"

We chatted away over the wall for quite some time. She laughed heartily at the tale of my being chased by the entire population of Bolton, and generally lapped up any morsel of information I could give her. She was particularly interested when I told her I had had the good fortune to visit Karno's house and meet his wife, and she wanted to know all about the furnishings, and most especially what impression I'd formed of her.

We heard a door open, on her side of the divide, and a voice called: "Hullo...!"

"Oh, do excuse me, I'm expecting a visitor," Edith said, and then called out: "I'm in the garden, darling!"

A young man appeared and strode down the garden towards us, and who should it be but young Freddie junior.

"Oh, hello there, Arthur," he sang out when he saw me. "Of course, you live with the Bells, don't you? I remember."

He stepped up to Edith and kissed her most familiarly on the cheek, which rather took me by surprise, I must say, but it was nothing compared to the surprise I got from the very next thing he said.

"Hello, Mama."

Mama...?

Freddie turned to me sheepishly. "Listen, Arthur..." he said. "I hope you don't think I was stepping on your toes last night. She's a pretty little piece, that Tilly Beckett, and I didn't realise she was spoken for, and all that. Uses her maiden name, you see, doesn't she?"

"Really, don't mention it," I said.

"No hard feelings?"

"Absolutely no harm done."

"Good man." Freddie checked his pocket watch. "Hey, hadn't you better be off if you're going to meet your good lady?"

I hadn't realised it was getting so late, so I excused myself and hurried on my way. I didn't want to humiliate young Freddie by telling him that a girl he liked had made up a fanciful story just to put him off, and anyway I was still thrown by discovering that our mysterious next-door neighbour seemed to be the lad's mother.

Which is why, do you see, I never quite got round to mentioning to him that Tilly and I were not, and never had been, man and wife.

149

For a good few years women had been angling and agitating for the vote, same as men, and a number of factions had emerged within the women's movement who seemed to find it hard to agree on anything much. The main bunch, the Women's Social and Political Union, which was the one run by Mrs Pankhurst and her daughters, had just, after five years of wrangling, decided that their colours should be green, purple and white, which smacked of compromise rather. After all, green is neither blue nor yellow, and purple is midway between blue and red, and white goes with everything, doesn't it?

The Guv'nor, never one to miss a trick, had put together one of his most successful satires on the subject. *The New Woman's Club*, it was called, although truth to tell it was less an impassioned discursion illuminating the issues surrounding universal female suffrage than it was an excuse to have ladies riding bicycles around the stage in their bloomers.

One of these suffragette types was holding forth to a small crowd when I approached Speaker's Corner. She seemed to belong to the more militant wing of the movement, as she was suggesting (at the top of her shrill voice) that there was nothing for it but to chain herself to the railings in front of Mr Asquith's residence and refuse food and water until he saw sense.

"You could be there for quite a while!" some wag shouted out, to general laughter.

Perhaps Tilly saw herself as one of these modern women, which is why she had made all the running and invited me to meet here. Or maybe it was all just a subterfuge to escape from the hapless Freddie junior. Maybe she wasn't even going to turn up...?

Then my speculations were banished into the ether, for there was Tilly, off to one side, watching the same performance. She spotted me at the same instant, and skipped over.

"Arthur, there you are!" she beamed, quite taking my breath for a moment. "I suddenly had the horrible thought that you might have taken the whole thing as a joke and not come."

"Well, joke or not, here I am," I said, and then couldn't stop myself from blurting out: "You look wonderful."

"Oh now," she said in a hushed voice, taking my arm and beginning to lead me away. "I'm not sure we should let my sisters hear you complimenting me like that, it might not be quite the thing."

"I'm sorry," I said. "Did you want to stay and listen?"

"No, no, she's a sideshow, really. You know," Tilly said as we strolled away in the sunshine, "there was a rally earlier this year, right here in Hyde Park, and thousands of people turned up to hear the Pankhursts speak. What do you think of that?"

I nodded. What I was actually thinking was that there must have been the most tremendous queue for the ladies' conveniences, but I judged it best not to speak that thought out loud.

"It was inspiring," Tilly went on. "After all, the vote is just one step on the road to full equality for women, and if anyone knows that a woman can be every bit as strong and smart and successful as a man, given the chance, it's people in our business, would you not say so, Arthur?"

"I would say so, of course," I said.

"Exactly! Look at Marie Lloyd, look at Vesta Tilley! They can top the bill as well as a George Robey or a Harry Randall any day of the week, can't they?"

She was right, of course. I didn't mention that whenever Vesta Tilley topped the bill she did so dressed as a man, or that Robey was the most successful pantomime dame in the country. I didn't want to quibble.

"So naturally I am in favour of votes for women," she went on, "although I don't need the vote to know that sometimes a girl has to be forward to get what she wants. You didn't mind me inviting you out, did you?"

And of course I didn't. My brain was still happily savouring the phrase "what she wants".

━━━

We found ourselves towards the end of the afternoon at Hyde Park Corner, where the carriages rattled through the great ornamental façade. Tilly, as befitted a New Woman, again took charge of the situation.

"Well now, Arthur, shall we take tea, or go our separate ways?"

"Oh, tea, definitely. That would hit the spot."

Tilly looked around for a moment, then pointed up Piccadilly.

"The Ritz is just a short walk away," she said disingenuously. I could almost hear my pocketbook screaming a protest.

"It is," I agreed. "Or ... we could take a cab ... to..." I caught sight of a convenient hansom just at that moment and stepped out to flag it down as my mind floundered for a suitable destination.

"To...?" said Tilly, as I opened the door for her to step in.

"The Trocadero, why not?" I blurted out, both to her and to the driver. It was the only place that popped into my head. It wasn't the Ritz, but it was still decidedly fancy.

"Coo!" Tilly said.

The Trocadero was, as it still is, at the bottom end of Shaftesbury Avenue. A lot of the older music hall turns used to like to relax there of an evening, and I had been there with George Robey after work one night, listening to him holding forth in the famous Long Bar. I couldn't take Tilly in there, of course, as it was for gentlemen only, but there were also the rather luxuriously appointed restaurants on the ground and first floors.

We walked through the marbled hallway past a vast frieze depicting scenes from Arthurian legends, and then up the thickly carpeted staircase to the first-floor dining room. I surreptitiously managed to ascertain, to my relief, that I could afford a light afternoon tea here, as long as neither of us absolutely pushed the boat out, and so I guided Tilly to a table.

"This is rather grand, isn't it?" Tilly said in a hushed voice. "I was joking about going to the Ritz, you know."

I smiled nonchalantly, trying to convey the impression that I took tea in these surroundings whenever I pleased.

"You must be doing ever so well. Everyone says you are."

"And who is everyone, exactly?"

"Oh, you know, the supers and the chorus girls. I've just come back to Karno's from another job, with Doctor Potter's Performing Dogs. I was supposed to be his assistant. Sounds pretty glamorous, doesn't it? But if I tell you that my duties included following the little beasts around with a dustpan you'll see why I was glad to leave. He wanted me to go with them to tour Ireland but I told him the dogs were making me sneeze. So I'm back with Karno's now, and they're still all talking about you, you know. Freddie says you've made his life a misery, moving up like you did, because they all think it can happen to them now."

I was gratified to hear this, naturally.

"Oh look," said Tilly. "There's a friend of yours over there."

She was looking at a table across the room, where another couple were in the middle of a meal. The girl's eyes were downcast and she was picking at the crust of a sandwich, while her gentleman friend was dolled up to the nines and gazing directly at her with undisguised adoration.

"It's Syd Chaplin's brother, isn't it?" Tilly said. "Go and say hello, I don't mind."

"No, no," I said, "we're not really friends, exactly..." but then young Chaplin turned towards us and saw me gawping at him, so I pretty much had to go and pay my respects.

As I approached his table I saw that he was getting on the outside of a really rather enormous repast, roast meat, vegetables, as if to say money was no object. He leapt to his feet to greet me like an old chum, looking really quite pleased that I had rolled up. I got the impression that the conversation had been suffering a little bit of a lull.

"Good afternoon, Mr Dandoe!" he cried. "May I present Miss Hetty Kelly? Hetty? This is Arthur, one of my colleagues in Mr Karno's company."

"Delighted," I said, taking the girl's hand. She couldn't have been more than fifteen, slim and pretty enough, with pleasing features and nice brown eyes. She gave me a wan smile.

"Hetty is one of Bert Coutts' Yankee Doodle Dancers," Chaplin beamed. "They've been rehearsing at the Montpelier, in the next room to us. I popped in to watch and was captivated by this vision of loveliness you see before you."

I'd seen these Yankee Doodlers, a group of kids, eight or nine of them, dressed in Stars and Stripes outfits, yodelling about the land of the brave down at the Streatham Empire. The appeal of the act had escaped me, frankly.

"I see," I said. "And are you yourself American, then, Miss Kelly?"

"Naah," she replied. "I'm from Camberwell. My sister's going to America soon, though. She's going to marry a millionaire."

This titbit brought a flash of life to the girl's features for the first time, and it struck me that young Chaplin might have his work cut out matching up.

"Well," I said. "I mustn't interrupt your meal. I just wanted to wish you a good afternoon, and meet your charming companion."

"Thank you, thank you, Arthur, most kind," Chaplin gushed, and it seemed to me that he took my compliment to the girl as a compliment to his own good taste. I returned to my seat, where Tilly was all curiosity.

"So?" she said. "What's she like?"

"She's just a child," I said. "He seems utterly besotted, though."

And he was. Shortly afterwards Chaplin came over to speak to us. I introduced him to Tilly, of course, whereupon he bowed, kissed her hand and said: "Enchanté..." in a rather oozy way which made her smile – amused, I remember hoping, rather than actually charmed.

Chaplin turned to me. "What do you say, eh? Isn't she the most radiant creature you ever laid eyes on? Hetty, I mean? Did you ever see such perfect teeth?"

Which struck me as an odd thing to say outside of a horse fair, but still.

"Well," Tilly said, as Charlie swanned away. "She's certainly got him hooked, if she wants him."

"Poor kid," I snorted.

"Poor kid? What do you mean?"

"Well, all that 'radiant creature' nonsense. Must be quite hard to take, don't you think?"

155

"Hard to take?"

"Yes, being, I don't know ... worshipped like that."

"Well, for goodness' sake, man, what girl wouldn't want to be worshipped?" Tilly was looking off into the distance thoughtfully, and I had the distinct feeling all of a sudden that I'd made a wrong step. I glanced over at young Hetty Kelly, who looked as though she'd had quite enough of being worshipped for one day.

I noticed that Chaplin had left her alone. Just then there was something of a stir in the room, just a ripple, as though something had caught the collective attention. The musicians struck up with *The Honeysuckle and the Bee*, and a thin, reedy voice began to sing. I looked round, and of course it was Chaplin. He had a single rose clenched drippily in his two fists, and was tippy-toeing around the girl in what I imagine he thought was a bee-like fashion. She looked as though she wished the floor would open up and swallow her whole.

"*I'd like to sip the honey sweet from those red lips, you see-e-e-e...!*" he trilled, and when he reached the end of the song, and presented Hetty with his single red rose, the room broke into delighted applause. I turned to Tilly, but the scornful remark I was about to make at this nauseating spectacle died on my lips as I saw her applauding even more enthusiastically than the rest.

And for not quite the first time, and certainly not the last, I knew what it was like to be measured against Charlie Chaplin.

14
MUMMING BIRDS

THERE were a couple of dozen of us hanging about the Fun Factory the next bright late-summer morning, waiting to be told what to do and where to go. We chatted lazily in groups of two or three, smoking our cigarettes, casually taking the rise out of one another.

Charlie was beaming all over his little face, having waited for his Hetty early that morning and escorted her to her own rehearsal before heading on to ours. He described their stroll along Camberwell Road in terms that a romantic lady novelist would have baulked at – "walking in Paradise with an angel", etc. – going on and on about the divine smell of the soap she had used to wash her face.

I was only half-listening, as I was thinking about Tilly, who had cheerfully agreed that we should spend the following Sunday afternoon together.

Suddenly the group stiffened, as if coming to attention, and Karno was amongst us. He nodded a wordless greeting to the group at large, and then lighted on yours truly and Charlie.

"You two lads. A word, if you please."

Once in his office he left us standing while he shuffled through some paperwork, then he turned his most piercing gaze upon us, making us feel rather as though we'd been caught scrumping apples in his garden. That's how I felt, anyway. Charlie was probably still thinking about soap.

"Now then," the Guv'nor began, after clearing his throat with a little cough. "You've been with me how long now?"

"Just under a year," Charlie said promptly, the keen little soldier.

"Just over a year," I said in turn, keen to remind the Guv'nor of my (slight) seniority.

"Just so, just so," Karno nodded, steepling his fingers. "And you've both learned most of the rep? *London Suburbia*, *Jail Birds*, *Early Birds*, *The Casuals*, *Wontdetainia*, *The GPO*, *Perkins MP* and so forth?"

Chaplin and I nodded along as he ticked the sketch titles off.

"Well then, I think the time has come to complete your heducation. There's a company touring at the moment in *Mumming Birds*, and I'm going to pull a couple of lads out and stick you two in there, see how you go on. It's Syd's company..." Karno said, directing this remark particularly to Chaplin junior, "...so he'll see you settle in all right. That'll take us pretty much up to Christmas, and then we'll see what's to be done with you."

Another little cough, and Karno turned his attention back to his papers. The two of us stood a moment, unsure if we had been dismissed.

"Don't both thank me at once," Karno said, without looking up.

"Thank you, Guv'nor," Charlie and I both immediately said, exactly together, as though we'd been rehearsing it for years, and I saw Karno smirk. He knew that was going to happen, you see.

Outside the Guv'nor's office we were gathered up by Alf Reeves and delivered to the Miracle, where a company were to be running through *Mumming Birds* for the week. We would learn the parts we were to play, plus all the other ones as was the Karno way, and then we'd be dispatched to slip into Syd Chaplin's company like two freshly oiled cogs into a finely tuned engine.

Now *Mumming Birds*, as I'm sure you know already if you have taken any interest in the halls at all, was then and remains to this day Fred Karno's most successful offering.

The idea came from a one-off evening's gala entertainment put on by the Water Rats,[6] at which the Shah of Persia was a distinguished guest. This turned out to be a knowing burlesque of a typical night out in a music hall, in which celebrated performers did each other's turns, and all barracked each other relentlessly like the worst imaginable Saturday night at the Star in Bermondsey.

Most present will have forgotten the whole affair by the next morning, but not Karno. He turned it into a hit sketch, *Mumming Birds*, in which a music hall bill-within-a-bill was staged, featuring acts of excruciating awfulness, with the comedy coming from the raucous reactions and heckles of a fake audience, housed in two pairs of extra boxes constructed on either side of the stage.

The principal comic part was that of an inebriated swell, who would stagger in late, disturbing the first act, and thereafter continually clamber into or fall out of one of the lower boxes. In one of the opposite boxes you would find a naughty boy dressed in an Eton suit and armed with buns and a peashooter, and his guardian, a dotty and indulgent old uncle (or aunt, if it was Johnny Doyle).

The acts themselves, all introduced by a number man,[7] would be something like the following. A hapless vocalist would recite *The Trail of the Yukon*, followed by a female singer known as the Swiss Nightingale, who would massacre a ditty entitled *Come Birdie and Live With Me*. A moustachioed conjuror, who insisted on the term "prestidigitateur", would present a magic act of spectacular incompetence, and then there would be a "rustic glee club", or a double act called Duff 'n' Dire. Finally there was the Terrible Turkey, a self-styled champion wrestler, who would challenge all-comers to a bout for a small cash prize. Naturally, the inebriated swell would take him on, which was the excuse for the free-for-all climax.

We can only imagine the chagrin with which the King of the Water Rats, Mr Wal Pink, realised that his one-off gala show had provided the inspiration for his rival's greatest-ever success.

Mumming Birds was like a rite of passage. Karno would have two, three, even four companies performing it around the country at any one time, and a couple more in America, and all the big names had played in it at one time or another, so you couldn't be said to have truly arrived in the company until you had been 'blooded' in this sketch.

Both Charlie and I were, naturally, highly delighted to be reaching this landmark in our careers, and soon discovered that pretending to be a bad music hall turn required nice judgement. Charlie proved an excellent mimic, and was able to replicate pretty much everything the established company we were rehearsing with were doing, adding little physical embellishments of his own. I was a little more concerned to force the various characters to resemble myself than vice versa, but by the end of the week we were both deemed ready to go out on the road. I was quietly hoping against hope that a significant part of the tour would be in and around the capital, so that I could see Tilly and fan the small flickering flame of our romance. At lunchtime on the Friday I asked Alf Reeves.

"Alf?" I said. "Where are we due to play, do you know?"

"Aberdeen," he replied.

My heart sank. Even I knew that Aberdeen was in Scotland.

"And where after that?"

Alf stroked his chin and rooted around for the list, finding it in an inside jacket pocket. "Ah ... Greenock, Glasgow, Blackburn, then Hartlepool, Middlesbrough, Ardwick, Warrington, Southport, Burnley and Birkenhead. Who's a lucky boy then, eh?"

Only one of those sounded even remotely promising. "Southport? That's South, isn't it? Sunny South coast? Quite handy for London?"

"No, son," Alf said, clapping a hand sympathetically on my shoulder. "Not even close. It's near Liverpool."

Worse was to follow, though, as at the end of the day's play Alf warned Charlie and me to be sure and pack our bags as we'd be leaving for Scotland the next evening on the overnight train. This threw me into a panic, as it meant I would not be able to see Tilly on the Sunday, nor even at pay night on the Saturday to warn her I wouldn't be coming. And of course I didn't have her address, or know what theatre she was at, because I was such an utter chump, so I was stumped.

In the end I scribbled her a note, hoping that when I returned we would be able to continue where we were now being obliged to break off. It really wasn't the world's best or most romantic of notes, but the drafts I rejected were even worse.

I was going to pin it to the noticeboard at the Fun Factory in the forlorn hope that Tilly might spot it there, but in the end, as I was leaving the Bells' house in Streatham with my bag on the Saturday afternoon, I spotted Freddie K junior arriving next door to visit his mother (I still hadn't asked him about *that*), and handed it to him.

"Oh yes, of course, I know who you mean. Your wife...?"

"My wife, yes, that's the one. Thanks, Freddie."

I didn't disabuse him. I was in a hurry. And anyway, I didn't want him taking advantage while I was away, did I?

Now, if you ever find yourself in a position where you are embarking on a professional rivalry with someone you don't really know very well, then you could do worse than travel by train from London to Aberdeen with them. You'll know them a whole lot better by the time you get there, I guarantee you that.

Mind you, I thought at first I would be making the journey alone. In those days if you'd said to any of us that Charlie was a genius, we'd have thought you were referring to the particular kind of talent he had for missing trains, and it was only when we stopped at Rugby that I discovered he had managed to leap aboard the guard's van at the very last instant.

Now he was able to stroll along the outside of the train and find our compartment. He wasn't a happy chap. He mumbled a greeting, stowed his bag, then slumped down by the window with his chin on his fist. He hadn't shaved, his collar had come adrift at one side and his hair was all over the place.

It was the girl, of course. He was being forced to part from the gorgeous creature whose praises he had been singing non-stop the whole week, boring us all to tears, and naturally that was getting him down.

"It's only three months, and then you'll see her again," I said.

Charlie just grunted and stared out of the window, the very picture of melancholy. I thought he was overdoing it a bit, to be honest.

Three months – actually that felt like a long, long time. Everything could have changed by then. As the fields rolled by I found myself bleakly imagining meeting up with Tilly again, and she'd have got married in the interim to a greengrocer (not sure why I thought that particularly) and be heavily pregnant (not practically possible in that short space of time), and pretty soon I'd made myself feel very nearly as fed up as my travelling companion.

Chaplin perked up a bit when a steward popped his head in at the door to inform us that we could have supper now if we pleased, and he remarked that he had not eaten since breakfast the day before.

"Why ever not?" I asked, and he sighed a heavy melodramatical sigh before leading the way to the dining carriage.

As we waited for the main course to arrive, Charlie shoved bread rolls in his mouth and explained that it was not merely the thought of leaving Hetty behind in London that was the root of his depression; it was the fact that the budding romance was over entirely.

"Over?" I said.

"Dead. Dead. Dead as a door nail," he lamented.

"How so?"

"It was two days ago. I asked her to marry me and she broke my heart in pieces."

I was astonished. "You asked her to marry you? How long have you known the girl?"

"A week. It was the most profoundly affecting week of my life. I shall never forget her, and shall never again love so deeply nor so well."

"You asked her to *marry* you and you've only known her a week?"

"Well, yes, it was a test to see if she loved me, a hypothetical case. I asked her, supposing she were to be compelled to marry somebody, would she marry me or somebody else, and she said she didn't know, which is as much as to say she doesn't love me, so I said perhaps it would be best if we didn't see each other any more, again as a sort of test, and she agreed, can you believe it?"

I couldn't believe it. I wasn't exactly a leading authority on dealing with the fairer sex, but I think I knew better than to behave as Charlie had done.

"Then yesterday morning I arrived to escort her to work as usual," he went on, "and her mother appeared at the door in her stead and told me that I was not to see Hetty again, and that she had plans for her daughter which did not include consorting with a ragamuffin stage monkey four years her senior. I begged to hear it from Hetty's own sweet lips, and sure enough she was listening behind the parlour door and stepped forwards. 'Well,' I said, 'I've come to say goodbye again.' And do you know what she said in return?"

"'Goodbye?'" I guessed, and do you know I was bang on the button.

"Exactly!" Charlie cried, and shrugged, as if to say: "Women!" Which reminded him. "Hey, what about you and the girl you were with at the Trocadero?"

"Oh," I said, trying to put him off. "She's just a super in one of the Guv'nor's companies."

"You like her, though, don't you?"

"Oh yes, I like her well enough. I'll probably see her when we get back to London."

"Probably?" he scoffed. "You should have pursued her night and day, as I did with Hetty!"

We finally arrived in Aberdeen in the middle of the next afternoon, and Syd Chaplin was there to meet us. Well, to meet Charlie, of course. The brothers were obviously happy to see one another, and Syd plainly believed the sun shone out of Charlie's backside, which chimed pretty neatly with Charlie's view of the universe, so they had plenty in common.

Charlie and I had begun to rub along in a pretty friendly fashion, and Syd's attitude to me thawed accordingly over the next few weeks. That first afternoon, though, I just traipsed along behind their reunion, listening to their inconsequential catching up, and outside the station they merrily got into a cab to go off to the handsome digs they'd be sharing, while Syd squashed a piece of paper into my hand with the address of my lodgings scrawled upon it, and I was left standing alone on the pavement.

When I finally located the place, I realised I was in for a wretched old week. I knocked on the door of a tiny little shack down by the docks and a crone appeared. When I explained who I was, she beckoned me in with a bony finger and then showed me to a hammock, an honest-to-God *hammock*, slung across one end of a tiny kitchen. Not even a spare room, the kitchen, which was the main living room of the whole tiny place. Her husband, it appeared, was a fisherman, and was presently out at sea on his boat, and thanks to him the entire place reeked of fish.

It wasn't just the digs, either. The whole grim grey granite town smelled of fish. Every night in the theatre the grim grey granite audience, carved it seemed from the same stone as the buildings, smelled of fish. Every meal seemed to be fish, as well, apart from the breakfast, which was porridge that tasted vaguely of fish.

Charlie, meanwhile, was staying at the Imperial Hotel, where apparently there was no room for me, in a room adjoining his brother's.

The rest of the company was an agreeable enough assortment to knock around with. Jimmy Russell and Johnny Doyle were the main support for Syd as the Drunk, Russell the exasperated Master of Ceremonies, and Doyle in drag as the outraged Matron Aunt. There was Albert Darnley and Frank Melroyd, lovely Amy Minister, dotty Dolly Baker, Sara Dudley, solid old Ernie Stone, and the stalwart Karno couple George and Lillie Craig, who were usually to be found touring the country together. In fact they spent so much of the year in digs and hotels I'm not sure they even had a house of their own to go home to.

When I turned up at the grim grey granite theatre on the first morning for the get-in a sharp-looking young rake, who was, it seemed, also on the strength, introduced himself thusly: "Hallo, there. Chas. Sewell. Which is to say, Charles Sewell, but I go by Chas."

"You're not a Charlie, then?" I gagged, and his shoulders slumped a little.

"No, you see, that's exactly it, I've just got fed up of being described as "a proper Charlie", ha bloody ha ha, and what's more, you know, there's plenty of Charlies out there. Just look at the company for a start. There's Charley Bell, Charlie Mason, Charlie Corrigan, Charlie Marshall…"

"And Charlie Chaplin," I offered.

"Who?" Sewell replied blankly. Which I mention only because

it may have been the very last time in history that mention of that name elicited that response from a sentient human being.

Chas was a young chap, about my age probably, who was on his first Karno tour. We naturally began to knock around together, and also with Bert Darnley, who was an agreeably jovial sort of a type. He was maybe ten years older than me and Chas, and had been with Karno for years. He was still only a number four, but seemed to have no particular ambition to move up. Slow but steady, that was Bert. He'd certainly been around, had worked with (or near) all the greats and could name-drop for England.

Bert's experience often came in handy. He showed us the best pubs, the best digs, the finest cheap eateries, and he seemed to be on friendly terms with every publican, waiter, landlady, novelty act, chorus girl, gymnast, manager and stagehand we ever came across.

Bert, Chas and I developed a particular fondness for Scottish beers, and began to follow the scheme for life laid out by the great coster singer Gus Elen in his ditty *'Arf a Pint of Ale.*

For breakfast I never thinks of 'aving tea – I likes 'arf a pint of ale...

And so on through the day, with every meal supplemented by further 'arfs. It certainly struck a chord with me, especially later when my own favoured way to greet the day was with 'arf a bottle of Tennessee sipping bourbon, but we'll come to that. All in good time.

From Aberdeen we moved on to Glasgow, where you could hardly help noticing that the audience largely comprised blokes with eyes out, or else fingers missing or parts of their ears gone. These were shipyard lads. Tough houses.

The most popular acts on the bill, wherever we went North of the border, were in the Harry Lauder vein. These would typically march about the stage in their kilts or their tartan trews, and troll some ghastly laments about heather, and lassies, and things being "braw" or else "bricht", and so on and so forth.

Syd had the bright idea of pandering to the locals by changing the normal bill-within-a-bill of *Mumming Birds* to include a Scottish vocalist reciting a comically impenetrable Scottish poem. This backfired somewhat, as once the heckling and horseplay began from our unruly cast of characters the audiences would shout out: "Let him finish, you English bastards!"

When I wasn't out on the town with Bert and Chas, I used to like to walk and think. I couldn't help fretting that I had missed my chance with Tilly, and that by the time I got back to London she'd have struck up a romance with some other lucky chap. Had she even got my scribbled note...?

One Glasgow afternoon, left to my own devices, I wandered into Pickard's Museum. It was a gloriously barmy place to while away an hour or two, Pickard's was. For a ha'penny you could hear a demonstration of the gramophone, for example, or you could put a penny in a 'penny-winder' and glimpse what the butler saw in thirty seconds of flickering naughtiness. You could marvel at the inexpertly stuffed walrus, done by a taxidermist who had never seen one of these creatures alive and so had smoothed out all its trademark wrinkles, making it look like a giant dirigible. Or you could stroll into the theatre – if you could call it that.

I stood at the back bar nursing 'arf a pint of seventy shilling, minding my own business, watching the entertainment, such as it was, when I heard a hushed voice close by.

"Mr Dandoe, isn't it? Mr Arthur Dandoe?"

I turned, and there was a plumply pink-faced gentleman in his middle forties leaning on the bar beside me, decorated by a sheen of perspiration and a knowing smirk.

"You have the advantage of me, sir," I said. It was an advantage he decided to hold onto a while longer.

"I greatly enjoyed your performance yester-evening," the fellow said, and I acknowledged this by raising my glass an inch or so. "You're quite the coming man, I hear."

I regarded him curiously. He didn't seem to be the usual sort of after-show hanger-on. He'd have bought me a drink by now, for one thing.

"That's what you hear, is it?" I said.

"Oh yes, the estimable Mr Karno has his eye on you. And so do I. So do I." He took a sip from a tumbler of whisky and raised an eyebrow enigmatically.

"Oh you do?" I said.

"A fine employer, I've no doubt, our Mr Karno," the fellow went on. "But does he pay you what you are worth? This is the question you should be asking yourself, I think."

"The question I'm asking myself," I said, turning to look this smug chap full in the face, "is who the devil are you?"

He looked a little put out at this, as though naturally he was such a substantial figure in the world that I ought to have recognised him at once.

"Why..." he spluttered, fishing out a card from the pocket of his silk waistcoat. "I am Wal Pink, at your service, sir."

Now then. I'd heard that name. This was none other than the celebrated King of the Water Rats himself. Insofar as the Guv'nor had a rival worthy of the name, this Pink was it. His sketch *Repairs*, a couple of years previously, had been a first tilt at Karno's crown. Now, it seemed, Pink was back for another go.

"This is to give you fair and friendly warning," Pink said.

"Myself and a cadre of fellow sketch writers and performers, all Water Rats of long standing, are planning to incorporate. We have the backing, and we have all had enough of Mr Karno ruling the roost, distorting the marketplace, making our lives impossible. It is our intention to bring him to his knees."

I observed him frostily. "Really?" I said.

"Oh yes," Pink went on, "and make no mistake, you are either with us or heading for Poverty Corner. We have already secured the signatures of many of your colleagues – no, I won't disclose names – and when we are ready to put our plans into action their places will be secure."

"I beg your pardon," I said. "What *are* your plans exactly?"

Pink glanced around to make sure no one else was within earshot. "I will pay you twenty guineas on the date of your signature. In return you will agree to walk out on Karno and come to work for us – at an improved salary, mind – when you are signalled so to do, which will be when we are absolutely ready to proceed. Most, if not all, of your colleagues will do the same, I assure you, and it will thus prove utterly impossible for Karno to fulfil his many engagements. The New Wal Pink Company will step into the breach, thus supplanting him at a stroke and leaving his reputation in tatters. The so-called Fun Factory..." – here he became so excited that some spittle flew across the short space between us and landed on my bottom lip – "...will be finished!"

I looked at Wal Pink, his face flushed, a smug, sneery smirk on his sweaty chops, and I wanted nothing so much as to give him a hearty slap.

"I should be on my way," I said, draining my glass.

"You need time to think, of course," Pink nodded. "You have

my card. Step into my London office at any time and the arrangements can be made in a trice. Don't be left behind, now!"

I was going to show my disdain by leaving then, but blow me if he didn't jam his hat on his head and make for the exit a yard in front of me.

There was plenty to think about. Twenty guineas was not to be sniffed at, and I could well imagine many, if not all, of my colleagues biting his plump little hand off.

Could it really be that the end of the Fun Factory was nigh?

15
UNDER THE
HONEYMOON TREE

SCOTLAND had its charms, undoubtedly, but we were all glad to hit the road – the iron road – back to good old England and a week in Blackburn at the Palace. We came down by railway train on the Sunday. Bert Darnley, Chas Sewell and I set up a card school, while Charlie gazed mournfully out of the window in one of his poetical moods, occasionally sighing: "Hetty...!"

As we rattled along the insidious cunning of Wal Pink's scheme began to dawn on me. I looked over at Bert and Chas and found myself wondering whether the pennies they were laying down in wagers had come from Pink's coffers. I couldn't very well ask them if they'd signed up, though, could I, because what if they had? It was damnably cunning, the whole thing. Sad, in a way, too, I thought. The man had let his whole life be taken over by a rivalry – a rivalry, what's more, in which he could hardly hope to come out on top. (I know, I *know*...)

Mid-afternoon time George Craig wandered down the train to sort out our accommodation for the week, and eased his big, yellow-waistcoated belly into our compartment, wafting smoke theatrically from in front of his ruddy face. George ignored our moonstruck companion, as we knew he would – we all knew that Charlie would actually be rooming with Syd at a Grand or an Imperial somewhere, and there was no need to rub our noses in it. He thrust a note with an address on it at the other two lads, then looked over at me and said: "You're with me and Lillie from now on." He said it in a way that implied I knew why, as well, so I wondered if I was being punished for something. Perhaps he'd seen me talking to Wal Pink?

When he'd waddled off, Bert and Chas started ribbing me that management needed to keep a closer eye on me, ha ha, because of the demon drink, ha ha, but in truth I was no worse nor better than either of them were back then. And I was sure I'd be able to slip the leash, anyway, once we settled in, so I thought no more about it.

Once we arrived I traipsed off with George and Lillie, then, to these digs, where they, as respectable married folk, had quite a comfortable double bedroom. Across the landing, glory be, so did I, which was some compensation, I supposed, for being separated from the drinking party. There was already a trunk in there, set just inside the door, and I didn't think anything of that.

The landlady, a jolly, buxom, pink-cheeked old stick, laid on some tea and cake downstairs, which I wolfed down, anxious to catch up with the other lads to see if Blackburn's hostelries were open for business.

"Naah then," our hostess said as I made my excuses and headed out. "She'll not be best pleased if thee're late back, think on!" She said it with a smile, though, and so I gave her and George

173

and Lillie a cheery wave and stepped out into the evening, pondering the local linguistic peculiarity of referring to oneself in the third person. Didn't ponder it for all that long, though. There was drinking to do.

Near the theatre there were any number of welcoming establishments, in one of which I found my colleagues and spent an agreeable night off sampling the local ales. So agreeable, in fact, that I can't remember too much about it. Come chucking-out time we all went our separate ways, they to their respective pits, I back to my unexpected and luxurious double room.

I tiptoed softly up the stairs, not wanting "She" to be not best pleased, got myself into the big bed and stretched out in all directions like a starfish, as you do. Then I curled up and dozed off.

After a little while, who knows how long, I was woken by a creak of the landing floorboards. The door handle turned slowly, and the door opened, allowing a small figure to slip into the room. I wasn't too concerned – after all, this wasn't a haunted house that I had agreed to spend one night in to win some sort of inheritance. My beer-fuddled brain reckoned that this must be the owner of the mystery trunk trying to get his pyjamas or a shaving kit or something without waking me. Then the figure closed the door to again, plunging the room into complete darkness. I reached for the candle and matches which were on the bedside table.

The match flared, the figure gasped, turned wide-eyed to stare at me, and I found myself staring back in astonishment. It was Tilly Beckett. We gaped at one another until the match burned down to my finger, then I lit another one and we began gaping all over again.

"What on earth are you doing here?" I said when I had recovered some of my wits. Only about half of them, though, or I would have kept my voice down.

"Oh, Arthur," Tilly whispered, more pragmatically. "Such a silly thing has happened."

She came over and perched on the edge of the bed next to me, making me acutely aware of the fact that I wasn't fully clothed, and what's more that I was really pleased to see her.

"I got your note," she breathed. "Freddie brought it to me, and I was so disappointed, just then, at that moment, not to be seeing you the next day, when I'd been looking forward to it so much all week..."

This, as you can imagine, was music to my ears, as they say. The people who say such things. Poets and such.

"And Freddie's such a sweetheart, and he was right there and asked me what was the matter, do you see, and he said he could swing it for me to come and be in the same show that you were going off to be in for three months without even saying *goodbye* or anything...!" (Here she slapped me crossly on the arm.) "Except he couldn't fix anything until one of the girls was due to leave, at the end of last week, in Greenock, wasn't it? And so I've been taken on, haven't I? A featured artiste too. If the supers back at the Fun Factory get wind of it I shall be torn limb from limb! I came up from London this afternoon, and met up with the other girls this evening, Amy, Sara and Dolly. They seem very nice."

"This is excellent news!" I said. "But listen, there'll be merry hell to pay if they find you in my room. Where's yours? I'll help you with your trunk."

Tilly gave me a sheepish grin. "That's just it, you see. This *is* my room."

175

"Your room?" I said, not especially quick on the uptake (blame the beer).

"*Our* room. Freddie... Oh, Freddie thinks we're married, doesn't he, because of that silly thing I made up to put him off, so we're in married digs. I'd no idea until I got here. Oh, what are we going to do?"

We scratched our heads, tried to think what to do for the best, and in the end both of us felt the only sensible thing to do was to share the bed for the night – after all, there really was nowhere else for either of us to go – and try to clear the confusion up in the morning.

Tilly blew out the candle, and I lay there with my heart pounding and my mind racing, listening to the mysterious rustlings as she located and changed into her nightdress in the dark. Then the covers shifted, the bedsprings moaned and she slipped into the bed alongside me. A warm breath of her perfume wafted over me, and I clamped my mouth shut desperately, trying to make sure that she didn't get a ghastly gust of Northern ale in return.

I lay on my back with my arms by my sides like a corpse in a coffin, and if I can give you a hint of how I was feeling without being too indelicate, let's just say that if I had really been lying in a coffin there's no way the undertaker would have been able to screw down the lid.

All may have been well, though – I mean, I wouldn't have slept a wink, but nothing untoward would have occurred – except that after a minute or two her hair brushed my cheek and she whispered in my ear: "Aren't you going to give me a kiss goodnight?"

And that kiss goodnight went on, and on, and on, until the morning, when we found we'd both arrived at the conclusion that, well, if everyone thought we were married, then perhaps the simplest thing to do was to let them carry on thinking so.

It turned out to be the easiest thing in the world. George and Lillie greeted us at breakfast in the morning with that slightly prurient nudge and wink the older married couple likes to bestow on a younger, with a hint of: "We know what you were up to, we were young once!" mixed with the strange approval that goes with that for those who have validated their own life choices.

And at the theatre the rest of the company were charmed to meet Tilly, and were remarkably unsurprised that I would have kept her a secret. After all, why should they have known about her? What business was it of theirs? Bert had a wife and he barely ever spoke of her. He and Chas melodramatically lamented the loss of a drinking colleague, but both seemed thoroughly convinced that my excesses of the previous few weeks were now explained by my having been briefly off the leash.

The only one who seemed to give the matter even a second thought was Charlie. He had met Tilly, of course, at the Trocadero that time, when we hadn't mentioned that we were married, and I had also failed to mention the 'fact' once on our long train journey North.

"Delighted to see you again ... *Mrs Dandoe*," he oozed, when we met at the theatre, managing to invest that slight pause before her name with more suspicion than seemed humanly possible.

"Tilly, please. Not so formal," my 'wife' giggled as he took her hand and kissed it. "I still haven't got used to it, have I, Arthur?"

I fancy I smirked rather at this, and Chaplin replied: "Well, and you must call me Charlie. Now tell me all about your wedding day, this one's told us nothing at all!" And he hooked his arm in hers and led her away, the two of them chattering like a pair of old biddies. Tilly was enjoying herself, improvising happily. I gathered we'd had a small affair, family only, nothing too extravagant, in a little village church in Essex, on a lovely sunny day.

It suddenly occurred to me that we might both need to have our story straight at some point, so I hovered nearby committing Tilly's fantasy to memory as best I could. Charlie glanced over at me once or twice. I could see he was curious about something, but he couldn't quite put his finger on what it was.

━━━━

Charlie and I had begun the *Mumming Birds* tour on an even footing, but Sydney Chaplin's favouritism towards his younger brother was not to be confined to swinging him the swankiest digs, I discovered.

Our first forays into the comical mayhem of *Mumming Birds* were to be in the supporting roles of the Naughty Boy and the Magician. Charlie was ideally suited to playing the Boy, being slighter than me (slighter than almost everyone, actually), and it would mean that he would be onstage for the duration of the piece, so he snagged that part with his brother's approval. Meanwhile I went to work on my portrayal of the hapless Prestidigitateur – one of the better parts to play in the show-within-a-show, actually, because although he was supposed to be bad, he was bad in a hammy sort of way which was good fun to do.

I even got to feel the Power in action. It seemed to enable me to convey that even though the act I was portraying was bad, I myself was competent, and funny, and in charge, and I revelled in that feeling of strength.

During our travels in Scotland I'd found that I was getting more and more of a response as the Magician, and was quite happy with the way things were going. Charlie was trying to catch the eye as the Boy, but the part really involved little more than going: "Yah! Boo!" and chucking fruit about the place. Once we got going at Blackburn, I noticed the Boy becoming more and more rowdy and vocal during the Magician's act, almost as though he was trying to drown it out completely. I was so preoccupied and full of the joys of life, though, playing at husband-and-wife with Tilly, that I hardly minded.

At the end of the week Syd took me to one side in the pub after the last show.

"Ardwick Empire next week," he said.

"Right you are, skipper," I replied jauntily, anxious to get back to Tilly and my pint.

"I'm making a change there," Syd went on, catching me by the arm. "You'll be playing the Naughty Boy from now on, and Charlie's taking the Magician. Got it?"

"Um ... yes, I see," I said. "Any particular reason?"

"I don't have to explain myself to you," Syd muttered. "Just do as you're told."

So from then on I was the Naughty Boy, and to be honest more than a little cheesed off about it. Still, I quickly worked out that my new role gave me the opportunity to throw oranges at Charlie's top hat, and I became so proficient at this that the next time Syd took me to one side it was to tell me to pack it in. I put it down to all the Students v Staff cricket matches I'd played back at the college.

However I felt about what was happening in the theatre, there was always the prospect of a beer or two afterwards, followed

179

by the moonlit stroll, arm in arm with my pretend wife, back to married digs and the fraudulent conjugal pleasures we shared together. I don't have to paint you a picture, do I? I mean, I could do, but there's no way they'd let me include it in the book, so you'll just have to imagine.

Now I know what you're thinking. You're thinking: here we go. Two young people with bright and promising futures, she gets in the family way, and then it's all downhill from there. Misery, struggle, money trouble, before you know it more brats littering the place up, she drags him down, he resents her, she resents him for resenting her, and for ruining her looks and her chances of bettering herself...

We've all read that one, haven't we? Well, Tilly had read it too.

"I've seen too many girls fall for a baby," she said once. "And then you bump into them two years later and they look twenty years older. Grey hairs they haven't time to pluck out, and great red faces from boiling and boiling goodness knows what!"

Which is why, whenever we settled into a new town for a week on that tour, I would be dispatched to seek out the old red and white striped pole, trying to find "something for the weekend". I never quite mastered the art of going into a barber's shop and just acquiring the "something for the weekend" without the haircut. For some reason – probably just sound commercial good sense, actually, now I think about it – those particular items never seemed to be on sale until after the trim was completed. Sometimes I'd have to have a shave as well, before the old geezer in charge would admit to having any at all.

Mrs Rennocks, the landlady Tilly and I stayed with in Ardwick, cooed over the two of us newlyweds to such an extent we were hard put not to burst out laughing. Tilly filled in much of the detail of our make-believe wedding day in her parlour, I seem to recall. Anyway, Mrs Rennocks was adamant that she would only allow married couples to stay in her rooms, because once you let to single men, especially theatricals, they "got up to all sorts". We had to go out for a walk shortly after that, we were giggling so much, and ever after that "getting up to all sorts" was what we called it, and all sorts was what we got up to in her house for the whole of that week.

Charlie, meanwhile, was quite a hit as the Magician, and I remarked on this to Tilly in the pub after the show one night.

"Well, you would think that, wouldn't you?" she said, rather to my surprise.

"What do you mean by that?" I asked.

"It doesn't take a genius to see it," she said. "He's just copied exactly what you were doing, all your new bits, even down to that eyebrow thing of yours. I mean, he's funny enough, of course, but they're your laughs, really, when you think about it."

She was right, as well. He was a great mimic, Charlie, no doubt about it, and imitation is the sincerest form of flattery, they say, don't they? Well, I wasn't the first person to be 'flattered' by Charlie, and I certainly wasn't the last. Once Tilly pointed it out it really began to niggle with me, though, and the next night I picked out a couple of larger oranges.

I should have known it would take more than a couple of oranges to make a dent in Charlie Chaplin's progress.

16
THE KARNO
OF THE NORTH

"**DON'T** you know who we *are?*"

We arrived at the band call on Monday morning at the Middlesbrough Empire to find Syd in a terrible snit, rampaging around the stage gesticulating angrily at the theatre manager, a hapless individual named Blezzard, who was trying to placate him. I sidled up to George Craig, who was standing by the prompt desk watching these shenanigans with a face like thunder.

"What's up, George?" I whispered.

"Here," he hissed back, angrily thrusting a piece of paper into my hand as though it would be explanation enough. It was the publicity poster for the week's run, and I spotted right away that *Mumming Birds* was right down at the bottom of the bill, down among the wine and spirits, in other words taking second billing. It was quite a shock – it must have been years since a Karno company had been obliged to play second fiddle to anyone on any music hall stage anywhere.

I glanced at the top of the bill, and was mystified. If it had been a top-rank artiste, or some foreign turn with a global following and an ego to match, then maybe I might have understood, but it was actually another large company sketch, which would undoubtedly have its own substantial set and cumbersome cast cluttering up the place. The Arthur Jefferson Company, they were called, in something called *Home from the Honeymoon*,8 and this Jefferson was not shy of styling himself 'The Karno of the North'.

Syd broke away, exasperated, from the theatre manager – who crumpled into a chair, gasping for breath – and stormed over to the assembled Karno troupers.

"If it were not bad enough to be billed second, we are expected to go on before the interval!" he fumed. "I've complained till I'm blue in the face, but the fellow insists that the second half is promised to this other mob and he won't shift an inch."

"We're not going to stand for that, are we?" said Jimmy Russell, hands on hips.

"Well, what *else* can we do?" Syd exclaimed. There was a pause while heads were scratched, and then I suddenly burst out: "Withdraw!"

"What?" said Syd. "The Guv'nor would have my guts for garters!"

"Pull out!" I insisted, and Tilly squeezed my arm encouragingly. "Show we're not to be messed about. He'll back down, and if he doesn't ... well ... we'll set up somewhere else!"

I was talking off the top of my head, but Jimmy Russell took over my half-baked idea.

"Yes!" he cried. "There's a huge church hall just around the corner, that big dark red building. We set up in there. It could be done, Syd, you know it could. We'll wipe the floor with this mob, what do you say?"

There was a cheer from the rest of the company, apart from Syd, who looked as though the cares of the world had landed on his shoulders, and George, who was shaking his head, the big wet blanket.

"Come on, George!" Jimmy said. "How about it?"

"Lights?" George said, discouragingly.

"Borrow 'em!"

"Stagehands?"

"Bribe 'em!"

"Audience?"

"Go out and grab 'em!"

George was still shaking his fat head, looking terrified, and Tilly suddenly shouted: "Let's have a vote! Who's for pulling out?!"

Most hands shot up in the air right away. Everyone's, in fact, apart from George's, Syd's and Charlie's.

"This isn't a democracy, you know, chaps," Syd said, frowning. "It's all on me if it goes to hell."

"Which would you rather have to do?" I said. "Tell the Guv'nor that we rolled over for that chump? Or tell him that we wouldn't stand for it?"

Syd looked at Charlie, who shrugged. He looked at George, who mopped his brow with a big handkerchief. He looked at the rest of us, all raring to go. All of a sudden he smacked his fist into the palm of his hand.

"Let's do it," he said.

What a day that was. We got the set loaded back onto the carts, with our faces set firm against Blezzard, the theatre manager, who grabbed us by the sleeves begging us to turn round. Jimmy Russell managed to secure the use of the big church hall that he had seen for the week. It was promised to a temperance society for improving talks, but Jimmy managed to charm them round. Bert Darnley was dispatched to a theatre in Darlington which happened to be dark for that week, and returned with a cartload of lights and a small crew of eager stage workers.

And once it was all set up, early afternoon time, we all dispersed to the four corners of the town to spread the word. Actually, it was surprisingly easy to start the ball rolling. Tilly and I worked it together, and I'm sure the other members of the company had a similar approach. We would go into a pub, and over a drink or two we'd get chatting to the customers and mention the exciting news that the Karno company had pulled out of the local theatre and were setting up a rival show in a church hall. It didn't take long for the word to pass around the pub, then we would move on. By the end of the afternoon we were no longer bothering with the drink or two first. We would just poke our heads in through the doorway and shout the news, letting matters take their own course.

When the time came to return we made our way past the Empire, and saw the queue waiting to be let in for the evening's performance.

"Look at that," Tilly said. "He's not made any attempt to tell them that the Karno company is not appearing tonight. That's taking their money under false pretences, that is."

"We should tell them," I said. "It's only fair."

We intended to whisper the information here and there as we passed along the line, but in the event we only had to tell the people at the front of the queue and the news travelled faster than we could walk. It was like lighting the fuse on a firework, and as we watched the queue disintegrated before our eyes, with the Empire's audience running, scurrying, hustling away round the corner to the church hall of St John the Evangelist.

Hundreds were waiting there, the queue snaking away to the corner and away out of sight. George Craig was taking money hand over fist, and the big red hall was already crammed to the rafters. Tilly and I burst out laughing when we saw it, and we ran hand in hand to get ready.

The show that evening had a rather curious beginning. Jimmy Russell had secured the use of the hall by promising to share it with the temperance society, but the audience sat dutifully through a harangue about the demon drink from the excitable Mrs Muriel Staveley, and then were rewarded by a Karno company at the top of its game. First some party pieces from the likes of Johnny Doyle and Bert Darnley, and then the mighty *Mumming Birds*, which was rapturously received.

Afterwards we rubbed salt into the wounds by gathering to celebrate in the pub next door to the Empire, which we were pleased to discover had been less than half full.

Syd was holding court, flushed with success, at one end of a long table, with the other senior members of the company – Johnny Doyle, Jimmy Russell, George and Lillie Craig – in attendance. To listen to him and Charlie, you'd think it had all been Syd's idea. They were debating whether to send a wire now to Karno about the whole affair, or whether to wait and see how the rest of the week played out. I sat at the other end with Bert, Chas and Tilly for company.

On the opposite side of the room we could see the Jefferson party, similarly installed, like a mirror of ours, but mired in gloom. Their senior performers at one end, their junior fellows at the other, and then off by himself a slim figure of maybe eighteen years old, with springy red hair and a gormless smile stuck to his chops. No one seemed to be talking to him, and after a while he picked up his glass of beer and wandered over in our direction.

"Hullo," this ginger stripling said, a big ingenuous grin on his face as though he were incapable of imagining why anyone wouldn't like him. "I'm Stan."

"All right, Stan," I said, choosing to play the benevolent victor. "Join us."

This Stan plonked himself on the spare chair at our table, and raised his glass as if to say "Cheers!" as we introduced ourselves.

"So, not celebrating with your mates tonight?" I asked, nodding over towards the Jefferson company table.

Stan had just brought his pint to his lips, and snorted the froth off the top in surprise. "Celebrating?" he said. "After that stunt you lot pulled?"

Bert, Chas, Tilly and I smirked and clinked our glasses together. Stan leaned in close.

"They're all crapping themselves that word's going to get back to the Guv'nor and they'll all be out on the streets, so nobody wants to talk to *me*."

"Why's that?" Tilly said.

"Well, you see, he's my Dad," Stan said. "I'm Stan Jefferson."

"So if your Dad's 'The Karno of the North', then you're the Freddie junior of the North," I said. Stan grinned blankly at this.

"Difference is, Stan's old man's given him a go," Bert said. "Actually, Dad was dead against me going on the stage," Stan said. "He wanted me to go into the management side of things. Arthur Jefferson *and Son*, you know? Then one night I borrowed some of his clothes and did a turn at a place called Pickard's

187

Museum, do you know it? In Glasgow?"

I did know it, of course, and an unpleasant memory of Wal Pink's smooth, well-fed features flashed before my eyes. I blinked it away.

"So I walked out onto the stage in my borrowed trousers and my borrowed hat, and I did my borrowed *lines*, and it wasn't the greatest act in the world but it was the greatest feeling I ever had in my life. I saw Pickard standing at the back, watching me, and there, standing next to him … was Dad!"

"Crumbs!" said Tilly.

"He saw that I was a lost cause, I suppose, and now he uses me as a sort of comedy sticking plaster when something goes wrong with one of his shows." He glanced over his shoulder at the *Home from the Honeymoon* team, some of whom seemed to be giving him the evil eye and muttering darkly.

Bert and Chas made their excuses and slipped away, probably to another pub where there were girls, if I know them. Stan turned to me with another big grin.

"What about you, then?" he said. "How did you get started?"

"Well, you'll hardly believe this," I said, "but the fact is I borrowed my dad's clothes to do an act, and he caught me at it."

"No!" Stan guffawed. "How about that!"

And when you're eighteen, nineteen years old, that's all you really need to strike up a firm friendship with someone, isn't it? That you should have one thing in common?

Stan turned to Tilly. "And how about you, Mrs Dandoe?"

"Oh, like most people, really," she replied nonchalantly. "My family are in the business, so it was in my blood. My father has his own theatre, and my mother is a seamstress, she makes all the costumes for the shows."

188

This was news to me and I was intrigued. "So you first appeared at your father's theatre, then?"

She laughed at that. "I suppose I did!" she chuckled, and then she stuck her hand up and waggled her fingers at me.

"What's so funny?" I asked, but apparently it was a private joke between Tilly and herself.

Just then Charlie strolled over, clutching his little glass of port and a cigarette, and stood over us, a disapproving expression on his face.

"You're giving away company secrets, Dandoe, is that it? To this spy from the opposition?"

"Oh, come on, don't be so bloody po-faced!" I said, slapping Charlie hard on the back. "Anyway, I'm the one who's getting information. Did you know that Mr Jefferson gets his people to call him 'The Guv'nor'?"

"Well, perhaps he shouldn't after tonight's little embarrassment," Charlie snorted, then he stuck his nose in the air and went back to the top table to consider weightier matters.

Tilly, Stan and me, we rolled about. If you could have seen Charlie's pompous little face with its pointless little sneer, and if you'd had a good night onstage followed by a few ales, then maybe you'd have been holding your aching sides, too.

━━━

The rest of that week was a triumph, a rout, a slaughter. The church hall was packed to wheezing point night after night, and we had to do two extra shows on the Saturday. We cleared far more than we would have at the Empire, while *Home from the Honeymoon* et al limped along to cavernous empty houses. So much for 'The Karno of the North', we thought.

We all really took to young Stan, though – even Charlie did, once our victory was certain and he loosened up a bit – and we spent a good deal of our spare time in his company. And so we were delighted, naturally, to find that the following week while we were topping the bill at the first-rank West Hartlepool Palace, the Jefferson mob were not far away, in Hartlepool's somewhat lesser second theatre, the Crown, and we were able to continue meeting up for an after-show pint or three.

Stan, Tilly and I even managed to organise a bit of an outing for ourselves, one sunny day when we had no daytime rehearsals, taking a picnic out to the headland. Syd had taken himself off to visit a friend from his days on the Cape mail boats whose ship was in the Victoria dock for a spell, so when Charlie got wind of our day trip he tagged along.

We met up outside the hotel where the Chaplins were spending the week, Tilly and I sharing a knowing look at the grandeur of the place, compared to the modest lodgings we had been billeted in. Charlie himself was in beaming dapper form, dressed up to the nines (sometimes he simply wouldn't make the effort and looked pretty much like a tramp, which I'm sure, Reader, you will not be hard pushed to imagine). He skipped down the steps as though he owned the place and greeted the three of us with exaggerated formality.

"Mrs Dandoe," Charlie gushed, bowing low to kiss Tilly's hand. "I see you are looking particularly fetching today for our day out. This collar shows off your classical neck to particular advantage, and this tie, why, it's almost like a gentleman's tie, is it not? Not that it makes you look at all like a gentleman, I hasten to add. Anything but!"

Tilly simpered. It's the only word for it. She was indeed wearing a man's thin tie that afternoon, one of my own, as a matter of fact.

It was something of a fashion for the young ladies at that time to wear a high, stiff gentleman's collar and a tie, making a none too subtle point about equality for women. Charlie knew this perfectly well, of course, and so when he offered Tilly his arm in a parody of a courtly gesture he was gently mocking her. And when she took his arm, loving the fuss he was making of her, he was highly delighted, and winked over his shoulder at Stan and me.

The two of them set off chattering towards the sea, which glistened away on the horizon, leaving Stan and me to stroll along behind with the picnic basket. This had been prepared by our landlady, a nice widow named Mrs Budgen, who had been cooing over Tilly, seemingly convinced that she was going to need to build up her strength for a couple of decades of childbearing.

When we reached the headland, jutting out into the shining North Sea, we put the hamper down for a moment to fill our lungs with North Sea air and admire the view, the ships below, the docks down to one side and the beach curving away to the other.

Ahead of us Charlie trotted down a little slope onto the sands, then turned to catch Tilly as she skipped after him pretending to be running out of control, so that he had to grab her by the waist for a moment. He made some joke which we couldn't hear, smiling his toothy smile, and she threw her head back and laughed, leaning her weight against his arm.

Stan looked at me with a wry half-frown. "Charlie seems very familiar with your wife, doesn't he? Do you not mind?"

"As a matter of fact," I found myself saying, "she's not actually ... which is to say, we're not, strictly speaking..."

"What?" Stan grinned at me. "Spit it out, man!"

And so I told him about the misunderstanding with young

Freddie Karno which had led to Tilly and myself sharing our accommodation as man and wife. He gawped at me, his mouth open wide, and then broke out into great gusts of high-pitched laughter. His eyebrows flew so high I thought they would disappear off the top of his head, and tears poured down his cheeks.

Charlie and Tilly came running back up the hill to see what the fuss was about. I was laughing myself now, laughing helplessly at Stan, and Tilly, too, began to giggle at the pair of us.

"Whatever is so funny?" Charlie demanded, refusing to get drawn into the hysteria, as ever resenting any laugh that he himself had not generated, but I managed to signal, somehow, to Stan to keep his counsel.

We found that the laughter had taken the wind out of our walking sails for the time being, so lunch was declared. We found an agreeable spot where we could perch on those sort of grassy tussocks that you often find where the beach meets the land, and tucked into Mrs Budgen's picnic.

I asked Stan how the week was going for the Jeffersons at the Crown.

"Oh, not all that well, I'm afraid," he said. "Mr Spencer, the owner, he's talking about converting to a picture house."

"More fool him!" I scoffed.

"All the staff are walking around like condemned men. He'll not need above half of them, you see, just to show pictures. It's about as cheerful as working in an undertaker's."

"Madness," I said, and I'm sure that most music hall folk would have agreed with me then. For us the Bioscope was the part of the bill where the music hall audience upped and went to relieve themselves.

"Your father would never think of doing that, would he, Tilly?" I asked. "Turning his theatre into a picture house?"

"Not likely," Tilly snorted, breaking into a giggle at the very idea. "Not very likely at all!"

"Why must it only be real life that is captured on film?" Charlie mused. "Why should it not be performances by the very same people you might go to the music hall to see?"

"So George Robey, say, might come here one day and find himself appearing in the flesh at the Palace and also on film at the Crown?" said Stan.

"How can that be better, though, than seeing the real thing?" Tilly mused.

"It can't, of course it can't, and people will realise that soon enough," I said.

"I don't know," said Charlie. "Think about it this way. You could capture a perfect performance, just the way you want it, and then you never have to do it again, never have to step out in front of a crowd wondering if they're going to be captivated by your art or baying for your blood."

Suddenly Stan, Tilly and I all found ourselves choking on our sandwiches, and all at the same word.

"Your *art*?" I managed to scoff.

"Yes, my art. What's so funny about that?"

"Nothing much that I've seen," I shot back, and the others laughed along.

"It is an art, the art of comedy performance," he insisted. "I'm like any artist, trying to capture the essence of the human condition."

"And you do, you do, every time you fall on your face or get hit by a bun," I chortled.

"And the frustrating thing, it seems to me, is that once one's performance is honed to perfection, then that perfection can never be preserved, it can only be repeated, and deteriorate,

193

slowly but inexorably, as the artist strives too hard to regain the perfection he once created."

Stan and I shared a look, still amused by the pretentiousness of Chaplin styling himself an artist. Tilly, meanwhile, seemed carried away rather by the little fellow's eloquence, and was wearing an expression of intense interest as he directed his argument to her.

"If I were a painter, or a sculptor, or a writer, then my art would live on, would it not? In galleries, in museums, in libraries. Perhaps one day film will be able to do that for me, will become a new art form. What do you think, Mrs Dandoe?"

"I suppose that could be the way of it," Tilly said.

Life was good that afternoon, strolling up the coast in the sunshine with my girl and my new friend, and even Charlie was on his best and most amusing behaviour. I made sure to pair up with Tilly when we set off back to town, though. She was becoming a little too admiring of young Mr Chaplin for my liking.

Later, back at our lodgings after the show, I lay awake in the dark wondering whether either of us had actually won that argument at the picnic.

I said to Tilly: "You know, I think Charlie would be happiest if they stuffed him and put him on display in the National Gallery."

She giggled and drew herself closer to me under the blankets, and I soon stopped thinking about the art of comedy performance altogether.

17
TILLY'S PUNCTURED ROMANCE

TOWARDS the end of the week, George Craig loomed in the doorway of the dressing room.

"Just to let you know. The Guv'nor's in Manchester next week, and he's going to pop over to see us one night in Warrington, surprise visit, so, best behaviour, right, lads?"

"How's that a *surprise* visit, then, George?" Chas Sewell sang out. "You've told us about it now."

"I don't know, maybe he'll have a pink hat on..." George grumbled as he left.

I looked over at Charlie, and he was deep in thought. I knew what he was thinking, because I was thinking it too. Karno was coming to check on the two of us.

During the show itself Charlie was clearly distracted, mistiming a couple of bits of business, which was most unlike him. It was a notable triumph for Bert Darnley, though, who was having a rare old hit that week declaiming *The Trail of the Yukon*, and afterwards we were all making this the excuse for a celebration while Charlie sat in a brown study, nursing a single port. After a good long while, he got up and had a quiet word with his brother, then he left the pub.

At the end of the evening Syd came over to our well-oiled little group.

"Goodnight, lads," he said. "Keep the noise down, won't you? Oh, and one more small thing. Tomorrow Bert, you're Naughty Boy, and Arthur? You're back to the Magician. All right? Till tomorrow, then, toodle-oo!"

And off he went. Well, we were all a little worse for wear, and it took us a moment or two to process this turn of events. In fact it was Tilly who first pointed out: "That means ... that Charlie ... is doing the *Yukon* poem. Doesn't it...?"

Bert was utterly crestfallen. "Oh," he said, and then, after a moment or two: "Oh."

As Tilly and I walked back to our digs later, a thought struck me.

"Maybe I should do the old Magician quite badly for a night or two, keep Charlie's paws off it for when the Guv'nor comes."

"I don't know why you're both so sure he's coming to see you boys in any case," Tilly said. "He might be coming for something else altogether."

———

On the Saturday night, George stuck his head round the door again.

"Syd wants a word," he said.

"I'll see him in the pub," I replied.

"Now," George said emphatically, then went on his weary way. Bert Darnley grimaced at me and drew his thumb across his throat in an ominous fashion. I threw a pair of socks at him and headed along the corridor to Syd's room. Syd was there waiting for me, sitting facing the door like a judge in judgement, face like thunder.

"Dandoe."

That was all he said at first. He just looked me up and down with an expression of disdain for what seemed like minutes on end, until I could stand it no longer and broke the silence.

"I'll sit down, shall I?" I said.

"You do as you damn well please," Syd exploded. "That seems to be your speciality!"

Well. That wiped the smile off my face.

"Is it true...?" he began. "No, don't even answer that, because I know perfectly well it *is* true. You have been living as man and wife with one of the girl supers, staying in married lodgings arranged by our company manager, getting up to Heaven only knows what, despite the fact that you are not and never have been married. What do you have to say for yourself?"

So that was it. I suppose deep down I knew it was too good to last.

"Actually it's funny how it all came about..." I said.

"It is not funny!" Syd exclaimed. "Nothing about this sorry business is funny. I don't know..." – he began to massage his temples – "first the Jefferson business and now this. Do you have any idea of the responsibility involved in leading a Karno company? Do you? I am responsible for how this company behaves itself in the towns we visit. How the company appears. Which is why I will not tolerate drunkenness, and I will not tolerate moral turpitude!"

I must admit it was the first I'd heard about him not tolerating drunkenness. He'd have had to give himself a right ticking off more than once. And I noticed that he'd managed to turn this round so that it was all about him.

"So you're giving me the sack, is that it?" I ventured.

"I have no desire to see a promising career in ruins over this. Yours or mine. However, I cannot allow the current state of affairs to continue. The girl must leave the company at once and return to London. You may go with her if you choose to, or you can continue with us for the next week in Warrington and the rest of the tour."

Syd's eyes narrowed.

"If you leave us in the lurch, of course, you will have to explain that to the Guv'nor, and I imagine he won't take too kindly to being let down."

That was true. So there it was, as plainly as could be. My career, or my girl. I was facing the worst dilemma of my life. Up to that point anyway. Worse ones were to come, believe me.

———

I left Syd's dressing room in a daze. George Craig was outside in the corridor, and as company manager he was clearly privy to what had just been discussed. He hissed at me.

"It's too late now to find either of you anywhere to stop the night, so you've one more night at Mrs Budgen's, but if I hear any of your high jinks I'll be straight in there with a bucket of cold water, you mark my words."

"Steady on, George," I said. "We've been pretending to be a married couple, not a pair of wild rabbits."

I picked up my bag from the dressing room, already deserted. I looked into the ladies' dressing room for Tilly, but that was empty too. I headed down the stone stairs towards the stage door, and met Charlie coming the other way. As we passed each other on the landing, he smirked: "Well, so long, then, Arthur. It's been grand!"

198

"Eh?"

"I gather that you are leaving us, you and your ... wife."

"What's that to you?" I snapped back.

"Oh, nothing much," he trilled. "But I shall watch your future career with interest. Ta ta! Give my regards to the Corner!"

Meaning, of course, unemployment, poverty, failure, despair. I listened to his footsteps tripping gaily up the stairs, and a new determination took a hold of me.

Tilly wasn't in the pub, but Stan was, leaning on the bar.

"Hail fellow well met!" he cried out. "Or should I say *ale*, fellow? Ha ha! What'll you have?"

"Nothing, thanks," I said. "I have to find Tilly. She'll have gone to our lodgings, I expect."

Stan's face fell. "Oh. Well, then, I suppose this is goodbye."

I looked at him sharply. "What do you mean by that?"

"Well, next week we're for Wallsend, and you're off to Warrington, and that's a devil of a hike for an after-show pint. But I dare say our paths will cross again. Let's hope it's sooner rather than later, eh?" He smiled and shook me warmly by the hand.

I found Tilly sitting on the bed in our room back at Mrs Budgen's house. She gave me a rueful smile as I came in.

"You heard, then?" I said.

"Lillie took me to one side. Very serious." She took my hand and pulled me gently over to sit beside her. "How do you think they got wind of it?"

"Don't know. You didn't mention it to anyone?"

"Not a soul," she insisted. "What about you? Been bragging to any of the lads?"

"No, no. I may have said something to Stan Jefferson, but he wouldn't have let on. He hasn't even met Syd or George, has he?"

"I don't suppose it really matters, anyway, does it love?" Tilly said. "What's done is done. Nice while it lasted, all that."

"Wasn't it, though?" I grinned, and we pulled each other close.

"Do you think...? No, silly..." she said.

"What?"

"Well, I was wondering, do you think they'd let us stay if we actually did...?"

"Did what?"

"Did ... get married?"

We looked at each other, and we both seemed to be holding our breath for an age. It felt like we were both waiting for a clue from the other. In the end we could stand the tension no longer, and burst out laughing. We rolled back on the bed, making the springs squeak, and within moments there was an urgent rapping upon the bedroom door.

"Oi!" George hissed from the landing. "Pack that business in, do you hear me?"

Naturally this only added to our mirth, but we tried to keep the noise down as best we could. Once the first flush of hilarity had passed, the question of the marriage suggestion – or was it a proposal, even? – still hung over our heads.

"I think..." I started, but Tilly started to speak at the same time, so I stopped.

"No, you go on," she said.

"Well, I think we'd struggle to get the banns read, and a vicar out of bed, and my mother up from Cambridge, and the cake cut, all in time to catch the train for Warrington tomorrow morning."

"Yes. That's true," Tilly said carefully, neither relieved nor disappointed.

"So, I suppose all we can really do is make the best of a bad lot."

Tilly laid her head on my chest, and I looked up at the ceiling. "It's like a good old melodrama, isn't it?" she said. "'We shall be poor, but at least we shall be together...!'"

"Ha!" I snorted.

"It's not so very bad for me," she went on. "I'll get something soon enough, in the super way, or maybe dancing. Oh, but poor you! All the work you've put in to make your way at Karno's, and you're quite the coming chap, everyone says so. You and Charlie Chaplin, the next big Karno players."

There was a pause, a pause during which I'm pretty sure I was supposed to say: "Never mind" or: "It's not your fault." Or possibly: "What I have discovered with you matters more to me than my silly old career!" But I lay there thinking about Charlie's gleeful "Ta ta!" as his main rival flushed his big chance away, and I just couldn't give him the satisfaction.

"The thing is..."

"What?"

"What Syd Chaplin said to me was that they don't want this business of ours to be known about, because it reflects badly upon him, and upon the Guv'nor, so..."

"So what?"

"So in point of fact, I can finish the tour, this *Mumming Birds* tour, as long as..."

Tilly sat up. "As long as I am sacked and sent back to London on my own, do you mean?"

I shrugged, nodded. "That's..."

"That's about the size of it," she finished for me. Her face flushed with the sheer drama of it all. "Why that's even more melodramatic, isn't it?" she cried. "Choose between your career and your true love! Good Heavens! The rotten so-and-so! And so you told him to take his tour and shove it in his pipe. I wish I could have seen his face!"

I spread my palms apologetically, and a sudden frost descended upon the little bedroom.

"You did, didn't you? Arthur?"

I said nothing.

"You *didn't*?"

"You know Karno is coming to Warrington next week, and he's coming to look at me and Charlie, maybe make one of us up to number one…"

And I didn't say this, but I knew that if I did turn my back on Karno, and left the way clear for Charlie, then I would regret that for the rest of my days, and who knows, maybe I'd blame her for it for the rest of both our days, and so really what I was doing was the best thing for both of us…

"I see," Tilly said. "Hmm." She stood, and began to undo some fastening or other in her hair, preparing to go to bed.

"I don't think I'm ready to break with Karno," I said.

"No, no, of course not. You must do what's right for *you*, of course."

━━━━

In the morning, when I awoke from a fitful sleep, she had gone. I dressed and went down into Mrs Budgen's parlour. The Craigs were already ensconced at the table, munching away at toast and jam, seething. George and Lillie seemed to have taken the strange situation personally, as though our deception had been an affront not only to the state of matrimony itself, but to their marriage in particular.

202

"Have you seen Tilly this morning?" I asked. Lillie pinned me with an icy glare.

"Your *wife?*" she said, solely for the benefit of Mrs Budgen, who was hovering in the doorway with a teapot. "She had to leave early for the station. Had you forgotten?"

"Oh, that's right," I said, scratching my head. "I haven't woken up properly yet. She had to catch a train to...?"

"To London," Lillie said, turning to explain to our benign landlady. "Mrs Dandoe is taking a part in a new show and must start work on it at once."

"What?!" cried Mrs Budgen, stricken. "They'd split up a lovely young couple and send them to work at opposite ends of the country? That's hard! That's... Why, that's inhuman!"

"Well," I shrugged. "It's a good chance for her, I suppose."

"Sit down, young feller, and I'll bring you some bacon and eggs, that'll put a smile back on your poor face. Dear, oh dear, what a shame!" And she bustled off into the kitchen.

George sniffed. "You'll be coming with us to Warrington, then, I take it?"

I nodded.

"Very well. Just don't expect to carry on living in the style you have become accustomed to, that's all."

He was right about that. When Mrs Budgen returned she brought with her the last decent breakfast I had on that tour, but it could have been ash and potato peelings for all the mind I paid to it. I barely noticed George and Lillie's disapproving gaze, or Mrs Budgen's sympathetic twitterings.

All I could think was that I might just have made a terrible mistake.

18
A VISIT FROM
THE GUV'NOR

THE Wednesday of the following week, I was at the theatre in Warrington, sitting in the dressing room, with my Magician's moustache stuck on my upper lip and a bottle of Scotch hanging by the neck from my listless hand. I supposed the others were watching the first-half acts. I didn't know and I didn't care.

Has anybody here seen Tilly? T-I-double L-Y...?

Kelly, not Tilly, it was, of course, in the original. Kelly from the Isle of Man. That's one of the old songs you do still hear about the place.

She's as bad as old Antonio, she's left me on my own-ee-o...

Round and round I went, drunkenly murmuring that daft ditty to myself, wondering if I'd done the right thing. Were my prospects with Karno really so rosy? Should I not have put Tilly first? I saw the hurt in her eyes when she realised that she was returning to London alone. I already missed those eyes.

"Ah, young Dandoe, as I live and breathe!" said a jolly voice from the doorway, snapping me out of my melancholy navel contemplation. Who should it be but Alf Reeves, whom I hadn't clapped eyes on for a good few months.

"What ho, Alf," I sighed, half-heartedly affecting the posh dude greeting that we were all using back then, as a sort of in joke. Made us sound quite foolish to bystanders and passers-by, I've no doubt. And to Alf, I suddenly realised, as he'd been in the States and wasn't in on the gag.

"How's America?" I asked quickly, to try and wipe the puzzled expression from his features.

"Oh, Arthur, lad," he replied. "Nuggets of gold the size of your fist just lying around on the pavements over there!"

My eyes must have widened, because he shook his head in pity.

"America," I said. "Land of opportunity, isn't that right, Alf?"

"That's right," he agreed. "If you want the opportunity to get robbed or shot."

"Hullo, what's this?" I said. "Oh, you really shouldn't have..." Alf was clutching in his paws what looked like half a dozen bunches of assorted and colourful blooms.

"Oh? Yes? What?" he spluttered in momentary confusion. "Oh, the flowers, yes. For the ladies ... ahem, the ladies' dressing room, of course. Which would be...?"

"Along to the end and left," I said. "Are they perhaps for one lucky girl in particular?"

"Oh, well, one could hardly bring flowers for one and not all the others too, could one?" he blustered.

I knew perfectly well that he was drawn there by the chance to see little Amy Minister, to whom we all knew he'd taken a shine, and I hoped the path of romance would be smoother for him than it was for me.

"So the Guv'nor is in tonight?" I asked, and Alf slapped himself on the forehead.

"Oh, I wasn't supposed to say, was I? Never mind. Make it a good 'un, all right?" He shrugged the bunches of flowers in his arms, grinned and disappeared.

Performing was the very last thing I felt like doing just then. I had hardly slept since the weekend, not only because of the devastation of breaking with Tilly, but also because Syd and George had gone out of their way to find me the least hospitable digs imaginable, miles from the theatre and with a ten o'clock curfew, worse than useless for a theatrical. I had spent the last three nights in a costume hamper right there in the dressing room, which had given me a coating of dust on the roof of my mouth that the Scotch simply couldn't shift.

The interval drew close, and the time when all Karno hands would be turned to assembling our set, our fake theatre boxes and whatnot, behind the tabs. Suddenly there was an almighty kerfuffle in the corridor, and George, red in the face and dabbing a flop sweat from his big red forehead with a big red hanky, was shoving Karno personnel into the room for all he was worth. In came the glee club, the Terrible Turkey, the naughty boy, the aunt, the flappers, the supers and all, baffled and bewildered, and George held both his arms above his head for quiet.

"Listen, everyone. Listen. Terrible thing, just terrible...!" he gasped, trying to get his breath back.

"Whatever is it, Mr Craig?" one of the girls asked.

"It's Syd, Sydney, Mr Chaplin – he's terrible poorly all of a sudden! Green to the gills and limp as a wet rag! Mustn't be moved from his hotel room!"

206

George seemed to feel faint at the thought of it, and sat heavily in a chair, which had the effect of making him suddenly invisible in the crowded room.

A murmur went around, confused and concerned in roughly equal measure. What on earth was wrong with the man...? Whatever it was sounded awfully serious. The pressing point, however, everyone realised at once, was what was to be done about the performance that evening? No Fred Karno company worth its salt would ever scratch a show, even without its leading performer. Jimmy Russell and Johnny Doyle were the number-two stars, both had played the 'Swell' before, and they got their heads together quickly and practically.

"No, gentlemen," George interrupted firmly. "The solution has been decided upon by Syd himself from his sickbed."

A pause perfectly honed by the old ham's many years on the boards, then: "His brother will stand in for him."

As one, the company gasped. Russell and Doyle both opened and shut their mouths wordlessly, as though trying to work out whether to be offended or relieved. For the rest of us it was the most exciting thing that had happened for weeks, and when Charlie himself stepped into the room, timing perfect, already clad in his brother's costume, and suddenly reeled about 'drunk' against the jamb of the door, it was almost too much for us to take in.

"Come along, come along, the set won't assemble itself!"

The room emptied briskly with an accompanying hubbub of chatter, and Charlie slipped over to a mirror to add a finishing touch or two. I slid along next to him and saw he was trembling feverishly with excitement as he applied some black to his eyelids. Not a time to be trembling, by the way.

"You're taking over from Syd?" I hissed. "You know Karno's in?"

"Of course I do," he whispered out of the side of his mouth.

"Do you know what you're *doing?*"

He turned and faced me, his purple eyes boring into my skull.

"Listen, Arthur. I've been a supporting player for well over a year. Syd was a number one in three months, you know? It's time I stepped up. I'm going to show him. The Guv'nor, I mean. Show him I'm up to it."

His concentration was frightening, and the audacity of it fairly took my breath away.

"So Syd is...?" I managed.

"Fine, he's fine," Charlie hissed. "It wasn't hard to put the fear of God into old George. A bit of green make-up we borrowed from that girl who sings the song about the frog prince, and a hot water bottle under the pillow."

I whistled.

"Well, the best of British luck," I said, as you would to a man facing a firing squad.

———

Needless to say he did brilliantly. In my opinion *Mumming Birds* that night was better than it had ever been. The amount of adrenalin pumping around that stage has rarely been surpassed in the history of British theatre, I dare say. It certainly cleared the cobwebs from my head. Charlie's Drunken Swell was everything that Syd's had been, and more. The falls were breathtaking, the timing heart-stopping, the audience in helpless paroxysms of joy. Of course, at bottom, it was a pitch-perfect imitation of Syd's performance, but with a fluency and virtuosity laid on top of every move and gesture that Syd himself would have cheerfully killed for.

For my own segment of the act, the faulty Magician's turn, well, it was the purest pleasure. Playing it opposite Syd, more often than not, was like a wrestling match, struggling to get my best moments out before he trampled all over them. With Charlie, that night, it was, I don't know, it was as if we saw into each other's minds and each had a share in controlling the other's actions. His movements dovetailed so perfectly with my own, and the timing was so exhilaratingly immaculate, that I felt I had time to just look out into the audience and watch them enjoying us. This was The Power in action, all right, and we both knew it.

Afterwards the backslapping and congratulations were so enthusiastic that the stage manager had to come round and hush us all up, as there were still acts trying to follow in our footsteps.

We quickly stripped off our costumes and packed away our paraphernalia, and then adjourned to the pub next door. Most of us were a little overwhelmed, I think. Bert Darnley, who had been seething mutinously at Charlie since being supplanted as the Yukon poet, was clapping him on the back and buying him a drink. George Craig slumped in the corner, positively smelling of relief. The three girls, Amy, Dolly and Sara, chattered away at Charlie's elbows – obviously two of them were having to share an elbow. Even the seasoned veteran Johnny Doyle was falling over himself to propose a toast and predict the brightest of futures for the younger Chaplin.

I was reflecting to myself, as I began to calm down from the thrill of it all, that if Charlie and I were indeed rivals, then he had surely stolen a march on me that evening. Most of my thoughts, though, were elsewhere.

Has anybody here seen Tilly? T-I-double L-Y...?

Finally that familiar dapper little figure pushed through the pub doors, and Karno was amongst us. He glanced around the establishment with the air of a man who very rarely set foot in such a place, and then came over to our group, which hushed and spread open to admit him.

A little cough.

"First of all ... a good evening to you all," the Guv'nor began, receiving a murmured "good evening" in reply. Another trade-mark little cough, and Karno continued. "Well now, I have seen Heaven knows how many performances of *Mumming Birds* in the past five years, and I have to say – and I don't say this lightly..."

You could feel the whole company tense as he held the moment. Charlie held his head high, trying hard not to beam with self-satisfaction.

"I have to say ... ahem ... that that were the finest rendition of the Magician that I have yet seen." He nodded at me and said: "Arthur."

With that, Karno turned on his heel and left.

There were gasps. Everyone looked at me, as though I had done something unspeakable, but I was just as stunned as they were.

Then Charlie crumpled, like a man whose skeleton had just been removed. Solicitous hands helped him to a chair, where Amy undid the top button of his shirt and loosened his tie. George peered closely at Charlie's bloodless face, and pressed a palm anxiously to his forehead.

"I hope to God he hasn't got what Syd's got," he said.

You wouldn't have wanted to spend much time with Charlie for the next few days, weeks even. He sank into a black depression, and it was all we could do to get a grunt of greeting from him for many a moon. Syd was dreadfully worried. Charlie only became animated onstage. He'd reverted to the Naughty Boy role after his single night in the lead, and to look at him during the act you'd think he was his old self, but once the curtain went down the oranges or buns or whatever missiles it was he was flinging about would drop from his nerveless fingers, and he'd slope off to his hotel room to wallow in more misery.

He was laying it on a bit thick, we all agreed. We'd all seen Karno cut him down to size on the night of his visit, and we all thought it was mightily unfair, to be sure. Unlike hapless old George Craig, the Guv'nor had seen clean through the subterfuge of Syd's illness. He knew Syd would certainly have painted his face green if he'd thought it would advance Charlie's career. The Guv'nor, quite simply, didn't like being led by the nose, and he decided to stamp his immaculately shod foot down.

I had troubles of my own. Every town we went to seemed grimmer and greyer than the one before it, and I could not wait for the tour to be over so we could get back to London and I could try and patch things up with Tilly.

Has anybody here seen Tilly? T-I-double L-Y...?

I wrote letters to her, of course, but the trouble was I really hadn't a clue where to send them. It hadn't occurred to us that we would need to know addresses when we were spending all our time together on the tour, but when she left without saying goodbye I realised I had no idea how to get in touch with her to apologise or explain.

Then one evening I was sitting in a corner of the dressing

211

room, writing another plea for forgiveness, when Amy Minister popped her head round the door.

"Writing to Tilly?" she asked brightly. "I've just been doing that."

"Really?" I said. Then a thunderbolt of a notion struck me. "I'll ... post it for you, if you like."

"Ho ho!" Amy laughed. "You just want to see what I've written about you."

"I don't ... I mean, I don't want to read it," I said, although actually I wouldn't have minded a quick peek. "I was just going to slip out and post this in a minute, and I'll take yours too if you'd like."

Amy saw the sense in that, and skipped off to fetch her letter to Tilly. A few moments later it was in my hand, and yes! Glory be! There was an address on the envelope! Which must be her lodgings, near to Finsbury Park, in London. I committed it to memory, as well as to my own envelope, and spent the next day or two with a lighter heart, waiting for the reply.

Nothing had come, though, by the end of the week, and there was nothing the next week at Burnley either. I told myself that she would maybe have sent a reply to Clara and Charley Bell's house in Streatham, in case the post missed me at the theatres. She could have sent a wire, though. Maybe I should send a wire?

Finally, after a spectacularly miserable week at the Argyle in Birkenhead, we were done, and the whole company headed South on the train to the capital at last.

I found myself sitting opposite Charlie for the journey. He was still making a meal of his Great Disappointment, unshaven, no collar to his shirt, staring out of the window at the rain, lost in his own little world. It suited me, as I was not in the mood

212

for conversation either. After we'd been rattling along for a little while, however, I suddenly realised that Charlie was looking at me.

"You'll be looking forward to seeing that girl of yours, I expect," he said.

I smiled wanly. I was indeed thinking about seeing her, but had no idea whether she would want to see me.

"It was unforgiveable, don't you think? You must think so."

"Yes," I said, Syd's face uttering the phrase "moral turpitude" springing immediately to mind.

"Karno's behaviour, that night in Warrington. To humiliate me so, in front of everyone."

"Well," I said. "Perhaps you pushed your luck, a bit, you and Syd."

"It was devastating, what he said, though, devastating."

"Oh, I don't know," I said. "He said I was the best Magician he'd seen in five years of watching the act."

Charlie snorted. "Oh, well, obviously he was only saying that to get at me, wasn't he?"

"Oh, is that so?" I bristled.

"Yes, yes, yes," Charlie waved a hand dismissively. "He knew that would be the surest way to drive the dagger home."

"Why is that?"

"Because he's set us against one another, hasn't he? Cooked up this, this ridiculous ... rivalry. Why, if it wasn't for that, of course, I would never have..."

He caught himself short, and turned to look out of the window again. I was puzzled, naturally, and after a moment I pressed him.

"Would never have what?"

"Nothing. Nothing..."

"Listen, Charlie, the Guv'nor is no fool. He knows what he saw that night, and he'll give you your chance, you wait and see."

"Well, maybe I don't want to wait for him to give me my chance. You know, Arthur, I've been giving serious consideration to leaving Karno's altogether."

I goggled at this. "You'd leave? To do what?"

"I could work," Charlie pouted. "I always found work before, and in any case, I've been considering a single act."

No wonder he'd been depressed. I remembered the solo turn he'd done at Forester's.

"You'd be a damned fool," I said vehemently. "Where are you going to find the chances you get with the Guv'nor? The scenes, the settings, the scale, and always top of the bill? I know he's capricious, and you mustn't get on the wrong side of him, but he's an absolute genius, no one to match him."

Charlie grunted. "Yes, well, anyway, I didn't say I was going to do it, just that I've been considering it. I've been thinking about things a lot."

No kidding, I thought. Charlie smiled and sat back in his seat, and a serenity settled on him that seemed to wash away the self-doubt and torment of the past few weeks. At that moment the sun came out from behind a cloud, as if in perfect synchronisation with his mood. Say what you like about Charlie, he had timing.

"And do you know what I realised, Arthur? Do you? I *should* stay, you're right. I should stay, bide my time, work my way up, as long as it takes. One day I'm going to have that little bastard over a barrel, and I'm going to make him grovel."

19
BESIDE THE SEASIDE

AS I made my way back to Streatham I couldn't help feeling a little flutter of anticipation. Little Edie Bell, still clutching Miss Churchhouse to her chest, was pleased to see me in one piece. She'd picked up enough snippets of conversation about the unfortunate Ronny Marston to imagine that I was doing dangerous work from which I might not return.

When I got a little time to myself think, I realised I had set a lot of store by there being a letter from Tilly. But there was nothing. Now I had to put my mind to what to do next. A little carefully reasoned detective work was called for, I thought, in the style of Mr Sherlock Holmes of *The Strand* magazine, so on my next free morning I smartened myself up and took the tram from Streatham to the West End, walking the last stretch up to Finsbury Park to save myself a few pennies.

I found Tilly's address easily enough, a terraced house in a residential street, but I didn't knock right away. I needed to walk up and down the street for a while, preparing what I was going to say and taking deep breaths.

Has anybody here seen Tilly? T-I-double L-Y...?

When my knock on the door was finally answered it was by a careworn landlady, hair hidden by a knotted scarf, traces of flour on her apron, who crossed her arms at the sight of me in my Sunday best, pursed her lips, and then said: "Which one of 'em have you come for, then?"

"Good morning," I said. "I wonder if I might speak with Miss Beckett?"

"Remind me," she frowned.

"Um ... around this height..." – I showed with my hand – "... fair hair, blue eyes..."

"First name of?"

"Tilly. That is, Matilda."

"No," the landlady shook her head firmly. "No Tillies or Matildas currently. I've got an Annie, a Louisa, a Mary who calls herself Marie, and two Elsies. Dancers, the lot of 'em. So they *says*, anyway."

She started to close the front door, and I quickly interjected. "Please!" She paused. Raised an eyebrow inquisitively.

"She was staying here, a little while ago, I'm sure. Can you remember if she said where she was going or what she was going to do?"

"Wait a minute..." I could almost see the cogs whirring round. "Beckett, you say? Matilda Beckett, now that do ring a bell. Going to see her, are you?"

"I hope so," I said.

"Wait here," she said, and disappeared into the back of the house. I allowed myself to hope she was fetching a forwarding address, but no, when she returned she thrust some letters into my hand and said: "Give her these when you see her, there's a good lad."

The door shut. I looked at the letters. Two from Amy Minister and three from me.

Now I was out of ideas. I had a little time to kill, so I wandered down to the Corner to see if I could find Tilly amongst the lingering unemployed, but no joy. Mr Holmes would doubtless have had some bright notion at this point, but I had nothing.

On the Saturday I found myself, as usual when in London, in the Enterprise for pay night, looking hopefully out of the window at the milling crowd of supers over at the Fun Factory. So Tilly had left her lodgings, but that didn't necessarily mean she hadn't found work in the Karno organisation somewhere. It would have been a step down to go back to super work, no doubt, but it was a possibility, surely?

Suddenly there were raised voices and the most terrible commotion from over by the Guv'nor's corner. A familiar portly figure pushed his way through the crowd, pop-eyed and red in the face. He banged the outside door open furiously with the heel of his hand and disappeared into the night.

George Craig.

"What happened?" I whispered to Bert Darnley.

"Sacked!" Bert hissed. "That business up in Middlesbrough, remember? When that Jefferson mob pinched our top billing? The Guv'nor said he should never have stood for it, should have got them to back down."

I glanced around, and caught sight of Lillie Craig, George's wife. She was as stunned as everyone else by this development, and let out a melodramatic wail: "Ge-o-o-o-orge...?"

Maybe it was this exhibition of the Guv'nor's ruthlessness, or this indication that nothing that occurred within his empire escaped his notice, but when it was my turn to collect my pay I felt a sudden overwhelming urge to demonstrate my own loyalty. I didn't know whether he knew about me and Tilly, but the thought that he might was making my heart race, so when he handed me my packet I found myself blurting out: "In Glasgow I was approached by Wal Pink, Guv'nor."

Karno looked piercingly up at me from behind his fold-up table. "Was you now?"

"He means to bring you down," I said.

Karno nodded slowly. "Thank you for telling me, Arthur," he said. "But don't fret. The matter is in hand."

I left him then, and went back to my pint of ale with the blood pounding in my temples. I didn't think I had surprised him at all, and so it was clearly the right thing to have done. I might even have done myself a good turn. And if the Guv'nor knew about his rival's plans, then I didn't give much for their chances of success.

I glanced over at the Fun Factory. Freddie junior would be there, of course, with the ledger and his fold-out desk, and it crossed my mind to see what he knew of Tilly, if anything. Not there, though, and not at that moment. I was still shaking...

The opportunity presented itself by and by. I contrived to bump into Freddie in Streatham as he arrived at the house next door.

"What ho, Arthur!" said Freddie. He was really desperate to be one of us, poor fellow.

"Freddie," I said. "I'm glad to have a chance to speak to you. There's something I need to clear up. You remember Tilly?"

"Your wife, of course. She was pleased to be sent to your company, I expect?"

"Yes, she was..."

"Bit of a sudden promotion from the ranks for her, to be sure, but I dare say she coped well enough, eh? How is she?"

"She's well, as far as I know," I said. "The thing is, you see..."

And I explained how the misunderstanding had played out, right up to the dressing down I got from Syd, where he accused me of moral turpitude. Freddie laughed fit to bust.

"Moral turpitude? Did he say that?!"

"He did," I assured him, "and he said the Guv'nor would take a very dim view of it."

"Oh well, ahem, I'm sure he would," Freddie smirked, affecting seriousness, and not especially well. "The old Guv'nor knows all about moral turpitude, of course."

"Really?"

"Oh yes, he's a great authority on moral turpitude. He himself is quite turpitudinous, don't you know. In point of fact, the old man..." Freddie went on, tears springing from his eyes, "often shows exemplary turpitudinousness!"

"My, my! Whatever is so funny?" a voice said, and I saw that my next-door neighbour was standing in her front doorway, watching us making fools of ourselves.

"Mama, there you are!" Freddie cried. "You remember Arthur? Invite him in for tea and we'll tell you all about it."

And so I found myself ensconced in the next-door parlour with Freddie, while our hostess disappeared below stairs to set a scullery maid to making tea. I leaned over and half-whispered, not wishing to be indelicate: "So, Freddie. Do I take it then that my neighbour ... is your mother?"

"Yes, hadn't you cottoned onto that? Yes, indeed, she is Mrs Karno."

"But I met Mrs Karno, at your father's house. At *your* house."

"Oh, you met Maria, of course. She's not really a Mrs Karno. They say she is, and all that, but they're not actually married. Mama is Mrs Karno all right. First and only. The old feller is desperate to divorce, but she's not having any of it. Still loves him, you see, despite everything."

"Despite what? What do you mean?"

"Oh ... *ahem*..." Freddie coughed, exactly like his father. "Never mind about that now."

Freddie's mother joined us then, and eagerly pressed me for news of my adventures working for her husband. I told her a little about the *Mumming Birds* tour, and about the Guv'nor's visit to Warrington to check up on Charlie and me. She hung on my every word, storing up every titbit, particularly about the Guv'nor himself – how did he *look*, what did he *say*, what did he *wear*?

"He's not told you yet about the thwarting of love's young dream, though, has he?" Freddie cut in. I shook my head to warn him not to lead the conversation there, but he ploughed on. "It's all right, Mama won't tell anyone, will you, old thing? And she might get a thrill out of it, eh?"

So I found myself recounting again the circumstances leading to my travelling as man and wife with Tilly, and sure enough, Mrs Karno was fascinated.

"She left without a word the next morning, and I have not been able to find any sign of her since," I finished. Freddie looked thoughtful.

"Well, I haven't seen her at the Factory lately. If she's working for the Guv'nor she'll be on the books, though, somewhere. I'll take a squint for you and let you know. How's that?"

Freddie was as good as his word, and sought me out at the Enterprise on Saturday night.

"Sorry, old man," he said, clamping his hand to my shoulder sympathetically. "She ain't on the strength, not since she was paid off for the *Mumming Birds*. Left no word, either, what she was moving on to. Don't know what to suggest, I'm afraid."

I thanked him and went to sit alone with my pint for a think. There was still one loose thread nagging away in my mind. Essex... Surely Tilly had said that her father owned a theatre in Southend-on-Sea? If that was where her family home was to be found, maybe a little further sleuthing would uncover a useful lead, even the girl herself.

So the very next time I had a day off – which was a little time coming, as the Fun Factory was more factory than fun just then – I took myself up to Fenchurch Street station and caught a London, Tilbury and Southend service to the coast, Mr Holmes pursuing *The Case of the Missing Show Girl*.

The town's theatre – the New Empire, it was called, probably still is – sat on a busy road off the main street, flanked by rows of shops, haberdasheries and the like. It boasted an impressive façade that towered above the surrounding buildings.

Since I was searching for information, I judged my best bet might be to speak to the stage door chap, maybe stand him a pint, but the stage door was locked and barred. I was stuck, then, with the front of house, and the bored-looking girl in the box office.

"Good day," I began, tipping my hat. "Could I speak to Mr Beckett?"

"I don't know a Mr Beckett," she replied. This flummoxed me momentarily, having not thought through my interrogation beyond this point, and she went on: "We have stalls or gallery for this evening, if you would like to make a purchase."

I saw I would need to push a little harder. The New Empire maybe wasn't a theatre that the Karno company frequented, but his name was a thing to be reckoned with nonetheless.

"I work for Mr Fred Karno in London," I said. "He asked me to speak to Mr Beckett on a matter of some urgency."

The girl's demeanour changed at once.

"Oh, I see," she said. "Would you wait here a moment?"

She disappeared into the interior, and shortly I was joined in the foyer by a slender fellow, quite bald, with a broad smile slapped on his face.

"Good morning," he oiled. "I understand you represent Mr Karno?"

"Indeed," I said. "And he has charged me with speaking to Mr Beckett. Do I ... have the pleasure...?"

"Oh, dear me, no. I am the manager. My name is Conquest."

I inclined my head to him and said: "Dandoe."

"I am very much afraid that we have no knowledge of a Mr Beckett" Conquest said. "There is no employee of that name, nor is there any member of the Southend-on-Sea Theatre Company, the owners ... of this..." He wafted his hand around to indicate the premises as he tailed off.

This was very puzzling, and I said so. Perhaps there was another theatre in the town, I suggested, but Conquest regretted that there was not.

Thwarted, I took my leave and wandered along to the main street. So much for my Sherlock Holmes adventure, I thought. Even Dr

Watson would have made a better fist of it. There seemed nothing for it but to return to London none the wiser, but then my eye was taken by a jaunty little fellow bobbing along the street from door to door delivering the midday post. A Holmesian ploy suggested itself.

"Excuse me," I said, as the postman approached. "Would you know the name of Beckett around these parts?"

"Beckett? Beckett...?" he said, stopping to scratch his head in a pantomime of 'man thinking'. I jiggled some coins encouragingly in my pocket, and this seemed to speed the process.

"There's a Beckett back o' the Esplanade," he said, "which is down to the end 'ere, left, second right, number 34, and another up on the hill the other way, next door to a pub called the Lion. And another out Prittlewell way an' you could try..."

A minute or two later I had quite a few suggestions, and he had a shilling he hadn't had before.

And so, a not inconsiderable expenditure of shoe leather later, I found myself walking up the path of what struck me as an unprepossessing little house for a theatre owner. The door was eventually opened to my knock by a middle-aged lady, red in the face, not best pleased to be disturbed.

"Good afternoon," I ventured, raising my hat.

"Who are you?"

"My name is Arthur Dandoe," I said. "I am trying to find an acquaintance of mine, a Miss Matilda Beckett. I wondered if she might perhaps be here?"

The woman frowned at me, giving me to understand that this was not likely.

"Who is it, my dear?" said a man's anxious voice from inside the house. "Is it one of ... *them*? Offer him tea. Yes, and make him say 'thank you'..."

223

The woman tutted to herself, as though this was always happening, and then said: "Would you like to come in for a cup of tea?"

"Thank you," I said, at which the woman turned and said to her unseen companion: "Satisfied?"

"Well, who is he then?"

"Some friend of Tilly's," said Mrs Beckett (for so she apparently was), regarding me with suspicion.

There was a brisk wrestling match in the narrow hallway, and Mrs Beckett was replaced by a kindly looking little fellow who smiled owlishly up at me from behind little round spectacles.

"Friend of Tilly's, you say? Gordon Beckett. Delighted!" He ushered me into a small parlour where he fussed about, plumping cushions. "I'm sorry about just now. We have to be careful, you see, but you can always spot them. They don't drink tea, number one, and number two they can't say 'thank you'."

"Who can't?" I asked.

"The Germans. They try, of course, but it always comes out 'Sank you'. Sometimes they'll click their heels together, too, they just can't help it. So," Mr Beckett said, clapping his hands and sitting forward on his chair. "You've news of my Tilly, then, have you?"

"Well, as a matter of fact," I said. "I was rather hoping you might have."

His face fell, and he looked into the fire and went silent. Over tea, brought in by Tilly's mother a short while later, I brought them up to date with Tilly's movements, such as I knew them, over recent months. They hadn't heard from her, it appeared, since the previous Christmas, and were anxious for such titbits as I could supply. The name of Fred Karno brought its usual excited reaction.

"Karno, eh? That's good, though, isn't it? She's fallen on her feet then," Tilly's father said. Her mother, meanwhile, glowered over a sewing project, which she was working away at with fast, efficient fingers, but she was listening avidly, I could tell.

"Mrs Beckett was disappointed ... well, we both were," Mr Beckett hurriedly corrected himself as his wife flashed him a glare. "When Tilly left. The theatre ... it's no sort of life for a young girl, really, is it? It's not ... respectable."

He caught himself then, worried suddenly that he might have offended me, but I nodded for him to continue.

"There was a young man, you see, here in the town. His father is Mr Harrison, who has the ironmonger's, and is on the council, could even be the mayor in time, they say. And we were more or less certain that he, that is the son, John, was about to ... which is to say, he would have ... except..."

"She'd have had that ironmonger's if she'd only waited, the flighty little piece!" Mrs Beckett burst out.

"Tilly told me you had your own theatre," I said, after an awkward pause.

Beckett brightened. "Did she say so? Well, young man, indeed I do. Would you like to see it?" He'd already jumped to his feet and was reaching for his coat, so I agreed, even though I'd done more than enough walking for one day. We slipped out of the front door and set off down the street into the town.

"It's quiet at this time, well, you can see, can't you? So there just aren't the audiences at the moment, but in the summer, oh, you should see the place. Folk come down from London, you know, oh yes!"

We reached the seafront, where one or two people were walking along the esplanade or strolling on the sand. They were well wrapped up, though, as there was a bitter wind whipping in off the sea.

"There she is, young feller, my pride and joy," Beckett said. I scanned the façades of the buildings, looking for the telltale ostentation of a playhouse, but saw nothing. I glanced at old Beckett, who was looking in the other direction altogether, in fact he was pointing down onto the sands. I followed his gaze, and there was a red and white striped tent, tall and thin, about seven feet tall.

"This is your theatre?"

Beckett nodded. "This is where the magic happens."

"You're a Punch and Judy man," I said, the light dawning.

"Man and boy," Beckett beamed. "My girls used to help out, you know, when they were younger. I'd let them stand on a box and have a go, sometimes. Not the whole show, you know, but a small part. Tilly were a fearsome crocodile when she were a nipper!"

Suddenly I understood Tilly's mirth as she'd wiggled her hand in front of my face. It had been a naked Mr Punch. Her father stomped over to the Punch and Judy stand and tested its sturdiness, pushing it from side to side.

"Well, I should be getting on my way..." I said. Beckett suddenly grabbed my arm and pointed out to sea.

"You know what's out there, don't you?" he said urgently, all joviality gone.

"The sea?"

"Beyond the sea," he hissed.

"What?" I whispered, caught up in his mood.

"Germans!"

"Germans?"

226

"Germans. Oh yes. He sees 'em."

"Who sees them?"

"Mr Punch, he sees 'em, he knows what they're up to."

"Aha."

"When they come we'll set fire to the pier, Mr Punch and me, and they'll be forced to move on down to Margate or somewhere, or straight up the Thames, that's what they might do. I'm right here, aren't I? I'm Johnny-on-the-spot. All that wood, it'll go up like billy-o..."

"Dad?!"

My heart stopped.

The voice came from behind us, and it was Tilly's voice. Unmistakably so. I turned round to see ... not Tilly, but a kind of worn-out, grey, harassed version of her, clutching a small tear-stained child in one arm, and manoeuvring a bassinet, presumably containing a further infant, with the other.

Beckett trotted over to relieve her of her burden. "Hallo, soldier," he said to the miserable child as he took him, but the boy wanted to know who I was before he even considered the possibility of smiling.

"Alice, this is Mr O'Dandy, he's a friend of Tilly's. Mr O'Dandy, this is Tilly's sister, Alice."

I didn't bother to correct him, but simply raised my hat to Tilly's sister, who managed a tired half-smile in return, before turning to her father.

"Dad? I'm going to the house to see Mum. Can you come and help me with Thomas?"

Beckett addressed his reply to the boy. "Of course I can, we'll go home and have some toast, shall we? Would you like toast, Tommy?"

Alice had already steered her bassinet around and started walking away, evidently too fraught for further social niceties. I suddenly realised why Tilly had been so very determined to avoid inadvertent motherhood and its life-changing implications.

"Thank you for calling by," Beckett said. "The station's straight up that road, can't miss it."

We shook hands, and he held on a moment longer than I was expecting.

"You will tell her, when you see her, just drop a line to your old man, girl?"

"Of course," I said.

"And if you get the chance, take her to Wales. They won't come there. Will you do that? We'll hold 'em off as long as we can, Mr Punch and me."

I watched them go, then headed forlornly for the station, miserably humming the familiar old tune to myself:

Has anybody here seen Tilly? T-I-double L-Y...?

PART III

20
THE FOOTBALL MATCH

In the spring of '09 I was wondering whether Karno had actually forgotten all about me. What had happened to all that talk of Charlie and me being the next big players? It had all gone quiet since his visit to Warrington, and I hadn't seen Charlie for months. Still, there was nothing for it but to muddle through, until I turned up at the Fun Factory one Monday morning and was told that Karno wanted to see me. I trotted up the stairs to his office, and found him with his nose buried in some paperwork, as usual.

"You wanted to see me, Guv'nor?"

Without looking up, Karno gave his trademark little cough. "I hear good things, Mr Dandoe, I hear good things," he said then. "Time you were a number two, I think."

"Thank you, Guv'nor," I said.

"*The Football Match*, Harry Weldon's company. Rehearsing at the Montpelier."

I stood there, pleased as Punch, of course, waiting for more.

Such a momentous step up surely merited a little speech, a pat on the back. Karno looked up, frowned.

"Still 'ere?" he said.

I ran all the way over to the Montpelier to join my new company, thrilled to be taking a big step up at last, and wondering gleefully what Charlie would think when he heard about it. If only Tilly had been there to share the moment with...

Has anybody here seen Tilly? T-I-double L-Y...?

I pushed through the doors into the back of the stalls, ready to introduce myself, but the place appeared to be empty. Then I noticed a small wisp of smoke rising from the front row. The smoker turned to look over his shoulder. It was Charlie.

"Aha!" he cried. "Have you been assigned to this punishment detail as well?" He stood to shake my hand. "Unbelievable!" he said. "To put us with that great blowhard Harry Weldon! What have we done to deserve *that*? Still, at least I'm to be a number two at last."

"So am I," I said.

Chaplin frowned, taking this in, and then nodded slowly. "Hey," he said. "You heard about George Craig, didn't you?"

"What about him?"

"Well, he's gone to work for Wal Pink."

I whistled. "Wouldn't mind being a fly on the wall at that dinner table," I said, and Charlie grinned. Lillie Craig was still with Karno's, of course.

"Here," Charlie said suddenly. "Watch this. Fred Kitchen taught it to me..."

He took the cigarette from his mouth and flicked it nonchalantly over his shoulder. It spun up in the air and dropped behind his back, where he kicked it away squarely with the heel of his

232

shoe. The cigarette end flew through the air, showering sparks as it went, and bounced neatly off the bald head of a stocky fellow in a waistcoat and shirtsleeves who was emerging from a side door.

"Good trick," I said.

The newcomer looked up to the ceiling to see where the cigarette end had come from, as we were the picture of innocence, then he came over.

"Are you the new number twos?" he said. "I'm T. Ellis Buxton, company manager. Now, you'll forgive me, but this show is an organisational *night*..."

Buxton's attention was caught by something over my shoulder. I looked round, and Buxton was already scuttling over to greet a new arrival. Not exactly tugging his forelock, but making a tugging gesture near where a forelock might have been had he had any hair left.

No such worries for the newcomer. He had a shock of red hair, sprouting in all directions, and the colour seemed to have leeched down into the face beneath.

"Good morning, Harry," Buxton smarmed. "Can I bring you a cup of tea, or ... or ... or...?"

"No tea, ta, T.," the newcomer said, with the air of one wheeling out a practised witticism. "Best get on wi' it."

"Right, of course, yes," Buxton said, beckoning frantically to me and Charlie with his hand flapping behind his own buttocks. We approached.

"These are the new men, Harry," Buxton wheedled. "This is Arthur Dandoe and Charlie Chaplin."

"Syd's brother, right?" Weldon barked in Charlie's face. "You don't look like 'im."

233

Charlie's eyes narrowed at the blast of ale on the big man's breath. Beer for breakfast. "Syd's my half-brother."

"Thought so. That explains it then." Weldon's face set in a self-satisfied expression, and he folded his arms smugly.

Buxton jumped into action. "I thought this one for Ratty, and the other for..."

"Wrong, *Books-ton*, wrong. T'other way round. This 'un don't look like a footballer, he looks like a gust of wind'd carry 'im off. He looks like a good fart'd knock him over completely. He can be t' villain..." – here he prodded Charlie in the chest – "...and that'un thier can do Ratty. Got me?"

"As you say, Harry, as you say, quite right, quite right," Buxton fluttered, mopping his brow with a hanky.

"All right, I'm off. I'm on the course at eleven with Harry Tate, if the weather holds up."

Charlie was astonished. "But aren't you going to rehearse?"

"What for? I know what *ah'm* doin'. You're the one as needs to re'earse, boy."

And Weldon gave us a last contemptuous sneer, turned on his heel, and left.

"I told you it was a punishment," Charlie muttered.

It was left to our predecessors in the roles of Ratty and the Villain, a pair of anaemic youths called Gilbert Childs and Will Poluski junior, to walk us through the act. At the end of the day the two of them were slapping each other on the back with glee as they made their way out. I couldn't help feeling they looked like a couple of chaps who had just been released from jail.

Charlie and I repaired to the pub to discuss the matter over a beer (me) and a port (him).

"There's not a laugh in the thing until Weldon comes on," I pointed out.

"Aye, and I'll bet that's how he likes it, too," Charlie said grimly.

"You know," I mused. "Just because there's never been a laugh before Weldon comes on up till now ... doesn't mean there can't be laughs before he comes on *from now on*, does it?"

A slow grin spread over Charlie's face. We chinked our glasses and a little pact was made there and then. Me and Charlie against Mr Harry Weldon, esquire.

———

The Football Match, it has to be said, was one of the Guv'nor's greatest spectacles, and Stiffy, the lead part, was perhaps the greatest star vehicle he ever devised.

Where in *Wontdetainia* he had created an ocean liner onstage – and the ocean too, on that first night! – and in *Mumming Birds* another whole theatre inside the theatre, in *The Football Match* he did no less a thing than staging an F.A. Cup Final.

The 'scenario', as laid down, kicks off at a pub called the Bull, where a football team, the Midnight Wanderers, are put through their paces by Ratty, the team's star forward. We discover that there is an insidious plot afoot to fix the match, to which end a 'Villain' is lurking on the premises. Stiffy, the team's goalkeeper, a 'figure of manly beauty', arrives late and three sheets to the wind, and the villain sidles up to offer him wealth beyond the dreams of avarice to throw the game.

The climactic scene was the match itself, between the Midnight Wanderers and the Middleton Pie-Cans. A full match would be staged, with twenty-two players, a referee and a crowd of spectators. Stiffy would first try to hand the game to the Pie Cans, then he would have an attack of conscience and decide to thwart the villain's machinations. Finally the whole thing would be brought to a close with a violent rain storm, and a great amount of energetic mudslinging, before the referee declared the match abandoned.

It always had to be the last act on the bill because of the mess, and the company would feature one hundred people onstage at one time or another. It's little wonder that Mr T. Ellis Buxton had so little hair left.

A key part of the spectacle was a huge panoramic backdrop with a great crowd of spectators painted on it. A mob of real supers lined up in the foreground on a raked ground row, big ones at the front and small ones at the back standing higher up the rake, cunningly sorted to give an illusion of perspective. Behind them was the cloth, which was very cleverly done, so that the living faces seemed to merge into the painted ones.

And there were slits in the cloth, so what you were sure was a painted face could suddenly be replaced by a real one, one of a team of supers swarming around behind on stepladders, who would shout out a line, then withdraw and reappear elsewhere. There were arms sewn to the front of the cloth, very light, that were made to wave handkerchiefs and even throw little hats into the air by bursts from the giant electric fans concealed at floor level. It was a stunning coup, one of Karno's finest.

My first sight of the famed backcloth came a couple of days later. I turned up for work to find that there was to be no principals rehearsal, as Weldon was 'indisposed'. I rolled along to the Fun Factory to find everyone there in a frightful panic. The cloth had been taken down and rolled wrongly while still wet and muddy from the rainstorm the last time the act had played, and whole sections of it were utterly ruined.

The whole panorama was laid out on the factory floor, and Alf Reeves was close to despair.

"I don't suppose you can paint faces, can you, son?" he said.

"I don't know," I said, feeling sorry for him. "But I'll give it a go."

I hadn't painted anything since I was a child, but it quickly turned out that I had a real knack. I found I could produce pretty good representations of faces I knew from memory, and I began to enjoy slipping people I knew into the football crowd.

I painted in my brother Lance, my father, Mr Luscombe and The Rotter from Cambridge. I painted in Charley and Clara Bell, and quite a few Tilly Becketts, before I was finished. Not that she was on my mind or anything...

Has anybody here seen Tilly? T-I-double L-Y...?

Now, the other brilliant stroke Karno pulled in *The Football Match* was this. Every night we'd enact a cup final right there on the stage, twenty-two players, a referee and dozens of supporters. And everywhere we played there'd be a handful of famous footballers right up there with us.

Charlie Athersmith, for instance, and Jimmy Crabtree, who each played for England above a dozen times, and were in the legendary Aston Villa team that had won the League Championship five times back in the nineties, not to mention the double in '97. Crabtree's sartorial quirk, if you like, was to play in a neckerchief, while Athersmith had been known to grab an umbrella from the crowd when it was raining, and carry on galloping up and down the wing underneath it.

237

The outside left for England opposite Athersmith when he was in his prime was 'Flying' Fred Spiksley of The Wednesday, and he was another Karno regular. Then there was Billy Wragg, a great slow beanpole of a centre half, who won the Cup with Nottingham Forest in '98, Tommy Arkesden of Derby County, Joe Clark of Hibernians, Jack Weat of Birmingham City – all pretty much guaranteed a round of applause in their respective home towns.

By and large, these footballers were in their mid to late thirties, and had finished their playing careers. All of them belonged to the first generation of professional players to reach the end of the road and realise there was still a living to be made for a few more decades. If you got them all together for a pint they could really wear you down talking about money.

The greatest pleasure of all for me, though, was that all of these greats of the game were introduced onto the stage by the referee, who was none other than Mike Asher, my old mate from *Jail Birds*, who reckoned I still owed him a few pints for saving my life on that tour, and I didn't argue.

"Did you know?" he said indignantly as we relived that escapade, "that every *Jail Birds* company now has a 'Lumpy' in it? And do we get any credit for that? Do we heck as like! I reckon Syd told 'em it was all his idea!"

So, come the first night of the show – well, the first for Charlie and me – the two of us had got together some bits of business to kick things off with a bang. We still hadn't been vouchsafed a single rehearsal with Harry Weldon himself, indeed the great man didn't even arrive until midway through the evening's bill, and the stink of beer on his breath was strong enough to make a unicyclist wobble unsteadily as she passed through a cloud of it in the wings on her way onto the stage.

Up goes the curtain, and there are the Midnight Wanderers all ready to go through their paces. Ratty the forward – yours truly – steps forward to lead the session. Except I can't find my shorts, and so I borrow Stiffy's, which are too big for me, so that every time I raise my arms above my head down they come to half mast and I have to snatch them up again. When the rest of the team, behind me, begin to copy my actions exactly, then you had a training routine like nothing you'd ever seen before. It was a simple gag, but it had the place in a roar.

I glanced into the wings to give Charlie the nod to enter, and caught sight of Weldon, pop-eyed with amazement, his big mouth wide open, and T. Ellis Buxton standing next to him laughing fit to bust. On comes Charlie as the villain, in a typical Edwardian villain's get-up: the top coat, the cane, the spats and a voluminous Inverness cape. He has his back to the audience at first as he sneaks around our exercise room, then he suddenly turns to reveal a bright red nose, which brought him a big laugh. Then he falls headlong over a dumbbell and catches his cane on a punching bag, becoming involved in a fight with it when it swings back and hits him in the face.

I saw Weldon's great red face slide slowly out from behind the tab, like a sunrise turned through ninety degrees. His eyes were out on stalks: he couldn't believe what was happening. There'd never been so much as a snigger before his entrance, remember, and now there was a veritable riot! All he could think, in his beerfuddled brain, was to stop it, somehow, anyhow.

So out he comes, far too early. He's not been introduced, so all he can do is stand there, while Charlie whirls about him, looking for a button which has popped off his trousers. Charlie picks something up, then throws it away in disgust. "Those confounded rabbits!" he cries, and Weldon grabs him hard by the arm, trying to hold him still so he can bring him into focus.

"Quick! I am undone!" Charlie says to him, ad lib. "Have you a pin?"

And Weldon just stands there, looking at him, lost. He doesn't know if he has a pin or not, or whether he's even supposed to have one. He thinks he might not even be in the right theatre...

Afterwards the other members of the troupe patted us both on the back and were fulsome in their praise, especially Buxton, who was in full flow when Harry Weldon stuck his big, angry face into our dressing room.

"I was just saying, Harry," cried Buxton enthusiastically, "that I can't remember ever seeing the show go down so well!"

Everyone looked at Weldon, and I had the distinct impression that he'd come in to tear a strip off our hides but couldn't now do it without losing face.

"Aye," he said, after a heavy pause. "That were ... all right."

And if looks could kill, Charlie and I would both have left the theatre that night feet first.

———

Touring the country with *The Football Match* took us right into the summer of '09, and Charlie and I were at daggers drawn with Harry Weldon more or less all the way. Harry was a Northern comic with a thick accent and what Charlie called a 'cretinous' style. His speech also came with a strange trademark gurgling noise in his throat, possibly due to the fact that he seldom took to the boards without pouring at least eight pints of ale down it. In the North he would go down well, whereas in Plymouth,

Southampton and Bristol he was a lot more hit and miss, shall we say.

In Belfast the audiences didn't take to Weldon at all, and neither, as it happened, did the press. The paper there gave him a terrible panning, calling him an "incomprehensible boob gargling away like a broken pump", while Charlie and I were described as "bright" and "promising" and we were the ones given credit for "bringing the house down".

At the theatre that evening Weldon was incandescent, as well as pretty much tanked to the gills. He was supposed to give me, as Ratty, a couple of slaps, to liven me up after taking too much of the 'training oil'. On this night, driven to fury by the critic of the *Belfast Evening Telegraph,* he let me have it full in the face. I saw stars, I'm telling you, and the blood streamed from my nose and down my jersey, which fortunately was a red one.

Later, in another scene outside the turnstiles at the football ground, he suddenly stepped backwards, knowing full well that Charlie was close behind, and crushed him against the wall. Charlie slumped down to the floor, making an extra laugh out of it, but we could all see he was badly winded.

Afterwards there was a dreadful scene. Charlie was beside himself, and tried to brain Weldon with one of the dumbbells. I had to get between them to break it up, even though I wanted to floor Weldon myself for the thump he'd given me.

"Leave him be," I said to Charlie. "He's only jealous."

"Jealous?!" Weldon scoffed. "Of you two? Why, I have more talent in my arse than you have in your whole bodies!"

"So you have," I retorted. "You can use yours to talk out of."

The footballers, too, were not particularly fond of our leader. They were a venal bunch, and Weldon never let an opportunity go by to taunt them about how much money he made. The bad feeling all came to a head the week we were at the Exeter Hippodrome. One night after the show, the footballers beckoned me, Charlie and Mike Asher over to their smoky cabal in the pub.

"Eh up, boys," Fred Spiksley whispered. "You fancy mekkin' a bob or two?"

"What's up?" I asked.

"Exhibition game."

From time to time as it travelled the country the *Football Match* company would play against a local team, to drum up publicity or goodwill, and we'd usually get a decent crowd along to see our handful of ex-internationals play. They liked to see as well whether the comedians had two left feet. I'd played in a couple of these matches and not done too badly. Scored a goal in off my knee in Bury, I did.

"It's all sorted out," Fred said. "Arthur Chadwick, the manager of Exeter City, he played for England alongside Jimmy Crabtree there. Nah then. We're getting a bet down with Chadwick and his lads. They'll match what we put down, and we play winner-teks-all wi' t' gate money on top. Now, are you in?"

Mike, Charlie and I looked at each other.

"How much?" Mike said.

Crabtree blew a column of smoke up to the ceiling and eyed us coolly. "Twenty quid. Each. We're all in for t' same. And when we win you'll triple it, easy."

I exhaled slowly. Twenty quid! That was more than a month's money, and it would about clean me out if it went wrong. I looked at Mike and Charlie, and they were clearly thinking the same.

Jimmy Crabtree leaned over conspiratorially. "They're expecting to beat us easy, like. Bunch of old crocks and actors like us.

But Buxton reckons we're getting Jack Fitchett next week, used to play for Plymouth, and Bob Sharp, who were Bristol City skipper not so long back. There's the five of us regulars, you lads are decent enough, and that gives us a right good chance, I reckon, eh, lads?"

The other four, Spiksley, Athersmith, Arkesden and Wragg, nodded seriously in agreement. Crabtree looked us right in the eye.

"In?"

After a beat, Mike, Charlie and I put our hands out.

"In!"

"Good, good lads!" said Spiksley. "Now all we need to do is make damned sure that silly arse Weldon don't get wind on it!"

There seemed a fair chance that he wouldn't, as well, as he spent most days on a golf course somewhere or other. We reckoned without the deviousness of Arthur Chadwick, the Exeter City manager, though, who turned up at the theatre the night before the game, introduced himself to our number one and said how much he was looking forward to the match.

Well, once Weldon knew there was a game he hadn't been invited to he insisted on coming along. What's more, he insisted on playing centre forward as well, and playing to the crowd with his slapstick antics. He barged his own teammates off the ball, he crocked Fred Spiksley with a boot to the ankle, he gave away penalty kick after penalty kick, and even though Tommy Arkesden and Charlie Athersmith were inspired the final score was Exeter City 6, the Fred Karno Company 3, with Weldon having contributed a hat trick of own goals.

"That went well!" he cried as we trooped off the pitch at St James's Park, beaten and flat bloody broke.

That evening after the show we convened in the pub next to the theatre, Mike, Charlie, the footballers and I, nursing the frugal half pints of ale we could now barely afford, hoping against hope that some flush punter would feel like treating us. The mood was sombre, resentful, and when Harry Weldon, the big ginger goof, swaggered over to join us you could almost hear the teeth grinding.

"So tell me again," Weldon gurgled. "You lot played for however many years, and in all that time you had a maximum wage. Not a minimum wage, a *maximum* wage."

The footballers glowered at him. This was a sore point.

"So none of you *duffers* has ever topped four quid a week. I make twelve times as much as that!" he cried. "That means I make more in a week than the whole Aston Villa team. Hey, I'll tell you something else, an' all. I could make twice as much again as I do now! No, three times as much!"

"What the hell are you talking about?" I muttered sourly.

"I could! What's Marie Lloyd make? A hundred? A hundred and twenty a week? I know for a fact that Arthur Roberts gets a hundred and sixty. What do you think of *them* potatoes?"

The footballers looked pretty sick, I can tell you.

"Yes, but Arthur Roberts and Marie Lloyd, they're solos, aren't they?" I said.

"Pah! I know that!"

"Karno'll never pay that sort of wage. The only way you could make that sort of money is if you left and set up as a solo turn yourself."

"Well, who's to say I mightn't just do that!" Weldon blustered.

"You'll never do it," I said.

Weldon puffed himself up indignantly. "I might!" he insisted.

"No, you won't," I said. "You haven't the nerve. You're tied to Karno's apron strings so tight you'll never be able to let go."

"What do you know abaht it?" Weldon spat.

"George Robey says so," I said. It stopped him dead in his tracks.

"Robey? George Robey said that, abaht me? That I'd never have t' nerve to leave Karno?"

"He did."

"When did he?"

"Just before he said that you'd be nothing without Karno's name on the bill," I said, giving the knife an extra little twist.

Weldon looked as though all the air had been let out of him, and he left for his bed shortly afterwards. I'd probably pay for baiting him, but he'd asked for it, and the footballers clubbed together and bought me a drink, which wasn't like them. And whether what I said had anything to do with what happened later, well, who knows?

21
HE OF THE
FUNNY WAYS

FOR weeks after that ill-fated exhibition game Mike, Charlie and I were absolutely on our uppers. Losing twenty quid was enough to cause us all considerable grief in the belt-tightening area. The footballers seemed to spend all their free time trying to get Harry to bet with them, but he would always throw his hands up at the sight of a pack of cards or the little paddle they used for the three-coin toss.

"A fool and his money are soon parted!" he'd gurgle, backing away. "You lot should know that, with your *maximum* wage!"

A little relief from penury came in the shape of my old friend Mr Luscombe. He was always eager for titbits about the world of the theatre, and so I had kept up a friendly correspondence with him. He had gone down from Cambridge that summer, after (by his own account) burning brightly in another Footlights extravaganza at the end of his last term, and he was now obliged, to his chagrin, to make a start in the family import-export (or it may have been vice versa) business.

It was a surprise, then, when he presented himself at the stage door of the theatre we were about to grace with *The Football Match* in Sheffield, of all places, at the Empire Palace.

"You made the piece sound so enthralling I just had to see it for myself," he gushed.

I introduced him to Charlie and Mike. "This is Mr Luscombe..." I began.

"Oh, come come," Luscombe cried. "No more of that master-servant nonsense. I have left the college for good and all. You may all call me Ralph, and jolly pleased I am to make your acquaintances!"

He pronounced his first name to rhyme with 'safe', and that was the first time I ever knew it. After the show, which he *adored*, he wanted to have a late supper at a nearby restaurant. I tried to plead poverty, but he was adamant.

"Don't worry about that, it's all on me," he said, far too loudly. Charlie and Mike were almost audibly salivating, and the footballers seemed to have a sort of sixth sense where free food was concerned, so the upshot was that Luscombe stood a whole bunch of us a handsome meal, just about our first since Weldon's dozy antics in Exeter had bankrupted us all.

Now during the course of this splendid repast, the subject of Luscombe's own theatrical endeavours came up, and Fred Spiksley had the notion of sneaking our generous host into *The Football Match* – probably, if I know Spiksley, in the hope that he might stick around and provide more free dinners.

There were, of course, very nearly a hundred people involved in the act, and it turned out to be a simple – or perhaps I should say cheap – matter to persuade one of them, a super by the name of Claude, to stand down and let Ralph Luscombe take his place for a night.

Luscombe wasn't just standing onstage cheering, either; he actually had plenty to do. He was one of the fellows running around behind the back of the painted backdrop, clambering up and down the little ladders, sticking his head through the slits here and there to shout "Play up, Pie-Cans!" and the like.

Well, he was the happiest soul you could ever hope to see.

"For I on honey-dew have fed, and drunk the milk of Paradise," he beamed seraphically afterwards, reliving the sheer thrill of it all.

I fully expected this to be a one-night-only treat, but the next evening he appeared at the stage door and thrust another ten bob into Claude the super's hand, whereupon Claude the super trotted off to the pub to spend his windfall and Luscombe gleefully took his place again.

He stayed with us all of that week, and all of the following week in Derby too, living the life of his dreams – as well as, I'm ashamed to report, being ruthlessly fleeced by my colleagues. But still, he was enjoying himself, and because we were using the backdrop I myself had painted back at the Fun Factory, onto which I had painted Luscombe's likeness here and there, when he stuck his head through to shout his lines it really did look as though the painting was coming eerily to life.

At the end of that second week, however, he came hurtling into our dressing room at the end of the act, face white as a sheet, a cold muck sweat on his brow.

"In the audience!" he gasped. "I saw him! Large as life!"

"Who, for goodness' sake?" I said, holding him by the shoulders to get him to calm down.

"Brother...!" Luscombe wheezed.

"Your brother? What on earth's *he* doing here?" I said, baffled. I knew Luscombe major, of course, as he too had been a student

248

at the college. A painfully serious individual, who seemed to regard his time at Cambridge as something of a nuisance, keeping him from the business of import and export, profit and loss, for which he was born. Frankly, you'd have been as likely to find the Archbishop of Canterbury at the Palace in Derby as the elder Mr Luscombe.

"Oh, he's looking for me, of course," Ralph Luscombe sighed, sinking into a chair. "They told me, my father and my brother that I should be dispatched to our South American office if I didn't cease my infatuation with Dame Theatre. Oh, I'm for the high jump now!"

We were last on the bill, so the audience were already on the loose. I peeked out into the corridor to see if the coast was clear.

"Ho! You there! Dandoe!" a voice rang out.

"Mr Luscombe, is it not?" I said, pulling the door closed behind me as I stepped out. "From the old college? What a surprise!"

Luscombe major was puce with indignation – or perhaps his stiff white collar was too tight.

"I mean to take my brother with me back to London at once. Where is he?"

"Your brother?" I said, scratching my head (as people do when puzzled). "Whatever makes you think he might be *here*, of all places?"

"A letter, damn your cheek! He wrote to our mother, and the envelope was franked in this God-forsaken town! I knew I'd find him here, amongst you low-lifes and vagabonds! And I have!"

With that he shoved past me into the dressing room. I peered over his shoulder, and saw only the innocent faces of Mike, Charlie, Fred Spiksley ... and a wicker costume hamper which Charlie Athersmith was sitting on, lighting up a pipe.

"Mr Luscombe?" I said. "A thought occurs. Would you follow me this way?"

I led him to the stairs which led up to the stage. We had to pause there to allow a seemingly endless procession of semi-clad chorus girls to pass by, which discomfited the elder Luscombe no end.

"You see, your brother and I were friendly, as I'm sure you know, and so when I painted this..." - we stepped out onto the stage behind the fire curtain, where the *Football Match* backdrop was still hanging in plain view - "I took the liberty of using his likeness. Here, you see, and here, and again here..."

"No, no, no, no, no..." Luscombe's brother said, pacing in front of the cloth, and poking at it with a suspicious finger. "I saw him, I saw him *speak*!"

I slipped around behind and stuck my face through one of the hidden slits in the design. "No, sir, I'm afraid not. It was an optical illusion, d'you see?"

"What the...?"

I quickly moved to another position and popped my face through there. "It's very convincing, do you not agree?"

Luscombe major blustered. "It can't be ... I mean to say, I *saw* him. I saw Ralph ... didn't I...?"

He came with me, as meek as a little lamb, down to the stage door and out into the open air. A little cloud of chorus girls in feathered headdresses bustled by us, and he averted his eyes until they were past and twittering along the alleyway towards the front of house. A fellow with a ginger beard followed close behind, clutching a carpet bag, excusing himself gruffly as he squeezed through.

"But ... the letter?" Luscombe senior ventured, no longer sure of his ground.

"I'm sure there will be a perfectly reasonable explanation when you see him," I said. "Do give him my regards, won't you?"

In the distance ahead of him the feathered headdresses all turned right and out of sight. Something caught in the breeze swirled around Luscombe the elder's distracted feet as he walked away, and then was whisked up the alleyway towards me, coming to rest in a puddle a yard or so away.

It was a ginger beard.

———

Every time we brought the *Football Match* to a new town, I would be sure to attend the band call on the Monday. My intention, of course, was to run my eye over the other acts on the bill and see if Tilly might somehow be amongst them.

Has anybody here seen Tilly? T-I-double L-Y?

It was not as far-fetched a hope as it might sound, as the music hall kaleidoscope would spin and change the multi-coloured view every week, and coincidences of that kind would often occur. No such luck, though.

I did see one familiar face, though, the week we were at the Palace in Leicester. There was a solo act, tucked away in a graveyard slot, right after the interval while people were still finding their seats, who was billed, rather endearingly, as 'He of the Funny Ways', and who should it be but Stan Jefferson?

We greeted one another like old pals, and sat together in the stalls to catch up.

"Well, I left the old man, finally," Stan explained cheerfully.

"How did he take it?"

Stan grinned. "Ah, not well, actually. The phrase 'Never

251

darken my doorstep again!' was bandied about pretty freely. He'll get over it. But what about you? And what about the lovely *Mrs* Dandoe? Is she with you?"

"Not this time," I said.

"Shame. I suppose there wasn't a part for her in a sketch about football," Stan said.

'He of the Funny Ways' had very funny ways indeed, to my way of thinking. That evening Charlie and I watched Stan from the wings, and he had a struggle at first just getting the audience's attention after they'd been to the bar at the interval. He did it, though, and by the end of his five minutes every night that week the crowd were laughing again and ready to enjoy the rest of the turns.

"It's pretty simple stuff, though, isn't it?" Charlie sniffed, and it was, he was right, but Stan was able to win an audience round with ... well, with his funny ways. I didn't believe Charlie when he tried to put Stan's act down. He was cleverer than that. He saw another potential rival, that's what he saw.

On the last night, in the bar, we wished one another luck.

"What's next?" I asked Stan. He shrugged.

I turned to Charlie.

"Stan would do well with Karno, don't you think?"

Stan brightened, but Charlie sucked air in through his teeth, doubtful, discouraging.

"It's not as if *we* could actually do anything, though, is it? The Guv'nor likes to dig up his uncut gems for himself. He doesn't really go to the smaller houses, and he doesn't like being pushed into things – remember Warrington?

I supposed he had a point, but Stan's chin had just about hit the floor. I decided to drop the subject. "It was just a thought," I said.

"Yes, well, maybe one day, like," Stan said, but that day seemed a long way distant.

——————

It was the autumn of that year, 1909, a sunny afternoon, and a little group of us were standing out in front of the Bells' house. Clara was there, and Edie, clutching her dolly, the ubiquitous Miss Churchhouse, as usual. Charley Bell crouched down, poking away at a flower bed with a trowel. Mrs Karno was ruffling the hair of her little lad Leslie, and quizzing me for gossip about the Guv'nor and his empire. Suddenly I realised that Clara and Edith Karno were no longer listening to me, but were looking at something behind me, in the street. Their faces had hardened, and Charley Bell was slowly rising to his feet.

I turned and there was a brougham gliding slowly past, the driver holding the grey horse at a gentle trotting pace. If I hadn't been able to see the passengers I would have recognised it easily enough, as it was the Guv'nor's pride and joy, painted maroon, with gleaming brass fittings, with "Fred Karno's Comics" painted boldly on the door. Inside I could see Karno and Maria, the woman he'd introduced to me as his wife, chatting away, laughing, affecting not to notice whose houses they were passing.

"Oh, my dear," Clara sighed. There was a resignation in her voice that told me this wasn't the first time this sort of thing had happened.

"It's quite all right," the real Mrs Karno replied stoically.

"Coming back," Charley Bell muttered, and sure enough, the maroon brougham had executed a languid turn at the far end of the road and was about to trot past again.

"Well, then," Edith said. "Let's give them something to laugh at, shall we?"

She reached over and grasped Edie's dolly, cradled it in her arms and began to coo over it as though it were a real baby. Charley and Clara joined in, and Edie and Leslie too, thinking this was a fine game.

I watched as Karno's brougham glided past again, with the Guv'nor and his mistress themselves playing at happy families, and saw the moment Karno spotted that his wife was nursing a baby. His jaw dropped, and, as the carriage pulled away, I could see him leaning out to get a better view, almost braining himself on a lamp post as he disappeared around the corner.

———

The next time I saw Karno was at the Fun Factory. He called me into his office, and I sat across the desk from him as he tapped a pencil on his fingers. A little cough, and then he smiled, as if not quite knowing how to begin. My first thought was that Syd had finally told him about the moral turpitude thing and I was going to be sacked.

"So," he said eventually. "How did you and young Chaplin take to Mister Harry Weldon?"

"Charlie said he thought it was a punishment," I said.

Karno laughed. "So it was, so it was," he chuckled. "But not for you, for Harry Weldon. He was throwing his weight around, so I thought I'd send him a couple of arrogant young upstarts to shake him up a bit. And you certainly did that, by all accounts."

He smiled, looked down at his hands.

"You're living with the Bells, then?"

254

"When I'm in town."

"So you'll have realised that ... ahem ... that your next-door neighbour is, or *was* rather, my wife?"

I was on my guard, now. "Yes," I said.

"Does she...? Erm, that is to say, have you had the chance to speak with her?"

"I have," I said. "She often asks about the various goings-on."

Karno's eyes narrowed.

"The shows, I mean, she's always very interested in what shows I have done, and all your many successes."

"Quite so." Karno tapped a pencil against his teeth.

"And you know that t' child who lives there with her is my son?"

"Leslie? Yes, he's a grand little chap."

"You don't think him too skinny?"

"No, not at all."

"I am concerned that she doesn't feed him well."

"Oh," I said. "Don't worry about that, he eats like a horse, he just runs it off, you know."

"You would tell me if you thought he was badly treated?"

"He is not, I assure you, Guv'nor."

"Right." Karno coughed again, and leaned forward onto the desk. "Now listen to me. What I have to ask you about is rather a delicate matter, and you don't really need to know the ins and outs of it all, but I happened to see, as I was passing t'other day, just in the area, you understand, I happened to see ... a certain ... babe-in-arms."

"Oh?"

"Don't give me that," he snapped. "I need to know who is t' father of that infant and I need to know it this minute."

"The father?" I said, quite taken aback.

"Is it Bell? Is it?"

"No..."

"Is it you, you randy little sod? Because if it is..."

"No, no!" I cried out, alarmed at the turn things were taking. "It was just a doll, that's all!"

"A doll?"

"A child's toy. Your wife bought it for Edie, the Bells' daughter. It's very lifelike. It's a toy!" There was an awkward pause, and then he smiled again. It seemed to cost him a little effort, but he was trying to signal a return to the jollier mood of a few moments earlier.

"Well!" he said. "Ha ha! Enough of all that. I have some news for you. I need to send a *Mumming Birds* company to Paris for a month. You can go and give that very *very* fine Magician I witnessed in Warrington, and you can take young Chaplin along, as he is so desperately keen to play the drunk. Paris, eh? The Folies Bergère! How about that!"

"Thank you very much, Guv'nor," I said, relieved.

"Now then. Is there anything else I can do for you, young Dandoe?"

"Anything you can do for me?"

"Yes. Is there anything else that I..." – he patted himself on the waistcoat – "can do for you?" – and offered both hands across the desk to me, palms up. Ordinarily I would just have been pleased to be on my way, but he seemed keen to make amends for his earlier sharpness, so I felt momentarily emboldened.

"Well," I said. "I saw someone who would be a fine addition to the company. He was working as a solo, but I've seen him in a skit as well. His name is Stan Jefferson."

Karno looked curious, alert. "Jefferson? Any relation to 'A.J.' Jefferson? Calls himself the 'Karno of the North'?"

"His son," I admitted. "You remember when we first met in Cambridge, and you said I had 'it'?" Karno nodded. "Well, I'm pretty sure Stan has 'it' too."

"I see..." the Guv'nor mused, more to himself than to me. "That'd be one in the eye for old A.J., and no mistake... Ha! His own son...!"

I edged towards the door.

"I'm obliged to you." Karno sprang to his feet to usher me out. "See, this is good, isn't it, Arthur? I help you, you help me. That is how things ought to be, don't you agree?" He caught himself there, speaking in rhyme, and smiled broadly. "There's an idea for a song, half written already, ha ha! Enjoy yourself in gay Paree, lad, an' I'll see you in a month!"

22
OUI! TRAY BONG!

WE left for Paris on a Sunday morning. Charlie did his usual trick of almost missing the boat train, and it was only when we got to Dover that we realised he had travelled down in the guard's van as per usual.

Charlie had been to call on Hetty Kelly to tell her that he was going to Paris, only to be told by her sister that Hetty herself was there already with the Bert Coutts Yankee Doodle Dancers, so he was aflame with romantic imaginings. He didn't keep them to himself, either, while the rest of us tried to while away the crossing playing cards.

"The most romantic city in the world!" he kept sighing. "It can hardly fail."

The late autumn weather was filthy, with heavy rain keeping everyone below decks, and our first view of the continent was through a foggy curtain of water. The outlook was hardly more thrilling on the train journey from Calais, as the countryside was flat and uninteresting, and the rain grimly persistent. Charlie's excited chatter continued unaffected, however, and to tell the truth as we approached Paris I began to feel a little thrill myself. We saw a golden luminescence lighting the underside of the rain clouds in the distance, and Charlie pressed his nose against the window.

"Is that it, do you think?" he asked. "There! There! Is it?"

"Oui, oui, c'est Paris," said a French gentleman sitting nearby without looking up from his newspaper, using the tone of voice a parent might use to a child he has already told several times to sit still and be quiet.

"Oui! Tray bong!" Charlie exclaimed. When Ernie and I wrinkled our noses in puzzlement, he launched into a song, inviting us to join in as if we must know it:

Hip, hooray! Let's be gay!
Boom diddy ay! Ta-ra-ra!
To each little Frenchy dove,
Standing drinks and making love,
We fairly mashed the ladies with our Oui! Tray bong!

"Sit down, you idiot," I said. "Before you destroy the *entente cordiale* completely."

———

On the short drive from the Gare du Nord to the small hotel where we were to stay, on the Rue Geoffroy-Marie, Charlie was once again a bundle of energy.

"Look!" he cried, pointing at some café or building. "Just like a Pissarro. I'm getting out and walking..."

"Just wait, can't you?" I said. "If you start walking you won't know where the place is."

The place, when we got to it, was enough to dampen even

Charlie's enthusiasm; small rooms, with freezing-cold stone floors, like cells in a monastery. The Bastille, Charlie called it, and it was a great incentive to get out and about.

Charlie was quickly dressed up to the nines and knocking impatiently on my door. I myself only ever had the capacity to dress up to the sevens, maybe seven and a halfs at the outside, but enough to pass muster. The two of us stepped out and strolled over to the Folies Bergère, where we were to catch the Sunday night performance before starting in ourselves on the Monday.

And it was quite an eye-opener, I can tell you, after the months of traipsing around the ale-drenched halls of Northern England, to set foot in the thick-carpeted foyer of the Folies Bergère. You never saw such a glamorous place in all your life. An orchestra played as gorgeous ladies checked their wraps and fur coats, baring their creamy white shoulders. Huge mirrors and vast chandeliers made the room twinkle, and it seemed somehow that we had arrived at the very centre of the whole world. We climbed a plush staircase to the promenade of the dress circle, where bejewelled Indian princes in their pink and blue turbans, and military officers of all nationalities, it seemed, French, Turkish, British, in their peacock uniforms and plumed helmets, had congregated to watch the world go by. And you could get good old British Bass Ale there too. It was like a vision of Heaven.

We ventured into the theatre to get a flavour of the entertainment, which was as different from a night at an English music hall as champagne is to ale (although, as I say, you could get ale). Women, women, dancing girls, flesh, quivering, wobbling, girls, moving or in teasing tableaux as far as the eye could see.

In one number the dancing girls were wearing flesh-coloured body stockings which left nothing to the imagination, except, obviously, what they looked like without the flesh-coloured body stockings on. In another an alluring array of female pulchritude twinkled and glittered behind giant feather fans on a huge glass and gilt staircase.

In between these fleshy parades there were turns, musical and comical. I felt a little sorry for one act in particular, a tall, loose-limbed youth of about my age, who came on to do a few wistful and melodic numbers by himself. A solo male singer stood very little chance of holding the crowd's attention after dozens of scantily clad girls had just departed the scene, and although he actually had a thoroughly tuneful and agreeable singing voice, the place simply emptied in front of his eyes as he warbled away about this and that, and occasionally the other.

More successful at holding the audience in their seats was a sketch by the celebrated local comedian Max Linder. He cut a dapper figure in his forlorn pursuit of a lady, with his louche moustache and his sleepy eyes, and although I could not follow the dialogue I picked up enough to be impressed.

The headline act was a familiar figure, none other than Little Tich himself. Tich was a huge star in our home country, of course – Marie Lloyd used to say that the only people she would ever share top billing with were George Robey and Little Tich – but in Paris, well, he was a god.

For this engagement at the Folies Bergère he had chosen not to employ his usual bag of tricks, not even the trademark Big Boots. Instead, he hurled himself onto the stage dressed as a grand lady in a glamorous court dress with a long train.

"Je m'appelle Clarice!" he cried, and proceeded to chatter away in a mixture of French and English, both with his strangely deep-voiced Kentish accent, while waving a large feathery fan and becoming inextricably tangled up in his costume. His act was, as always, grotesque, yet perfect, filled with little touches and movements that kept the place in gales of laughter, as the miniature lady tried to hang onto her dignity. The little genius climaxed his spot with a wicked gnome parody of a dancer called La Loïe Fuller, who had earlier that evening cavorted around the place in a sheet with tremendous po-faced seriousness, and whom we later became accustomed to seeing in the wings, seething.

Charlie and I hurried around backstage at the end of the show, he ostensibly to seek news of Hetty, and I because, well, backstage seemed like it might be a pleasant place to pass the time. The magic word "Karno" gained us access, and Charlie scurried off to quiz some of the regulars while I loafed against a wall in a corridor, smoking and watching the comings and goings. Dancing girls thronged, completely uninhibited by my presence. Indeed, I picked up a number of appraising glances, and seemed to be the object of some finger waving from one group in particular, who were offering, through the international language of mime, to treat me to a drink and more besides.

I straightened myself up and headed in their direction. Just then, however, there was a tremendous screeching from one of the other dressing rooms, and the gangly singer I had felt sorry for earlier suddenly bolted from a doorway ahead of me, followed by a bottle of champagne, hurled with great force by someone inside. It hit the corridor wall right by my head and smashed, drenching me from head to foot.

Out of the room then shot a little whirlwind of a red-faced French woman, who continued a screamed tirade at the young singer, while he cowered on the floor with his knees up to his chin waiting for the storm to pass. The woman punctuated her shrieks with angry kicks and slaps, and finally blew herself furiously up the stairs and out into the street. Faces (and more besides) disappeared back into dressing rooms, and the young singer picked himself up and dusted himself down.

"Ah, mon ami, je suis désolé, désolé!" he cried, when he saw that I was (a) soaked in fizzy stuff, and (b) covered in broken glass.

"All right, it's all right," I said, trying gingerly to brush the debris off.

"Oh, you are English?" the singer said. "I apologise a thousand times, sir. Marguerite, she is..." His English let him down and he gave a miserably eloquent shrug. "Come, come..."

He showed me into his dressing room and positively insisted that I borrow one of his jackets, which fitted me well enough (and was something of a step up on the one I had been wearing, truth to tell), and then he led me out to the dress circle bar, where he furnished us both with a drink.

"I am Maurice," he introduced himself. "Maurice Chevalier."

"Pleased to meet you," I said. "I'm Arthur Dandoe, with the Fred Karno company."

"Ah!" Chevalier cried. "But you will do very well here, I think. Above all the audience loves *spectacle*. *Danses et sports* – sketches, I mean, anything where there is lots and lots to look at." Here he made a little firework display with his fingers. "For me it is different," he went on. "I am just one man. The manager, Monsieur Banel, he likes me, but the critics not so much, and the crowd, well, who wants to hear a sad song when there are so many pretty girls to look at?"

"Thank Heavens for them," I said.

"Indeed, my friend," Maurice said, raising a glass to that sentiment.

263

"Perhaps you should find yourself a sketch," I suggested. "Like Max Linder."

Just then Charlie came into the bar, looking dejected, which is to say, he looked like someone doing a pantomime of the word 'dejected', scuffing his feet on the carpet. I beckoned him over and introduced him to Maurice, but Charlie was barely able to force a smile.

"Whatever's wrong?" I asked.

"Hetty's troupe, the Bert Coutts Dancers. They were here last week..."

"I remember them," Maurice nodded. "The Yankee Doodle-doodle girls, no?"

"That's right," Charlie agreed mournfully. "They left yesterday."

"Perhaps they haven't gone too far," I said, thinking they might still be playing somewhere in Paris.

"Huh," Charlie grunted. "They've gone to Moscow."

"Oh! And you like one of these little girls?" Maurice sighed. Charlie nodded glumly. "Ah, what are we poor fellows to do? Your girl is in Moscow, and mine throws a bottle at my head if I even look at one of the dancers. What am I supposed to do? Wear a blindfold backstage? The naked ladies are everywhere!"

Charlie and I smirked at this like schoolboys.

"And what about you, mon ami?" Maurice said, patting me on the shoulder. "Is a woman making of your life a misery also?"

Before I could reply, Charlie butted in, flapping a hand dismissively. "He had a girl, but he's lost her."

Maurice looked stricken. His hand flew to his mouth. He assumed the tone you assume when questioning the recently bereaved.

"I am so very sorry. How did this happen?"

"No, no, no, she's not dead, he's lost her. He doesn't know where she is."

"Ah! I see! Well, in that case let me introduce you to an old acquaintance of mine, Mademoiselle Absinthe..."

You'll have heard, no doubt, the ancient crumbling witticism that absinthe makes the heart grow fonder. It certainly makes the time pass agreeably, although I must admit I can't remember a great deal more about that first week, for some reason.

Seriously, though, I do recall that Charlie would take every opportunity to watch Max Linder's act. He liked, as we all did, Max's onstage persona, the hopeless romantic optimist, but he was chiefly fascinated by Max's success with the films he was making for Pathé Frères. He dragged me along to see a couple of Max's short features one afternoon, in a right fleapit of a Parisian cinema, it has to be said, and the comedy was agreeable enough, but not a patch on watching Max onstage at the Folies, in my view.

In the bar after the evening performances Charlie would corner Max and interrogate him about the 'art of cinematical performance', as he insisted on calling it, trying to get his new friend to agree that cinema could be every bit as artistically satisfying as the theatre. Max would just smile and wink at the gaggle of beautiful ladies who would clamour for his attention.

There were plenty of distractions for a group of young men at the Folies Bergère, and some took enthusiastic advantage, particularly Ernie Stone, who could barely open his eyes to do the show by the Friday. Some of us, though, preferred to venture out into Paris and sample the nightlife, and Maurice was an effervescent and energetic guide. I think he was partly driven to stay out all night by the desire to avoid the alternative, which was being harangued some more by the fearsome

Marguerite. Charlie, meanwhile, was looking for romance.

One evening we were idly watching the ladies promenading in the circle bar. Charlie and I were wearing our *Mumming Birds* stage costumes (he the Drunken Swell and I the Prestidigitateur) and in consequence may have appeared to be rather more prosperous than was actually the case. Whatever, one of the more than usually spectacular ladies fluttered her eyelashes at young Charles as she glided past, and then languidly let a long white glove fall to the floor as she began to make her stately way up the staircase. Charlie leapt to his feet to retrieve it for her, a knight in shining armour, and he flashed his most winning smile – the one with all the teeth, you've seen it – as he handed it back, no doubt accompanied by some gushing compliment. Maurice and I could see that she didn't have a clue what Charlie was saying, and he came trotting back to us to enlist our friend's help as she swanned out of sight.

"Maurice!" he gasped. "This dame arouses my concupiscence!"

"I beg your pardon?" I said, choking on my drink.

"She ... you know, she is very..."

"Isn't she though?"

"You like this girl?" Maurice said.

Charlie did an irritating little mime, in which he was both himself and Cupid, and showed us the little arrow striking him in the heart.

"You like this girl?" Maurice said again, deadpan.

"Oui! Tray bong!" Charlie said. "Now can you write some lines on a card in French so that I may..."

Maurice understood, and turned the corners of his mouth down as he nodded, a very French-looking gesture.

"...court her as a lady of her elegance deserves to be courted?"

"But of course," Maurice said, businesslike, borrowing a little pad and pencil from a passing waiter. "What would you like to say?"

"I have loved you from the very first moment I saw you," Charlie said. I was taking another sip at that moment, unfortunately, and some cognac went up my nose.

Maurice frowned. "Vraiment? You want to say that to *this* girl?"

"Yes, yes. Also write: 'I adore you, you are a bright shining star illuminating the firmament...'"

"Very well," Maurice shrugged and scribbled at the same time (a French thing). "But if you like I can arrange this for you very easily."

"Really?" Charlie said. "Arrange what?"

"Arrange ... a liaison with this girl."

"That would be very... I mean, yes, yes, go, go! Oui! Tray bong!"

Off Maurice trotted in the wake of the goddess in question, while Charlie clutched his little cue cards nervously.

"So," I said. "You are finally going to dip your toe in the water?"

"This is the most romantic city in the world," Charlie replied. "And I am in the mood for romance."

Shortly Maurice returned. "All is set, Charles. She will await you in the foyer at the end of the performance."

"Mon ami!" Charlie cried, and kissed Maurice on both cheeks, before indulging in a little jig of joy and excitement. "I must go and prepare!" He put one finger to his lips as if miming thoughtfulness. "I need to buy some flowers, of course. Adieu, my friends, wish me luck! This could be the start of one of the grand romances of our time!"

He skipped off towards the great gilt staircase that led out to the main entrance. I watched him go, then turned to Maurice.

"So it was just that easy? To arrange a liaison for our friend?"

Maurice shrugged and signalled the barmaid for a top-up. "But of course," he said. "I just hope he can afford her..."

267

23
LA VALSE
RENVERSANTE

AT the end of the first week Little Tich's stint as the headline act was to end. On his last night an extraordinary thing happened. As Tich took his final curtain call, a man in a black cloak leapt to his feet, clambered up onto the apron and waved a broad-brimmed black hat about his head, shouting: "Get up, all of you. On your feet! Pay homage to the world's greatest artist, a genius! Greater than Irving, greater than Lautrec!"

The audience duly rose to their feet in a standing ovation, and in the wings I turned to Maurice, who was joining in the applause, my whole face a question.

"It is Lucien Guitry," he confided, as the cheers rose to the rafters. "He is the greatest actor in all of France."

Eventually Guitry waved the crowd's acclaim to a hush, and kissed Little Tich on both cheeks. He had to kneel to accomplish this, looking rather like an emotional father reunited with a long-lost child, and while still down there on his knees, he begged:

"Please, maître ... do not leave us without letting us see one more time ... the Big Boots!"

A roar of delight went up – "Big Boots! Big Boots...!" – and what could Tich do but oblige? He sent for his great flat, narrow, clacking wooden shoes, and performed his extraordinary acrobatic routine, knocking his hat off, then leaning right forward to grab it. It culminated, as ever, in a cheeky wink, and then the mischievous dwarf rose right up onto his toes until he was nearly seven feet tall, to a tumultuous ovation.

Charlie was utterly enchanted by all this. The very French notion that the music hall entertainer could actually be acclaimed an artist – a *genius*, even – seemed to strike a deep chord within him (yes, over-modesty was never a flaw of Mr Chaplin's). He practised one of Tich's moves – the one in which, in order to keep his toes clear of the stage, he would be obliged to change direction with a sort of swivel of the hips while his feet were level with his waist – until he had perfected his own variation on it. You'll have seen Charlie do it many times if you've seen his films, which I don't doubt that you have.

In fact it is not too fanciful to suggest that Charlie's Little Tramp was germinated on that trip to Paris. If you took the physicality of Little Tich and mixed it with the hopeless romanticism of Max Linder you wouldn't be too far off, I reckon. Whether that is fair or not, Charlie's later success did end up making life difficult for old Tich at the Folies, by the way. Once 'Charlot' made his name on the silver screen the word – somehow – went out that Little Tich had actually stolen Chaplin's act and the Parisian crowds, incredibly, began to boo him. Broke his heart.

Little Tich's replacement for the following weeks was a singer, a great favourite, returning from out of town for a new long-term residency at the Folies. She arrived trailing an entourage of at least thirty dancers and sundry other hangers-on as befitted the greatest star in France at that time. Her act was a spectacular affair, all top hats, fans and feathers, carefully choreographed so as to direct all eyes towards the irresistibly glittering bauble at the centre. Her name: Mistinguett.

Right away you could see that Maurice was smitten, not deterred by the fact that the lady was a good fifteen years his senior nor that there were significantly easier pickings to be had amongst her dancing chorus, all of whom had seemingly been selected for their lustrous dark hair. He hung on Mistinguett's every word and followed her around the place like a puppy with its tongue hanging out. If she wanted a drink, or a chair, or a newspaper so she could bask in her own brilliant reviews, then Maurice would scamper off to fetch it.

In the circle bar after the show she would be surrounded by fawning admirers, some of whom were from the finest families in Europe, and poor Maurice would be condemned to the fringes of her circle, summoned occasionally to fetch and carry while Mistinguett herself would continue to bathe in compliments and turn her radiance on the world.

The front-runner, when it came to competing for Mistinguett's attentions, was a rather po-faced chap in a fancy military uni-form, one of those with brushes on the shoulders, whose face, adorned by a twiddly little twirling moustache, seemed to be incapable of smiling. This, as you can imagine, is not a charac-teristic designed to endear a fellow to a bunch of comedians at the best of times, and we all loathed him heartily. The chap's name was Alfonso, if you please, and, yes, all right, he was the King of Spain.

Night after night we'd sit with Maurice, watching this creature fawn solemnly over Mistinguett, vainly trying to make our friend see that he stood no chance, and to drag him off to the revels we'd enjoyed previously, but he was having none of it, not wishing to miss a moment in her company.

Charlie was vicariously thrilled by Maurice's romantic infatuation at first, but after a while even he began to drift off to find diversion elsewhere. He began to pursue a secret amour of his own – "pitching woo", as he was wont to call it – encouraged by his new acquaintance, the debonair romantic Max Linder. We took a rise out of Charlie whenever we could, saying we hoped he could *afford* her, and so forth, and wondering what the etiquette for leaving a tip might be, and so it probably wasn't surprising that he kept the details of his activities more or less entirely to himself. Ernie Stone discovered then that Charlie had struck up a rapport with one of Mistinguett's *chansonettes*, and we pretty much lost interest. Whoever it was that said: "Where ignorance is bliss, 'tis folly to be wise", well, they were onto something.

Anyway, one heady evening things turned decisively in Maurice's favour. Mistinguett was holding court, as usual, in the long circle bar. Champagne was flowing, and everyone was laughing and relaxing, except, that is, the tightly buttoned-up King Alfonso XIII of Spain.

The orchestra in the foyer began to play a jaunty little waltz, and Mistinguett raised her head like a hound picking up a scent and held out her hand alluringly to her beau.

"Danse avec moi, Alphonse!" she sighed.

Alfonso was not keen, it seemed, to make a public spectacle of himself, even for *la belle* Mistinguett. He remained bolt upright with his hands behind his back.

"Ma'mselle," he began, "si on veut danser, je..." His Majesty's French wasn't up to it, and he began again in English. "Mademoiselle, if you wish to dance I shall throw you a ball the splendour of which you have never seen the like of which."

"Non!" Mistinguett cried petulantly. "Ici! Maintenant!"

Chevalier leapt to his feet as though an electric shock had been passed through his chair. He stepped forward, clicked his heels and offered the fabulous Mistinguett his hand. "Enchanté!" he said, and stood trembling before her like a man at the edge of a chasm. The gorgeous creature looked at the long Chevalier for a long moment, and a smile began to play about her lips. She slowly laid her hand on his, then watched as he bowed low. You could see her wondering what she was letting herself in for.

The music reached the end of a phrase, and as it began a new sequence Chevalier suddenly reached forward, snaked a long arm around la belle Mistinguett's waist, and swung her bodily around. She shrieked with surprise as both feet left the floor, and then held on for dear life as Chevalier galloped frantic circles around the room on his great long legs, one-two-three, one-two-three. He'd clearly decided to seize the moment, and give Mistinguett a dance she would never forget.

People at other tables jumped to their feet to watch, clapping their hands and laughing, and Mistinguett's big skirts swept their chairs aside, sending bottles and glasses flying.

A waiter came scurrying over to start clearing up, and just as he bent to start sweeping up some broken glass into a dustpan around came the whirling, swirling couple again and sent him sprawling. The crowd hooted with glee and pressed themselves against the walls to keep clear of the mayhem. Chevalier and Mistinguett, locked together now, bounced giddily off the bar, and a champagne bottle was dislodged by the impact and sent rolling towards the edge.

Round and round they spun, without tiring, and you began to feel like they would never bring the dance to an end. Certainly Chevalier showed no inclination to release Mistinguett now he had her in his arms, and she was not complaining either.

I found myself standing next to Monsieur Banel, the manager, who had tears of laughter streaming down his face.

"Hey, Monsieur," I said. "How do you like this new sketch of Chevalier's? Not bad, eh?"

I saw surprise, then calculation, then delight flit across his features, before he waved the orchestra to finish, and embraced the couple, who had come to a standstill in the middle of the room.

"Magnifique!" Banel cried, mopping at his face with a big white kerchief, as my friend the interpreter whispered: "Magnificent!"

"Mistinguett et Chevalier ensemble! Ça sera une sensation!" Banel beamed, and you could almost see his mouth watering at the prospect of putting this spectacle on his stage.

The two dancers were still holding onto each other and gazing into each other's eyes, panting, oblivious. Banel turned and led the tumultuous applause which suddenly broke out, before urgently ushering his staff to begin to clear up the debris. King Alfonso XIII of Spain, meanwhile, was tight-lipped, bitterly regretting not seizing the moment.

The two lovebirds began work on their new sketch the very next day, and by the beginning of the week following it was ready to make its debut at the Folies. I didn't see much of Maurice during that time, although whenever I did he was effusive in his gratitude for my having suggested to Banel that the wildly energetic dance would make a fine comic routine. The sketch, entitled *La Valse Renversante*, was an immediate triumph, a *succès d'estime*. They worked it up so that the two main characters, absorbed only in the dance and their besotted devotion to one another, danced obliviously around a set which was like the foyer of a grand hotel. They smashed and overturned furniture, discombobulated the hotel's staff and guests as they passed to and fro, with great timing and finesse actually, and finished up with a brilliant coup whereby they rolled themselves entirely up in the carpet, still dancing, leaving just their heads sticking out of the top of the roll for the last chords of the music.

It was a sure thing, you could tell the first time you saw it, and the thing that really sold it above all was that you could see right off that Maurice and Mistinguett had fallen for each other and weren't just putting it on for the act, and a Parisian crowd loves a real-life romance almost as much as it loves looking at semi-naked ladies. As their first week wore on it seemed to take them longer and longer to unroll themselves from the carpet for their bow, as they were unwilling to disengage from the embrace, until one night the curtain went down with them still wrapped up together, the audience cheering and hooting. Afterwards I asked Maurice what had happened.

"We could not unravel because ... of my embarrassment. To be so close to that ravishing creature, you understand...?"

"Surely you could have hidden ... your embarrassment...." I said. "With a bow? Or perhaps your hat?"

"Yes, perhaps," he agreed solemnly. "If only I could persuade her to let go of it."

Back to the first night they performed it, and of course they were thrilled. Banel was delighted that his faith in Chevalier had been vindicated, and there was much back-slapping and cheek-embracing all round.

Max Linder, beaming with pleasure for his friend, kissed Maurice on both cheeks.

"Pas seulement la voix, eh? Mais aussi le *corps* magnifique!" he cried.

"Celebration!" Mistinguett declared above the hubbub, and the whole party decamped to a fancy restaurant a few streets away, which in my memory is illuminated in gold by three massive chandeliers. There was some sneaking out by the stage door, too, because Mistinguett wished to avoid the attentions of King Alfonso XIII, and Maurice had not been home to mad Marguerite for a week and a half.

The huge room was packed with the fashionable *beau monde*, with barely a spare seat anywhere, but somehow the appearance of Mistinguett galvanised about twenty waiters into action, and we were all shortly seated at a massive table created from numerous others that had been pushed together and covered in new white tablecloths.

Before long the champagne and bonhomie were flowing in broadly equal measure, and we were getting on the outside of some huge platters of shellfish, which were served on what seemed to be upturned bin lids.

Suddenly Maurice hissed: "Look! It's Charlie!"

And indeed there, on the far side of the room, was young Mr Chaplin, enjoying a tête-à-tête with a young lady. Maurice hailed him at top volume.

"Hey! Charlie! Ho!"

Charlie looked pretty shocked to see us. He said something to his dinner companion, who was sitting with her back to us. She had long black hair, curled into ringlets, so I gathered, even in my champagne-and-cognac-fuddled state, that this was probably one of Mistinguett's chorus girls.

"Come!" Maurice shouted. "Join the party!"

Charlie put his hand up to say that no, he and his paramour were just fine over there, but it was Maurice's night, and he was not taking no for an answer.

"Come on! Both of you! I insist!" he cried, as he got up and in a handful of gangling strides crossed the restaurant to Charlie's table. I was leaning drunkenly over the back of my chair, giggling at Charlie's discomfiture.

Mistinguett now, full of the joys of life, saw her new young lover had left her side and peered around for him.

"Tell them!" Maurice shouted to her, across the heads of a number of late diners, some of whom were irritated to be disturbed by this boorishness, while others seemed to be enjoying the little free cabaret, as I was. "Tell them they must join us! This is our night, the night for celebration!"

"Qui est-ce?" Mistinguett called.

"C'est Charlie," Maurice called back, indicating with his open hands. "Et sa jolie demoiselle."

"Mathilde? Mais elle doit être ici, avec nous! Mathilde! Mathilde! À moi, vite-vite...!"

Charlie's companion could hardly refuse such an insistent invitation from her distinguished employer, and so she turned to face us.

The busy chatter of the restaurant seemed to retreat suddenly, leaving only the pounding of my own blood in my ears.

It was Tilly Beckett.

24
A WOMAN OF PARIS

I woke to screaming, not sure where I was or what was happening. I was still trying to unscramble my wits when a tiny figure burst into my room and stood, sobbing, on the mat in her bare feet.

"Monsieur Art'ur! Monsieur Art'ur!"

It was Amélie, the thirteen-year-old *première danseuse* from the Folies, who was staying with her mother and sister in our hotel.

"It is Monsieur Charles! He is..." Here she broke off, choked with emotion. "Dead!"

There is an undeniable frisson of excitement when you think you might have killed someone with the power of your bare hands. A moment of raw masculinity, something like that. And France, as a nation, and as a legal system, recognised the crime of passion as a legitimate defence, so I might even have got away with it.

I had the grandmother and grandfather of all headaches, though whether this was from the drink or from being run into a wall like a bull I wasn't sure. I lurched up into a half-sitting position, and grunted: "*Dead?*"

I just about managed to focus my eyes on little Amélie, who was looking at me, appalled, as though horror was piling upon horror. Her hands flew to her mouth, and then she filled her lungs and let out another almighty scream as she fled.

I got myself to the basin, which seemed to be full of pink water, like some sort of medicine. I splashed my face with the stuff and it got even pinker. Aha... That would be blood then. I then caught sight of myself in the shaving mirror and realised why Amélie had run for her life. I looked like an ogre, battered, swollen and bloody, with a fat lip, one eye half closed and a lump like a goose egg on my forehead.

I grunted, and shambled my aching carcass into the next room to check on Chaplin.

I could see – actually any fool could have seen – his chest rising and falling, but he'd taken such a battering that all the screaming and palaver hadn't woken him up, and there was blood trickling from the corner of his mouth. I gave a little harrumph of satisfaction.

As I shuffled across the corridor I passed little Amélie cowering in the corridor.

"He'sh not *dead*, more'sh the piddy..." I snarled, then went back to bed.

Of course, we'd kicked off at the restaurant. Tilly stood up, and I met her halfway across the room.

"Tilly?" I said, still not wholly believing my eyes.

"Hullo, Arthur," she said, keeping hers downcast. "I'd better ... you know..." She hurried over to answer Mistinguett's summons.

"Well?" I said, turning to confront Charlie. "What have you got to say for yourself?"

"I really haven't done anything wrong, have I?" he bleated shiftily.

"Haven't done anything wrong?" I shouted. "You know, you *know*, that I have been looking everywhere, trying everything I know for a *year* to try and find Tilly, and now here I find you blithely sitting here having a secret romantic dinner with her as though it was nothing!"

"Listen, I couldn't tell you, could I? She asked me not to."

Maurice was putting two and two together. "Mathilde? *Mathilde* is the girl? Oh là là...!" Apparently French people do actually say that when surprised.

"That's right!" I bellowed, "and this little weasel has been sneaking around with her behind my back!"

I grabbed a fistful of his shirt front and pulled him up onto his feet to oblige him to face me like a man. I planted myself foursquare, feeling the need, I must admit, to keep my balance against the effects of the celebration, and gathered myself to deliver Retribution with a capital R.

The room gasped as I swung my fist at Chaplin, who ducked, lightning fast, and then scurried away on all fours between my feet and stood up behind me. The indignity of it! I lumbered round to confront him again, swung my fist at his head, and he did the same thing again, popping up behind me like a jack-in-the-box.

Now the whole restaurant seemed to be laughing and cheering, which only enraged me more. I was trying to kill him, and the little bastard was scoring laughs off me!

It was too much. I gave up on the haymakers and jabbed my fist forwards at his face, trying to slow him down. He swayed left, making me miss, and then swayed right, and I missed again. I drove another big punch at his chin and he disappeared between my feet once more. This time when he popped up behind me he kicked me up the backside.

279

Hoots of laughter were ringing round the restaurant now, and I changed tactics, my cheeks burning with embarrassment. I decided to give chase, and Charlie dodged away around one large round table and then another. We found ourselves suddenly facing each other across a smaller empty table. He feinted one way, and I matched him. He made to go the other way, and I blocked. He went one way and then the other, and I mirrored his moves, and then grasped the table and hurled it aside to grab him in a bear hug. He turned to flee, but wasn't fast enough, and I managed to grab hold of him from behind, pinning his arms.

Before I could work out what to do next, though, Charlie ran up the white-shirted barrel chest of a fat gentleman sitting at the table opposite – yes, *ran up him* – and twisted out of my grasp, so that he was now horizontal, with his feet on the fellow's shoulders either side of his pop-eyed gasping red head, and his hands on mine. On the way up his feet kicked over a large plate of mussels, which went flying down the cleavage of the fat gentleman's wife, and everyone at their table screamed. Charlie and I were momentarily face to face. He planted a kiss on the end of my nose and sprang to freedom.

I roared incoherently with rage, but all of a sudden I couldn't move. Strong hands had taken hold of my arms and legs, and I suddenly found myself being carried bodily out into the street by four burly waiters, with applause inexplicably ringing in my ears. As they shoved me roughly through the glass doors and dumped me onto the pavement, I saw to my satisfaction that Charlie was being similarly dumped some six feet away, and prepared myself to continue hostilities right away. However, Maurice had followed us out and barred my way, while Ernie had hold of Charlie, who otherwise, I think, might have just bolted into the night.

"Non, my friend!" Maurice urged. "You must not fight in the street, it will be a night in prison for both of you."

I saw the sense in his argument, particularly as two gendarmes were at that very moment eyeing us suspiciously from across the boulevard.

"He's right," Ernie said, although Charlie needed little persuading to back down. He wasn't expecting what Ernie said next, though. "We'll settle this back at the hotel, come on. Queensberry Rules, like Englishmen."

Ernie, of course, had been a prize fighter in his time. He was only a lightweight, but he was certainly imposing enough to bend Charlie to his will, and I was mustard keen. Maurice waved and blew a kiss through the picture window at Mistinguett, who was peering out into the night, and by her side I saw Tilly, also watching, her expression unreadable.

At the hotel we went straight up to Ernie's room. He made us take off our shoes so as not to disturb people in other rooms, and Charlie and I stripped down to shirtsleeves and braces. Ernie stood between us, a hand on each of our chests, and said: "Right, let's do this thing. No kicking, no gouging, and hands off the family jewels. You get me?"

We nodded, tensed, and Maurice began to snigger. We glared at him.

"I'm sorry," he giggled. "It is all so ... noble!"

Now that he couldn't back out of it Charlie was as ready for battle as I was, and when Ernie stepped back he came at me, landing a couple of light blows to the sides of my head, which I swatted away derisively. I thumped him on the chest, which took some of the wind out of him, and then we went at it in earnest.

Charlie danced around on his toes to begin with, trying to stay out of my reach. There were none of the crowd-pleasing comedy antics he'd employed in the restaurant, apart from one occasion when I rushed him, trying to get to grips, and he sidestepped so that I ran headfirst into a wall. I gave him a ringing thump on the ear, which slowed him down a bit, then he tried to brain me with a chair, but Ernie pinned his arms by his sides and gave him a stern talking to, which I'm not sure he could hear, on account of the ringing.

Finally I caught Chaplin with a big flailing open-hand slap which rattled his jaw and echoed off the bare walls like a gunshot ricochet. He stepped back and put his hands up, then began to feel in his mouth for loosened teeth. There was blood on his fingers, and I think he had bitten his tongue. I waited, poised to finish him off.

"C'est fini!" Maurice cried, and led me to the far side of the room. I was too tired to protest. I looked up and saw that there was blood on the wall and on the ceiling.

And the next thing I remember is that silly girl screaming and waking me up.

In his autobiography, by the way, if you care to take a look at his account of the month we spent in Paris, you will find that Charlie says he had this fight with Ernie Stone. I suppose this is so he doesn't have to mention me, or the fact that he was entirely in the wrong and deserved everything he got. It also makes him sound like a tough little scrapper, doesn't it, to have fought an ex-professional boxer to a standstill. We can't both be right, can we?

I didn't speak with Tilly for several days, even though I now knew where she was and how to find her. Partly I wanted to wait until I was at least presentable, having received absolute proof that my face was capable of scaring children, and partly I was cross with her for not making herself known to me.

I saw her, though, now I knew to look for her. In fact I could hardly believe I'd managed to miss her. It was the dark hair that had thrown me, as all my daydreaming (and night-dreaming, for that matter) of her had recalled her lovely fair locks. But there she was, not only one of Mistinguett's chorus, wearing very little, this fact concealed artfully behind a pair of giant feather fans, but also as a shocked hotel maid trying to keep vases and glasses from crashing to the floor as *La Valse Renversante* whirled on its merry way. I took every opportunity to watch her in action, but couldn't quite bring myself to approach her backstage.

I didn't speak to Chaplin either, and he didn't speak to me. I wasn't interested in his self-justifying wheedling, and in any case his mouth was so sore that he couldn't have spoken even if he'd tried to. The Drunken Swell appeared even more drunken than usual, while much of the change to the Magician's appearance was fortuitously masked by his moustache.

On the last night of our month in Paris, with the prospect of the boat train for Calais first thing in the morning, I finally decided that it was time. After our last performance of *Mumming Birds* I dodged my share of the packing up and slipped around front of house to watch the second half of the bill, which contained Tilly's appearances, and then I went backstage.

I determinedly checked every crack and crevice of all the dressing rooms, much to the flirty glee of the Folies Bergère dancers, but Tilly was nowhere to be seen. At last Maurice beckoned me into his room. Mistinguett was there, and the two of them were drinking champagne.

"Join us, mon ami," Maurice said, looking for another glass. "We must cheer you on your way, eh?"

"Thanks," I said, "but I was looking for Tilly. Mathilde, I mean."

Maurice turned to Mistinguett, and they began an animated exchange in French which I couldn't follow. He was protesting about something and she was forbidding him to do something, if I understood the pantomime correctly.

"She... ... um ... Mathilde is doing something for Mistinguett, and Mistinguett is doing something for Mathilde. An admirer, you see, and they have left together already. I am sorry."

"Where have they gone?"

"I cannot tell you, I am sorry. She will not allow it. She has high hopes for Mathilde and this nobleman, he is a Count from Prussia, it could be a very advantageous match." He shrugged his apologies. "Have some champagne with us, my friend, and let us talk of other things."

I reeled out into the corridor again and stumbled towards the stairs. Before I could make it out into the evening air, however, there was a little whistle from behind me, and suddenly Maurice was by my side.

"L'escargot d'Or," he whispered. "Rue de Rivoli. Bonne chance, mon ami, et vive l'amour!" Then he embraced me, kissed me on both cheeks, and trotted back to his room. I mentioned he was French, didn't I?

Shortly afterwards I managed to locate the restaurant where Tilly was apparently having a late supper with some continental nob. L'escargot d'Or had a large front window and the brightly lit tables could clearly be seen from the street. I spotted a good vantage point from which to look in, behind a sort of cylindrical wrought-iron installation, so I loafed there and tried not to look too suspicious. I spotted Tilly quickly enough, at a table with two military gents in fancy blue uniforms – not quite as fancy as King Alfonso's, but still – and another girl. I realised I had nothing, no plan of any kind. I fantasised briefly about making a scene and starting a fight, but even though it was my own fantasy the two foreign soldiers gave me a good sound beating.

Through the window I saw the Prussian count take Tilly's hand and bring it to his lips, paying her a compliment of some kind, and she laughed. I remembered that laugh. I hadn't heard it for a year. A steady reeking trickle of steaming liquid suddenly began to run under and over and into my shoes. Suddenly the gulf that had grown between Tilly and me was brutally apparent. She was being wined and dined by the aristocracy in a fancy restaurant, while I was outside in the cold, hiding behind a *pissoir*.

A Frenchman emerged, adjusting his clothing, and gave me a quizzical look, and I found myself walking away with my regrets, one of which was definitely choosing that hiding place. As I walked and walked it came to me that spending this last evening watching her from afar was maybe all I had left of my dream of us ever being together again, so I turned myself round and headed back up the boulevard.

And not a moment too soon, either, because as I made it back within sight of L'escargot d'Or, there was Tilly and the Prussian on the pavement outside. A moment later a carriage hoved into the picture (closed, with a fancy crest on the side, a bit like the one the Guv'nor had off the Duke of Chatsworth). It stopped alongside, and the driver jumped smartly down, saluted his highness and held the door open as Tilly stepped inside.

I froze, horror-struck, thinking that this might actually turn out to be the last glimpse I ever got of her. Then, to my surprise, the nobleman closed the door to the carriage while still standing there on the pavement, took Tilly's hand (through the open window) and kissed it, saluted, nodded curtly to the driver, turned smartly on his heel and went back into the restaurant.

I watched the carriage go, carrying Tilly out of my life. Then, with a mind of their own almost, my feet began to stride after it, faster and faster, until I was fairly pelting along. I dodged in and out, weaving through the late-night promenaders, until up ahead the carriage slowed to take a corner across me into a narrow street. If I'd carried on running I'd have flattened myself against the side of it. Quickly I grabbed the handle, wrenched the door open and flung myself inside.

"Arthur!" Tilly squealed. "What do you think you're doing?"

"Bit of excitement for a Saturday night," I said, sitting down heavily on a plush leather banquette opposite her, gasping for breath.

"Get out, for goodness' sake!" Tilly hissed. "This is Count Adalbert's personal carriage! If he finds out you were in here molesting me I don't know what he'll do. Challenge you to pistols at dawn, most likely."

"Who's going to tell him?" I said. Tilly agitatedly indicated the driver, and I shook my head. "He didn't see me."

"He will, though, when we stop, and he escorts me to the front door! Whatever were you thinking of?"

"I wanted to talk to you," I said, trying to keep a bleating tone out of my voice. "We're leaving in the morning."

"Well, you had all week to talk to me, didn't you, or were you too busy knocking poor Charlie's teeth out?"

"*Poor* Charlie, is it?"

"What's that supposed to...?" she started crossly, but then our conveyance slowed and turned into a drive. "Oh God, we're nearly there, this is it. Come here, come here...!"

Tilly slid sideways along the seat, urging me to do the same, and as the carriage came to a halt she waited with her hand poised on the door handle. As soon as she heard the driver clamber down from his perch on the one side she wrenched the door open and shoved me out the other. The carriage was thus between me and the flunkey, and he was none the wiser. Neatly done. I peeked around the back wheel and watched him gallantly guide Tilly up the steps to a pleasantly appointed town house with lights still burning inside. As she disappeared inside, the driver bowed from the waist, and then as he snapped back upright he clicked his heels with a crack, not unlike the noise Little Tich's wooden clackers used to make, before hopping back up to his seat and clip-clopping away.

Ten minutes later the front door opened just for a heartbeat, and a small figure slipped out. She skipped quickly down the steps, peering around from side to side into the ornamental bushes, until I stepped out.

"There you are," Tilly said. "Let's walk, come on." She slipped her arm in mine and we headed off along the wide, tree-lined boulevard. Even though the hour was late, there were still several couples strolling along in the lamplight. It seemed to be quite the done thing.

There was so much to say that I couldn't quite summon up what should be first. The silence stretched on for an achingly

287

long time, until I heard myself uttering the following timelessly charming and witty opening gambit: "I like your hair."

"What?" Tilly said, turning to look at me, and as she did so I saw for the first time that the hair tumbling down beneath her hat was actually the gold colour I remembered. "Oh yes, that wig. I just had to take it off. Such a relief! Mistinguett likes all her girls to be dark, you see. We are not really people, we are scenery."

"How did you come to be with her?"

"Do you know it was straight after, you know, the end of that Karno thing – well, the end for *me*, anyhow..." She shot me a sharp look and I felt a surge of something acid in the pit of my stomach. "What was that, a year ago? I came to London, without an idea what I was to do, and my dancer friend Angeline – you remember her? Pale thing, puked up on the *Wontdetainia*? She was coming to France and said why didn't I come too, so I did, and we started dancing at the Folies. I say dancing, it was posing, really, assuming alluring postures."

She let go of my arm and demonstrated some of these, which made me smile, mostly with relief that we were starting to relax together.

"Then Mistinguett asked me to join her troupe, and that's been me ever since. She's lovely, although she does treat me rather like you would a pet. And you? Charlie seems to think you're still Karno's blue-eyed boy."

"Does he?"

"Oh yes, I've been listening to him going on and on about how he could be the next number one to lead a company, just as long as it isn't you, and how he has such and such a thing in his favour, and you have so and so. I like him, but he will talk about himself, that boy."

"Did he not tell you I've been looking for you?"

"Have you? No, he didn't mention that."

"Why didn't you say something when you realised I was at the Folies?"

"Why didn't you?"

"I didn't recognise you, did I?"

We turned a corner and found that we had walked to the Champs Élysées. Neither of us wanted to turn back, so we kept on walking towards the Arc de Triomphe.

"I wrote, you know? Over and over. Then I went to your address and your landlady gave me my own letters back to give to you if I saw you. I even went to Southend."

"You never did!" she gasped.

"I did. I met your mother and father. I saw your father's theatre. On the beach...?"

Tilly nodded slowly, acknowledging the demise of that little fabrication of hers.

"I met your sister, too."

She stopped, and turned to face me. "Well then, you know what Fate had in store for me if I'd stayed there. A screaming brat on each arm and another on the way."

"Not to mention a thriving ironmongery."

She laughed. "They really didn't keep any of my secrets, did they? Well, things are different now. Dear Mistinguett plans to marry me off to a Prussian Count who wants to whisk me off to the Hohenzollern, whatever that is."

"Is that what you want?"

"Well, a girl could do worse, it seems to me. Than becoming a countess, I mean."

"I see."

"I feigned exhaustion tonight to get away early. Keeping him keen, you see."

We strolled along in companionable silence, but inside I was churning away madly, trying to think, think, *think* how to bring up the matter that was eating me up.

Eventually the pavements began to seem emptier, and we were no longer walking past all-night cafés and bars, but shops and business premises closed up for the night.

"We should turn back," Tilly said. She stopped, obliging me to circle her so we could retrace our steps. Now or never, I thought.

"Listen," I said, my heart in my mouth. "That time, when we were married, remember?"

"Of course I remember. I don't pretend to be married to all the fellows, you know."

"Not a day goes by that I don't wish I'd said something, or done something, different."

She disengaged her arm from mine and walked ahead.

"You made your choice. It was me or Karno, simple as that. And you chose Karno."

"It wasn't as simple as that. We hardly even talked about it..."

"I was ready, you know, to throw in my lot with you," she said softly.

"Do it then! Do it now! I'll chuck Karno and we'll make an act together, you and me!"

"What *act*, what do you mean?"

"I don't know, we'll think of something! It doesn't matter what it is, we'll make it work, and we'll be together. That's the important thing."

She turned to face me, there in the street. Tears were glistening in her eyes but she wasn't crying.

"And then what? Every time you saw a Karno company on the bill, or heard someone say how well Charlie was doing now, it would be my fault, wouldn't it? My fault for making you choose me."

"I want to choose you, I should have chosen you, I would *always* choose you," I said fervently. "Always and only!"

I held my breath, as if I realised suddenly that the whole future course of my life, and hers, could be decided by what she said next.

"Well, that was then, wasn't it?" she said finally. "I've got a life here now. A different life. With Mistinguett and Count Adalbert of Prussia."

She put her arm in mine again, and we walked along together. I tried to think of something else I could say, but nothing came, and in any event I was choking. In no time, seemingly, we reached the house where she was staying and it was time to say goodnight.

I found a stub of pencil in my pocket, scribbled the Streatham address on a scrap of paper and gave it to her.

"Send me a postcard from the Hohenzollern," I managed to croak out.

She reached up and put her hands on my shoulders, then gave me a quick peck on each cheek. Very French, I thought. Very sisterly.

"Take care of yourself, Arthur Dandoe," she said, and then skipped lightly up the steps to the front door.

I turned and walked until I recognised where I was and eventually found myself back at the hotel where I was staying for what little was left of one more night only. It took hours and hours, but I didn't really care. I didn't really see the point of anything any more.

25
THE TOSS OF A COIN

"HARRY Weldon has up and quit."

Charlie and I looked at one another, then across at Fred Karno. Our jaws hit his desk in amazement.

"Yes, would you believe he's got it into his fat head that he wants people to come and see him for a change, not the Karno Comics, and d'you know what? I say the best of British luck to him. He's going to sing comical songs, if you please, and if he can get a booking outside of Lancashire by the end of next year then I'll eat my hat. Not just my everyday hat, either, I'll eat t' big hat."

He jerked his thumb over his shoulder at the cupboard where all Karno comics knew the big hat resided, waiting to take you down a peg or two if you got too big for your outsized Karno comedy boots.

"What does this mean, boys, I see thee struggling to calculate? Well, I'm going to need to find myself a new number-one comic, as *The Football Match* still has bookings to fulfil. There's Will Poluski, maybe, and there's the two of you. So who reckons they could fill Weldon's shoes, eh?"

"I could do it," Chaplin blurted out, quick as a flash. "I'm ready. I know all the moves, and I've got some ideas too..."

"I'm sure you have," Karno interrupted. "What about you, Mr Dandoe? Do you think you have what it takes?"

I tore my eyes away from glowering resentfully at Chaplin, and answered: "Yes, Guv'nor. I'm ready to step up, if you want me to."

Now Chaplin was glaring at me, although what else he expected me to say I can't imagine. Karno leaned back in his chair and interlocked his fingers behind his head.

"I'm inclined to think that young Poluski let Weldon push him around too easily, and he can wait his turn until he gets himself some gumption. So here's my problem. Two promising candidates, but only the one opening. What to do, what to do...?"

He knew perfectly well what he was going to do, of course. He was just toying with us. We held our breath.

"All right," he said, sitting forward again. "Here's how it is." He took a gold sovereign from his waistcoat pocket, showed it to us and poised it on the end of his thumb. He looked at Chaplin, and said: "Call it."

Chaplin was aghast. "Guv'nor?" he wheedled. "You're surely not going to decide something as important as this on the toss of a coin?"

"If I want to do so then I shall," Karno said. "Call it, Mr Chaplin."

Chaplin looked plaintively at me for support, but I just shrugged my shoulders.

"Very well," he said, conceding defeat. "Heads."

The sovereign spun and twinkled in the air, and then tinkled onto the desk between us. We all peered in to look, and 'heads' it was. Chaplin smirked triumphantly.

"Interesting..." Karno said, building suspense like the master showman he was. He was a master showman, I mentioned that, didn't I?

He coughed.

"All right," he said then. "Listen carefully. *The Football Match* opens at the Oxford on Saturday next. There is a matinée and an evening performance. In one of these performances Mr Dandoe will play Stiffy the Goalkeeper, and in the other, Mr Chaplin, you will play the part. After this I will make my determination and my decision will be final. Follow?"

We both nodded, brain cogs spinning, competitive juices already beginning to flow.

"Mr Chaplin, you won t' coin toss. Will you take first or second turn?"

Now this was clearly a matter worthy of serious deliberation. The evening bill at the Oxford would certainly be rowdier than the matinée, and if the act went well the audience would potentially be more demonstrative. A calmer atmosphere, though, often meant that an audience was more attentive to details, and easier to control.

"Well?" said Karno, tapping his fingers on the desktop. You didn't want to make him lose his patience.

"First," said Chaplin hurriedly. "I shall go first. And he should not be allowed to watch."

"Happy not to," I said.

"Well, there it is," said Karno, getting to his feet and fixing us with a stony eye. "I expect all this to take place in t' proper spirit," he said.

Truth to tell, the two of us had not spoken since the night of the fight in Paris. I think the last words that had passed between us were Chaplin sneering: "Call that a punch?" just before I relieved him of a molar. We'd studiously avoided each other's company on the train from Paris to Calais, on the ferry from Calais to Dover, and then on the train back up to London. I wasn't going to extend an olive branch. Now, though, it seemed we were going to have to put a diplomatic face on things, for the Guv'nor's sake.

Charlie forced himself to offer his hand and look me in the eye.

"May the best man win," he said through gritted teeth.

"May the *better* man win," I corrected him. I hadn't spent all those years eavesdropping on old dons' dinnertime conversations at the High Table of a Cambridge college without picking up some pedantism of my own. Sorry, I mean pedantry, don't I...?

"I'm sure I shall," Charlie smirked.

"Good, good," Karno said. "All right, now run along, children."

He made a show of going back to his paperwork: his habitual way of making his performers feel like there was always something to do that was more important than talking to us. As Chaplin and I reached the door he gave one of his little coughs.

"Oh, ahem ... Arthur?"

I turned to look at him. Actually we both did.

"Could I just have a quick word? In private?"

"Of course, Guv'nor," I said, enjoying the look that flitted across Chaplin's face.

"Shut the door."

I did so, on Chaplin.

"Have a seat."

As I sat down, Karno perched on the corner of his desk.

"I like you, Arthur."

"Thank you, Guv'nor."

"And you like me, don't you?"

"Of course I do, Guv'nor."

He gave a little cough, and for one awful moment I thought he was about to proposition me. You just thought that, too, be honest. It might have been easier to deal with all round if he had done, because what he actually had in mind was this: "You want to beat young Chaplin, don't you, at this little contest of mine?"

"Whatever it takes," I said.

"Well, then, perhaps if ... you could help me out with a little something, then maybe I should be able to help you in return, d'you get my drift?" He smiled in a friendly sort of a way. It was terrifying.

"What ... could I help you out with, Mr Karno?"

The Guv'nor stood, patted me on the shoulder, then began to pace the room.

"Have you seen my wife of late?"

"Well, no, I have been in Paris for the last month," I pointed out.

"So you have, so you have. But you are ... friendly? With her?"

"I think so," I said.

"She's still a handsome woman."

"I'm sorry?"

"Attractive. You think her attractive, I take it?"

"I ... suppose ... so..." I ventured.

"Good, that's good," Karno said. "That is as it should be. No need to beat about the bush. We are grown men. Men of the world. Eh?"

Karno paced up and down the small office, coughed again, then fixed me with his beady eye.

"When our marriage ended, as it sadly did – no fault on either side, just one of those unfortunate things – she was persuaded by unscrupulous men that her best interests lay not in the divorce which would have made things right and proper between us but in our remaining manacled together in a union that is little more than a sham. A sham, I tell thee, devised by lawyers with the sole purpose of milking me for every penny they can squeeze out!" Here he paused, and took out a handkerchief with which to mop his brow. "Because of this I am unable to make an honest woman of Maria, and am unable to move on with my life, leaving that unhappy chapter behind me."

"I see," I said, more to fill the pause than anything, because I didn't see yet, not really.

"Good, Arthur, good, I knew ye would," Karno said, and returned to his chair behind his desk, leaning forward again to rest on his elbows. "Now the fact is, I can see no way out of this legal impasse without the help of someone such as your good self."

"Me? What can I do?" I asked, not sure I was going to like the answer much.

"Well. You say you are friendly with my wife, correct?"

I nodded.

"*Very* friendly, right?"

I shrugged.

"Just so. Now if you were to – how shall I put this...? If you were to become even *more* friendly with Edith – an attractive woman, as you yourself said just now – to the point where you could persuade her to indulge in a liaison of a ... um ... carnal character. That would give me grounds, do you see, for a challenge in t' courts, she wouldn't have a leg to stand on, as it

297

were, and the whole damned thing would be done and dusted in a trice."

"I don't know..." I began.

"Of course, of course, you take some time to think about it, eh? That's only reasonable. You have a bit of think. In actual fact, if you have any qualms at all about what I am asking, it would not be essential – preferable, I think, but not altogether essential – for you to *actually* engage in a liaison with Mrs Karno, just so long as you were prepared to swear an affidavit to the effect that you had done so. There would naturally be questioning, in court and so forth, concerned with verification, and a knowledge of certain..." – here he coughed one of his little coughs – "...certain ... *intimate* details would no doubt be, um, helpful, but I'm sure someone of your skills could carry that off without breaking sweat. Eh?"

So there it was. The road to success, for me, was paved with cruel seduction, or perjury, or a combination of the two. It was set before me as plainly as that. Ruin my wife, and I'll make you a number-one comic.

Karno watched me anxiously. "Just our little secret, all right?" he said, with a wink.

━━━━

Well, as you can no doubt imagine, I gave this matter a fair bit of thought over the next few days. In fact I doubt whether I spent a waking moment thinking about anything else.

Half the time I thought feverishly about the glittering prize that had been dangled in front of my greedy young eyes. To be the number one of a company of Fred Karno Comics was all I had dreamed about since I had come to London. And as if that wasn't enough, the brass ring came with the additional bonus of depriving Chaplin of the same.

The other half of the time I was thinking about what I would have to do to get it.

Was it possible to do what Karno asked, and still escape with my own reputation intact? Only if I could make it appear that I was a hapless victim of circumstances myself, which would mean pretending to actually fall in love with Edith Karno, becoming besotted with her, and sustaining that pretence for how long? Weeks? Months? *Years*...? Otherwise it was a straightforward proposition – seduce the woman, and then turn on her in court.

How could I do that to Edith? How could I do that to Freddie junior and Leslie, her sons? To Clara and Charley Bell, her dearest friends?

And yet ... and *yet* ... I could find myself the number one of a company of Fred Karno's Comics, which was as near as damn-it-all saying 'made for life'. Karno looked set to rule the roost for years and years to come, always provided he didn't sink all his money into some God-forsaken scheme to set up his own entertainment resort on an island in the Thames and take himself to the very brink of bankruptcy, anything like *that*.[9]

I passed the whole of that week in an agony of indecision, until, on the Saturday I awoke and realised that I would in all probability see Karno that evening at the Enterprise when I went to get paid. Perhaps I should make some progress.

I spruced myself up, slicking down my hair and popping up to the High Street for a nice close shave. I spent some little time shilly-shallying over what I should wear, trying to decide which of my (two) suits and (three) ties were most ideal for philandering in. I shined my shoes. Twice. I sat on my bed, feeling slightly faint. I opened the window. Let some air in. Began to shiver in the November chill...

Then I heard Clara and Charley go out of our front door, taking Edie and Miss Churchhouse up to the Common for a stroll, and I got a grip of myself. Come on, I said out loud. Now or never. Faint heart and all that.

I felt rather odd as I knocked on Edith Karno's front door. It seemed utterly unreal, somehow, to be calling on her with this purpose in mind.

The door opened, to reveal not the maid I was expecting but Edith herself. "Mister Arthur Dandoe!" she cried when she saw me. "Well! I think I can guess what *you* are after!"

I was speechless. Terror-struck. How could she *possibly* know? I felt my face burning as she turned and disappeared into the hallway. When she returned a moment or two later she had a letter in her hand, which she thrust at me.

"Here you are, this is what you've come for, isn't it?" she said. "Delivered to our door by mistake. Is this what you've been waiting for all this time?"

I looked down at the envelope. It was addressed to me, and had come from Paris. From Paris! All thought of my strange mission fled from my head, and I began to retreat down the steps.

"Yes ... yes, that's right. Thank you very much."

"I would have popped round with it shortly, you know, but you beat me to it," Edith smiled. "A lady's handwriting, if I'm not mistaken – but don't let me pry."

She gave me a conspiratorial wave, then closed the door. I took my letter onto the Common and tore it open eagerly. It was from Tilly, of course, the first I had ever had from her, and it contained unexpected news.

"My dear Arthur," she began. I liked the sound of that, and I read it again. Then she went on:

"Events have taken such a surprising turn here since you left. Maurice's combustible fiancée[10] became so distraught at his relationship with Mistinguett that she attempted suicide by poisoning – unsuccessfully, thank God. However, he feels duty bound to take care of her as she recuperates, and so *La Valse Renversante* has come to an abrupt end. I feel sure it will be revived shortly, but without me, for I have determined to return to England. Amy Minister – you remember her, of course? – has helped me out. I've got an audition with Fred Karno himself, no less, next Wednesday in the afternoon at his house, while his wife is out at the shops, so fingers crossed for me, hey? With a bit of luck I shall not be unemployed for long! Shall we meet for tea afterwards, say four o'clock at the Fun Factory?"

She closed then with the two words "your Tilly", which made my head spin. I could hardly believe it. Tilly was coming back, and wanted to meet. The possibility that she might come to work for Karno, and that I might soon be a number one, able to pick and choose the members of my company, why, suddenly it was all falling into place perfectly. I was walking on air, I can tell you.

When I pitched up at the Enterprise later that evening, I was surprised to see Fred Spiksley, Jimmy Crabtree and Billy Wragg already ensconced in a corner, their habitual fug of smoke hanging over their table.

"Evening there, lads," I said. "Wasn't expecting to see you till Monday."

"Aye," said Fred. "Yon Charlie asked O'Neill to bring us down early. Couple of things he wanted to work on, he said, so we thought why not, if he's payin'...?"

"Is that right?" I said, looking around to see if Chaplin was there, and he was, deep in conversation with Syd not far off, not paying me any attention.

So, I thought to myself, it's going to be like that, is it? All's fair in so-and-so and also of course in you-know-what. I realised it might be a very good idea to get these lads on side as soon as possible, so I clapped my hands together and opened my mouth to offer them all a drink on me. Before I could do that, though, Karno himself walked up and clapped me on the back.

"Arthur, my boy, come with me. Someone I want you to see."

I followed him around the bar and there, beaming fit to split his face in half, was Stan.

"Took your advice, you see?" Karno said. "Got to help one another in this business, haven't we, eh?" He gave me a look laden with meaning, and then turned to Stan. "What does your Dad have to say about it, eh, young Jefferson?"

"Well, to tell the truth, I've not told him," Stan admitted.

"Ha!" Karno cried. "I'll bet you've not, neither! Oh, I meant to ask," he said, turning to me and snapping his fingers as though this had only just occurred to him. "Have you by any chance seen Mrs Karno since we spoke?"

"This very afternoon," I said, neglecting to go into any details.

"Good lad," the Guv'nor said, patting me on the back. He then drifted off to circulate amongst his flock, and Stan pumped my hand enthusiastically.

"So, I've to thank you, have I?" he grinned. "I thought as much!"

"Well, I only mentioned your name," I said. "What happened?"

"I went to a Karno pantomime when I was in Manchester and presented myself backstage afterwards. He was there, the Guv'nor

– *your* Guv'nor, that is – said that he'd heard all about me and took me on there and then. I've been rehearsing *Mumming Birds* these last few days and start at the Hippodrome in Hulme next week."

"Marvellous news," I said, punching his arm. "So you're a Karno man now."

"I'm only sorry I shall miss all the fun next weekend," Stan said. "I hear it's between you and Charlie for Harry Weldon's number-one spot."

Just then Freddie junior passed by, and I grabbed his arm. "Hey, Freddie, meet Stan. Stan, this is Mr Fred Karno *junior*."

Stan turned, grinned his happy grin, and stuck out his hand. Freddie shook it, and gave me a puzzled look.

"Stan's the new boy," I explained. "Your dad's just taken him on."

Freddie's face darkened. "Oh, for pity's sake!" he cried. "Another one?" And he pushed off through the crowd, looking for something to kick.

Just before closing time big Billy Wragg came up to me, took me to one side. I was a bit surprised. He was a quiet lad, Billy, just used to sit at the table with the others, puffing away, drinking along, while Spiksley or Crabtree made the running. Not one to take the initiative.

"If you want," he said, "we could work on a bit of – what do you lads call it? Stuff?"

"Business," I said. "What sort of thing do you have in mind, Bill?"

"Whatever you think," Billy said. "I know Charlie's all for trying something new with Fred and Jimmy, like, and I thought mebbe you wouldn't want to get left behind..."

We arranged to stay behind after rehearsals the next week and see what could be done. Of course, I understood perfectly well that Fred and Jimmy would be touching Charlie for a few quid for their "help", and that Big Billy would expect similar. I offered him a generous – I thought – remuneration, with a bonus to be paid if I was successful on the night. I reckoned I'd be able to afford it then, and it might give him the incentive to put plenty into it.

Of course I didn't realise then just how much he would put into it.

26
DON'T DO IT AGAIN, MATILDA

EVERYONE attached to the Karno organisation, and plenty who weren't, got caught up in the contest as it drew nearer.

I was reliably informed – well, I say reliably, it was Mike Asher who told me – that a book was being run and some substantial sums were being laid down on me and Charlie. That should have put me on my guard, knowing the footballers as I did. I noticed Fred Spiksley and Jimmy Crabtree hanging back rather, trying not to get involved, keeping their powder dry for young Mr Chaplin's sake, but I didn't think there was much they could really do to actually undermine me. Not without losing their jobs, anyway. I actually looked forward to rubbing their noses in it once I took over as the new number one.

Anyway, Billy Wragg was my man. After the large cast rehearsal was finished the two of us started working on a piece of business, or 'stuff', as Billy called it. Obviously there wasn't much leeway to add to what was already there, but we were able to come up with a couple of ideas to embellish the football action passages of the piece. In our best little sequence we worked it so that Billy would stop the ball and instantly brace his leg behind it so that I, as Stiffy, could throw myself full-bloodedly into a save, giving it everything. When we showed it off to the rest of the company later, the meaty slap of the two of us colliding made the other players wince, and drew a smattering of spontaneous applause from those watching the rehearsal. I knew we had a winner.

I had the Wednesday off, and was looking forward to meeting Tilly at the Fun Factory later that afternoon. I hadn't done anything more about the 'favour' that Karno had asked of me, and I supposed I should grit my teeth and get on with it, if I was going to.

Clara Bell seemed to know as much about my neighbour as anyone, so I had in mind that a chat with her might be useful. I poked my head into the kitchen, where I found Clara warming her hands on a fresh pot of tea.

"Clara?"

"Hullo, Arthur, my lad. What are you about this fine morning? No rehearsals today?"

"No, that's right," I said.

"Tea?" Clara asked, her hand poised on the teapot handle, and I nodded and took a seat at the table while she fetched another cup.

"I wanted to ask you about the lady next door. Edith." I said.

"Oh?"

"How did she and the Guv'nor come to split?" I asked. Clara gave me such a piercing glance at this that I flushed bright red.

"I was only wondering," I went on hurriedly, "because she speaks of him so fondly, always wants news of him."

"You are her friend, I know you are," she said, after a moment or two, and I nodded keenly. "I have heard her speak of how much she enjoys your little chats. The view she gets from Freddie, and I am afraid from most of us, is rather jaundiced about her husband, you see, knowing what he is and what he has done. That's why you are like a breath of fresh air to her. Worshipping him the way she does. The way you do."

"I do?"

"Oh, of course you do, you silly boy. It's perfectly plain. And I don't know if it's really my place to bring you down to earth. Perhaps it's better if you don't know."

"Don't know what? Tell me."

Clara took a sip of her tea, and then decided to begin. And once she began, there was no stopping her. "It was ... not a happy marriage. She was seventeen when they met, working in the box office at the Theatre Royal in Stockport. He was a gymnast with his act the Three Karnos, and he set his cap at her right away. Her parents, though, didn't like him, and thought Edith was too young to marry, so they eloped. Very romantic, but he treated her as a slave, all along, right from the first. She'd sell tickets for his shows, then be in his shows, and then scrub the stage once his shows were finished while he and everyone else was in the pub. She was still a child, and he was a bully, that's all, she was like a piece of property to him."

Clara paused, took another sip of tea.

"What he started to do, you see, eventually, was say she had to be nice to a particular theatre manager, so that they'd get more bookings, and so she would be, to please him, but then he would get it into his head that she must have gone as far as his filthy mind imagined she would, and he would fly into a jealous rage.

He'd beat her black and blue, time and time again. He brought a doctor to her once, and when he saw her the doctor threatened to horsewhip him on the spot, that's how bad it was. She has a scar, just here, on her cheek. Have you seen it?"

I shook my head. I had, though.

"She covers it well, but she'll have it till the day she dies, like a little crescent moon. He did that to her, threw her to the ground and stamped on her face with his heel."

The image of Karno's smart, shiny little shoes flashed into my mind.

"She stayed with him, though," Clara went on. "There were the children, of course, but she adored *him* still despite it all, if you can believe that. There was Freddie, the eldest, you know him. And Leslie too. In between there were six more that, well, they just weren't meant to be, poor little scraps. And when each one died he'd beat her again, like it was her fault."

Clara took a moment to compose herself.

"It wasn't just the beatings, though they were bad enough. It was the mistresses, too. When little Leslie was born ... what is he now? Seven? The brute had set up a second home, on the very same street, with that ... woman..."

"Maria?"

"One of his Amazonian chorus girls, she was then. We all knew about it, everybody did, except poor Edith, and we hadn't the heart to tell her. Introducing her as 'Mrs Karno' to everyone, he was, it was disgraceful, with his real wife still recovering from the birth of his own child. Well, one day he decided he'd let Edith know that he had a mistress now, and one who would ... do things that she wouldn't do. Wouldn't *dream* of doing. So he delivered a packet of photographs. Oh, such things, they were!

The two of them, naked as the day they were born, in a field if you please, cavorting around, posing, doing ... well, anything you could possibly imagine, and then worse."

"You don't mean...?"

"I *do* mean. Well, Edith could hardly turn a blind eye any more, then, could she? When she left him, finally, she came to us, you know, and we took her in. Charley went and told Karno straight that Edith was under his protection now, and we got her and little Leslie a room next door. Karno was furious, but he couldn't fire Charley, too many people would have had something to say about that, and Charley would never leave. But he's never got the leads he deserved, Charley, because of it. Been a number two for, ooh, ten years now."

"So why did they never divorce? Edith and the Guv'nor?" I asked.

"Edith went to a solicitor at the Variety Artistes Federation, who said to her that she should seek a separation, not a divorce, as that way Karno would have to support her while she raised his sons. He fought her in court, though, and was winning his case, spinning his ridiculous sob story, until I brought those photographs into the judge. Edith would never have done it, but I knew where she kept them, and I wasn't going to let him get away with it. The judge allowed that they should be separated, and determined that Freddie should be left with his father for some reason I couldn't fathom then and still cannot now. Something to do with the chance of one day being brought into the family business. It's a miracle that boy has turned out as well as he has, a perfect miracle."

I was finding it harder with every passing minute to imagine that I would ever be able to oblige Karno with his request.

"Does she ever...? I mean, has she been alone since she and the Guv'nor separated ... or have there been...?"

"Good Heavens! What sort of a question is that?"

"I'm sorry," I said, flustered.

"Of course not, is your answer! She is a saint, that woman, a saint. She'd no more break her marriage vows than she'd cut off her own right hand. The very idea!"

"I see."

"She has two satin pillows on her bed to this very day, one with 'EDITH' embroidered upon it, and the other with 'FRED'. I do believe she'd take him back, even now."

I must have looked pretty crestfallen, for she said: "There now, that was more than you wanted to know, wasn't it? He's not a bad man to be working for, I dare say, if you can manage to stay on the right side of him. And it's not really any of our business, now, is it? More tea...?"

I didn't need tea, I needed the open air. I needed to think. I grabbed my hat and strode out to the Common.

———

Clearly what the Guv'nor had asked me to do was beyond the pale, and equally clearly the man I had idolised since I came to London had feet of clay. In fact was little short of monstrous.

Nonetheless, the tantalising vision of a near future in which I was the lead comic of a Karno company of which Tilly was a member, well, could I really pass that up? I could find somewhere else to live, far from Streatham and the protective Charley Bell. I could find a way of avoiding Freddie junior, for the next ... well, for the rest of my life. Couldn't I...?

Tilly was doing her bit that very afternoon. I reckoned if I was going to go through with this, then I really should do it as soon as possible. I wasn't sure how far I actually had to go before the weekend and Karno's big decision. Perhaps I would be able to make him see that his scheme was madness? Perhaps the attempt itself would be enough to show him that in fact he was in the wrong?

The one thing I couldn't get away with doing was nothing at all.

I decided that I should bring some flowers if I was really going to 'pitch woo', as Charlie would no doubt have called it, to a married lady. Whether I actually thought that flowers would make a difference, or I was just postponing the moment again, I can't now quite recall. Whichever it was, I found myself browsing at a florist's barrow at the bottom end of the Common for some considerable time.

"If you wait until they turn they'll be cheaper, is that what you're thinking?" the crone in charge eventually enquired. I laughed off her sledgehammer sarcasm.

"No, no, I beg your pardon. I just wanted to be sure I get it right. Difficult ... choice," I said.

"Courting, are you?" she said. "Here, let me help you out, sonny." She quickly gathered a two-bob bouquet together for me and thrust it into my arms. "Never a woman born yet that wouldn't swoon at the sight of that little lot."

I thanked her, paid her, and was turning to leave, when she called me back and stuck something into the lapel of my jacket.

"Lucky heather," she whispered.

"Thanks," I said. "I've got a feeling I'll need it."

A few minutes later I stood by the gate of next door's house.

311

Actually maybe it was longer: I may have walked around the block a couple of times. And nipped into a pub for a stiffener. Anyway, I stopped there at the gate and took a deep breath. I just about felt like I'd screwed my courage to the old sticking place, when a voice hailed me from across the street.

"What ho, Arthur!"

I turned, and there was young Freddie striding towards me with a big grin on his silly chops, just the very last person I wanted to see. He spotted the flowers clutched in my fist, of course, right away, and punched me jovially on the arm.

"Flowers, eh? Who's the lucky gal?"

"Ha ha! No one, no one!" I said.

"Oh? Have you got a secret admirer yourself, then? Some fellow sweet on you, is it?"

"Don't be an ass, Freddie."

"I'm just going to see Mama. Are you going out, or do you want to come in and say 'Hullo'?"

"I'm ... er..."

"It's all right, you can if you want. I'm sure she'll like to see you. I'm just killing time while Maria's out shopping," he said cryptically.

"What?" I said, and he laughed.

"Maria's out shopping. That's just what I call it. She goes up to town for the afternoon, looking at shoes and so on, deciding she'll maybe get them next time, or the time after. And while she's out, that's when Dad does his auditioning. He doesn't call it the Fun Factory for nothing, you know!"

"Sorry, what?" I said.

"Come along, Arthur, you're not usually this dim. The Guv'nor is *auditioning* a young lady, and he does it when Maria is out shopping, because she's an extremely jealous woman and he doesn't want her to know what he's about."

The truth was dawning slowly on me now, although I didn't want it to.

"Likes to see just how super the supers really are, if you follow me?"

I nodded, but was barely listening. In my mind I was hearing Tilly's voice, reciting her letter: "I've got an audition with Fred Karno himself, no less, next Wednesday in the afternoon at his house, while his wife is out at the shops, so fingers crossed for me, eh...?"

Freddie was still talking. "I walked in on him once, not long back, *auditioning*, and got a pound pay rise so I wouldn't tell Maria. Ha! I'd tell you who the girl with him was, but it wouldn't really be fair, would it? I see her on pay night. Think it's her, anyway. I only got the briefest look at her *face*, to be honest. Eh? You with me?"

I laughed along with him, hollowly, my mind racing.

"In fact sometimes I amuse myself on a Saturday night by ticking them off in my head. She's been 'guvved', she's been 'guvved', I *saw* her being 'guvved', 'guvved' *twice* to my certain knowledge, 'guvved', 'guvved', 'guvved' and so on. I should put a little 'g' next to their names in the ledger, shouldn't I? Baffle future generations of accountants!"

His bawdy grin turned to a look of concern as he saw my expression.

"I say, are you all right, Arthur? You look rather pale."

"Here," I said, slamming the bunch of flowers into his chest. "Give these to your mother!"

I set off at a run down the street.

Too agitated to wait for a tram or an omnibus, I ran up Streatham High Road towards Brixton. Got passed by a tram, which would have got me there sooner if only I could have calmed down to wait for it. Cursing, ran on up the hill. Lost a scarf – it blew off from round my neck. I didn't go back for it. Up to Coldharbour Lane, red in the face, panting, sweating. Into Vaughan Road, seeing the Fun Factory, lit up by the winter sunshine, seeing Karno's house. Stopped, gasping, leaning on somebody's garden wall, trying to get my breath back...

The door of Karno's house opened, and Tilly stepped out. She was smiling, and gave a little wave back to the occupant, as the door closed.

She set off walking along the street towards me, saw me, smiled.

Karno's face leering down at her.

"Hullo there, you!" she said, as she got close.

Karno unbuckling his belt.

"Guess what!" she asked, brightly.

Karno giving a little cough.

"I passed the audition!" she beamed.

Karno's lips leaving a wet smear on her cheek.

"Didn't you hear me? I got a job..."

Tilly's face changed. I saw her read in my eyes that I knew perfectly well what her audition had consisted of.

She said, in a small voice. "It was for you, Arthur. So I could be with you."

But I didn't hear her. All I could think of was ... her. Being 'guvved'.

"Leave me alone," I said. "You ... disgust me."

She walked away, of course. Her head bowed, one hand over her face, not a sound. She walked away from me, to the end of the road, turned the corner and disappeared from view.

I didn't know what to do with myself. I sat on the pavement, rested my head on my knees, closed my eyes. It began to rain, a sudden, heavy shower. Within a couple of minutes I was soaked through to the skin, but I couldn't bring myself to get up.

After a few minutes I heard a front door bang and glanced up. There was Karno, strutting across the road to the Fun Factory under a bright red umbrella, exceedingly full of himself, clip-clopping lightly around the puddles in his shiny little shoes. I wondered if they were the same shoes he'd used to stamp on his wife's face, to scar her for life. It made me think of the other people he wasn't worried about scarring for life. Me, for one. I felt a volcanic anger building up inside me. I scrambled to my feet and followed.

He'd just started talking to Alf Reeves about some theatre plans of some sort when I kicked the door of his office open. I stood there in the entrance like a drowned rat. He got half the way up to his feet and opened his mouth to speak, but I beat him to it.

"You!" I shouted. "You're a monster!"

"Are you drunk?" Karno said calmly.

"Not yet!" I roared. I grabbed his bottle of Scotch from atop his cabinet and took a big, spluttering swig from it.

"What is this about?"

"I'll tell you!" I cried. "It's about me telling you where to stick your stupid contest, and where to stick your bloody job!"

Karno's jaw dropped. "You *what?*" he said.

"You heard me," I snarled, pushing my face right up to his, nose to nose. "Stick it where the sun doesn't shine, because if the only way to keep it is to compromise your poor wife, well then clearly it's not a job worth having and I'll find some other bloody thing to do!"

I had no idea what that other thing might be, and to be honest that big swig of whisky was beginning to make me feel dizzy, but I was rather enjoying myself. The smoke in my nostrils from all the bridge burning I was doing had an exhilarating tang.

"Do I take it that you are resigning from the company?!" Karno shouted, trembling with fury.

"You can take it up your arse!" I roared, rocking back on my heels. "That poor woman still loves you, you know, even though you have got yourself another so-called wife, and are betraying *that* one with any available trollop whenever *her* back is turned!"

"Resignation accepted!" Karno yelled, banging his fist on the table as if it contained a rubber stamp to make things official.

"Fine!" I shouted, my face an inch from his.

"No!" another voice cut in, strongly, firmly.

Karno and I were stunned. We'd been so wrapped up in our fury that we'd almost forgotten Alf was still in the room, yet there he was, red in the face and visibly quivering with suppressed rage.

"You *what?*" Karno said, slowly turning to face him, hands on hips.

"I said, no," Alf said, with a dreadful calmness. "No, Arthur is not resigning from the company, nor are you going to sack him. I won't allow it."

"Oh-ho!" Karno bellowed nastily, turning an interesting puce colour. "Is that so?"

"Yes," Alf said, ice cold. "That *is* so. Or do you want me to tell everyone what you asked this boy to do?"

"You can do exactly as you damn well please!" shouted Karno, but the wind was leaking from his sails.

"This is what is going to happen. You can play out your contest on Saturday, even though it is silly and demeaning to this lad and to young Chaplin, both of whom deserve better from you..."

"*He* doesn't," I muttered.

"...and then you may come to whatever decision you think proper at the end of the evening. But I shall be there, too, and I will feel obliged to see that no travesty of justice is done, do you understand me? Fred?"

Karno glared at Alf for a moment, but Alf held his gaze.

"Fred?" he said again, with steel in his tone. "Do you hear me?"

"Very well," Karno said through gritted teeth, after a long, long moment in which he seemed to be weighing up Alf in his mind, reappraising him. "Very well then. But I shall stop the money for that door out of his wages." He turned to Alf with exaggerated deference. "Unless *you* think that would be inappropriate?"

"No, that will be perfectly acceptable," Alf said, holding himself erect. "Now come along, Arthur – time we left, I think."

I let Alf guide me out of the office, and out into the wet street. I was astonished.

"What on earth did you think you were you doing?" I shouted. Once we were clear of the Fun Factory Alf's superhuman composure suddenly deserted him. He grabbed at his heart and leaned heavily against a lamp post.

"Saving your life, you young fool!" he gasped. "Now get me a bloody brandy!"

27
BREAK A LEG

$\mathcal{SO}$ we come to that most peculiar of days at the Oxford, when Charlie Chaplin and I went head to head.

The Oxford – gone now, pulled down and replaced with a Lyons Corner House – had the reputation then of being the handsomest music hall in London. It was certainly one of the most prestigious places to play. George Robey made his name there in the 1890s, you know, and it was always a favourite of his.

I was there in plenty of time for the matinée, even though I wasn't to be in it, or even allowed to watch it. Once or twice a couple of strangers popped their heads in at the door and stared curiously at me, before whispering to one another as if to say:

"There he is, he's one of them!"

At some point during the first half – *The Football Match* was in the second – Chaplin came to pay me a visit, all dressed up in Stiffy the Goalkeeper's roll-neck jumper and long pantaloons, and shut the dressing-room door behind himself.

"Listen, Arthur," he began, shuffling from one foot to the

318

other. "It's embarrassing, this, isn't it, to be set against each other like this?"

I shrugged.

"You know, it's not really how it should be, is it?"

I shrugged again.

"But seeing as we are ... rivals, as such, I didn't want there to be any bad feeling between us..."

I raised a quizzical eyebrow.

"So I wanted to apologise, you know, for Paris. I should have told you when I recognised Tilly. Even though she asked me not to, I don't know why, it's none of my business. But I should have told you."

"Yes," I said, "you should have."

There was a pause.

"And ..." he ventured, "I suppose I shouldn't have then begun to court her behind your back, that was ... not really on, was it?"

"No," I agreed. "It wasn't."

"So. I just wanted to say that I'm sorry for what happened. Friends?"

Charlie stood there offering his olive branch of a handshake, and I let him for a moment or two, before finally nodding and taking his hand.

Left to my own company, I fell once more into the black musings which had occupied my mind over the previous few days. Tilly, the girl of my dreams, the girl I had been desperately seeking for a whole year, had thrown up her new life in Paris and returned to find me, *me*, and I had rejected her. And try as I might to envisage ways of making that right, I still couldn't shake the mental picture of Karno 'auditioning' her.

Maybe I would have to leave the Karno organisation and

make my own way as a solo, daunting though that prospect was. I remembered Stan's recent travails as 'He of the Funny Ways', and how glad he was to have joined the security and sheer creative enterprise of Karno's Fun Factory, and my heart sank into my boots. There was Wal Pink, of course, but who knew what he was up to?

Suddenly there he was in the doorway. Yes, Wal Pink, large as life, as if I'd conjured him up simply by thinking about him.

"What the hell are you doing here?" I said.

"I've come to see your contest of course, Arthur," he oiled. "At the Water Rats dinner last night everyone was talking about it."

"So, you've not yet brought the Fun Factory to its knees, then?" I asked.

"Give me time, my boy, give me time. Our plans march forward apace, and sooner rather than later we'll..." Pink caught himself. "Well, well, never mind what we'll do. I just wanted to be sure and let you know that my offer still stands, whenever you wish to avail yourself of it."

"Yes, well, if I do, you'll be the first to know," I said. "Now if you don't mind?"

"Of course, of course, you need to ready yourself. Break a leg!"

And he trotted off up the corridor as if he owned the place. Just the sort of distraction I needed at that moment.

Shortly I realised that Charlie's big moment was drawing nigh, because a tidal wave of studded boots clattered along the corridor as the Midnight Wanderers and the Middleton Pie-Cans headed towards the stage.

Then I heard the synchronised smashing of boots on the apron which signified that the opening warm-up scene was under way, and I could make out some muffled laughter trickling down to

320

the dressing room where I was still sitting. Some more laughter I judged to mark the entrance of Will Poluski junior as the Villain, and then it must surely be time for Stiffy to appear ... and sure enough, yes, there was Chaplin's first big cheer.

Long before the end of the sketch I had crawled into a costume hamper with my fingers in my ears, worn out with the stress of trying to read what I could hear of the audience's response. It seemed to my increasingly frantic imagination as though the whole act was running twice as long as before, maybe three times. I could only assume that was because of all the brilliant new sequences Chaplin had added, and my heart sank lower and lower as the blood pounded in my ears.

After an eternity of torment there was suddenly a blaze of light. I looked up to see Mike Asher in his referee's outfit holding the lid of the hamper up and gazing down at me.

"There you are!" he cried. "Whatever are you doing?"

"I lost my ... er ... never mind," I said, clambering out awkwardly.

"And with instinctive improvisational skills like that, how can he fail?" Mike crowed, and I punched him on the arm.

"Well?" I said, kicking the door to. "How was it? How was he?"

"Young Mister C? Oh, he was a revelation! Such panache! Such finesse! He's still up there now taking the audience's applause, even though the act finished a quarter of an hour ago and there are four synchronised unicyclists trying to form a pyramid behind ... ow!"

He rubbed his arm where I had thumped him again, looking faintly aggrieved.

"*Really*, how was it?"

"You really want to know?"

"Of course!"

Mike shrugged. "Ennnh..."

"Well, what does that mean?"

"Ennnh... It means ... it was all right, I suppose. Nothing special. Not quite as good as Weldon. Nowhere near as good as he thinks he is – well, how could he possibly be? Started well, but lost them in the middle I'd say."

I was fit to burst now. "What do you mean 'lost them in the middle'? What *happened?*"

"Well, it was rather peculiar," Mike said. "He started in on this new bit of business he'd worked out with Fred Spiksley and Jimmy Crabtree. It was kind of a sentimental interlude, right in the middle of the biggest action bit, and I don't know if they messed it up or something, because the audience just seemed to get, well, a bit bored, really, and he never got them back. Afterwards Charlie was furious, and Fred and Jimmy were trying to apologise, but Syd was just fending them off and shooing Charlie away. Who knows?"

"Ha!" I punched my fist into the palm of my other hand. "He ballsed it up, in other words!"

"Well, it wasn't bad, as I said, it was just ... ennnh."

Even though I hadn't seen it, I knew in a flash of inspiration what Charlie had done. He'd been faced with an audience desperate for entertainment, and he'd tried to give them 'art'. Art with a capital 'A'.

Well, I thought. *Ennnh.* That'll do me. Perhaps the game wasn't entirely up. Not yet.

The bar at the Oxford was heaving with well-oiled Karno folk. It was the place to be that night, and no mistake.

My old drinking pals Bert Darnley and Chas Sewell came over at once to wish me luck. The lads had seen Charlie's performance in the matinée, and were rubbing their hands together with glee.

"It's an open goal, I'm telling you!" Bert crowed.

"It's true," Chas insisted. "You're odds on, now, that's the word."

He nodded over to the far end of the bar, where Fred Spiksley and Jimmy Crabtree were taking money hand over fist. They had been running their book all week, but grumbling and moaning the while about how the odds on Charlie and me were so level that they would struggle to make a killing. Now, though, it appeared that everyone wanted to bet on me, and Fred and Jimmy were taking the bets on, I presumed out of loyalty to Charlie's cause and the fervent guilty hope that they hadn't helped to sink it. It occurred to me that I could really put the cat among the pigeons for them if I let on how much reason Karno had not to favour me.

Billy Wragg saw me looking over the business they were doing, and raised his pint to me in a cheery salute. Then Alf Reeves appeared at my elbow and guided me away to a quiet corner.

"Now then, Arthur," he said. "You're well prepared?"

"I am," I said.

"Good," Alf said, fixing me with a serious look. "Now listen. You go out there and do your best. Don't go half-hearted, thinking the Guv'nor won't give you a fair crack of the whip. He's a businessman first and foremost, and if you show him you're the better bet he'll pick you, never mind what passed between you. My word on it. All right?"

"Yes, Alf," I said, feeling better every moment that passed. "Thanks."

He nodded, patted me on the arm, went about his business, and George Robey, of all people, wandered over.

"Hail fellow well met!" he boomed, as was his wont.

"George," I said, shaking him by the hand. "What are you doing here?"

"I wouldn't miss this, my dear chap. Never been anything like it! Positively gladiatorial! Comedy as combat! Could be the next big thing."

"Oh, I don't know about that," I said.

"Yes indeed. I'll tell you what you need. You need a fair damsel's favour to wear to the lists. That's right. Excuse me, my dear..."

George waylaid a passing wench by placing his hand on her arm.

"I wonder if I might trouble you for a handkerchief?" he asked with exaggerated courtesy. She turned with a smile to give him what he asked for, and it was Tilly, of course. When she saw me she flushed, and we stood speechless in front of one another as George twittered on innocently.

"Here you are, Sir Arthur," he said, handing me the handkerchief. "Tuck this about your person, and when you are victorious, as surely you must be, then you can claim the hand of the fair Lady...?" Here he raised an inquisitive eyebrow.

"Matilda," Tilly murmured frostily.

"Lady Matilda, quite so, as your own. And you, my dear, must be sure to claim your prize!"

He ground to a halt, finally, seemingly unaware that the temperature in the vicinity had dropped a good few degrees, and let Tilly go, which she did with considerable dispatch, weaving away through the throng. George watched her appreciatively, then gave me a hearty nudge.

"Pretty little thing," he said. "There, now, don't say I never do anything for you."

Ralph Luscombe was there, of course. My patron, as he insisted on calling himself. I had written to him about the contest, and he couldn't keep away, despite the ongoing threat from his brother to send him to South America.

"I have five pounds riding on you. Spiksley is adamant that Charlie will still win, but I have every confidence, every confidence, old chap."

He paused to sip his drink, a dry sherry, and let his eyes roam around the busy bar.

"This really is the most tremendously exciting evening," he enthused. "Look, there is Fred Kitchen, and Johnny Doyle, and George Robey, and Jimmy Russell – oh listen to me, you know all these fellows. Good Heavens! Is that not Marie Lloyd?! My my...!

I began to feel oppressed by the weight of expectation pressing down on my shoulders. Time to leave, I thought.

"I need to go and get ready," I said to Luscombe, who winked conspiratorially.

"Of course, my dear fellow, no need to explain to me. I am in the business, after all. Best of British!"

———

Later I stood in the wings by myself as *The Football Match* got under way. I was nervous, yes, but confident too. My chief concern was not about the act, which I knew was a banker. It was whether the Power would be with me now, when I needed it the most.

The Power, you see, was by its very nature a thing only partly under my control. The part of it that derived from my own skill and my own personality, well, that was up to me to deliver. But part of it depended on establishing a rapport with that particular audience on that particular night, and that always carried an element of the unknown.

This is why, in short, so many comedians turn to drink.

Will Poluski was getting some nice laughs as the Villain, more than he was used to since he had now incorporated some of Charlie's touches, and then there was my cue.

On I strode, out into the lights, out where I belonged, and within half a minute I knew that this was one of those nights when the Power was oozing freely from my very fingertips. The audience positively lapped me up, and enjoyment ricocheted around the auditorium.

This was going to be a good one.

My first scene with Poluski went like a dream. I could see a veritable ocean of happy faces beaming back at me. I picked off the moments neatly, not too showily, leaving something in the bank for later.

The second scene, too, went breezily enough, and I knew the best was yet to come.

Then it happened. A cry, clear as a bell, came from the stalls below me.

"Oi! Goalie! You stink!"

I was stunned at first. I could see the faces looking up at me, and picked out the speaker quite easily. He was looking me right in the eye for one thing, a smug grin on his stupid face. For another clue, all the people around him had turned to look at him.

I shall never forget that face. The man was large, and his features were ruddy and pockmarked. He was bald on top, and the back of his head was surrounded by a crazed halo of ginger hair. His nose was huge and swollen, and seemed to be divided into two distinct yet uneven lobes, so that – there is no particularly delicate way to phrase this, so I'm just going to say it – so that it looked like nothing so much as a pair of testicles.

My apprehension of this peculiar vision was the work of an instant, as the Power was exercising its particular control over the seeming passage of time.

What the Power does, one of the ways in which it works, is it corrals an audience together, shapes it into one organism with one mind, and then you can take it with you wherever you wish to lead it. That one discordant voice, shouting from the one-and-sixpennies, shatters the fragile illusion. Suddenly it is not one audience in front of you, one single entity, suddenly it is hundreds of different entities with hundreds of different faces, each of whom may have its own separate opinion. It's like trying to ride three horses at once, and all three want to go in different directions.

The Power, if it is with you, can retrieve this situation. You bend the audience to your will, and mould them together once again. The solo act can address his tormentor directly, and humiliate him or win him over, thus isolating him from the whole or absorbing him into it. For the team player, such as myself on that night, it's trickier, but still feasible, and I set about it with a will. We continued, and shortly I felt it again, felt the Power emanating from me, embracing the room, caressing it into submission.

Laughter rolled in from the back of the stalls in waves, and I rode it like a bareback rider. Comfort, confidence, control, all returned.

Then it came again.

"Oi! Goalie! You stink!"

I looked out into the stalls, and Mr Testicle-nose had his arms crossed and was smirking triumphantly back at me. Those in the neighbouring seats were beginning to grumble at him, but he was unperturbed.

Yet again I felt the reins yanked from my grasp, but gathered them up again. On I pressed, and the sketch was so reliably funny, and this fellow's opinion of my performance so unsupported by the public at large, that I soon had them again where I wanted them. There was an extra edge to the laughter now, as if people wished to show this witless, gonad-faced rogue what it was to be lonely.

I was building up now to the climactic part of the scene before the actual match itself begins. It was a nice moment, and required the timing to be just so. Sure enough, right at the crucial split-second there was his rasping bellow: "Oi! Goalie! You stink!"

The joke shattered in pieces at my feet, and so perfectly was it done that I found myself distracted by the sudden suspicion that a deliberate sabotage was being done, and a distraction like that, trust me, is instant death to comedy. Time seemed now to be speeding up for me where before it was supernaturally slowed, and I barely remembered that I was supposed to exit the stage so that Mike Asher as the Referee could begin the cup final. I caught one last glimpse of Testicle-nose sneering at me, and for that moment I wanted nothing more than to just leap down into the stalls and smash his idiotic face in. To my intense gratification, I then saw a right-thinking individual lean forward from behind the fool and cuff him really hard around the ear.

This pleasant image revived my spirits as I waited in the wings, composing myself to embark upon the final scene, Stiffy the Goalkeeper's finest hour, listening to Mike introducing the various players one by one. Each attracted a huge roar, and the atmosphere, as ever, was not so very far from that of a real football match. My heart was racing, and a muck sweat was trickling down my spine, but I comforted myself with the thought that from now on Testicle-nose could shout whatever he liked and nobody would be any the wiser.

On I went, to an encouraging roar of my own, and the big match pantomime began to trundle along on its well-rehearsed way. I risked a single glance towards my enemy, but couldn't pick him out. Maybe someone had sat on him.

Things were once again going well. All my thoughts now were of the special bit of business I had worked out with Billy Wragg. I had tried nothing new so far, but this, if it came off, would draw gasps from the crowd and, I hoped, even Mr Karno himself.

Here came the moment. The ball was loose in the centre of the apron. Billy would brace his leg behind the ball and I would dive at his feet at full pelt. Every time we had practised this there was a satisfying reaction from our colleagues, as there was a really meaty smack. It was a variation on rolling with a punch, really. A really hefty-seeming collision, but nobody got hurt.

The Power was with me again by this time, and I saw the whole thing in every detail.

The ball.

Billy's big tree trunk of a leg telescoping out.

Myself, leaping, flying through the air.

Billy's boot, not disappearing behind the ball, but rising up and over it.

Myself, puzzled as I flew unstoppably towards him.

Billy's boot, with all his considerable weight behind it, crunching into my kneecap, with all my weight behind that.

There was a gasp all right. The collective intake of breath nearly brought the tabs down.

I knew something was terribly wrong. A cloud of pain engulfed me, and the world seemed to grind to a halt. I looked up at Wragg, a malicious gleam in his eye as he followed through. I could see the hairs standing up on his great white ham of a thigh, braced against my knee. Then I looked out into the stalls. Every face I could see had an appalled expression on it. Mouths were open, horrified hands were flying to eyes, blood was draining rapidly from features. I saw one woman gasp and then suddenly lurch forward retching into her handkerchief.

This wasn't good, not by a long chalk. I hadn't been in show business all that long, but even I knew that if your audience had started retching then you'd probably lost them. Suddenly I wanted to retch myself, but somehow I gathered myself together, remembered where I was and what I was doing. I dragged myself up – how, I don't know – with all my weight on my left leg, and I reached down behind and thumped my right leg back into line with a wet sort of crunch.

Flashing lights twinkled madly at the edge of my vision and I felt on the verge of fainting. As I'd thumped it, the knee had made a wet sort of crunching, squelching noise, but everything seemed to pop back roughly where it was meant to be, and gradually my head seemed to clear. Suddenly, stupidly, I began to believe everything was going to be all right. I tried, gamely, to step to my

330

right and the leg just buckled under me, sending me sprawling. I registered more horrified gasps from those close enough to see the detail of what was going on.

I saw Testicle-nose, mopping his freckled brow with a spotted kerchief.

Looked into his eyes.

And then I passed out.

PART IV

28
THE SOCIALIST

THE college was a quiet place over Christmas. The young gentlemen had all gone down to celebrate with their families at their various piles, or else in the South of France and even further afield. Only the usual handful of elderly single dons were still in residence to be attended to over Yuletide. Not a deal of point even pinning up the mistletoe, to be frank.

My time with the Karno company would have seemed like a strange, far-off dream, were it not for the stud marks from Billy Wragg's boot on my knee, and the nine-inch scar running North-South where the surgeon had opened up my leg to root around in there for the halves of my shattered kneecap. Not to mention the crutch I still needed to hobble about on a whole month and a half later.

So there I was, back in the ivy-clad embrace of college life, and back in the bosom of my family. Not that they made a deal of a fuss about it. When I first arrived back, I limped painfully into the kitchens to greet my mother, who was just then engaged in making several hundred mince pies, by the look of things, each of which would bear an imprint of the college crest, and she looked up, smiled and said: "Hullo, dear," then carried right on with her work. I wondered if she'd even noticed that I'd been away for a couple of years.

I found my brother polishing shoes, and he squinted semi-curiously at the crutch I was leaning on.

"Hurt your poor little leg, is it?" he said with withering mock concern.

"Broke it," I replied, not particularly wishing to go into details.

"When I was fighting the Boer," Lance said, without a pause in his shoe shining. "Bloke standing next to me had his leg shot clean off, and he still drove off the bastards with an empty gun and a bayonet. Hopped after them, he did, screaming like a banshee."

"Oh?" I said nonchalantly. I was secretly impressed, as Lance very rarely spoke of his time in South Africa.

"Yeah," he said. "So don't be such a cissy."

Welcome home, Arthur.

———

My father was delighted to have me back at the college, thus, to his way of thinking, proving that he had been right all along and the theatre was "something I needed to get out of my system". He was planning to have me back in harness for the start of the new term in January, and to that end was diligently working on my fitness. The doctor had told me that I should be perfectly mobile again once I had built up the muscles in my leg that had wasted away through forced inactivity, and what better way to accomplish this, my father reasoned, than resuming college rounds?

And so I found myself every morning, noon and night limping

around the old circuit, past the still-ghastly Wren chapel, past the red-brick library, past Pitt the Younger, past the Master's Lodge and its lily pond, down to the New Court that was older than many a college's Old Court, back up under the arch between the kitchens and the dining hall, and back to the fireside at the porter's lodge.

As I walked I pondered over and over again the same question: what the hell *happened*?

I had only my own vague shadowy remembrances and a smattering of anecdotal evidence to go on as I struggled to make sense of it all.

After I passed out at the Oxford I was carried from the stage unconscious, thus missing the traditional cry of: "Is there a doctor in the house?"

There was, apparently, a deal of confusion as to what would happen then. At that point there were over a hundred people on the stage, twenty-two footballers and eighty supers, not to mention my pal Mike the Referee. Kent and Keith, a right pair of banjo-toting chancers, saw their chance of saving the day in front of Fred Karno, and were trying to drop the tabs in so they could begin some of their inane crosstalk, but before that calamity could occur, why, what was this?

Another Stiffy the Goalkeeper pranced onto the stage, in identical costume, but with two fully operational lower limbs, and the sketch, the well-oiled machine, resumed where it had left off and played to its triumphant conclusion almost as if nothing at all had happened.

Yes, Charlie Chaplin saved the day! He was the hero of the hour! My one consolation was that I remained spark out and missed the whole thing.

When I awoke I quickly wished that I had not. The pain in

my knee was excruciating, and to make matters worse I had been laid on a chaise longue backstage just a couple of yards away from what seemed to be a victory celebration.

A doctor had materialised, and he had secured some ether. He was not especially expert in administering it, however – Mike Asher told me afterwards that he suspected the man was actually a veterinarian – so the next few minutes I passed in a sort of dreamlike semi-consciousness, from which I retained only fleeting and impressionistic recollections, such as:

The anxious face of Ralph Luscombe peering over the doctor's shoulder.

Chaplin being carried around on the shoulders of Fred Spiksley and Jimmy Crabtree.

Karno leaning over me, and saying: "You had yer chance, an' you blew it!"

Ralph Luscombe in urgent discussion with Alf Reeves, frowning, nodding.

Tilly clapping and smiling, and then embracing Charlie when the footballers finally dropped him to the ground.

The whole crowd of them parting as I hovered magically in mid air and passed amongst them – I appreciate now that I was being carried from the building – and faces looking down at me, some pitying, but most laughing.

The shock of the cold night air as I was bundled towards a waiting hansom.

Wal Pink shaking his head sorrowfully, and saying: "You know, funny thing, I told him to break his leg..."

Loafing against the wall outside the stage door, the malevolent leering face and ginger halo of Mr Testicle-nose, tucking a bunch of fivers into his jacket pocket.

Syd Chaplin glancing furtively at me, and then ducking back into the warmth of the theatre.

Then the ether won its final victory over my senses, and when I woke once more it was the next day, and I was in a hospital bed.

Winter sunlight streamed in through the windows. I looked around and saw several bunches of flowers by my bedside. My right leg was bandaged and plastered from hip to ankle, and itched damnably, although blessedly the pain of the night before had receded. I could not get up and move about, so I resigned myself to lying there waiting for an explanation to present itself, which in due course it did, courtesy of my first visitor, Mr Alfred Reeves, esquire.

"What ho, Alf!" I said feebly, as he hoved into view.

"Good afternoon, Arthur," Alf said, taking a seat by my bed. "How does it feel?"

"Sore," I said.

"I'll bet," Alf grimaced at the plaster cast on my leg. "Still, it will be right as rain in a month or two, I'm told, and for that you can thank your college chum."

"Mr Luscombe?"

"Splendid young fellow. He has secured you the very best of care from a specialist surgeon who it seems is an old friend of his family, so things could be much worse."

I nodded. "He's a good sort. And is he ... well, is he *paying* for all this, too?" I waved my hands to indicate the hospital room, which was well above the average, in my estimation.

"Oh, by no means," Alf said. "He offered, but it was not necessary to trouble him."

I frowned. "Who then? The Guv'nor, I suppose? Takes care of his own?"

"Wrong again," said Alf. "No, any and all bills are to be sent, at her express instruction, to Miss Marie Lloyd."

Well, I was flabbergasted. I had never met the lady, although I knew her by sight, of course, for hers was one of the most famous faces in the country.

"What?" I said. "But why on earth would...?" And words failed me. Alf fixed me with a glistening gaze, apparently moved by what he had to say.

"It took a deal of courage to stand up to Karno the way you did, Arthur me lad, and it has not gone unnoticed. Edith is not without good and loyal friends in the world, and they appreciate what you did for her, appreciate it very much. Marie Lloyd is one such, and I am another, and let me assure you that you will find us grateful. There it is, let me not go on about it, for I shall embarrass us both."

So, it appeared that I had acquired the aspect of a knight in shining armour. No one but myself (and Tilly, of course) knew of the provocation I had for bearding the Guv'nor in his den that day, and the story being put about by good old Alf was that I had taken an heroic and righteous moral stand against my scheming boss on poor Edith Karno's behalf, with a selfless lack of regard to the damage this might do to my own prospects.

And once I was recovered enough to return to Streatham I found that Charley and Clara Bell could not do enough for me, and Edith herself and Freddie K junior were frequent and attentive visitors. I had cakes, and sweets, and jellied fruits, and endless cups of tea, and plumped pillows, until I began to feel quite the fraud. It began to oppress me, to be honest, which is how I came to consider returning to Cambridge for a spell, and now that I was here it was harder and harder to imagine ever going back.

The new term came around, and the college filled up once again with bright young things. I was finding it easier every day to move around, now, with the help of a cane from the porter's lodge's lost property cupboard, even though the knee still looked like a badly made mailbag, improbably lumpy and haphazardly stitched.

I kept my head down and got on with my various duties. I did the rounds, I took over O and P staircases again, I fetched, I carried, I laundered, I swept. I served the port at High Table, although not yet able to manage the heavier trays with any confidence.

I even caught one young gentleman sneaking in after the gates were locked, as Ralph Luscombe had done years – was it years? – earlier. I couldn't give chase because of the knee, of course, but I did manage to trip the fellow up with my cane and extract gate pence from him.

My father was disgustingly happy about how things had turned out, and rarely passed up the opportunity to share his vision for the future with me. This involved passing on more and more responsibility to me and beginning his own slow easing into a comfortable and prestigious armchair of a retirement, during which he would stroll around the college as a much-loved institution.

My own mood was dark, however. The disappointment of the showdown at the Oxford weighed heavily on me, but even that was not as burdensome as the recollection of how things stood between myself and Tilly.

It was still hard to even think of her and Karno together that afternoon.

Karno unbuckling his belt.

It was even harder to remember her small voice saying: "It was for you, Arthur. So I could be with you..."

Karno giving a little cough.

There was not even much comfort in the memory of the magical time we spent together on that tour masquerading as man and wife, for I had messed that up, and then just as surely messed everything up again.

More and more I would slip out of the front gate once dinner was done, and nip down to the river for a swift pint or three at the Mill. There I would usually sit by myself, trying to force my brain not to think about Charlie as a number-one comic. Beer helped, but not much, even though I was now following the advice of the great Gus Elen and having at least'arf a pint of ale at every meal, including breakfast, and another meal or two besides that I'd invented between luncheon and supper.

I puzzled away relentlessly at the events of that night at the Oxford. The more I thought about it, the more I thought I had something. I remembered Spiksley and Crabtree running their book on the contest between myself and Chaplin, complaining that we were too evenly matched. I remembered their special rehearsals with my rival, and Billy Wragg offering his services in a similar regard to me. Then Charlie's performance went badly, thanks to the two of them, and the odds suddenly became a lot more interesting. Was it not possible that the footballers had deliberately sabotaged Charlie, so that they would then be able to take heavy bets on me from the likes of Ralph Luscombe, knowing that Wragg was going to ruin my chances in turn? It was more than possible. The swine were easily selfish enough and venal enough to devise a scheme of that sort.

I vented my furious imaginings on the footballers, then, as Charlie and I seemed to be mere pawns in their game. In fact, I reasoned, the whole contest had actually been decided on the toss of a coin in Karno's office.

Even though I was not, now I think of it, happy, I had decided that the college was going to be my life from now on. How could I return to the Fun Factory now? My relationship with Karno was surely in ruins. And how could I even contemplate the humiliation of working under Charlie, still less having to meet Tilly again. I tried to put the whole thing from my mind, but it was hard, it was hard.

One afternoon I popped into a cake shop – Fitz's, around the corner from the porter's lodge – to collect some pink coconut confections that a Mr Vermont on one of my staircases was particularly fond of, and who should be there taking tea with a bunch of hangers-on and acolytes but The Rotter, Harry Rotten-burg, large as life, the progenitor of the mechanical brontosaurus which had propelled me into show business. Well, regurgitated me into show business.

I could not resist introducing myself.

"What ho, Rotter," I said, at his shoulder. He was in mid-anecdote, and turned to see who had dared to interrupt his flow. His florid face clouded as he tried to place me.

"Dandoe," I said. "*The Varsity B.C.*" I turned to his companions while he digested this. "I got eaten by a mechanical dinosaur. Marvellous fun."

"Indeed! Indeed!" the Rotter cried once the light had dawned, standing to pump my hand warmly. "How do ye do, my dear fellow? How do ye do? Will you join us?"

I held up the box of coconut treats by the string, and explained that, sadly, I was expected back at the college.

"Well, look here, you absolutely *must* come to the show..." He snapped his fingers at a disciple, who fumbled in his coat pocket and came up with a small fly sheet. "Tonight we try out my latest. Come and see!"

And so that night, instead of disappearing down to the pub to wallow in misery and ale, as had become my habit, I took myself off to see the show at the New Theatre. It was the first night of a Footlights effort, written, naturally, by The Rotter himself, a self-styled musical satire entitled *The Socialist*, ridiculing the political ideas being espoused by Mr Shaw, Mr Wells and the Fabian Society.

The idea of the piece involved a college succumbing to socialism, with hilarious consequences. The students marked their own examinations, and awarded each other firsts. In a society where everyone is equal, you see, what is the point of a second-class degree?

Now this show may sound flimsy and insubstantial, but it forcibly reminded me of something else I had turned my back on. Those Footlights boys were not a patch on the Fun Factory journeymen I had been used to working with, but watching them made me think of what it was like to be on the stage. It made me think of the Power, frankly, and whether I would ever feel anything so intoxicating again. I found I missed it like a physical pain.

Then there was the ridiculous play itself, with its "Yah-boo-sucks to the workers!" It brought home to me that if I were to continue as I was, as a college servant, then I would always belong to that downtrodden and unregarded class, always be a-tugging my forelock, always be serving the port, making the beds and clearing up after the young gentlemen.

Whereas at the Fun Factory, it struck me, one man was reckoned superior to another only by virtue of his talents. And when we Karno boys were travelling from city to city, peering out of the railway train windows at the factories and cobbled streets where the workers lived, or at the fancier toffs' dwellings on the hills, did we really see anywhere we would rather be? We were the chosen ones. We could do the things, and go to the places, and live the lives they could only dream of...

It was useless to dwell on it, though. That part of my life was over. Karno was done with, comedy was done with, for I could not bear to start from scratch somewhere else, or as a solo. Chaplin, our rivalry, was behind me, and Tilly – *ah, Tilly!* – how could I look her in the eye again?

Nothing, I thought, would induce me to go within fifty miles of the blasted Fun Factory ever again.

Until one spring morning a crisp white envelope arrived at the porter's lodge bearing my name.

An invitation to a wedding.

29
LET ME CALL YOU SWEETHEART

EASTER Saturday was a sweltering hot spring day, and I found myself dressed to the nines and crammed into Brompton Oratory together with the cream of the British music hall. As the matrimonials were concluded I glanced around the assembled crowd and felt the honour of being invited to this gathering, for you could hardly have afforded such a bill unless you were the Royal Command performance itself. The first of those, incidentally, was still a couple of years off, I think I'm right in saying, and Marie Lloyd was not invited to take part – how about that? Too saucy, apparently. Nor was Fred Karno, the single biggest draw in the world of the music hall, invited to submit a contribution to the entertainment.

Marie Lloyd was at this particular do, though, as were George Robey, Gus Elen, Albert Chevalier and many more, as well as theatre managers and impresarios from across the capital. Alf Reeves was clearly a popular figure on the music hall scene, and there was quite a turnout to celebrate his nuptials. Happy though I was for old Alf, it wasn't my friendship with him that had brought me all the way down from Cambridge. It was his bride, lovely little Amy Minister, who had been on that *Mumming Birds* tour with me so many months before. She was friendly with Tilly Beckett, you see, and it was the chance of seeing her that had enlivened my every waking moment since the invitation had arrived, and had sent me running for the London train at the crack of dawn.

The Karno organisation was such a sensitive and hierarchical monster that Alf and Amy had had to restrict their invitations to the top level, or else invite absolutely everyone, so only the top number ones were there. Fred Kitchen, Billie Ritchie, Jimmy Russell and Johnny Doyle were in attendance, and so, sitting together near the front, were Syd and Charlie Chaplin. The whole affair's culminating act of diplomacy was the installation of the Guv'nor himself as Alf's best man. Anything else was unthinkable.

Karno had been the very soul of generosity, and had not only volunteered the use of the entire fleet of Karno company omnibuses to transport the assembled multitude to the reception, but had also offered up the Fun Factory itself to host the occasion.

After the nuptials were officially concluded, we spilled out into the sunshine and crammed higgledy-piggledy into the conveyances like a bunch of kids going to the seaside. The non-Karno people were not aware that the lower levels were strictly for the senior performers, of course, so I found myself cheerfully crammed on the open top deck between the celebrated Mr Elen and Miss Lloyd, who waved at a few dozen star spotters on the pavement below.

Off we rattled over the river towards Camberwell, and I took the opportunity to introduce myself to the great Marie.

"Miss Lloyd?" I said. "We haven't met, although I have written to you to thank you for your generosity when my knee was broken. I am Arthur Dandoe."

347

"Of course you are!" the great comedienne cried. "I recognises you, Arthur, an' I recalls your letter. Most gracious it was. I'm very pleased to make your acquaintance at last."

"Let me say again how grateful I am for your help," I said. "It was much appreciated."

"Well," Marie said, leaning in and confiding in hushed tones. "What you did was much appreciated by me, and all of Edith's friends, so let's say no more about it."

She patted me on the chest in a friendly manner, and I only discovered later that she had slipped a five-pound note into my inside pocket. I did feel something of a fraud, I must confess. Didn't give it back, though.

The Fun Factory was transformed for the reception, with cream-coloured ribbons and yellow flowers, and running along the back wall was the big backdrop from *The Football Match*, which had been painted over so that the crowd were sporting buttonholes and top hats.

I was seated with Edith Karno and her party, next to Freddie and across from Clara and Charley Bell. They were all delighted to see me and treated me like some kind of martyred hero, which was a little embarrassing.

The wedding party processed to the top table, and as they did so some unseen hand flicked a switch on the big fans so that the arms on the backdrop waved in the air. Nice effect.

Alf and Amy made their way to the position of honour, wreathed in smiles. Then came Karno and Maria, who tried to ignore our table completely as they passed, but Karno caught sight of me there and turned to stare, his eyes narrowing in surprise. I stared right back. I didn't work for him any more, and I didn't care what he thought of me.

Then came the bridesmaids, two of Amy's sisters and – my goodness! – Tilly Beckett, looking a real picture, with her hair fully restored to its natural golden colour, and her green eyes twinkling with happiness for her friend. I couldn't take my eyes off her.

As luncheon was served I turned to Freddie.

"That crowd scene will need a bit of cleaning up after this, won't it?" I said.

"Oh, *The Football Match* is long gone," Freddie said. "Did you not hear?"

"Hear?" I asked. "Hear what?"

"Oh well, a few days after that business at the Oxford – must have been the very day you left for Cambridge, I should think – young Chaplin went down with bad laryngitis. Couldn't say a dicky bird. Well, if only *you* hadn't..." He waved a fork at my knee, and I completed his thought.

"...hadn't been crocked, I would have been right there to step in, wouldn't I?" I sighed. "So, what, Will Poluski did it? Or who?"

"No, the Guv'nor pulled the show entirely, scrapped it, cancelled all the bookings."

"He did *what?*"

"He got wind that some of those football fellows had mucked about with the shows because of some gambling scheme that they had cooked up, and he was so furious that he took it as a perfect opportunity to sack them all. I've never seen him so angry. He swears he'll never employ any of them ever again."

Ha, I thought. Retribution! Justice! Comeuppance! Eat that, you money-grabbing swine!

"Do you know, I thought it might be that way," I said. "So Billy Wragg broke my knee on purpose, d'you think?"

Freddie shrugged. "That one was sacked before the curtain hit the apron," he said. "The Guv'nor did it himself. He was livid."

I could see Syd and Charlie Chaplin sitting together at the opposite side of the room. "So, if not *The Football Match*, what is Charlie doing now?"

"New piece," Freddie said, chomping on a bit of beef. "Called *Skating*. On roller skates. Two companies. Syd's number one of one, and Charlie's the number one of the other."

Suddenly I didn't feel like finishing my food.

After the meal there were speeches, of course. I remember Karno's best man speech well. He seemed to have the idea that we would like to hear a speech about himself, rather than the bride or groom particularly. After all, Alf and Amy worked for him fifty-two weeks of the year, so his story was their story, in a way, was how he set it up.

He told us a tale of how he had first come to London. Like many successful fellows, he enjoyed laying it on about how poor he had been to begin with, and even reverted to his thicker accent to remind us of his humble roots. He'd found himself on his uppers, and he and a pal had decided to work their way down to the capital to try their fortune. Young Karno had got hold of a glazier's kit, and they tramped from town to town mending windows and getting by that way. Until they hit a rough patch.

"We come to this village, see," the Guv'nor recounted, one thumb tucked into his waistcoat. "And we hadn't a bean, not even t' price of a cup o' tea, and there was no jobs to do. So we sat there on a wall, glum like, an' I says to Tom: 'See that shop winder over there? That winder could just break tonight, and in t' morning they'd be glad to 'ave it fixed.'

"That night I slipped back into that village, bunged a brick through this winder and a branch through that, an' when we came along in t' morning shoutin' 'Winders to mend?' the whole town come a-runnin'! An' that's how we made it down to London. Smashin' winders at night, an' mendin' 'em in t' mornin'!"

Sound familiar, that story? Thought it might...[11]

Karno then moved on to his solemn duty of offering a toast to the lovely bridesmaids. I saw a look pass between the Guv'nor and Tilly as he raised his glass, and struggled to interpret it. The image of the 'guvving' forced itself upon me for the umpteenth time, but his crooked smile looked, what...? Hopeful...? Or was I the optimist?

"So when are you coming back, then?" Freddie asked me suddenly. "Clara's kept your room for you, haven't you, Clara?"

"Of course I have," Clara said cheerily.

"Oh, well, I'm not sure the Guv'nor would have me back, after..."

"Oh nonsense," Clara said. "He's hardly spoken to Charley for nearly ten years, has he Charley, but he knows a good man when he's got one."

People were beginning to mill about, now, in search of drink and conversation, so I excused myself and went for a wander rather than let them pursue the matter. Almost immediately I bumped into George Craig, last seen storming out of the Enterprise after being summarily fired, making his way back to his table with a couple of frothing glasses of champers.

"Hullo, George," I said. "I thought you were working for Wal Pink."

"No, no," George said with an almighty wink. "I'm working for the Guv'nor. Don't you worry about that."

And off he went to join Lillie. I reckoned one way or another George must be a better actor than I'd ever given him credit for.

I found myself a vantage point where I could watch Tilly. She was smiling, fending off the drunken attentions of Billy Reeves, Alf's brother. I found myself close to the table where the Chaplin brothers were sitting, and when I glanced that way I caught Charlie looking at me. He beamed brightly all of a sudden, and bounced over to where I was standing. Grasping my hand and shaking it vigorously, he made a great business of inspecting my right trouser leg, as though he could see through it to the knee inside.

"Arthur! How marvellous that you are here! Are you recovered?"

"I'll manage," I said, holding up the cane I now walked with.

"Terrible business, that was, terrible. We were all terribly shocked, and worried about you, you know?"

A brief mental image from the Oxford surfaced, of Chaplin being carried around on shoulders celebrating while an incompetent veterinarian overdosed me with ether.

"And, you know, I'd much rather have won that contest fair and square, and I would have done, I think. Well, you know I would have, don't you? Deep down?"

"I ... er..." I spluttered, but Charlie was chattering away, a bag of nerves.

"And I know I didn't come to visit you, and I should have, I should have, but you haven't congratulated me on my success either, now have you?" And he poked me in the chest reprovingly.

"Well ... congratulations," I managed to make myself say.

"Thank you, Arthur, thank you kindly. Better man won, eh?"

"I didn't say *that* exactly," I said, but his nervous chatter just rolled over it.

"Good, good, and so ... are you back in harness, so to speak?"

"No, no, I'm just down for the day."

"So when can we expect you to return to the strength?" he said, punching me playfully on the bicep.

"I'm not ... I'm working at the old college again. I'm not coming back."

He was shocked for a moment, and then the relief washed over his features. He couldn't hide it.

"So-o-o-o! Cambridge's gain is comedy's loss, eh? Well, well, well. It's a great pity, in a way, because I really think one day you might have been almost as good as me."

"You what?!"

"And you know things really are going *tremendously well* for me just at the moment."

Suddenly, with a rustle of skirts, Tilly was beside him. I saw her slip her arm into the crook of his, and she was whispering into his ear before she recognised who he was talking to.

"Shall we get some champagne?" she said, and Charlie glanced at me apprehensively. She followed his eyes, and her mouth popped open into an O of surprise.

"Hullo, Tilly," I said, my heart racing. "I hope I find you well?"

"Yes," she said, collecting herself quickly. "And you? Your injury?"

I shrugged, nodded, held up my cane. I wanted to speak but no words would come. An awkward pause was developing, until Charlie clapped his hands smartly. "Well. Let us find ourselves some champagne, shall we?" He pressed his forehead to Tilly's in a two-turtle-dovey gesture then patted me on the arm in a way which made it clear that I was not invited along. "Delighted to see you up and about, old chap!"

I watched them go, arm in arm. So that was how things were now, I thought. Chaplin had my career, and he had my girl. Maybe he *was* just the better man, and that was that.

I began to feel I couldn't get my breath, that I needed to go outside. The desire to take back the things I had said to Tilly was like a physical pain. What did it matter if she had done what she needed to do in order to get herself a job with Karno? She had come back from Paris to be with *me*. What did any amount of 'guvving' matter? Really?

Suddenly Charlie was back at my elbow. "Listen," he said. "You're not going to make a scene, are you? All's fair in love and war, all that?"

I shook him off and headed for the street. It crossed my bitter mind that I should just tell him about Tilly's audition with Karno, and that such was his romantic inclination to place women upon pedestals that he might then have dropped her at once like a hot coal, but I couldn't really do that. I had done enough.

Outside the Fun Factory I lit a cigarette and loosened my shirt buttons, trying to calm down. It was late afternoon by this time, and there were groups of Karno performers hanging around waiting for the omnibuses to take them to the evening shows. They peered through the big double doors at the festivities inside, not venturing in.

I nearly didn't go back in myself, but I decided I couldn't leave after only that ridiculously brief conversation with Tilly.

Inside the tables were pushed to the sides, a band struck up, and dancing got under way. Tilly was sitting by herself now at the top table watching the happy couple twirling away. No time like the present, I thought, and limped over there.

She glanced up at me as I joined her.

"Lovely day," I ventured, and she nodded and smiled.

"That's Amy sorted out now, then," she said.

"I suppose so," I said, not sure quite what she meant.

"Her career is his career, now," Tilly explained. "Alf will manage the shows, and Amy can be in 'em."

"Good luck to them," I said.

"Well. It would not suit me," Tilly said firmly.

"In what way?"

"To have my career determined so by my husband's."

"I see," I said.

"Why should I not have my own career, that's all?" she said. "There's Marie Lloyd, over there look, as big a draw as any in the land, without any help from a husband. Why should I not be able to make my own way?"

I shrugged, then asked: "What are you doing at the moment?"

Tilly paused for a second. "*Skating*," she said then.

"With Charlie?"

"Yes."

She looked down at the table, and I realised I had inadvertently scored a point off her.

"And you?" she said. "When are you returning?"

"I'm not," I said. "That's it for me."

Tilly gasped. "Oh? What a shame!"

"Well," I said. "There it is."

"What a shame!" she said again, and I saw to my surprise that she was becoming upset. "Do you mean to say that you'd really...? Because of...? Oh, you are such a...!"

And she covered her face with her hands and fled from me, pushing her way through the dancers and out of sight. I sat by myself, wondering what had just happened.

The band reached the end of the number, and the dancers came to a halt to applaud them. I watched Alf and Amy, the two of them beaming and out of breath. I was just thinking of slipping quietly away, back to the railway station and up to Cambridge, when I saw a familiar figure, leaning over one of the tables helping himself, and I clapped him heartily on the back.

"Stan! Have you been here all along?"

Stan turned furtively and whispered: "No, I came to get the bus for tonight's shows and I just slipped in. I thought there might be cake. How's the leg?"

"Better, thanks."

It was good to see Stan again. He had been one of my visitors when I left the hospital – he had leaned on my injury, and brought me a gift of hard-boiled eggs and nuts, which made a change from candied fruit. And he'd been making real headway at the Fun Factory while I was away, building up a good reputation for himself.

"Wasn't that Tilly you were just talking to?" he said, munching away. "However did you let that one slip through your fingers?"

"I don't know," I muttered. "I just don't know."

"When I first met you you were pretending to be married, remember that?" he chuckled.

I nodded. How could I have forgotten it? I thought of little else. "They found out about it, though, and Syd gave me the choice to leave Karno or to split up with Tilly, basically."

"And you chose Karno?"

"Well ... I didn't really have the chance ... to actually choose one way or t'other... It's complicated," I said.

"But..." Stan frowned. "However did they find out?"

"Beats me," I said. "No one knew except her and me. We told no one in the company."

Stan had frozen, a piece of wedding cake halfway to his mouth.

"What's up?" I asked.

"You told me."

"Yes, but only you, and you weren't in the company then."

Stan still hadn't moved.

"What is it? What's the matter?"

"Well ... you told me about it that day we had the picnic in Hartlepool, remember? And we laughed so much..."

"I remember..."

"And later, days later, Charlie asked me what was so funny, and ... I knew you two were friends, so I thought what was the harm...? And I ... told him."

Our eyes met, and I knew we were putting it together in the same instant.

Charlie told Syd.

30
JIMMY THE FEARLESS

THE very next morning I sat in a rehearsal room at the Fun Factory, my good knee bouncing up and down with nervous energy.

Charlie sat opposite me, with Tilly. He was perplexed to see me there, you could tell that, and his toe was tapping out an agitated rhythm on his chair leg. Tilly, meanwhile, squinted at me, puzzled.

I looked levelly at Chaplin, enjoying his discomfiture. He had reminded me that it was war. How could I have forgotten?

Also present, and on tenterhooks, were Stan, Mike Asher and Ernie Stone, Albert Austin, the taciturn fellow I knew from *Jail Birds*, Bert Williams and his wife, and Emily Seaman, who was already fluttering her pretty eyelashes at Mike across the room – her husband George was touring in Scotland, I think, at the time – and a couple more I didn't know yet, Harry Daniels and Willy Parsons.

We were waiting for the Guv'nor.

Right at the end of the previous afternoon a large part of the wedding party had been breaking up. The omnibuses were there, loading up with passengers to spread laughter out all over the capital once (or twice) again. Some were staying on, the lucky few who were important enough to be able to take a night off. Suddenly a bunch of well-wishers had dispersed and the bridegroom was by himself for a moment. At last! I'd darted in to take advantage.

"Congratulations, Alf!" I'd said, pumping his hand heartily.

"Thank you, Arthur," he'd replied. He'd seemed distracted. It was his wedding day, after all, and rice had begun to rain down on both of us from the top deck of the nearest bus. I'd decided to get straight to the point.

"Thank you for inviting me," I had said. "I feel privileged."

"The least I could do," he had said, keeping hold of my hand. "And if there's ever anything else I can do for you, you only have to ask."

"There is one thing, as it happens."

"Name it," Alf had said earnestly.

"I want to come back."

As we waited, I thought about the gossip I'd picked up about Charlie. The thing about him, you see – one of the things, anyway – was that he was a truly masterful mimic and mime. Ask him to express an emotion or a fleeting thought even using just the body God gave him, and he was something of a marvel. If you asked him to *speak*, however, he was simply not impressive at all. It was his misfortune, then, to discover that many of the number-one roles he was now expected to shine in required him to master dialogue, and it was eating away at his confidence. It was getting to a point where there were serious mumblings about his position, and his bumptious and annoying confidence of the day before had been masking his very real concern.

359

Then the door banged open, and in came the Guv'nor, as if propelled by a hurricano. When he saw me there he half-stumbled on the threshold, but then pressed on regardless.

"All right you lot, listen to this," he said, gathering us to him. "It is to be an entirely new show, and you are to be the first to play it."

He clutched a script in his hand – I say a script, it was barely more than a few jottings on the back of a receipt for something or other, but that's all his scripts ever amounted to – and he had clearly been in the grip of his legendary creative power. Stan grinned at me. This was exciting. Charlie looked as though he'd been given a week to live.

"The name of the piece is..." He scrabbled for his notes. It was so freshly baked that he could hardly hold onto the thing without oven gloves. "There, that's it. *Jimmy the Fearless.*"

We raised our eyebrows at each other as though those three words conveyed the whole scenario, which of course they didn't. Charlie looked pale.

"Chaplin? You will be Jimmy," the Guv'nor went on, hauling Charlie to his feet and putting his arm round his shoulders as if to walk him through it. "Now Jimmy here ... is a dreamer. He likes nothing more than to lose himself in a penny dreadful, a penny blood, you know the sort of thing. Drives his folks up the wall. His father – that's you, Dandoe..." he said, pointing at me, but not looking at me, "...wants him to settle down, take things a bit more seriously, but no, it's all stories for Jimmy. With me?"

We all nodded vigorously. I closed my eyes and gave silent thanks, to God and to Alf Reeves.

"Right here's the nub of the whole thing," Karno said, and

360

we inched closer in anticipation. "Jimmy falls asleep, and he begins to dream of t' things he has been reading about. Pirates, Red Injuns, bandits, gunfights, swordfights, and so forth. Suddenly..."

"The dreams come to life!"

We all looked around to see who had dared to interrupt the Guv'nor in full flow. It was Stan, the light of enthusiasm shining in his eyes.

"Yes, exactly!" Karno cried, pointing at Stan, not at all put out. In fact he seemed galvanised by Stan's excitement, and began to pace around, waving his arms in the air. "We shall need backdrops painting, so we can switch locations in a flash, and it will be a tremendous adventure at breakneck speed, blah blah blah. You..." – here he indicated Bert Williams – "...are Alkali Ike, the leader of the bandits."

And he went on round the room allocating roles hither and thither. Albert Austin was the Injun chief, Washti-ni Wampum (or Wampum na-Washti: it varied from night to night), Stan and Mike were in the cowboy gang, and also pirates, Ernie would play the bartender in the bar where the big showdown was to take place, and Tilly the beautiful maiden who was held to ransom, and rescued by The Boy 'Ero himself.

The company broke into delighted applause, eager to get started, to flesh out the scheme the Guv'nor proposed. All but Chaplin. He shrugged and sniffed air out from his nose dismissively. He and Karno looked daggers at one another for a moment, then the Guv'nor turned to the rest of us.

"All right, there it is. Get on with it!" He turned on his shiny-shod heel and stalked out.

We threw ourselves into the rehearsals with a will. I had never played in a sketch with Stan before, and was amazed by the way ideas just streamed out of him. Gags here, bits of business there, and we all were carried along by the flow. The piece seemed somehow to be assembling around Charlie, who, in contrast, was a great leaden lump of disinterest bringing the whole thing down. I don't know what was the matter with him, but he seemed to have convinced himself that the whole idea was a bust, and just couldn't get himself up to the starter's mark.

Well, the Guv'nor could hardly fail to notice this when he stopped by to see how things were shaping up, and there was a bit of a scene between the two of them that was more diverting to watch than anything Charlie was contributing to the sketch itself.

"Injuns?" Karno said, after watching us run through what we had so far. "Very good. More of that dancing, that's funny. Alkali Ike? That's all funny too, you and your cowboys. We'll get some more shooting in there, we'll work on that scene when we get the firing caps." He turned to Chaplin. "Jimmy? We need more from you. The whole thing comes from you. We need more energy, more fizz, and we need to find a bit of the old wistful from somewhere too. At the moment you just look like you want to be somewhere else."

"Perhaps I do," Charlie said. The whole room froze and held its breath.

"What?" Karno said icily.

"Perhaps I think the whole thing is just a bit ... silly..."

"*Silly?*" the Guv'nor said, sticking his chest out.

Chaplin looked at his fingernails languidly. "Yes, silly. Cowboys and Injuns. Like something you'd put on for children. I don't know why you reckon so much to it, frankly."

362

"Well perhaps, then, you'd rather not take part in this *silly* children's show at all."

Chaplin shrugged, as if it was a matter of supreme indifference to him.

"In that case," Karno said, cold steel in his voice, "it is fortunate indeed that there is someone already in t' company right now who is ideally suited to take your place..."

My heart stopped.

Here it comes, I thought, all of a sudden. Unbelievably.

Out of absolutely nowhere.

Vindication.

Victory.

All around the room, eyes were darting at me in anticipation. Everyone there remembered the showdown at the Oxford, so if Charlie was being shoved aside, who was the next cab off the rank? Why, yours truly...

"Stan Jefferson," Karno said. "You're Jimmy. Chaplin? Take a fortnight off. Unpaid."

And he strode out of the place. A beat and a half later Charlie picked up his hat and followed, his footsteps echoing in the shocked silence.

━━━━━

No one was more surprised than Stan at his sudden elevation. Having said that, though, we were all pretty surprised. Staggered, actually.

"I want you all to know," he said, breaking the stunned silence, "it isn't going to make a blind bit of difference." He turned to me. "You, fellow, bring me tea, just a splash of milk, and be quick about it!"

This was followed by a huge Stan grin, and a great roar of laughter from everyone, which Charlie must have heard as he exited the building in his huff.

Stan was a crackerjack, coming up with gags for everyone, business loaded upon business, and without the dead weight of Charlie's disdain for the whole idea pulling us down, the thing began to fly. To give you just one idea as an example: Karno's brief notes called for Jimmy , the 'Boy 'Ero', to demonstrate his prowess with a six-shooter.

"'Tis not for naught I have been called the dead shot of the plains!" he would cry. "I have never been known to miss!"

And then, the idea was, he would shoot the topmost feather from the headdress of Washti-na Wampum (or possibly Wampum na-Washti, depending on which version Albert Austin had used when first introducing himself). The feather, of course, was tricked to vanish when the smoke cap in the gun was fired off.

Stan liked this effect well enough, but then he started to think. That feather is really small. What about the fellows up in the gods? What if the whole feathered headdress were shot off. In fact, what if the whole feathered headdress *and the Injun chief's hair beneath* were shot off, leaving him suddenly bald as a coot?

So Albert was tricked out in a bald wig to cover his own hair, then the Injun chief's hair, with two large plaits hanging down, and then the big multi-coloured feathered headdress, and the whole lot was attached to an invisible line. The first time Stan tried it in a rehearsal, he fired off the gun with a tremendous bang and a puff of smoke, and in an instant Albert was standing there, his head as bald as a baby's behind, a look of pop-eyed astonishment on his face.

Everyone was caught up in the excitement. I stayed behind after everyone else had gone and painted the backdrops. It was a labour of love, actually. I was able to bring to life the America I had read about in my penny bloods since I was a boy. Mighty snow-capped rocky mountains, great sweeping, bear-laden forests, dusty, sun-baked main streets, just ripe for a gunfight.

Tilly, too, was full of enthusiasm, partly because the fact that Charlie had opted out meant that she was there on her own merits and not just by his patronage. And although we didn't get round to discussing it, she must have noticed that having once chosen Karno over her, and once dropped her because of Karno, now I was braving Karno for her.

———

Come the first night, Stan was on pins with nerves, as he'd every right to be, of course. We were playing the show twice in a night, once in Ealing, and then again up in Willesden, huge Hippodromes both.

We assembled along with the other Karno companies that were playing the capital that week at the Fun Factory, to be ferried off in the Karno omnibuses. It was cold, especially for April, and Stan and I had bought ourselves hot potatoes from a street brazier, which we shoved in our pockets to keep our hands warm – an old Fun Factory trick.

"I still can't believe it," Stan grinned. "Me! A star comedian with a Karno show." I grinned back. I was happy for him. Really I was.

The buses arrived, and Stan and I made to go inside on the lower level, which was a prized perk of the lead performers, but Frank O'Neill barred our way.

"What's up, Frank?" I said. "He's a principal, isn't he?"

"Not yet he's not," O'Neill growled. "Up top, you two."

Nothing could take the wind out of Stan's sails, however, and we rode to West London, he and my teeth both chattering away in the late winter chill.

Stan still seemed to be shivering when the curtain went up at the Ealing Hippodrome, and I was a trifle alarmed as I watched him begin, waiting in the wings ready to join him onstage. He was reading his penny blood at the kitchen table, and slicing a crusty loaf of bread at the same time without taking his eyes from the page. In his nervousness he cut the loaf into a sort of spiral, so that when he came to pick up a slice to eat the whole thing was all still in one piece. I saw him realise what he had done, and smile at himself. Then he grabbed the ends of the loaf and pulled it in and out, playing it like a concertina, doing a little jig around the table all the while. The audience hooted with glee.

I didn't worry about him any more after that, because I knew full well what I'd just seen. I'd seen the Power.

The crowd at the Ealing Hippodrome quite simply loved little Fearless Jimmy and his adventures. I had time to take a peek out at the audience, and what do you know? I caught sight of a familiar face slap bang in the middle of the front row. It was Charlie, of course, dressed to the nines like a dude, and with a face of stone. I guess he still didn't think much of the idea. He was in a minority of one, though, that night.

The climax of the whole thing was a bit of business Stan and I devised between the two of us. Jimmy's dad (yours truly) would find Jimmy (Stan) asleep on the kitchen table, still clutching the forbidden volume, and would administer a fearsome thrashing with his belt. Stan would begin to cry, a particular effect all his own, and it brought the place down.

The audience were on their feet, cheering and stamping. All except Charlie, who sat there in his seat in the middle of the front row, stock still, his arms folded, his face grim as a rock, his purple eyes locked on Stan. I watched him as the curtain came down for the last time, watched as it wiped him from sight.

Then I turned to join in the celebrations. It was so thrilling, suddenly, the feeling that we had created the thing from scratch, and made such a hit of it. I forgot myself entirely and threw my arms around Tilly. After a moment I realised what I was doing, but she did not seem to object, and was hugging me back. We broke apart a little awkwardly then, and smiled at one another shyly. And then we turned and each hugged someone else. It was that sort of a night.

If possible, the second show at Willesden went even better. Three thousand people were packed in there – it was a real monster of a hall, the sort of place where you sometimes were caught out by a big laugh taking its own sweet time to roll in from the back – but they loved Jimmy too.

And there, in the middle of the front row once again, arms folded, impassive, unmoved, was Charlie Chaplin.

The next night, he was there again, at Ealing and Willesden both, sitting smack in the middle of the front row, not laughing. And the night after, same thing.

Some comedians, you know, find it impossible to laugh at other people working. There's just too much going on in the old brainbox. Thinking how they would do such and such a thing differently, how they'd have left more of a pause there, or less of one. All sorts of things rattling about between your thinking equipment and your laughter machinery, getting in the way, fouling up the works.

I asked one comedian (who shall remain nameless on account of the fact that I've forgotten which one it was, but believe me there are several it could have been) why he wasn't laughing at an act that had the rest of us in tucks.

"It's too good," was his reply.

Anyway, after a few days of this, and having ample reason besides to want to put Charlie's nose out of joint, I decided to do something about it. Knowing that he and Tilly were still seeing one another, I contrived to sit next to her on the Karno omnibus one evening as it trundled to the theatre.

"Stan is doing well, don't you think?" I began brightly.

Tilly smiled at me, a smile which warmed my cockles more than any hot potato ever could.

"Isn't he?" she agreed. "He's a little marvel, that boy."

"I think this could be the making of him, you know," I said, laying it on with a trowel. "I've heard lots of people say it. He could be the next big thing."

"Do you think so?" Tilly said.

"Oh yes. Charlie made a terrible mistake getting out of this sketch, you know."

"Well, good for Stan, I say. He deserves it. He's made it what it is."

"That's right," I said, loving her then for not suggesting Charlie would have been better than our friend. However, I wanted her to be sure to pass on the meat of this conversation to him, so ended with a topper. "Actually, you know, I've heard people say that now he's got Stan ... the Guv'nor won't be needing Charlie any more."

Her eyes widened. "You don't say. Coo!"

I wished I could have seen Chaplin's face when that one

arrived. There was something else on my mind, of course, and she seemed relatively kindly disposed to me just at that moment, so I found myself blurting out: "You remember when we were pretending to be married, don't you?"

"Of course I remember," she said, pursing her lips and looking at the floor. "But that was a long time ago, wasn't it?"

She gave every impression of wanting to quit this conversation, but we were on the omnibus, so there was nowhere else for her to go just then.

"Do you never wonder why it came to such a sudden end, that time in Warrington?"

She frowned, puzzled. "Well, Syd Chaplin found out about us, didn't he, and put a stop to it."

"Yes, but we never knew, did we, *how* Syd got to find out about us?"

"Well, he must have... I suppose I thought..." she tailed off. Like me, she'd been so dumbstruck by the speed of events back then that she'd never tried to work it out. It seemed an insignificant point compared to the collapse of our happy idyll.

"Charlie," I said.

"What about him?"

"Charlie knew about us, and he told Syd."

Tilly looked at me, baffled. "But ... why would he? He's your friend..."

"That's not all," I said. "Charlie knew about us in Hartlepool. He got wind of it off Stan. Stan assumed he knew about it already, you see, but Charlie, right, didn't spill the beans until just before the Guv'nor was coming to sneak a look at both of us, remember? Him and me, in Warrington. He waited, waited, waited until he could use it to put me off. What do you think of *that*?"

369

"Yes, yes," Tilly said, wafting her hand distractedly and turning away from me. "I'm sure it's all about *you*, Arthur, dear."

━━━━━━

By the end of that week *Jimmy the Fearless* was running on rails. Two-a-nights will do that for you. We'd all settled into our roles, all the effects were coming off, and Stan was in blistering form. The response in Ealing was rapturous – with the exception always of one member of the front row – and we moved on to Willesden in high spirits.

There, however, things took a bit of a funny turn.

We all knew that Fred Karno would make the pilgrimage up from the Fun Factory at some point to check on the progress of his newest creation and asset, and as he hadn't been seen thus far we all assumed it would be this, the last show of the week, that he would grace with his presence.

It started well enough. Stan sat at the table sawing away at the loaf of bread and reading his penny story. Some of the audience were already giggling when suddenly a voice cut through.

"Hey! Jimmy! That's not how you cut bread!"

It threw Stan, you could see it. He peered out over the footlights, a puzzled expression on his guileless face, and then he tried to carry on. The bread-concertina gag went for nothing, but Stan just shook his head and got onto the next bit.

A minute or two later I heard the voice again. This time it was loud enough to be heard onstage, but not so loud that the rest of the huge theatre knew what was happening: "Jimmy? Jimmy? Jimmy? Jimmy? Jimmy? Jimmy...?"

It was a relentless, insistent, brain-emptying chant, and Stan could hardly not look out into the stalls again to see what the fellow wanted. When he did, the voice stopped, but something else happened which I could not see, because Stan took half a step back in astonishment.

I was waiting in the wings to enter as Jimmy's dad. It was not yet my cue, but I thought, to hell with it, I'm going out there. Let the bastard take us both on if he dares. So I stormed out onto the apron. My part required me to be loud, and forceful, and I was double that. The voice could have continued niggling away for all I knew or cared, no one could have heard it. Stan saw what I was doing, and skipped into step with me. We built up a head of steam together, and got the sketch back on its feet. I caught Stan's eye, and he gave me a merry wink, so I knew he was back.

Inevitably, in a sketch as long as *Jimmy the Fearless* was, there were changes of pace, lulls and lacunae, quieter passages between the louder and more frantic parts, and after a little while the voice returned to its insidious malicious work.

"Jimmy? Jimmy? Jimmy? Jimmy? Jimmy? Jimmy...?"

Stan and I spotted him at the same moment. A dozen rows back, bang in the middle. He saw Stan spot him, which was, of course, the whole point of the imbecilic little chant he'd set up, and when he knew he had his full attention he pointed straight at my friend, and then pinched his own nose, in the international language of mime gesture for indicating a bad smell.

Stan blinked at the man.

I didn't, though. I had recognised him.

For the nose that he was pinching was a distinctive one. It comprised two uneven swollen globes, with a cleft in the middle, so that it looked like nothing so much as a pair of testicles.

I heard muted gasps from my comrades behind me as I strode

371

down to the front of the stage and glared out at the fellow, his bald head surrounded by a ginger halo. He saw me, of course, and his smug expression changed to one of some apprehension.

I raised my arm slowly and pointed straight at him.

"YOU!" I roared.

31
I'LL GET MY
OWN BACK

THE fellow blanched, and would, I think, have fled that very instant if he hadn't been hemmed in on all sides. Everyone else was wondering whether this was a part of the show, of course, because if it was it was quite interesting to watch, and if it wasn't, well, then it was even *more* interesting, wasn't it?

Who knows what might have happened next if Stan hadn't taken my arm and pulled me gently back into the fictional world of Jimmy the Fearless.

"Come on, Dad," he said softly.

As I thrashed away at poor Jimmy with my belt at the end of the sketch I was looking straight at the miserable ginger bastard. He was pinned there by my gaze, and I was thinking, just stay there, chum, just stay right there...!

Down came the curtain.

"Ouch!" Stan said to me, rubbing his stinging backside. "Hold something back, can't you?"

I wasn't listening, though, I was reaching for my walking cane, which was leaning by the prompt desk. All thoughts that the Guv'nor was probably out there, in the auditorium, had been driven from my mind.

Up went the curtain.

Warm applause broke out, perhaps not quite what we had become accustomed to that week, but still not bad. Stan walked out to take his bow. I followed him, then stepped over the footlights and leapt down into the audience. I took the brunt of the landing on my good pin, but my right knee still sent a blade of fire right up my other leg. I roared, a wild animal noise.

Some in the audience screamed at this. It must have been like that time when the Bioscope showed a train heading straight for the front row, and people believed it was about to burst through the screen.

I landed close to Charlie, who pulled his feet up in alarm like a child who's been told there's a crocodile under his bed. I saw clearly in his face that he feared I might be coming for him. I wasn't, though. I was after Testicle-nose, and old Testicle-nose knew it.

I raced as best I could around to the end of his row, ignoring the various whoops and shouts coming from all around, and began clambering towards him over knees and legs and coats, while he began to barge along the row away from me. The audience were cheering now, cheering me on. It might have been an act, or it might have been real. Either way, it was certainly added value for their one and sixpenny.

His arms were flailing. It looked like he was swimming desperately through a sea of people, but even so he still made it out into the aisle before I was near enough to snag him. He ran pell-mell up the side of the auditorium, and out through the exit. I was not far behind, and as I reached the foyer I saw him bursting out into the street.

I gave chase, myself pursued by several dozen excited audience members. I half-ran, half-limped with my cane, out into the night, and for a moment couldn't see my quarry. Then my little posse gave a disappointed groan, and a couple of them pointed at a shadowy figure, already quite a way off, heading for the railway bridge.

I was not done yet. I set off in pursuit, pushing myself along with my cane. It hurt like hell, but my blood was up.

Testicle-nose galloped over the railway bridge. A train passed below as he went over, and he was clearly silhouetted for an instant, and then entirely enveloped in steam.

Over the railway the road swung round and down to the left. There were shop fronts and any number of alleyways left and right that Testicle-nose could have darted into, but he was busily charging along in full view, a little way off, and so I still had hopes of catching him.

Testicle-nose let me get closer as he recovered his wind, and then suddenly jogged off again. He wasn't at full tilt now: he didn't feel like he needed to be. He just bounced along, constantly looking back, keeping the distance between us. I drove my complaining leg on and on. I was going to pay for this in the morning.

My prey looked around for traffic. There was none, and he darted across the road to a brick wall, about six feet high, with a wrought-iron gate set into it.

Testicle-nose looked back at me and grinned. Then he reached up, hauled himself onto the top of the wall, and then sprang down to land on the other side. He looked back at me through the iron gate, smirking, confident that my leg would not allow me to follow. He'd seen what happened to it, of course, at close quarters. I was made of sterner stuff, however, and fuelled by fury. I slapped my cane onto the top of the wall and heaved myself up. I looked down at that hated face, a twinkling drop of some sort of indeterminate liquid hanging at the end of his absurd hooter, and saw doubt creep across it. He turned and bolted as I slithered painfully down to ground level.

I needed a moment to recover after that, and looked around as I sucked air in between gritted teeth. I found myself now inside Kensal Green Cemetery. No light save that provided by Mother Nature. Gravestones loomed up in the dark on the left and right. Family mausoleums, some the size of a small house, lurked blackly in the middle of the lawns. Stone angels the size of a man stood guard over the departed, casting huge black shadows everywhere.

You'd have to be an idiot not to be able to find a hiding place in here, I thought to myself in despair, as I crunched slowly down the path, as inconspicuously as I could, looking for signs of life.

Fortunately, Testicle-nose was just such an idiot, and having lured me into the cemetery to spook me, had spooked himself. He was desperate to get out of there, and I heard his panicking feet on the gravel ahead, just before I saw his silhouette making for the outer wall on the far side of the graveyard, then leaping up and over it. I made a dash across the grass to grab him, and almost had his trouser leg, but was just too slow off the mark. No time to lose! Painfully, I hauled myself up after him, and half-dropped, half-fell on the other side, clutching my knee to protect it from the landing. I was on a towpath alongside a canal.

The canal gleamed in the moonlight, and stretched out straight as an arrow in both directions. The canal disappeared into a dark tunnel under Ladbroke Grove one way, and round a bend in the other direction, but he couldn't have made either, not without me seeing him.

So he was near.

Right in front of me two longboats were lashed to the bank. Neither had lights on, or seemed to be occupied at all. One of them sat perfectly still on the water. One of them bobbed gently up and down. Got you! I thought.

"Damn it!" I shouted aloud then, looking desperately left and right. I started off towards the tunnel, but then changed my mind and made for the bend in the other direction. "Damn it all!" I shouted again. Putting on a show, you see.

Because I knew where Testicle-nose was hiding. The only place he could be was in the little stairwell at the back end of the boat that led down into the long cabin. Softly softly (with a view to catching monkey), I slipped up onto the roof. After a minute or two he felt safe enough to emerge, inching carefully up the steps, peering round the edge of the barge, left and right along the towpath, everywhere but right above, which is where I was.

I whistled softly. He looked up, startled. And I kicked the sliding hatch which covered the stairwell. I kicked it hard. The front edge caught him squarely on his ridiculous conk. He fell back in a heap, stunned, and blood began to gush freely from both globes. I looked down triumphantly, but he wasn't out cold as I'd expected, and he scrambled to his feet. I picked up the nearest item to hand, which was a hand-painted green metal jug, design floral. I laid it alongside the fellow's head with a satisfying clang, which I should say reduced the capacity of the utensil by about half. Still he didn't go down, though, and he made a dazed spring for the bank, sprawling on his face on the towpath. I jumped after him, and immediately wished I hadn't. My knee gave beneath me, and I measured my length on the ground, screaming like a girl.

By the time I had pushed myself up to my feet with my cane, Testicle-nose was standing before me. The bottom half of his face was bloody, his nose was even larger than before and seemed to be throbbing. He didn't want to discuss the matter. His hand jabbed forward threateningly, and I caught the glint of a short, broad, nasty-looking knife. A fighter's knife. He smirked, as he had smirked in the theatre, only with even more malicious intent behind it now.

At that moment I suddenly remembered a lesson Ernie Stone taught me one idle evening. We were talking about fighting – he was once a boxer, you will recall – and he said this: "If a man pulls a knife on you, it's because he don't know how to use his fists."

Which was encouraging.

"He expects you to be scared, see, to freeze, to let him stand there deciding how to stick you. It's natural, it's going to be your first thought. So what you must do is punch him, right away. Punch him hard, knock him down. Don't even think, just punch!"

Good old Ernie. As it happens, I didn't punch Testicle-nose, I whipped up my cane and potted his nose with it as if I was playing a cannon in billiards. *Then* I punched him. Hard.

Really hard.

When he awoke, some little time later, I was sitting on his legs. He was face down, with the top half of his body hanging over the edge of the canal. I had his knife, and I had tied his hands behind his back with some rope I'd appropriated from the longboat. If I stood up he'd go into the water, and that would be the end of him. It didn't take him more than an instant to work this out, and he started wailing and wriggling.

"Hey!" I said. "Keep still, will you? You don't want to throw me off."

He saw the wisdom of this and desisted. A great snort came from him as he tried to breathe through a snootful of blood.

"Now then," I said casually. "You and I are going to have a little chat. All right?"

I'd had a minute or two to think while he'd been out for the count, and I'd decided it was quite a prize coincidence that this same fellow would barrack two separate shows that I was involved with in two separate venues in two separate parts of town. I mean, if he disliked our comedy so much why would he even bother to keep turning up for more disappointment?

"Pummmeeupp! Pummmeeupp!" he cried. I hooked my cane in the collar of his jacket, then rolled off his legs. He squealed in terror as he felt himself sliding towards the murky water, but I held him, and then yanked him up onto his back on dry land. I crouched by his head and shoved his own nasty little knife up one of his misshapen nostrils. That got his attention.

"All right, no more messing about, you got me?"

He nodded, very carefully indeed.

"So what do you think you were doing, eh? How would you like it if I came down to where you work and start having a go at you? Come down to where you're shovelling shit, or whatever the hell it is you do, and shout that you're not doing it properly. Eh?"

I jabbed his knife further up his nose, and his eyes widened.

"Thuck oth!" he hissed.

"Charmer," I said. "So, did someone put you up to it? Is that what's going on? Someone doesn't like Fred Karno, is that it? Is it?"

"Thuck oth!" he hissed again. "Thuck right oth!"

"You getting paid, are you, for heckling us? Oh-ho...!" I had reached into his jacket pocket, and come out with a little clutch of fivers. His eyes narrowed. "I don't really think you've earned these, have you, letting me catch up to you, and me with a busted knee and all."

Testicle-nose made a great effort to speak clearly and as menacingly as he could manage. "You let me up right now or it will be the worsh for you."

"This little sideline of yours is over and done with, you got me?" I said, still skewering his grotesque proboscis. "You tell whoever it is that's paying you that every Karno comic will know to look out for you, and if we ever see you again it will be the worsh for *you*. Got it?"

I withdrew the knife from his nose, at which he sniffed and snorted with relief. I grabbed his shirt front and pulled him to his feet, then spun him round and sawed away at the rope round his wrists. I felt him tense just before he was freed, and he might as well have sent me advance warning by telegraph. Sure enough, he took half a pace forward and swung a huge haymaker at my head. I swayed back out of the way of it, and then shoved him into the canal.

Let me say, as a postscriptum to this episode, on behalf of the brotherhood. Think twice before you heckle a comedian, because that rage is bottled up inside all of us, that desire to jump down and sort you out, and if you pick the wrong target you might just find yourself in a canal. If you're lucky.

By the time I'd retraced my steps to the Hippodrome, the *Jimmy* company and the Karno omnibus had all left without me, heading down to the Enterprise to collect their week's pay. I made the best speed I could to follow, by tram and cab. I'd done more than enough walking to last me a week, and my knee was on fire.

When I got there and pushed my way into the pub, the place fell silent. Mike, Ernie and Stan were over by the bar nursing beers and smoking, so I joined them. Slowly a hubbub of conversation started up again, but it wasn't the usual lively atmosphere by any means.

"What ho, boys?" I said. "Who's for another?"

They shook their heads mournfully, all three of them. That's when I knew something was up, those boys knocking back the offer of a beer.

"What's happened?" I said. "Somebody died?"

The other two looked to Stan, who was uncharacteristically downcast. He gave me a wan smile and said: "Charlie has been to Karno and told him he'll play Jimmy after all, and so that's how it's going to be."

My blood was still running hot. "Oh-ho! Is that so? Where's the Guv'nor? I want to talk to him."

"*He* wants to talk to *you*," said Alf Reeves, from behind me. "He's in his office. I'm to bring you over as soon as you show."

"Lead on," I said.

Alf and Frank O'Neill walked me across the street to the Fun Factory. We all fell into step, and it struck me suddenly that they were like prison guards leading me to the hangman.

Karno was waiting, almost in the dark. Just one lamp burning low. His fingers drummed on the desk. What was all this?

"Well?" the Guv'nor said. "What have you to say for yourself?"

"I hear you have put Charlie in instead of Stan," I said. "That's an utter disgrace. What have you to say for yourself?

"We're not discussing that," he snapped. Behind him, Alf closed his eyes and shook his head slowly.

"Well, what are we talking about then?"

"Jackett, the manager of the Willesden Hippodrome, you know him?"

I nodded, recalling a stuck-up little martinet with oiled hair who'd been strutting about the place like it was his personal fiefdom all week.

"He's demanding your head on a platter, or else he'll book no more Karno shows into his theatre for fear of a repeat of this atrocity."

"*Atrocity?*" I laughed. I still saw myself as the righteous victim, you see.

"Well, what would you call it?!" Karno exploded. "Leaping from t' stage and assaulting a member of the paying public!"

"But...!" I spluttered.

"For crying out loud, what were you thinking?" Karno shouted. "What possible justification could there be for such madness?"

"Well," I said. "The thing is..." I caught Alf's eye just at that moment, and he was staring at me hard, almost willing me to say nothing. It dawned on me that I was in real trouble.

"The only reason – the *only* reason – I'm not going to give him what he wants, is this. No jumped-up little prig is going to tell me how to run my company. I could buy and sell him and his theatre a hundred times over. The pompous little arse! Never been onstage in his life. Doesn't know what we have to put up with, and that's a fact."

I glanced at Alf, who was exhaling slowly, willing me to keep my mouth shut.

"That said," Karno growled, "this must never, *never*, happen again. I make myself clear?"

"Yes, Guv'nor," I said, casting my eyes to the floor penitently. Karno sat behind his desk, and wafted me from his presence with one exhausted hand. As I made my way back over the road to the Enterprise, I realised that that was the first time the Guv'nor had even spoken to me since the Oxford.

"Well?" Stan said anxiously as I walked in. "Are you out?"

"Nope," I said. "You're still stuck with me." The boys grinned, Mike handed me a pint, and I held it up to toast the assembled company.

Later I sat quietly to one side, looking out of the window at the Fun Factory, pondering the question of my ginger adversary. Someone had paid that rotten bugger to heckle Karno shows, but who, and why? He wasn't going to tell me, even when I stuck a knife up his nose.

I decided that, come what may, I would get to the bottom of it.

32
THE GREAT DETECTIVE

CHARLIE went ahead and took over as Jimmy the Fearless, after a week of haunting our performances like Banquo at the feast. He made a good fist of it, too, I had to admit, even though the way he had shoved Stan aside still rankled with me. With me more than with Stan, actually, I think. One night well into the run, Stan – now just one of the cowboy gang – stood at my shoulder watching Charlie as Jimmy cutting the bread into a concertina, listening to the audience lapping it up, standing there with a big silly grin on his face.

"I don't know how you can be enjoying this," I whispered.

"What do you mean?" Stan hissed back. "It's still my gag. That's my laugh, that is."

That was Stan all over. He didn't care who got the laugh, so long as there was one. I, however, was more inclined to give credit where it was due, and so Charlie's guilty backside, when presented invitingly to me for a fake lashing at the end of the piece, regularly got given what for with the Dandoe belt.

"Christ!" he complained one night, rubbing his buttocks.

"Did you really whack Stan that hard?"

"Absolutely," I swore. "It's what makes the ending."

It is interesting now to wonder what was really going on over *Jimmy the Fearless*. Charlie was such a hit in it that it was difficult for any of us to see what he had not liked about the idea in the first instance. He was good, too. I still have a cutting in my scrapbook, yellowed and curling, from *The Stage*,[12] which declares: "The best work is done by Chas Chaplin in the name part, and Arthur Dandoe as Jimmy's father."

You can see why I kept that one. Ever since Charlie had joined Karno all he'd been asked to do was mimic (and improve upon) other comics' creations. His brother Syd showed him the way in *Mumming Birds* and *Skating*, and Harry Weldon broke the ground in *The Football Match*. With *Jimmy the Fearless* he was asked for the first time to create a new character from scratch, and his confidence deserted him. Strange to think that, considering what he went on to do and to be, but still.

Stan always said that poor, brave, dreamy Jimmy grew up to be Charlie the Tramp, so maybe Chaplin actually never did have to create another character for himself.

One balmy Saturday evening I clambered to the top deck of our omnibus, to come face to face with Tilly and Amy Minister, shrieking excitedly and laughing their heads off.

"Whatever is the matter?" I asked.

"It seems I am to have my honeymoon after all," Amy babbled, all of a flutter. "Alf is to take a brand-new company to America!"

America! It struck me like a thunderbolt! The Land of the Free! The Land of the Fresh Start! The setting for so many of the adventure stories I had lapped up since I was a boy! Surely

Alf could get *me* on that trip? After all, was I not the hero of the great standing-up-to-Fred-Karno-over-the-tormenting-of-his-wife incident? Did he not say he'd do anything for me?

"And the best news of all is that Tilly is to come too!"

Their happy giggling began afresh, and I staggered to the back of the bus in a daze.

I had to get on that trip.

That night I sought out Alf at the Enterprise, grabbed him urgently by the sleeve.

"Alf?! Listen to me. You're going to America again?"

"That's right," he shouted over the hubbub at the bar. "And Amy is coming too! It'll be a grand adventure!"

"When?"

"Next month."

"Take me," I said. "Please?" Alf's face fell. "Take me," I urged. "I've had a bellyful of this country, and I really want to go to America."

"I don't think I can," he said.

"What?!" I yelled.

"I don't think I can," he said again.

"What do you mean, you don't think you can?" I cried. "Surely you could pull a string or two? For me?"

Alf frowned. "The truth is I've just about used up my credit where you are concerned, young man," he said. "And anyway, listen, this one isn't up to me. It's up to the number one, he can say who he wants, and he can say who he doesn't want, and if he doesn't want you that's it."

"He doesn't want me, you say?"

"No, lad, he doesn't."

"Well, who is the number one?" I asked, although deep in my

central nervous system I already knew what the answer was going to be.

"Why, Charlie Chaplin, of course."

———

I pushed my way through the crowd out into the street, and set off walking furiously to nowhere in particular. Thinking frankly murderous thoughts, I ran my finger along the handle of the knife I had taken from that ginger heckler before I shoved him into the canal, which was still in my pocket like a little trophy. I suddenly noticed for the first time that one of the sides was not as smooth as the other, and pulled it out to take a closer look. Sure enough there was a pattern of indentations, symbols, *letters*, carved in the grime, which spelled out ... what?

I turned the knife around, trying to catch the light from one of the street burners, and found a stub of pencil to poke away the muck that was caught in the grooves, and after a little amateur archaeology I had it.

"SS *Dover Castle*."

So our heckler was a seaman, was he?

And what was his game, anyway? There had been something so deliberate about what he did, the way he had seemed to know exactly the point to interject to cause the most disruption. And someone had paid the man, evidently, so who stood to gain? Perhaps Wal Pink was behind it? Perhaps this was the beginning of his great move against the Fun Factory?

Perhaps I could find out a little more. And perhaps if I did, that would go some way towards repairing my relationship with Karno. Perhaps I would be the hero of the hour. Perhaps, I reasoned feverishly, I would even be able to parlay that into a place on the boat to America?

So the following morning, having no rehearsals, I left Fenchurch Street station on the London, Tilbury and Southend railway service, as I had on my previous Sherlock Holmes-style adventure, this time heading for Tilbury Dock.

My plan, if you can dignify what I intended with the name, was to stroll nonchalantly around the docks until I came across the SS *Dover Castle*, and then to find a vantage point from which to watch the ship until I caught sight of the man with the ginger halo and the distinctive nasal features that I had so enjoyed rearranging a few nights earlier. After that...? Well, Watson, I was planning to play it pretty much by ear.

Once I strolled up to the docks themselves, however, it became apparent that this plan did not have a great deal going for it. For one thing access to the wharves was blocked off by enormous gates that were guarded by a pair of pretty rough-looking individuals who each looked nearer than I liked to the end of their respective tethers. For another there were literally thousands of men there milling about outside, eyeing the gates hungrily, hoping against hope that someone was going to come out and start recruiting casual labour, at which point they would tear each other to pieces so that the coveted jobs would go to the last left standing. And we thought the Corner was brutal! Comparing that to this would be like comparing a cricket match to the Colosseum. At least if you got into a scramble for work with some of the types down at the Corner you could take the wind out of their sails with a sarcastic remark about what they were wearing.

I elbowed my way through a crowd of surly-looking coves with dirty neckerchiefs – these seemed to be a badge of honour, or at least a credential, a bit like wearing a sign around the neck reading "Will Work Until Filthy For Cash" – and crossed the no-man's-land to the gates themselves. One of the guards regarded me coolly through the ironwork, slapping a large truncheon into the palm of his hand. He had a gun, as well, I could hardly help noticing, strapped to his belt.

"Excuse me?" I said, extra politely. The fellow didn't speak. He conveyed to me that I should continue speaking by blinking in a menacing fashion. Not easy to do.

"I am trying to locate a ship," I said.

"We have ships," the fellow said drily.

"Yes, ha ha, very good. A particular ship, I mean. Name of the *Dover Castle*."

"What business do you have?"

"What business?"

"Cargo? Passage? Or crew?"

"Passage. Yes, that's it," I busked off the top of my head. "I'm a passenger, of course."

The man brightened. "Oh, well, in which case, I'll just need to see your documents, then, please, sir?"

"Documents? Ah, well, you see, the thing is, I haven't yet arranged my passage. I just wanted to ... take a quick look ... at the ship ... and make sure, do you see, that she looks nice and seaworthy ... before I ... um..."

"I see, sir. And once you have had a quick look at the ship, I presume you will be returning with my gift?"

"Your...?"

"Yes, my birthday gift. I was born yesterday, apparently, so it's a day overdue. I do hope you have bought me something nice."

"Ah."

He leaned towards me and lowered his voice. "See those blokes behind you? There's hardly a one of them that hasn't tried at one time or another to slip through these 'ere gates. They're meeting an auntie from overseas. They're collecting an important package. The idea being, as I am sure a man such as you can fathom for hisself, that once inside they will be able to badger, plead or otherwise grovel their way into a day's paid work. Now it is my job to see that that don't happen, for that way chaos lies. Which is why no one gets through these gates without 'is documentation, or at the very *least* a union card from the Dock, Wharf, Riverside and General Labourers' Union."

I nodded. "Right-o."

"Now you seems like a nice gentlemen so I'm going to help you out. Firstly, you are more than a touch over-dressed for wharf work. And secondly, there is no *Dover Castle* here, and as far as I know never has been, so whoever sent you down on a promise that he could get you a position was 'aving a larf. Got me?"

I retreated, and strolled away, under the suspicious gaze of a vast throng of surly and unemployed dock workers. Clearly I needed to rethink my approach before I tried this again at another yard. I felt their eyes on my back all the way to the end of the road, where I turned a corner and found myself in a large open space. This was similarly packed with men, but these ones had their backs to me. All were watching a speaker, who was addressing them from a dais, backed by an embroidered banner proclaiming the very same Dock, Wharf, Riverside and General Labourers' Union just mentioned.

He was certainly a passionate orator, this chap, and he had this huge crowd in the palm of his hands. I paused to watch for a while, admiring his presence and technique. He had the Power all right.

390

"For we are at war!" the chap cried, pushing his flat cap to the back of his head. "Don't think that we are not! The owners would crush you if they could! And replace you with unthinking mules!"

"Aye, Ben! You tell 'em!" went the murmuring mob round about me.

"Lord Devonport – there is a man who will stop at nothing!" this Ben[13] went on, and a grumbling rose up. Lord Devonport, I gathered, was not a popular figure in these parts.

"He would know what our plans are, and what our strengths and weaknesses! And so he sends spies to move amongst us, listening, watching..."

This brought a wave of angry grumbling and spitting on the floor from the assembled.

"So let us all be vigilant, and seek out the interlopers!"

"Aye!" roared the mob furiously.

Except one voice behind me, which said: "Here's one!"

All about me heads turned to seek out the speaker. I myself looked round with a sort of detached interest, like a curious observer of the show.

The damned fool was pointing straight at me!

Well, things quickly began to get ugly. A tight ring of muscle-bound wharf hands hemmed me in, and I began to get barged from side to side. One flicked my hat off, but I was too closely packed in to bend and retrieve it, and wouldn't really have wanted to bend in any case. Questions jabbed in from all sides like hostile punches, and there were hostile punches as well (which jabbed in like, well, like questions).

"'Oo sent yer?"

"What you up to?"

"'Oo's yer master, yer lackey of the ruling class?'" Had all the jargon, that one.

"I'm not, I'm not, I'm not whatever you think!" I protested, but my cries were lost in the rising angry hubbub. What I was thinking was: for Heaven's sake, I am a *socialist*!

"Wait a minute, lads," a deep voice cut in, and there was a pause in hostilities for a moment. "This 'un's no spy. I recognises 'im, I do. Oh yes."

My heart missed a beat at that, I can tell you. The only person I could possibly imagine recognising me in this hell-hole was none other than Testicle-Nose himself. I'd walked, like a fool, like a dumb *fool*, into his very lair, where he was backed up by hundreds of like-minded friends and colleagues, and I was surely done for. A beating, and broken bones, at the very least. I'd probably end up with a nose like his.

I closed my eyes a moment, took as deep a breath as I was able, and turned to face ... someone else! Thank the Lord! It was a vast chap wading towards me through a sea of flesh, a head taller than those around him. He could clearly have torn me limb from limb should he have so wished, but a benign smile was spreading across his stubbly features.

"Yes, yes, I recognises '*im* all right. 'E's one of Fred Karno's boys, ain'tcha, son?"

I could have kissed him, except that that would almost certainly have made things worse.

"Yes! Yes, I am! That's what I am! Not a spy! I'm a comedian! A comedian!"

My saviour pointed a vast finger not unlike an uncooked Cumberland sausage into my face. "*Football Match*. You was the centre-forward, the one with all the tricks. Tilbury Empire."

"Yes! Ratty! That was me! Well, well, well!" I cried.

"So what-choo a-doin' down 'ere?" mused the giant. "Pickin' up some tips from our Ben, is it?"

I glanced up at the dais, where the spittling orator was still in full flow, but casting angry looks over towards the distraction we were causing.

"No, no, no, nothing like that. We ... we ... are preparing a new show. Yes, that's it!" I clapped my hands as inspiration struck. "A new show set right here in the docks. And we wanted to make sure we get everything just so. *Wharf ... Birds*. That's what we are calling it. *Wharf Birds*."

An excited hum of chatter swirled around me now from my erstwhile attackers, thrilled at the prospect of being immortalised onstage. I reached into my coat pocket and pulled out a fistful of free passes that I had lifted from Alf's office, with the thought that they might grease a wheel or two along the way. I thrust them at the giant, who grasped them with child-like glee, and then obligingly carved me a way out of the mob.

"Just one thing," I added, once we'd made it to a little bit of open space at the edge of the rally. "Do you know a ship called the *Dover Castle*?"

The giant's brow creased in a mighty frown. "I don't know it, no..."

"Right. I see. Oh well, I'd best be off..."

"But," he went on. "If it's a Castle, it'll be one of the Union-Castle Line, they're all the Something Castle. *Pembroke Castle*, *Kinfauns Castle*, *York Castle*, *Dunottar Castle*, all sort of names like that. You should ask at their office. Now, where is that...?" After a moment he snapped his fingers. "Of course, I knows it. Fenchurch Street." I sighed. I'd risked life and limb, and the answer was right back where I'd started that morning.

Nice one, Sherlock. I thanked him and scuttled back to the railway station as fast as I could.

━━━━

Once back at Fenchurch Street I located the offices of the Union-Castle Mail Steamship Company soon enough, and ventured up the steps. A doorman in a natty lavender and black livery held the door open.

"A very good afternoon, sir. Cargo, Passage, Accounts or Staff?"

I'd had some time on my return train journey to consider my plan of action a little more carefully, so I replied: "Staff."

The liveried greeter jerked a thumb towards a dark corridor and returned to his post. I followed this corridor to a staircase, which led down into a basement.

There I found a veritable warren of corridors, with small offices leading off to either side, and some light provided by high frosted windows at street level. Dust hung and swirled in the sunbeams, which blinked at the passage of feet on the pavement above. Everywhere there were packets of papers bound together with string, just stacked on top of each other in piles, which made the corridors so narrow that I had to edge along sideways to make progress.

I reached the end of the corridor, and an office that was larger than the ones I had passed. A man sat behind a desk there, also lost in filling in some form or other, and he muttered without looking up.

"Be with you ... be with you in a mo ... ment."

I tucked my hands behind my back – this, by the way, is pantomime language for 'a man of substance', which is why the Royals do it – and inspected my surroundings. On the wall was a large map of the world, with coloured pins variously scattered about its surface. The largest concentration by far seemed to be in the vicinity of the Cape of Good Hope. Next to this were two framed portraits of military gentlemen, which I inspected while I waited.

"Lord Roberts, Commander-in-chief South Africa, and General Kitchener," said a voice behind me. The clerk had finished his paperwork and had come out from behind his desk to greet me. "It was our very great honour to transport these fine gentlemen both to and from the conflict, along with many of our brave lads."

"Really?" I said. "My brother fought the Boer with the Essex. Perhaps you transported him as well."

"Very possibly, very possibly. I must say that even though I myself never set foot ashore I still saw things I never hope to have to see again. Some of the injured we brought back home…" Here he stopped and clapped his hand to his mouth, realising that I had not said how Lance had fared out there.

"My brother doesn't like to talk about it," I said. "He was at the relief of Kimberley, I believe, and, fortunately, returned from the adventure whole."

"Good, good," the fellow gasped, pulling out a handkerchief and mopping his brow. "Well, my name is Turnbull."

"Dandoe," I said. "Arthur Dandoe."

"Welcome to Bleak House, Mr Dandoe. And how may I be of service to you?"

"I have a message for one of your crew members," I said. This was the story I had concocted. "I wonder if you could tell me where he might be found?"

"I see," Turnbull said, returning to his desk and reaching for a ledger. "What ship?"

"The *Dover Castle*," I said.

"*Dover Castle … Dover Castle…*" he murmured, licking his fingertip and flicking through the pages. "Here… And the name…?"

"I'm afraid I don't know," I said.

"You don't know the name of the person for whom the message is intended?"

"I don't, but perhaps if you could tell me where the *Dover Castle* is, I could…?"

Mr Turnbull was having trouble digesting the information. "You have a message for someone, but don't know *who*?"

"No, but as I say, all I really need to know is…"

Turnbull stepped out from behind his desk and strode to his door.

"Mr Handley? Mr Bunn? Step in here a moment, if you would."

In short order we were joined by a couple of junior clerks, eager to please.

"This gentlemen has a message for a member of the crew of the *Dover Castle*, but he does not know the *name* of the recipient."

"Doesn't know his *name*, Mr Turnbull?"

"What does he look like?" one of the junior clerks ventured.

"Yes, do we have a description?"

"Look," I said, "all I really want to know is where the *Dover Castle* actually is and I'll pursue the matter myself."

"But if you can describe the man you seek…"

"…we may be able to identify him for you."

Actually, I thought, if they could tell me the heckler's name, that might be very useful. And they were so very keen to help, so I said: "Well, he has a bald head, with a crown or halo of gingery hair, and but one other distinguishing feature that I can think of.

His nose. It is grotesquely huge, and divided into two globes, not at all unlike..."

Turnbull held up a hand. "Say no more, sir." Mr Handley and Mr Bunn were smiling knowingly at each other, and Turnbull was now running his finger down a column of the ledger before him.

"Here we have him, yes indeed, the very fellow. Moulden, his name is. He's a second mate on board, as you yourself said, sir, the SS *Dover Castle*."

"He was in this very office not three days ago," Handley said. "And his nose was even more of a spectacle than usual. He was swearing all kinds of bloody revenge on whoever it was who'd made it so, as well, and..."

"Yes, thank you, Mr Handley, that will do," Turnbull said, as he wheeled his chair around to consult a chart on the wall behind him. "I'm afraid your message will have to wait, Mr Dandoe. The *Dover Castle* is one of the six steamers we have carrying the mail to the Cape, and on to Natal. It's a five-week run there and back, leaving every Thursday afternoon, and so Mr Moulden will have departed yesterday from Southampton."

"I see. Gentlemen, I thank you," I said. "Good day to you."

"Is your message perhaps one that could be wired ahead?" Turnbull enquired. "Could I ask, are you a family member, or a potential employer? Or..." – he winced apprehensively – "a *police officer*, perchance?"

"No, indeed," I replied.

"You would not be the first," Turnbull said. "Or perhaps a detective?"

"No, no, no. In point of fact ..." I said, not really knowing why I said it, "...I am a comedian with the Fred Karno company."

This news went down big, as I had a feeling it would.

"Oh, well, in that case," Turnbull said, beaming. "I suspect then that we know who your message is *from*. Eh, Mr Handley? Mr Bunn?"

Handley and Bunn nodded vigorously.

"I beg your pardon?" I said, surprised, since, of course, there was no actual message.

"Oh yes. One of Moulden's former shipmates on the *Dover Castle* is now in the music halls, and a colleague of yours. We remember him well, do we not?"

"Indeed we do, Mr Turnbull," said Bunn.

"Quite a character!" said Handley.

I frowned. Suddenly I had the urge to shake the information out of them, but managed to hold myself in check.

"I have his picture right here. He signed his name upon it... Now where did I...? Ah, here we are! See?"

Turnbull handed over a postcard-sized publicity photograph, of a kind that music hall stars would have to give out to admirers. I looked at the picture. The face was unmistakable, and even if it had not been, the signature was legible enough.

Suddenly I had a vivid flash of an image that I recalled from the night at the Oxford. I had been feeling the effects of the ether, and it all felt like a dream, swimming in and out of focus, but yes, it was this same face and the creature Moulden together, wasn't it? Outside the stage door there? Moulden tucking some cash into his pocket, smirking, and this fellow glancing anxiously over to see if I'd seen him?

It was Syd Chaplin.

33
TIED UP IN NOTTS

CHARLIE Chaplin was in Nottingham, and he was furious. What a waste of a day!

He had just travelled by train the twenty or so miles over from Leicester, where he was starring as *Jimmy the Fearless* at the Palace, and now he was striding angrily across the western edge of the Old Market Square. Last time he had been in the town, the previous autumn, the Goose Fair had been on, and the big helter-skelter had been standing over there, opposite H. Samuel's the jewellers. Now the square was just a big open space, people scurrying hither and thither about their business, with the shops on one side and the Exchange on the other. Robin Hood won an archery contest here, they kept telling him last time, he remembered.

It was a warm day, and he stopped to cool off and calm down. He was early, with a few minutes to spare before the meeting to which he had been summoned, and so he took a seat on a bench, lit a cigarette and wafted his face with his hat.

The nerve of that Billy Wragg! Chaplin reached into his pocket for the letter, with its Nottingham postmark, and scanned it one more time. He'd looked it over on the train as well, and probably knew it off by heart.

"Dear Charly," it read. "Things hav gon hardly for me since the football match got canseled and I got sacked off mr Karno. I hav tried to find sum work but nothin doin. I am on me uppers. I no you are at Lester this week. I seen a bill. Come over to Nottinham on tuesdy to the white statue in the front of the thetre royal. Come at mid-day. If you do not come and pay me five pounds I will rite to that same mr Karno and tell him all what I done for you, and that is a promis.

"Your faithful frend, Wm Wragg esq."

Blackmail! That's all it was! The letter had been waiting for him at the Palace when the *Jimmy the Fearless* troupe arrived for the band call on Monday morning, and he had nearly had a seizure. He'd wired Syd at once, and the reply came back, two words only. "Pay him."

Chaplin looked around at the busy square as he finished his cigarette. This was Wragg's home town, of course, he remembered. He played for Nottingham Forest, didn't he? In the Cup Final, no less.

He watched people criss-crossing the square in front of him with disdain. These humdrum little provincials with their scrubbed faces and their limited little lives. How he despised them, and feared them too. Despised their low sense of humour, their inability to appreciate the nuances in his work, in his art. Feared that if he was to fail in the music hall, then he might end up amongst them, like them, one of them.

How tired he was of touring to towns like these. He felt like he'd been doing it all his life. He had, almost! What with the

Eight Lancashire Lads, starting in 1899, then with Mr Gillette's *Sherlock Holmes*, and then that pompous ass Wal Pink's Company, Casey's Circus and now with Karno's these last three years, there could hardly be a dismal, boxy-housed, grey-stone, cobbled-street, corner-shopped conurbation in the country he hadn't spent a week in at one time or another, in rain and shine, boredom and joy.

America, that was what he was looking forward to. A fresh start, new horizons, different towns, different people, a sense of adventure, of scope. Of freedom. It was trite and obvious, he knew that, but in the vast open spaces of America he felt he'd be able to breathe. Not like here.

Tilly would be there, too, he found himself thinking. She hadn't been as excited as he'd hoped when she'd heard the news, though. He'd made sure that she knew that he had requested her, but that seemed to be the very thing that was sticking in her craw. She was attractive, no doubt, but independent too. And did he really want her? Or did he just want her because Dandoe wanted her?

At least Dandoe would not be making the trip, which would simplify things. Not only with Tilly, but also with the company. Too funny by half, that was the trouble with Dandoe. He'd taken a bit of fixing, but it had been worth it. There was only room for one number one. Young Stan Jefferson was funny too. He'd tried to have that young man dropped from the America company as well, but Alf had said he was the perfect understudy. Which he was. Too damned perfect. Just as long as he knew his place.

Chaplin checked his watch and saw that it was five minutes to the hour. Let's get this over with, he thought to himself, and set off briskly up Market Street.

Once he reached the Theatre Royal he saw the white statue

401

quickly enough. It was an immodest marble tribute to a local hosier, set on a plinth maybe eight feet high. He'd seen it before but not particularly remarked it.

There was no sign of Billy Wragg, Chaplin noted impatiently. There was only an old gypsy woman, wearing a threadbare shawl and a tattered bonnet and holding a basket of lucky heather on her lap as she sat at the base of the plinth. He strolled over to look at the front of the Royal, which was presenting a piece by Mr Shaw, it seemed, while the Empire was just up the street there, where the town's music hall entertainments were to be found. He strolled back towards the statue, glancing up the streets to the right and left to see if he could catch sight of Wragg's lanky frame, but there was no one even remotely like the big brute in the vicinity.

"Lucky 'eather, dearie?" said a voice at his feet. Chaplin glanced down at the old gypsy woman. Like all theatricals he would admit to being somewhat superstitious, and he found himself fumbling in his trouser pocket for a sixpence, which he handed over. The crone struggled inelegantly to her feet, and pinned some heather to the lapel of Chaplin's jacket, drawing him in closer as she did so.

"There you go, me ducks," the gypsy said.

"Thank you, mother," said Chaplin.

"I'll tell your fortune if you likes," the crone offered.

"No, thank you, I don't have the time right now," Chaplin said, turning away. She tugged at his sleeve.

"Come on, now, Charlie, don't be like that."

Chaplin turned back, startled, and frowned. "You know my name?"

"I knows a good deal more than that," said the woman, a teasing smirk on her walnut-brown face.

402

"I suppose you saw me at the Empire?"

"No, I never did, me ducks. I'm sure you were a sight to see."

"So," Chaplin ventured, intrigued now. "What else do you know, exactly?"

"Oooh, let me see. I knows you are here to meet a fellow, a tall fellow. I knows you are here to give him an amount of money. I knows your name is Charlie and his name is William."

Chaplin peered suspiciously at the witch's face under the battered bonnet. "What is this? How do you know me, and how do you know his name?"

"Did I not give him the name my own self?" said the gypsy.

"What do you mean?" Chaplin said, perplexed.

"Why, it was my father's name, Billy's grandfather."

"You mean you are...?"

"Billy Wragg's mother, that I am."

"His mother? You are his mother? Well, where is Billy?"

"He's not come. He sent me instead."

"Why?" said Chaplin.

"He's frit. He warn't sure you'd come alone. He says you might send chaps to thrash him for his impertinence."

"Chaps? What chaps? Whatever is he talking about?"

"Sailors, he says. One of 'em with a great big red nose, like two great ... t-t-tomatoes. Nasty piece o' work, by all accounts."

"Oh, *him*? Don't worry about him. Listen, I assure you I mean Billy no harm. He asked me to come, and here I am."

"And do you mean to pay him what he asks for?"

"Well, I wanted to talk to him about that," Chaplin said. He had the money but he had no intention of handing it over without some assurance that there would be no repeat of the footballer's demand.

"Did he not do what you asked?"

"Yes, yes, he did, but..."

"Did he not break some other chap's leg, just as you wanted?"

"Well, I didn't exactly specify, but I suppose it worked out all right," Chaplin said, glancing around to see that no passers-by were close enough to eavesdrop.

"And would it not be most embarrassing for your good self if others were to learn of what you asked my Bill to do?"

"It would, it would," Chaplin conceded hurriedly. Suddenly he felt very uncomfortable having this conversation out in the open air, and he was anxious to be away. "So I give the five pounds to you, is that the arrangement?" he said, fumbling in his jacket for a pocketbook.

"That would be ... acceptable," the old gypsy woman said. Chaplin withdrew the notes from their hiding place, and held them out for her to take. When she reached for the payment, however, he suddenly twitched his hand back.

"Tell Billy," he said firmly. "No more after this. This is an end to the matter."

"Oh no, Charlie, no, no, no. This is not the end. This is just the beginning."

Chaplin started. He looked around in bewilderment. The old crone had not spoken, she was just grinning up at him. It was someone else.

A man's voice. A voice he knew.

Out from behind the plinth, where he had cleverly managed to conceal himself when his accomplice had pulled Chaplin close to affix the lucky heather, strolled the very last person on earth Chaplin wanted to see at that precise moment.

Arthur Sebastopol Dandoe.

Me.

Chaplin recovered himself after a moment.

"What is your intention?" he said sourly. "You go to Karno and it's your word against mine."

"You are forgetting my witness," I said, indicating the ancient gypsy crone with her basket of lucky heather.

"Billy Wragg's mother?" Charlie said with a sneer. "Who will believe her?"

"Oh, come on, catch up!" I laughed. "As if Billy Wragg would send his mother to meet you. Do you not recall my friend Mr Ralph Luscombe? He has stood you supper many a time."

The gypsy removed her bonnet and a tangled grey wig to reveal a slicked back gentleman's barnet, and a stark line across the forehead where the edge of the wig had been. Pale white male forehead to the North, and weather-beaten walnut make-up and fake warts to the South.

"What ho, Charlie!" Luscombe cried. Then to me he said: "I thought that went rather well, didn't you?"

"I liked 'frit'," I said. "That was most convincing. And 'me ducks', that was excellent."

"Yes, I was pleased with those suggestions, from our local friend the stage doorman, no less."

"I wondered about 'chaps', though. You said 'chaps' rather often, and it didn't quite strike right."

"Do you know, I wondered about that too," Charlie said, bitterly. "I never dreamed for a moment that it was you, though. It made me wonder if the woman had perhaps fallen on hard times from something higher, you know? Congratulations, my friend! You are quite wasted in the import-export business. Johnny Doyle should look to his laurels."

Luscombe glowed. "Thank you! Coming from you that's ... well, I am overwhelmed!"

They shook hands, the two of them. Quite sporting of Charlie, actually. I clapped him on the back. "Well, you look like you could do with a drink. Shall we adjourn?"

I led Chaplin off to the pub on the corner, which we had frequented during our week in Nottingham the previous autumn, while Luscombe trotted round to the stage door of the theatre. We had bribed the stage doorman to let us use a dressing room, some make-up and the street crone get-up from the Shaw play, whichever one it was. Cost us a couple of pints, that's all.

In the pub we settled into a booth, where I got on the outside of a pint of Marston's, and Charlie sipped a large port as per.

"Aaaaahh!" I said, a large sigh of satisfaction.

"So?" Charlie asked. "Are you going to tell me the purpose of that little charade?"

"I needed to know, that's all," I said.

"To know," he said, wary.

"I already knew that you shopped me and Tilly to Syd in Warrington," I said. "I knew you did it to put me off when the Guv'nor came to inspect us. I knew that you took up with Tilly in secret – well, we already had that one out in Paris, didn't we?"

"I'll drop her," he said quickly. "You can have her, I'll give her back."

I laughed. I could hardly wait to tell her he said *that*! "I don't think she'd take very kindly to being passed around like a piece of luggage," I said. "But anyway. I knew that orang-utang Moulden was a friend of Syd's, and I knew that he'd been sent to heckle me and Stan to help you, so I was interested to hear just now that you know him too. *Very* interested."

Charlie sipped his port, and wouldn't meet my eye.

"Of course, who better to tell him the precise moments to cut in so as to do the most damage? There was something else about that night at the Oxford that was niggling away at me, though. When my knee was broken by that oaf Wragg, and I was carried from the stage, you suddenly sprang from the wings to continue the performance in my place, did you not?"

"You would have done the same for me, I'm sure."

"But that was only a matter of moments later. And yet I saw you between the shows, in the bar, in your own clothes, not in Stiffy's costume. How could you have had time to run around backstage, find your costume, get changed, and leap out to save the day, all in the time it took to shovel my sorry carcass out of the way? How could it be *done?*"

Charlie said nothing.

"You knew, that's how. You knew it was going to happen, so you were ready. Now I wanted to know if you had paid Billy Wragg to break my knee. Actually, your turning up at all in response to that letter was proof enough for me, but it was nice to hear it from your own lips."

"You wrote the letter, of course?"

"I did, and Ralph posted it. He's been here for a couple of days. His family's firm has an office here, so it all worked out rather well."

"I didn't mean... I mean... I was horrified by what happened... I..."

"Save it," I said. "Not interested."

Chaplin took a sip of port, his eyes calculating. "What are you going to do?" he asked, flatly.

"Well, now," I said. "Alf Reeves is taking you to America, right?"

407

Charlie nodded carefully.

"And Tilly is going too?"

Charlie nodded again.

"And Mike Asher? And Stan Jefferson? And Albert Austin?"

"Yes."

"But not me. Now why would that be, I wonder? I'm one of the gang, aren't I?"

Charlie looked at me coldly. "But why? Why do you even want to go?"

"I've always wanted to go to America," I said. "It's the Land of the Free, isn't it?"

"Yes, but ... I'm sorry, what I meant was, after what we were just talking about, I can't believe you'd want to go with me."

"I don't," I said. "You aren't going."

That stopped him dead in his tracks. He gave a little gasp. "I'm not going?" he said eventually.

"You're not going."

"And how am I to explain that, pray?"

"You don't have to explain it. Just miss the boat."

"Just miss the boat. Oh, you mean rehearse the show, behave for all the world as if I'm looking forward to going, and then ... just miss the boat?"

"Exactly."

"Madness!"

"Nonetheless."

"And if I don't go along with your lunatic scheme?"

I leaned in towards him, and fixed him with a beady glare. "I'll finish you," I said.

34
THE WOW WOWS

JUST as I was working my devious scheme to land myself a berth on the ship to America, Mr Wal Pink's great plot to topple the Guv'nor from his perch on the topmost rung of the music hall ladder came tumbling down around his ears.

Pink stormed into the Fun Factory one afternoon, is how we heard it, to beard the mighty lion in his den. He was fuming, and as soon as he caught sight of Karno's innocently enquiring expression he blew his top.

"You have shut me out of every theatre in the country, sir! Damn me if I know how ye've done it! But I ask you – is it fair, is it honest, is it *reasonable?*"

"Is it reasonable, Mr Pink? Is it reasonable to approach a man's employees and try to bribe them to break a legally binding contract with him?"

Karno wore a chilling half-smile, and a frisson of fear crackled around the Fun Factory, flitting like ball lightning between all those listening in, some of whom – maybe all – had taken Pink's money. The Guv'nor knew! He knew!

"Somehow!" Pink spluttered, caught out. "Somehow you have done this thing! And I tell you squarely that I regard it as conduct unbecoming a gentleman, an artist and a fellow Wow-wow-water Rat!"

With that, he turned on his heel and left, accompanied by the sound of his own footsteps, and his challenge to Karno's supremacy – not that it had ever amounted to a very great deal – was at an end.

What Karno had done, quite simply, was let it be known by all the theatre owners and managers that Pink was planning to deal with, that if they ever booked in a sketch by a Wal Pink company they would never again see a Karno outfit on their premises. And how did he know which ones were listening favourably to Pink's overtures? Why, George Craig told him, of course. George Craig, who was so ostentatiously 'sacked', then quickly snapped up by Wal Pink, made privy to all his plans, and then returned to the Guv'nor's welcoming embrace.

"The matter is in hand," he'd said, hadn't he?

"You have to get up pretty early to put one over on the Guv'nor," I remarked to Stan when we heard about this.

"What time?" Stan said.

Now Karno had any number of shows in his locker that would have had America rolling in the aisles. There was *Jimmy the Fearless* for a start off, that was practically a love poem to the place. There was good old *Mumming Birds*, of course, which had been playing successfully over there for at least four years.

But no. Karno had got it into his head that America was positively teeming with secret societies, and so he had devised a new piece in which a fellow is put through all sorts of ridiculous trials at a campsite by a river in order to gain entry to one. He named it *The Wow Wows*, a little dig at the Water Rats, and the delicious memory of Wal Pink's exasperated stuttering.

And Pink got his revenge eventually. You remember I mentioned the very first Royal Command Performance, in 1912? And the notable absentees on that prestigious occasion, Karno amongst them? Well, guess who was one of the producers charged with booking the acts by their majesties. King Rat Mr Wow-wow-Wal Pink himself.

The main character in *The Wow Wows*, fortunately for Charlie, was a version of the stock posh buffoon Archibald Binks. Syd had gamely devised no end of ghastly puns and silly business which Charlie could slavishly copy, and it was just as well, because Charlie wasn't exactly throwing himself into rehearsals with a will. He had fallen into a black mood, listless, not taking care of himself, not shaving, turning up once for work in carpet slippers and the trousers from his pyjamas under his coat. We'd all seen this before, of course, when he was pining for Hetty, and again after his disappointment in Warrington. I knew what was getting him down this time, of course.

Poor Alf Reeves was tearing his hair out at Charlie's performance. The American tour was a big deal for him. I don't think I'd realised how perilously close his relationship with the Guv'nor had come to breaking point. If you think the Guv'nor was not perfectly capable of being a fellow's best man and then sacking him before the same summer was out, then I haven't described him well enough. In short, Alf needed a hit.

"Take Charlie to the pub, snap him out of it," he'd say, and I would dutifully make the offer, but he wasn't to be tempted, of course.

I, on the other hand, was in mighty fine fettle. Stan, Mike

411

and I chattered excitedly about America, and how grand it was all going to be, how much we looked forward to it all. Added to this, Tilly was exhibiting a definite thawing towards me, and from time to time she would join us in the pub after work as part of the gang, almost like the old days. Of course, once we were there we invariably talked about whatever could be the matter with Charlie, but it was a step in the right direction.

On the Saturday evening before we were to leave I headed up to the Enterprise in a fine mood to collect my last wage packet in the King's pounds sterling. Charley Bell and Freddie K junior were walking up Coldharbour Lane with me, as we'd just travelled up from Streatham on the same tram.

"I wish to God I were going with you," Freddie kept saying. "I've about had a bellyful of theatre administration, I'm telling you."

"Maybe your father knows what he's doing," Charley consoled him. "It's as well to have a trade of sorts that you can fall back on."

"Exactly," Freddie said heatedly. "I'd like to have it to fall back on, not to be stuck actually bloody doing it fifty-two weeks of the year."

He had the supers to deal with over at the Fun Factory, and Charley went along to keep the lad company, so we went our separate ways at the corner of the street and I sauntered over towards the pub.

I didn't make it there, though.

Halfway across the road I glanced up, and there, leaning on the big outside window sill with a tankard in hand, was the man Moulden.

I stopped in mid-stride. It was definitely him. I'd have

recognised that nose anywhere. I prepared to take to my heels, but just then he spotted me.

"There!" he bellowed, pointing straight at me. To my horror, three other burly fellows also set down their drinks and began to give chase. He'd brought some mates with him! Or maybe they were second mates, or stewards, or bandsmen, who knows? I didn't hang about to find out, I just legged it as fast as I could back down Coldharbour Lane.

Moulden and his chums were quite sprightly for big lads, and I was still hampered by my painful knee. I realised quite quickly that I wasn't going to make it back to the crowded hubbub of the Brixton Road, where the dozens of eyewitnesses might have given them pause, so when I saw my chance I ducked down a side alley between a couple of shops. I stayed still in the shadows there, and heard the clatter of four big pairs of boots as they rushed by.

I tiptoed back up to the street end of the alley and peeked out with a single eye. I thought I might be able to double back to the sanctuary of the Enterprise before they worked out where I was. No such luck, though!

They had reached the corner of the block, and then stopped, realising that I had given them the slip. Now they were coming back towards me, checking each entrance as they came. I retreated down the alleyway to seek refuge, but sadly the outlook was less than promising. The alley opened out into a square back yard, shared by two shops. The walls were at least eight feet high, certainly too high for me to scale quickly, and there were some rubbish bins, which would perhaps give me cover for about four seconds, maybe five. I started to drag the bins to the back wall to use them as a leg-up, but it was hopeless.

"'Ere's our rabbit, lads!" came a shout.

I turned to face them as they walked slowly into the yard, enjoying the anticipation of the mayhem to come. Moulden's pals spread out behind him to either side. Two of them had something hanging from their hands, little ugly-looking weapons, like little black cloth bags of shot. One fellow was clearly going to be relying on his bare hands, which were absolutely massive, while Moulden himself had got hold of a piece of wood about two feet in length.

"Mr Moulden," I said nonchalantly, and his eyebrows shot up when he realised I knew his name. "Brought your sisters with you, I see."

This brought a growl from the largest of the monsters behind. I tried the only spin of the dice I could think of.

"I'm sure your employers at the Union-Castle Line will be most interested to hear how you spend your leisure time," I said.

Moulden's eyes narrowed as he took that in. I knew more about him than he thought I did. But then he smiled, a nasty, mean-spirited smile which spread out beneath his grotesque twin-globed nose.

"You ain't a-going to be tellin' 'em anything," he sneered. "Is he, boys?"

His cohorts growled their agreement. I suspected this wasn't the first beating they'd worked on together. They were a nice cohesive unit.

"Let me tell you what we were a-thinkin' of," Moulden drawled nastily, tap-tap-tapping the palm of his hand with his piece of wood.

"Please," I said, all politeness.

"We thought we might start on your leg. Not the one which so unfortunately was broken by that there footballer. No, not that one. The other one. The good one..."

I smiled and nodded, affecting a casualness which I did not feel. This was going to be awful.

"Then perhaps we'll start on your face. Your face is by way of bein' your fortune, after all, Mr Actor Man."

I sighed. America, that's what I was thinking, wistfully, just at that moment. It was almost as if I could see the coastline of the New World drifting slowly away from me, further and further into the distance.

"Shall we, gentlemen?" Moulden said, and his burly chums hunched forward, eager for the action to begin.

Moulden took a step towards me. I balled my fists, resolved to get a few good shots in at that great hooter before they took me down.

He swung his wooden bar back, ready to lunge, and then...

Footsteps, blessed footsteps, hurrying down the alley towards us! And a whistle!

The sailors turned, and parted, so that I could see that salvation had arrived in the shape of a couple of police constables, who were galloping breathlessly down the narrow passageway, backed by a number of interested local citizens.

"Now then!" cried the older of the two officers. "What's going on 'ere then?"

"Nothing," Moulden muttered. "Just some old friends having a friendly chat, is all."

"I assure you, officers, that it was very far from friendly. These gentlemen intended to do me serious harm."

"Oh-ho! Is that so?" said the senior constable.

"What, this? No, no..." said Moulden, dropping his makeshift club. His chums followed his lead, and let their weapons fall to the ground. "It's all a misunderstanding."

"It's a very serious business, that's what it is," said the younger constable, pushing the end of his truncheon up against the end of Moulden's nose, which was a touch I very much approved of.

"Even so, no actual harm seems to have been done, so I am inclined to let you be on your way, unless this gentleman insists on taking the matter further. Do you, sir?"

I held the moment, ever the professional, and then said grandly: "No, you may release them."

I had no more desire to traipse down to the police station than Moulden and his mates had, and besides, I had recognised PC Charley Bell and PC Freddie Karno junior, as well as the uniforms from *Jail Birds*, so I judged that all in all we might have been greeted with some puzzlement once we got there.

Moulden slunk past me and down the alley towards the street. As he did so he leaned over to me, his beery breath filling my perfectly formed nostrils, which must have been such a provocation to him, and he said: "Tell Syd he still owes me. Right?"

Once out on the street again, Charley and Freddie sternly watched the sailors on their way, tapping their truncheons against their palms in the approved manner. Once we were sure that they were gone we burst out laughing, patting each other on the back, and positively panting with relief.

"You two are absolute life-savers!" I gasped, as we headed back towards the Fun Factory.

"What did they want?" Freddie asked.

"I don't know," I dissembled. "Money?"

"It's a good job it were dark down there," Charley grinned. "I'm not sure these suits'd pass muster in broad daylight!"

I went into the Enterprise then, while Freddie and Charley returned to the Fun Factory. The Karnos' home pub was quiet, as most of the performers would still be onstage at that time of the

416

evening. Our company, of course, rehearsing the wretched *Wow Wows* by day, were there early, drowning their sorrows.

Charlie Chaplin was there, sitting by himself in a corner, nursing a glass of port and smoking a cigarette, with all the cares of the world on his shoulders. He looked up at me as I entered the room, and I saw no hint of surprise in his eyes at seeing me unharmed. Alf Reeves grabbed my arm.

"Look at him," Alf whispered, glancing over at our morose lead comedian. "Whatever is the matter?"

"Maybe he doesn't think much of *The Wow Wows*," I said.

"It's not just that," Alf said. "Have a word with him, see what you can find out, will you? There's a good lad."

Alf thrust a pint into my hand and I wandered over to Charlie's table. The dark purple eyes flicked up at me as I sat, and then down into the port glass again.

"Evening, Charlie," I began brightly. "You'll never guess who I just bumped into outside."

"Go on. Who?" he mumbled into his drink.

"Mr Moulden, our heckling chum."

Charlie looked up sharply at this.

"Oh yes," I went on. "He and three of his pals seemed quite intent on rearranging my features. Said something about breaking my other leg. I don't suppose you would happen to know anything about that, would you?"

Charlie looked genuinely appalled. "No, I... You must believe me, Arthur, I would never... I mean, how awful! How did you...? I mean, how did you escape them?"

"A little help from the local constabulary," I said, taking a sip of beer.

"Good Lord!" Charlie was distraught.

I glanced over to the far end of the bar, where Freddie and Charley Bell were now gleefully reliving their daring rescue. I considered that I would have to repay that favour somehow and a delicious idea struck me.

"Hey, Alf," I sang out. "You know what Charlie says would cheer him up?"

"No? What?" Alf said eagerly.

"If Freddie were to join the American company. You could fix that, couldn't you? And you were saying yourself only the other day that we were a trifle under strength."

"I could ask the Guv'nor, certainly," Alf mused. "Would that cheer you up, Charlie?"

I gave Chaplin a nudge in the ribs, and he gave Alf a thin smile and half a nod.

"Right!" Alf said, and he trotted straight out of the pub, energised, leaving half of his pint still rocking in the glass on the bar there.

"Are you sure?" Charlie said. "I mean ... is Freddie going to be any good?"

"Well," I said, raising my glass. "What do *you* care?"

"That's right," Charlie winced. "He can be bloody terrible for all I care."

He slumped back into the same miserable posture he had been in when I first arrived. I knew what he was thinking, of course. It wasn't just about missing out on the American tour. He was wondering how he was going to explain it away afterwards and still keep his job with Karno. I leaned over and hissed into his ear: "You don't have to care, but if Alf should manage to pull this off you can still be pleased for the lad. Got that?"

I went back to the bar. Syd Chaplin and most of his company had just come in from their evening's performances, and he saw me leaving Charlie in his miserable stew. His antennae twitched, and he planted himself squarely in my way.

"Now listen," Syd began. "You leave him alone, d'you hear?"

I grabbed the front of his jacket and pulled him close. "Mr Moulden sends his regards," I snarled. "He's looking for you, he says. Him and his friends."

Syd went white, and I let go of him, straightening his lapels where I had crumpled them in my fists. I wasn't sure, but I thought Syd was as surprised and shocked as Charlie had just been. Maybe those sailors weren't actually lurking for me after all. Maybe they were looking for *him*. Interesting...

Shortly afterwards Alf returned from his chat with the Guv'nor, and whispered a few words in Freddie junior's shell-like. The lad sprang to his feet with a yelp, beaming all over his chops, and Stan and Mike jumped up too and began to clap him on the back. I watched as Freddie pushed through the ever-growing throng, over to where Charlie was sitting, and pumped his hand gratefully.

And Freddie was coming to America.

35
SHIP AHOY!

IT was a happy and excited company which gathered at Euston station for the boat train to Liverpool, none more so than Freddie Karno junior, who was embarking not only on his first trans-Atlantic voyage, but also on a whole new career as a performer. The momentous decision had been taken too late for him to have even one single rehearsal, but we would be working on the show during the six-day crossing, so we'd be able to bed him in. Freddie had decided to perform under the name Fred Westcott rather than Karno, for fear of American audiences expecting to see the great man himself and asking for their money back.

On paper, at any rate, the paper that Alf Reeves was clutching in his fist as he counted up the big pile of trunks and bags van on the platform alongside the luggage van, our party was sixteen strong.

There were three married couples. Alf Reeves himself and lovely Amy Minister were one, then there was George and Emily Seaman, and Fred and Muriel Palmer. There was a trio of well-seasoned senior Karno troupers that I didn't know all that well, namely Albert Williams, Frank Melroyd and Charles Griffiths, and Albert Austin, whom I knew from *Jail Birds* and *Jimmy the Fearless*. There were the four musketeers – myself, Stan, Mike and young Freddie – and there was Tilly Beckett.

There was also, naturally, our number-one comedian, Chaplin, C., who was still unaccounted for. I knew why, of course, but I kept an eye out for him. I thought the phrase "I'll finish you" was pretty unambiguous, but you never know, do you?

Alf shooed us all aboard, much like a mother hen would if poultry travelled by locomotive transportation, watching all the while for Charlie to make one of his trademark dashes down the platform. Albert Austin, who was under the impression that the sun shone from Charlie's nether regions, was the last to give up hope entirely and he stepped up into the carriage as we moved off.

"Never mind, Alf," we consoled Reeves. "He'll get the next one for sure."

Although I knew perfectly well that he wouldn't.

We arrived later that day at Liverpool Docks and got our first look at our home for the next week or so. It was the RMS *Lusitania*, no less, one of the mighty Cunard liners that plied the trans-Atlantic route to New York.

Whew! That first sight of her towering above us, her four mighty funnels thrusting into the autumn sky! Most of us stopped and gazed up, our mouths open. Even those hardened old pros George Seaman and Frank Melroyd, who had been to the States before, and who had been telling us how hard it was touring that massive continent, well, they pushed their hats back on their heads and admitted to a touch of awe.

And if that was not excitement enough, even better news awaited us once Alf had ushered us up the gangplanks and into

421

the belly of the mighty vessel. For in exchange for an agreement to perform entertainments in the evenings for the first-class passengers we were to be permitted to count ourselves amongst their number. First class to New York!

Once we had become accustomed to the splendour of our accommodation – the sumptuous cabin Stan and I were sharing had two bedrooms and a lounge, and as much floor space and furniture as my old family house in Cambridge – we explored the gangways and staircases, the ballrooms and the dining rooms and the viewing platforms like kids in a sweet shop. No, a sweet *factory*.

If this was indeed to be the start of a new chapter in my life, then I could hardly wait to read the rest of the book.

As the time to make steam approached, we got word that Alf had scurried back to the railway station in a cab to see if Charlie was on the last possible train from London, but I didn't give that possibility much thinking time. There was too much else to see, and stewards to bring me a glass of champagne and a bowl of strawberries to eat while I watched the crowds of well-wishers gathering on the quayside to wave the *Lusitania* off.

After a few minutes I strolled outside and leaned on the rail, looking down at the throng, feeling rather grand.

A whisper of petticoat, and a familiar perfume, and I had company.

"Remind you of anything?" Tilly said, leaning on the rail beside me.

"Of course," I said. "The good old *Wontdetainia*. You know, I thought that contraption was the size of a real ship until I stepped onto this beast. She's impressive, isn't she?"

"Wonderful!" Tilly said, her eyes sparkling as she smiled at me.

"Just be careful not to throw up on anyone down below," I warned. "Or else you'll be out on your neck like your friend..."

"Angeline," she laughed. "You remember that fellow with the top hat? He was most put out."

"I think he'd brought his own hat, if I remember aright," I said, and we both laughed.

There was a pause, then, amiable enough, but with a hint of awkward matters still left unspoken between us. Perhaps now we could clear the air?

"So, we're going to America," I said. "Just like back then."

"Yes," she said, "we had such plans, didn't we, as I recall? Back then?"

"We did," I said, remembering the elaborate story that we had concocted around our insignificant super characters. "I wish we could turn back the clock."

"Calendar," she said. "You want to turn back the calendar if you want to go back that far. Turning back the clock will take an age."

"Right you are," I said. "What I meant was: I wish that in Warrington, when Charlie and Syd blew the whistle on us, that I had left with you, chosen you, rather than Karno's."

"You said that in Paris," she said. "That was why I came back to London, because of what you said in Paris. Do you remember? Always and only."

"There has only ever been you, Tilly."

"And then you were so ... bitter suddenly, so cruel, after my audition that day."

"I know," I said. "I know. I wish I could take it back. Could I?"

She looked out over the wharves, her expression unreadable. I ploughed on.

"Freddie told me, you see, just that day, just that afternoon,

423

what an audition with the Guv'nor actually meant, and I found I couldn't bear the thought..."

"...of me and Karno together?" she finished. "Give me some credit, Dandoe. Every show girl knows what an audition with Karno is supposed to consist of. Supposed by *him*, at any rate."

"So, what, you mean...?"

"Well, there are ways and ways to play a scene like that. You can play it his way, and trust him to be a man of his word, or..."

"Or what?"

"The trick is, you see, to make him feel like you could do whatever he asks, if only he could help you with what *you* want, and once he's taken care of that, well then, all things are possible. But 'possible' is not the same thing as 'going to happen right now'."

"Are you saying you didn't actually...?"

"Are you saying you actually want to know?"

"No, no, I don't want to know," I said emphatically. "It is none of my business. What I want to do is apologise unreservedly for my actions that afternoon outside the Fun Factory, and reiterate, in the strongest possible terms, whatever I said in Paris that made you come back to London in the first place."

Tilly looked at me for a long moment. I watched as the sea breeze caught the curls of her blonde hair and blew a couple of strands into the corner of her mouth. She brushed it back in place.

"Well," she said, with the most marvellous smile I had ever seen in my life. "That's all right then. Apology accepted."

We hovered on the very edge of an embrace for a long moment, but in the end both turned back to the rail and looked down again. It seemed to an inexperienced seafarer's eye like mine that some more or less final preparations were being made, and that departure was actually imminent. The crowd lining the quayside was the densest it had been, and handkerchiefs were being waved and dabbed to tearful eyes.

"This tour of America feels like a fresh start, doesn't it?" I said. "New World, all that?"

"Mmm," she agreed.

"Perhaps it could be a fresh start ... for us, too."

"For us two?"

"For us two, too."

"I'd like that," Tilly said eventually, slipping her arm in mine and sliding closer along the rail. "You know what the best thing about this magnificent ship is?"

"No?"

"Well now, you know that all the other ladies in our company are married ladies, Amy of course, now, and Emily, and Muriel?"

"So they are."

"Which means that I have no one to share with. I have one of these marvellous luxurious cabins all to myself. Just rattling about in there, I am. Hardly know which chair to sit in first."

"Is that so?"

"Perhaps you'd like to take a look, later?"

My heart skipped. "I would like that," I said.

"Then that's settled," Tilly said, and laid her head on my shoulder, as she had on the *Wontdetainia* all those long months ago.

And just for a moment there, just at that very moment, do you see it? Let's just hold onto that, stretch it out as far as it will go. Just at that precise moment everything was working out perfectly. How long did that last, do you think?

"Is that Alf down there?" Tilly suddenly said, breaking from me. "Whatever is he doing?"

Down on the quayside I could indeed now see Alf Reeves. Beside him an ominous pile of Karno trunks was accumulating, dumped on the dock by fast-moving ship hands. A minute later Stan was there too, and then Frank Melroyd, and then in a rush the rest of the Karno troupe was scurrying down the gangplank onto the dock, with bags and loose clothing stuffed under their arms.

Alf was inching along the ship, looking up at the passengers arrayed as we were along the rail for departure. He caught sight of the two of us, and suddenly began beckoning furiously.

"We'd better see what's what," I said, with a sinking feeling in the pit of my stomach. You don't want a sinking feeling, not when you're on board a ship. Tilly nodded, her mouth set grimly.

We found our way through the crowd to the shipboard end of the gangplank, and hurried down onto the quay. Alf strode towards us and turned us bodily around to usher us back.

"Go get your things and then step off, as quick as you can. They're leaving in about ten minutes!" he cried.

"Why?" I shouted. "What's happening?"

"We're not going."

"Not going?" I yelled, frantic. "Why not?"

"Not without Charlie Chaplin," Alf said. "He's not here yet, so we have to take another boat."

"What?!" I howled. "We can go without him, surely to God?!"

"No," Alf insisted. "He's the number one, and we have to wait for him."

"But what if he's decided not to come?" I said. "We can manage without him. Stan is just as good, he's understudied the whole piece. And at least he's been *trying*. Let Stan take over."

The other members of the company had gathered around us,

426

and there was a murmur of encouraging assent to this plan. To be honest, I'd already prepared this argument in my head, but I'd not planned to be having this conversation until we were well under way to New York, or even there.

Alf was adamant, however.

"No, we're making other arrangements, once we know what's happened to Charlie," he said.

"Listen, Alf," I said, trying to sound as reasonable as I could. "Why do we not go, now, on the *Lusitania* here..."

At this there was a sigh from the assembled ranks, who had seen the trappings of luxury and had them snatched from their grasp.

"...and leave a message for Charlie to make his own way as soon as he can. Is that not the sensible option?"

"Yes, let's go back on board," said Frank Melroyd, turning to look for his trunk. He was not alone in this. Even Amy looked ready to defy her new-minted husband if there was a chance to regain the use of those gold-plated taps.

"I really think we should wait for Charlie, you know," said Albert Austin, the crawler, and Alf jumped in to stamp his authority on the discussion.

"Arthur, Tilly, go and get your things, right now, or leave them on there, I don't care which, but the company is not travelling today. I am making other arrangements. Understood?"

Tilly stared at him for a beat, and then turned and ran up the gangplank to fetch her belongings. I glanced from her retreating figure to Alf and back again.

"But...!" I said.

"But me no buts!" Alf shouted. "Run!"

And so, shortly afterwards, we all sat on the quayside on our travelling trunks, watching the lovely, the gorgeous, the impossible (as it turned out) dream that was a first-class crossing on the *Lusitania* ease out of Liverpool Docks and steam away into the distance. All around us the crowds cheered, hats were waved, and a brass band played a happy farewell, and we sat, our chins in our hands, thinking of what might have been. If Charlie had sauntered up then, at that very moment, I believe he would have been torn limb from limb.

It was dark by the time Alf returned from the booking office. Finding alternative passage for a party of sixteen was not proving an easy matter, and we were obliged to traipse off glumly for a miserable supper and a night in a cramped hotel, four in a room, and Tilly sharing with the Palmers. So much for our fresh start, I thought, as I lay awake listening to Mike Asher snoring, and wondering how my scheme would play out.

It was only when we were all back at Liverpool Lime Street station the next morning that we realised we had lost Charles Griffiths. We discovered later that he had bedded down for a bit of an afternoon kip in his luxurious first-class cabin. When he awoke he was well on his way to New York without us. The purser was, evidently, most agitated, since Griffiths was occupying a first-class cabin on the understanding that the Karno company would be performing regular entertainments along the way, and now there was only him. Griffiths was extremely sanguine about the situation, however, and said that he would happily honour the obligation to work his passage, and he did.

"I just did a load of Gus Elen's songs," he explained when we caught up with him. "I knew 'em – I've 'eard 'em often enough. Went down a storm, I did. Why wouldn't I? He's a copper-bottomed guarantee, is old Gus."

Alf had dragged us all back to the station, and it was there he

428

outlined the new plan he had been able to make, and the groans when we heard it, dear oh dear.

"We have a passage booked on another ship," he announced. "The RMS *Cairnrona*. Leaving from Southampton."

"Wha-a-at?" went up the cry of dismay from all throats.

"I have wired to Charlie to meet us there, and we shall travel by train first to Birmingham, then to Reading, and then on to Southampton. It's the cheapest way, 'cos it means not carting all this stuff across London. So let's make the best of it, shall we, and head for platform 4."

There was a decidedly mutinous muttering, but the company began to shuffle off. Alf grabbed my sleeve and pulled me to one side.

"Not you, Arthur," he whispered. "I need you to do something for me."

"Oh yes?" I said.

"Here," he said, thrusting a ticket into my hand. "I'll take care of your bags. You go back to London. Find Charlie for me, and get him onto that boat. I've wired the little bastard time and time again and he hasn't replied. I can't think what he's playing at."

I could, of course. "What if he doesn't want to come?" I said.

"Bring him anyway," Alf said, with a dangerous look in his eye. "You can persuade him if anyone can, or else I've missed my guess."

I gave my dream scenario one last go. "We can manage without him, you know, Alf. Stan is just as good, and how's America going to know the difference? They don't know Charlie Chaplin from a bar of Five Boys chocolate, do they?"

"You're right, lad, you're right," Alf sighed, looking tired. "But if Karno finds out I've left on an American tour without my number one, then that's it for me. I've pushed my luck once too often as it is, and on your behalf more than once, I might say, so I'm asking you to do this for me. Can I count on you?"

He was gripping my forearm now, and wearing the look of a desperate man. I hated to see him that way, so what else could I say?

"Yes, Alf, you can. I'll find the little bastard, and I'll bring him."

36
ALWAYS LEAVE
THEM LAUGHING

AS I travelled back to London, having not expected to return there for at least six months, I had plenty of time to consider how the land lay. Even though I was disappointed that my scheme to leave Chaplin behind had come to grief, and was mortified at missing out on a first-class ride on the *Lusitania* as a consequence, nonetheless I found myself beaming happily as the Midlands rolled by outside the carriage window.

It was Tilly. Tilly was the reason for my sunny mood. And in the end what did it matter how we got to the States, and who else came on the trip? The important thing was that we would be together again. Charlie's name hadn't even come up in our reconciliatory conversation the day before, and she had not seemed at all agitated that he might not make it to the ship in time, unlike Albert Austin, who had looked close to tears.

So while I'd much *much* rather he stayed behind with his career in ruins, if he absolutely *had* to come with us to America, in order that *we* could go to America, so be it. I could bear it.

Once I reached the hustle and bustle of the capital once more time was not on my side, so I made all haste to the address on the Brixton Road where Charlie lived with his brother.

The Chaplins rented a top-floor flat above a parade of shops – there was a butcher's and a baker's but disappointingly nowhere that I could see to buy custom-made candle holders. As I approached I found myself on the wrong side of the road, so I paused on the pavement and looked across, trying to judge where number 16 was to be found while awaiting a break in the traffic. I had my target in sight and was just about to step out when I glanced to my left and got the shock of my life. There, leaning indolently against a wall, flicking through a newspaper, was none other than the creature Moulden.

Really, this was too much.

He had not spotted me, fortunately, so I quickly retreated to a safe distance up the road and found a vantage point from which I could spy on him. What was he doing there? Every few seconds he would glance up from his reading – if indeed he was actually reading – and he'd eye the doorway opposite, the one which I had determined led to the Chaplins' flat. He was keeping watch, that's what he was doing. It defied belief that he could be expecting me to turn up, so he must have been waiting for Charlie, or for Syd. Then, with a heavy sigh, I spotted one of his cohorts, the fellow with the enormous hands, a little further along, also keeping watch. He was sporting a rather natty beret. Very nautical.

I considered for a moment, and decided that the fact that they were not expecting me would not for a moment prevent them from attempting to resume our last encounter where it had left off.

Damn it all!

I needed to get in to see if Chaplin was at home, and there was precious little time before I would have to make for Waterloo and the boat train. What was I to do? I inched carefully along the pavement towards Chaplin's address, taking cover wherever I could find it, falling in step behind a fat gentlemen for a few strides, then ducking into a grocer's a few doors down to pretend to shop.

An ailing white motor van bearing the legend 'Pears Soap' oozed and parped along the street towards me. As it drew level with me I nipped out into the road and trotted alongside it until I was level with Chaplin's front door, which happily was ajar, and then I darted into the darkened corridor. I made it unseen and quickly ran up the stairs to the top flat, where I pounded on the door.

There was no response from inside. I banged again and again, and shouted Charlie's name, but to no avail. I gave up and sat on the stairs to think, and after a couple of minutes I realised I was being watched. At the foot of the stairs was a child, a raggedy street urchin, looking back up at me.

"You 'is friend, are you?"

"Yes," I said, "but he's not in."

"He's in there all right," said the urchin. "He just don't want to see nobody, is all."

"Is that right?" I said.

"Yeah," the kid said. "He comes out for smokes. I fetches 'em for 'im, don't I?"

"That's why you're waiting?"

"Right."

"Well, perhaps I'll wait with you."

"No skin off my nose," said the child, and we sat in companionable silence for a while. I lit a cigarette, gave one to the kid and checked my watch with increasing anxiety, reckoning that there was barely time to make it down to Southampton and catch up with the rest of the company. I was damned if I was going to miss the boat as well.

"You in an 'urry, are you?" the urchin asked, languidly puffing out a cloud of smoke.

"Somewhat," I said.

"Only if you wants to get in and see 'im, there's a key just there, on top of the door frame."

I leapt to my feet and felt with my fingertips, and blow me, the kid was right. I saluted him, opened the door and went in.

It was dark in there, and didn't smell especially pleasant. The curtains were drawn against the world, and on the kitchen table there was a lump of bread and some cheese, both of which were rock hard and bore signs of mould. The parlour seemed cosy enough, with a pair of matching chunky armchairs arranged beside a fireplace, which didn't seem to have been home to a lit fire for a while.

I found my way along to a bedroom, and eased the door open gingerly. And there I found him, curled up on top of his bed, his knees drawn up to his chest. Piles of cigarette ends littered the floor, along with several empty bottles which had contained intoxicating spirits of one kind or another. The room smelled of a pub the morning after a busy night before. At the end of a really busy week.

I drew closer to the bed, trying to see if Charlie was breathing, because I suddenly had the ghastly apprehension that he might have done something foolish. No, I could see a shallow rise and fall there, and a quiver of his stubbly lips. Drunk, not dead, thank goodness for that.

I reached out a hand to shake him, but suddenly stopped short.

Here was a thought.

Chaplin ... *dead?!*

He wasn't, but he could have been. He could very well have been. He had clearly embarked upon a dramatic decline, and if no one arrested it there could surely only be one end.

I sat heavily on a chair as ramifications rushed in, clamouring for attention, clouding my head, drowning my reason. Revenge, revenge for all he had done to me, the dirty tricks, the double dealing, stealing my girl behind my back, smashing my knee, queering my pitch with Karno. And then there would be a clear sunlit run ahead, with Tilly, and with Karno's in America, without this little bastard gumming up the works. Revenge, revenge was here, within my grasp, if only...

I wouldn't even have to do anything, would I? Just turn my back, that would be enough. Leave now and say I couldn't find him, and let nature, his self-dramatising depressive nature, take its course. The outcome wasn't certain, though, I feverishly reasoned. Someone else could find him in time. Syd, Syd could be back at any moment...

I could ... could I? Pick up a pillow and ... finish him? The boy had seen me, but boys could be bought. Moulden was outside, but maybe that would be a good thing, maybe he would even be *blamed*...

I stood slowly, leaned over, looked down at his grubby face, caught a whiff of his foul breath.

That frail frame, curled to protect itself from a cruel world. As I loomed over it all I could think of, marvelling suddenly, was the Power it contained. I thought back to the times I had been with Chaplin onstage, and considered then what I had seen, without the resentment, and the competitiveness, and the bitterness. Some of the finest moments of my life, when the audience was eating out of the palm of my hand, and the Power coursed through my tingling veins, had been shared with him, with Charlie Chaplin. I saw in that moment that I would never, could never, match him, and saw too, I think, what the world would miss if he were to expire theatrically, self-indulgently, in this pit.

"Hey! Charlie!" I said, taking myself by surprise. "Wake up, man!"

He did not stir, so I began to clap my hands together as I called him up from the depths of his drunken stupor.

"Hey! Charlie! Come on, up you get!"

Slowly he roused himself, and looked around to see where the noise was coming from. When he saw me he squinted, as if trying to make his eyes focus. Then he recognised me and scrambled into a sitting position, pressing himself back against the head-board to try and get as far from me as possible.

"What?!" he cried anxiously. "What are you doing here?"

"I've come to get you," I said. He began to tremble, as though I had just confirmed his worst apprehensions.

"Why?" he stammered. "I did what you said, didn't I? Didn't I?" He had the look of a man not sure whether he was awake or still dreaming a nightmare.

I looked at the state he was in, unshaven, filthy, hollow-eyed. I supposed he hadn't eaten in days, and had subsisted only on drink and cigarettes. What a depression he had fallen into, and all because of me. It was all terribly dramatic, of course, and woe is me, but even so, I found myself feeling ashamed.

436

"Come on, old chap," I said, more kindly. "I mean to say I've come to get you, to take you to America. Get some things in a suitcase, for goodness' sake, and be quick about it. We've a train to catch."

Chaplin looked at me as though I was a creature from another world. I decided to leave him to pull himself together. I went through into the other rooms and opened the curtains, then opened the windows to let some air in. I disposed of his mouldering left-over food, and found a dustpan and brush to deal with the fag ends.

When I went back into the bedroom he was still sitting there just as I had left him.

"What do you *mean*?" he said, still baffled.

"America, come on, chop chop!"

"But ... the boat's already left... Aren't you supposed to be...?"

"We're going on a different one, and it sails tonight, so get yourself moving, will you?"

Chaplin blinked up at me from the bed. "Why? What made you change your mind?"

"Let's say I decided I'd rather do Alf a good turn than you a bad one. I'll explain on the way, but for now you really must get on with it!"

He seemed suddenly to realise that I was neither a figment of his own imagination nor joking, and leapt from the bed. He was a whirlwind of activity now, grabbing fistfuls of shirts here, and a violin there, a Latin textbook, if you please, some carpet slippers, what cigarettes he had left and a packet of lucifers, some ties, a boater, socks, and he stuffed them all any old how into his travelling trunk.

"Ready!" he cried, standing to attention. He looked better already. The light had returned to his eyes, and he seemed invigorated once more.

"Good," I said. "Let's make tracks."

Chaplin dragged his trunk over to the front door, and then snapped his fingers as he remembered something.

"One minute," he said, scrambling around in the drawer of the bureau until he located a pencil and a scrap of paper. He scribbled on it quickly, and then slapped the note on the table. I glanced at it as he did so, and saw that it read: "Off to America, love Charlie."

For Syd, of course. Which reminded me.

"One slight problem," I said, as we stepped out onto the landing. "That unsavoury ginger geezer is loafing about outside. I reckon he must be waiting for words with your Syd."

Charlie twitched his mouth from side to side, thinking.

"Show me," he said.

We tiptoed down to the street door, which was still ajar, carrying his trunk between us.

"There, see?" I said, as Charlie peered carefully out. "And further down that way is his chum, the chap with the neckerchief and the beret, see him?"

Charlie nodded, and withdrew into the shadows. "They'd be upon us before we got to the corner. Wait, I have it..." He inched back to the door and whistled softly a couple of times. In a few moments we were joined by the street urchin I had met earlier on.

"Arternoon, Mister," this youngster said cheerily. "Ciggies, is it?"

"Not this time, my friend," Charlie said. "Look over yonder. You see that fellow?"

"The one with the prize 'ooter, you mean?"

"Exactly. And you see ... *that* chap, there, with the beret?" The urchin nodded. "Here's a shilling. Go and tell that one that *that* one wants to speak to him urgently."

The kid flipped the shilling up in the air and caught it deftly. "You're the boss," he said, and sauntered out into the street. Charlie watched him go, and after a moment or two his protégé was leading Moulden by the arm down the street to our right.

Charlie gripped the handle of his trunk and I grabbed the other end. He was a changed man, a livewire.

"Ready?" he hissed, and I tensed. "Let's go!"

We darted out of the doorway and belted off up the street to the left. We made it to the corner, and Charlie started to turn to find us somewhere to conceal ourselves, but before we could nip out of sight I saw that Moulden had realised he'd been had, and he and his mate were hurrying diagonally across the road towards us. There was no earthly point in hiding now, we just had to run for it, so we pelted straight up the main road.

Charlie looked back, and his eyes widened. We were badly hampered by his trunk, and Moulden was only a few yards adrift. He was going to catch us for sure.

Then, blessed relief, I heard the ting-ting of a tram bell warning us to move over, and a northbound tram slid alongside. Gathering the last of my breath I shouted to Charlie: "On!"

He jumped up onto the tram's backboard. I shoved the trunk up after him, and made my own leap, landing there – just – on my knees. Blast it, that hurt!

Moulden's chum in the beret had fallen badly behind, but Moulden himself wasn't giving up his quarry so easily. A nasty grin spread beneath that bulbous twin-lobed pitted red nose, and he managed to get a hand on the pole. Next he would pull himself aboard, but before he could I lashed out a boot at his fingers, crushing them. With a howl he let go his grip and sprawled on the road in a heap, and Charlie and I watched him dwindle into the distance as the tram rattled away up the Brixton Road. We looked at one another then, breathless and sweating, and both began to laugh.

———

We caught the boat train from Waterloo station with not an inch to spare, Chaplin-style, and as the locomotive headed towards Southampton Charlie seemed to regain a little of himself with every passing mile. Having started the journey looking very much like – well, not to put too fine a point on it – a *tramp*, he finished it spruced and gleaming like a thoroughgoing dandy. He contrived to shave along the way, which must have taken considerable dexterity, for there was not a scratch on him.

So high were his spirits now, from one extreme direct to the other without calling at points in between, that he was not much interested in any explanations from me. He preferred to beam at the passing countryside, and burble about America, the land of opportunity. I suppose, in a way, he must have felt like he'd been spared the noose, as he would not now have to invent an explanation for Karno that would enable him keep his job. He would have to make some sort of excuse to Alf Reeves and the company, but that was small beer by comparison.

As we neared our destination he suddenly leaned over and put his hand on my knee.

"Thank you, Arthur," he said, with a quite dazzling smile (those teeth!). "Friends?"

"Friends," I said, and we shook on it. He just loved doing *that*, didn't he?

And at that moment we were friends, I think, and I was glad I had relented, not just for Alf's sake, but for Charlie's and for mine. After all, I thought, so Charlie Chaplin comes to America with us. What's the worst that could happen...? (Hint: read his autobiography and you'll find out.)

━━━

Once at Southampton we were collected at the dock gates by a functionary of the Thomson Line, and led to the RMS *Cairnrona* on foot. As we made our way along the quay we found ourselves passing by a steam packet with a lavender-grey hull and two red and black funnels. The name on the stern caught my eye.

"Well, well," I said. "How about that?"

"What is it?" Charlie said.

"Wait here a minute," I said. A little way off I could see a starched busybody of a fellow in a braided uniform heading towards us. His white peaked cap bore the same name as the ship, and I put on a gentlemanly air and accosted him before he could drive me away.

"Ahoy!" I said. "Are you from the *Dover Castle* there?"

"I am, sir. What is your business?"

"Are you the captain, might I ask?"

"No, sir, I am not. I am Dawkins, the purser. Can I help you?"

"Indeed," I said. "The purser, is that so? It so happens that I am acquainted with Mr Turnbull, from your London office on Fenchurch Street. Do you know the gentleman?"

"I do," said this Dawkins.

"You have a fellow on your boat, name of Moulden," I said.

"What of it?"

"I have a message from him," I said. "He wishes you to know that he has retired from the seafaring life, effective immediately, and you should take steps to replace him as quickly as possible."

"I see," said Dawkins, frowning. "And did he give a reason?"

"He said – I'm sorry to have to say this, Mr Dawkins, but remember I am merely the messenger – that the ship's purser was an insufferable prig and that he could not bear to spend another moment in his company."

Dawkins stiffened, and his face turned a sort of purple colour.

"He also gave me to understand that you would be pleased as Punch, because this would give you the chance to scour the docks for a young boy more to your taste. Does that mean anything to you?"

The purser's eyes bulged with outrage. "And what is *your* name, sir, if I might ask?"

"My name?" I said. "My name is Sydney Chaplin. I bid you good day, sir."

I left him standing there with steam coming out from beneath his starched white cap, and rejoined Charlie and our guide, pleased with a very tidy bit of business.

Shortly we came to the dock where the *Cairnrona* was berthed, and I got my first look at her. A modest little vessel, black-grey smoke already beginning to billow from her single funnel.

The Thomson man noticed that I had stopped, and retraced his steps with a look of concern.

"Something wrong, sir?"

"Not exactly the *Lusitania*, is it?"

He grimaced apologetically. "Few ships are," he said.

Once we joined the rest of the company on board it was plain to see that not everyone was as pleased to see Charlie Chaplin

442

as Mr Alfred Reeves was. Talk about the prodigal! He took him, and embraced him, and pinched his face as though checking he was flesh and blood and not an apparition come to torment him. Have you ever seen a mother who has mislaid a child, exclaiming that when she finds the errant infant she is going to tan his hide and make him wish he'd never been born, but then when the little rogue hoves into view it's all hugs and kisses and never-leave-me-agains? Like that, exactly like that.

At one point, Alf managed to free an arm from this embarrassing display and grab me by the hand to offer his heartfelt, if silent, thanks.

The rest of the company, however (except for old Charlie Griffiths, who was floating off in the lap of luxury somewhere past Ireland by now), stood and seethed. Arms folded, lips pursed, eyes boring holes in the back of the Chaplin skull.

I found out why when the welcome party dispersed and I could grab a word with Tilly.

"I don't suppose by any chance we have ... first-class cabins?" I said.

"There isn't even a first class on this bucket," Tilly said. "There's second class, and there's third class, but there's no first. What's the point of that, I ask you?"

"I see, but it's not *so* bad, is it?"

"I'll tell you what it is, it's a converted cattle boat, and I'm not even joking."

No wonder Charlie got such a muted welcome.

Later, as the *Cairnrona* steamed out into the Solent, and on into the English Channel, I leaned on the rail and watched England slide by. I was filled with anticipation, for I had dreamed of travelling to America ever since I had whiled away my time in Cambridge reading the good old penny bloods. I had a great sense of well-being all at once, because I felt things had been resolved between myself and Charlie. I had had my victory, but had not, in the end, rubbed his nose in it. I had also, don't forget, scored a point over the creature Moulden, too.

Yes, I had a great feeling of optimism, a feeling that everything was going to turn out fine. I didn't know then that instead of heading to New York, where we were due to perform, we were actually en route to Montreal. Nor did I know that the propeller was going to give way, leaving us adrift for three whole days in the middle of the stormy Atlantic, at the mercy of wind and waves and mal de mer. And I didn't know that my rivalry with Chaplin was destined to erupt into strife, bitterness, alcoholism, ruin and murder. That was all still to come.

Tilly joined me, and slipped her arm into mine.

"The cabins are not quite so grand as on the *Lusitania*," she said. "But I do still have one to myself. "Want to take a look?"

Yes, I thought, this is all going to turn out just fine.

NOTES

1. The university proctors' assistants who were responsible for enforcing the curfew.

2. Film star Jack Hulbert began his career as a clog-dancing luminary of the Cambridge Footlights.

3. *The New Accelerator* (1901).

4. The Corner, also known as Poverty Corner, was where unemployed theatricals and turns would lurk by day in the hope that employers would recruit them there in an emergency. It was near Waterloo station.

5. In later years Billie Ritchie indignantly claimed to be the originator of Charlie Chaplin's Tramp character.

6. The Water Rats is a society of music hall and variety artistes who organise events for charity. The roll-call of notable King Rats down the years includes such luminaries as Dan Leno, Wal Pink, Joe Elvin, Frankie Vaughan, Les Dawson and Bernard Bresslaw.

7. A number man would introduce the turns and place cards

bearing their names and descriptions on an easel.

8. This sketch featured a couple of burglars masquerading as butler and maid in a large house they are disturbed in the act of robbing. It formed the basis of the 1927 Laurel and Hardy silent film *Duck Soup*, and a talkie remake from 1930 entitled *Another Fine Mess*.

9. Which Karno did, when he established the Karsino on Tagg's Island in 1912. It was very nearly the ruin of him, and he never entirely recovered his pre-eminent position thereafter.

10. Marguerite Boulc'h, a singer, then spent a decade in Russia, before returning and reinventing herself as the singer Fréhel.

11. This anecdote is arguably the basis of a classic sequence in *The Kid*, Chaplin's 1921 First National film, with Jackie Coogan as the Tramp's window-smashing child accomplice.

12. *The Stage*, 28 April 1910.

13. Ben Tillett, of the Dock, Wharf, Riverside and General Labourers' Union, would play a prominent role as a leader of dock strikes in 1911 and 1912.

NOTES ON
CHAPTER TITLES

1. COLLEGE LIFE
The title of a music hall hit song by Billy Murray, 1906.

2. THE SMOKING CONCERT
The title of a classic Fred Karno sketch.

3. OH! MR PORTER!
The title of a music hall song which was part of the repertoire of the great Marie Lloyd.

4. THE VARSITY B.C.
A Cambridge Footlights show of 1907.

5. THE HOUSE THAT FRED BUILT
The House that Jack Built was a successful Fred Karno pantomime of 1906.

6. A NIGHT IN AN ENGLISH MUSIC HALL
The alternative title for the classic Karno sketch *Mumming Birds* when it toured in America.

7. THE MAYOR OF MUDCUMDYKE
A piece of bill matter sometimes used, as at the 1912 Royal Command Performance, by George Robey. He was also the Prime Minister of Mirth.

8. FRED KARNO'S ARMY
During the Great War there was a popular song among Tommies at the Western Front which went like this:

We are Fred Karno's Army
A jolly lot are we,
We cannot shoot, we cannot fight,
What bloody use are we?

And when we get to Berlin
The Kaiser he will say
Hoch, hoch, mein Gott,
What a jolly fine lot
Are the boys of Company A.

A variation featured the lines: 'Fred Karno is our general, Charlie Chaplin our O.C.'

9. WONTDETAINIA
The title of a classic Fred Karno sketch.

11. JAIL BIRDS
The title of a classic Fred Karno sketch.

12. IT'S A MARVEL 'OW 'E DOOS IT BUT 'E DO
The title of a song by the great coster singer and comedian Gus Elen.

13. THE NEW WOMAN'S CLUB
The title of a classic Fred Karno sketch.

14. MUMMING BIRDS
The title of a classic Fred Karno sketch.

15. UNDER THE HONEYMOON TREE
The title of a music hall favourite, sung by Ella Retford.

17. TILLY'S PUNCTURED ROMANCE
The title of a 1914 Keystone movie, starring Charlie Chaplin, Mabel Normand, Marie Dressler and Mack Swain.

19. BESIDE THE SEASIDE
I Do Like To Be Beside The Seaside was written in 1907 by John Glover-Kind, and became a music hall hit for singer Mark Sheridan.

20. THE FOOTBALL MATCH
The title of a classic Fred Karno sketch.

21. HE OF THE FUNNY WAYS
This was young Stan Jefferson's bill matter as a solo comic.

22. OUI! TRAY BONG!
The title of a music hall hit of 1893 for Charles Chaplin senior. A typical 'Gay Paree' number, it is about a weekend jolly in the French capital enjoyed by the singer and his pals Jones, Tom and Harry.

23. LA VALSE RENVERSANTE
A noted cabaret sketch, featuring Maurice Chevalier and Mistinguett.

It was also later a successful film, produced by Pathé Frères, the company that also produced Max Linder's films. Chevalier made a handful of other silent films with his friend Linder, but did not really come into his own as a movie star until the arrival of sound.

24. A WOMAN OF PARIS
A 1923 United Artists film, written, produced and directed by Charlie Chaplin, starring Edna Purviance, and also Maurice Chevalier.

26. DON'T DO IT AGAIN, MATILDA
The title of a 1910 music hall hit for Harry Champion.

27. BREAK A LEG
A well-known theatrical superstition involves wishing this injury on someone about to perform.

28. THE SOCIALIST
A Cambridge Footlights show of 1910.

29. LET ME CALL YOU SWEETHEART
The title of a popular song of 1910, featured in the 1938 Laurel and Hardy film *Swiss Miss*, with Oliver Hardy singing and Stan Laurel on sousaphone.

30. JIMMY THE FEARLESS
The title of a Fred Karno sketch of 1910.

31. I'LL GET MY OWN BACK
A title taken from the music hall songbook of Sir George Robey.

34. THE WOW-WOWS
The title of a Fred Karno sketch, particularly devised to play in America.

35. SHIP AHOY!
The title of a music hall hit for male impersonator Hetty King. The song was also sometimes known by its catchy first line: 'All the nice girls love a sailor...'

HISTORICAL NOTE

Although many of the characters in *The Fun Factory* are based on real people, the incidents and relationships depicted contain a measure of speculative invention on my part.

Arthur Dandoe was a real person, a member of the Fred Karno company, and he toured the UK and America with Charlie Chaplin and Stan Jefferson (later Laurel), the three of them performing hundreds of shows together and living virtually in one another's pockets for several years.

Despite this there is only one reference to Arthur in Chaplin's massive 528 page house brick of an autobiography - imaginatively entitled *My Autobiography* - and no mention at all of Stan, who was Charlie's understudy and roommate, and by all accounts (bar Charlie's own) a close friend.

The single reference to Arthur that you will find, should you be inclined to look, is to an incident on the night Charlie left the Karno company in Kansas City to take up a job offer with Keystone Pictures. He writes: "A member of our troupe, Arthur Dando (sic), who for some reason disliked me..."

Is it just me, or is there a wealth of contempt in that casual mis-spelling of Arthur's name? Anyway, Charlie goes on to describe a leaving present that Arthur prepared for him:

> "It was an empty tobacco box, covered in tin foil, containing small ends of old pieces of grease paint."

451

Charlie seems faintly puzzled by this. According to Stan Laurel's account he should have taken a closer look. That wasn't grease paint in that tin, and the clue to the gift's true nature was in the accompanying card which Arthur had inscribed: "Some shits for a shit."

Stan suggests that Arthur didn't actually go through with this gesture after he came across Charlie alone on stage, "cold, unsentimental Charlie", crying.

Some commentators believe that Stan Laurel was omitted from My Autobiography because he was the one genuine threat to Chaplin's supremacy over the world of comedy, the one performer who could actually hold a candle to the genius. For myself, I was fascinated by the kind of man who could have come up with that leaving present, and the relationship that is somehow defined by it.

I have tried, as far as possible, to stick to known chronology as far as the actual careers of Charlie Chaplin, Syd Chaplin, Stan Jefferson, Fred Karno and Arthur Dandoe are concerned. The one real liberty that I have taken with the Karno company's productions is that I have brought the Wontdetainia forward a year or two, because it sounded so great. Karno genuinely did have that ingenious ocean liner constructed, just as he cannily employed hard-up ex-professional footballers including Messrs Athersmith, Crabtree, Spiksley and Wragg in his spectacular Football Match.

When I started writing I was attracted to this period of Chaplin's career precisely because it was covered so imprecisely and unreliably in his own autobiography and the many various biographies, which naturally rely heavily on his own account. It seemed a dark, shady area that gave me a lot of elbow room. Then AJ Marriot brought out his book Chaplin: Stage by Stage, which shone a great forensic searchlight beam onto the whole period. It not only details where Chaplin was and what he was up to day by day throughout his Karno career, it also pulls the great man up on a surprisingly large number of inaccuracies and deliberate obfuscations, taking him to task in a most entertaining way. I recommend it, it's a lot of fun.

Charlie Chaplin did tour the UK in *Mumming Birds* and *The Football Match,* and did take over from Harry Weldon as the lead comic in the latter, only to succumb to laryngitis and miss out on what seemed at the time to be his big break. He did play for a month at the Folies Bergère, and did also pull out of *Jimmy the Fearless,* either sulking or in a funk, only to take over after a week when he saw what a success Stan Jefferson, his understudy, had made of it.

Fred Karno was the great comedy entrepreneur of the pre-First World War years, and most of the big names of the time worked either with him or for him at some time. The Fun Factory was his headquarters off Coldharbour Lane in Camberwell, and a spectacular hive of activity it must have been. He was a notorious and not especially subtle user of the casting couch, and his marital situation was pretty much as complicated as I have described, as were his bizarre attempts to resolve it.

Arthur Dandoe worked with both Chaplin and Jefferson on *Jimmy the Fearless* and several other shows. He then went on to share in some of their adventures in the States before their paths diverged. Most of the rest of what Arthur does in the book is fiction.

ACKNOWLEDGEMENTS

I would like to acknowledge the assistance of the Arts Council of Great Britain which was invaluable in enabling me to complete this project.

I would also like to thank Ben Yarde-Buller of Old Street for taking a punt, and James Nunn for the splendid cover.

Thanks to Jo Unwin, Rob Dinsdale, Robert Kirby, Charles Walker and Richard Dawes for your enthusiasm and skill. Also to Jo Brand, David Baddiel, Mark Billingham and Al Murray.

And special thanks to David Tyler. The next one's for you.